HAVENWOOD FALLS
VOLUME 1

A HAVENWOOD FALLS COLLECTION

KRISTIE COOK   E.J. FECHENDA   SUSAN BURDORF

Published by

Ang'dora Productions, LLC

5621 Strand Blvd, Ste 210

Naples, FL 34110

Havenwood Falls and Ang'dora Productions and their associated logos are trademarks and/or registered trademarks of Ang'dora Productions, LLC

Cover design by Regina Wamba at MaeIDesign.com

ISBN 978-1-939859-31-0

CONTENTS

OTHER HAVENWOOD FALLS BOOKS

Covetousness by Randi Cooley Wilson

More books releasing on a monthly basis

Also try the YA line, Havenwood Falls High, launching October 2017

Stay up to date at www.HavenwoodFalls.com and subscribe to our newsletter

FORGET YOU NOT

BY KRISTIE COOK

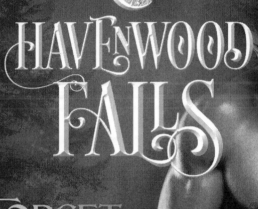

~ A Havenwood Falls New Adult Novella ~

Havenwood Falls

Forget You Not

KRISTIE COOK

ABOUT THIS BOOK

Welcome to Havenwood Falls, a small town in the majestic mountains of Colorado. A town where legacies began centuries ago, bloodlines run deep, and dark secrets abound. A town where nobody is what you think, where truths pose as lies, and where myths blend with reality. A place where everyone has a story. This is only but one...

Two years ago, Kaela Peters nearly killed her fiancé by ripping his throat out. Once she gained control over her vampire urges, she hoped to rekindle their love, only to find him on one knee again—now with her best friend. She can't blame them for their betrayal, though. They've been compelled to forget that she even existed. But she can't forget them, so when she receives an unexpected job offer far away in the Colorado mountains, she seizes the opportunity to escape her past and the painful memories.

If only she'd known she was running right into her true past and memories that cut even deeper.

Her real name isn't Kaela Peters, Havenwood Falls and her new job are not what they seem on the surface, and the love of her life isn't the ex in Atlanta. As she starts piecing together the fragmented memories of her past and her moroi heritage, the passion of old love reignites. Until she discovers that the triggering of her vampire gene may have been foul play with dire consequences—and Xandru Roca, the epic love she'd left behind, has something to do with it all.

BOOKS BY KRISTIE COOK

Soul Savers

A Demon's Promise

An Angel's Purpose

Dangerous Devotion

Dark Power

Sacred Wrath

Unholy Torment

Fractured Faith

Genesis: A Soul Savers Novella

Awakened Angel: A Soul Savers Novella

Supernatural Chronicles: The Wolves (A Soul Savers Tie-In Novella)

Wonder: A Soul Savers Collection of Holiday Short Stories & Recipes

The Book of Phoenix

The Space Between

The Space Beyond

The Space Within

For those who never gave up on me, who supported me, who believed in me

And to the authors who have put their trust in me

It's wonderful to be back. Back among the mountains that remind us of our vulnerability, our ultimate lack of control over the world we live in. Mountains that demand humility, and yield so much peace in return.

~ Alex Lowe

CHAPTER 1

*N*othing screamed badass vampire chick more than hiding behind a menu while your ex-fiancé and former best friend sucked each other's faces three tables over and five booths down. I could hear their lips smacking and smell their horn-dog pheromones from my small table at the back of the restaurant. As if hiding wasn't pathetic enough, I couldn't stop stealing glances at them from over the top of the laminated cardboard in my hands, some sick part of me reveling in the painful twists of my heart and knots in my gut. *That's supposed to be me.* My eyes squeezed shut to suppress the threatening tears as I slid further down in my seat.

Ugh. I'm such a freakin' masochist.

"Kaela Peters, you are such a fucking masochist."

My eyes popped open at the sound of my roommate's raspy voice to find the redhead plopping down in the chair across from me, her green apron bunched up in one hand. One of her brows lifted as she stared at me with big, blue eyes, gnawing on her plump bottom lip, painted as scarlet as her hair. The color was all the more vibrant against her unnaturally porcelain-white skin. Sindi was also a vampire; in fact, in a much more traditional way than I was. Her coloring, for example—pale like vampires should be while my skin was still the olive tone it had always been. Her eyes had stayed the same, except when she fed from the vein, and then they sort of glowed, but mine made a permanent change from brown to a greenish-gray when I turned. We hadn't figured that one out.

After enduring several long moments of her glare, I finally shrugged and widened my eyes with as much innocence as I could muster. "What? It's not like I followed them here."

"Not this time."

My eyes began to drift over to the happy couple once more before I snapped them back to her. I didn't fool her, though. She noticed, if rolling her eyes was any indication.

"I guess you're at least taking my advice," she muttered as she unfolded her long legs and stood to tie her apron around her small waist. "But when the hell were you going to tell me?"

My brows pinched together at the sudden change in her tone, from snarky to … pained. It took a lot to hurt Sindi's feelings—her heart was possibly tougher than her indestructible body. Another of the differences between us. My body could heal itself in a short time; hers healed immediately. My skin burnt and blistered in the sun, but she'd burst into flames. I still needed oxygen (though not as much as a human), and she didn't. My heart still beat, while hers was silent. But could it still be broken? What could I have done to do so?

"I'm sorry," I said, "but tell you what?"

She blew out a quick breath. "It's okay, Kaela, I get it. When you joked about moving far away from here and your past, I was serious when I said you should. I'll miss you, but it's what you need. But don't lie to me about it."

"I really have no idea what you're talking about." Actually, muttering about moving away hadn't really been a joke, but not something I'd done anything about. Yet. My eyes stole another glimpse of the cuddling exes at the thought of leaving, and I sighed. I really was too much of a masochist.

Sindi's hands landed at her waist, and her long fingers tapped against her hip bones as she let out another huff. "Whisper Falls Inn? Job offer? You left the email open on your laptop this morning. How could you not even tell me that you'd applied? And Colorado? Really, Kaela? Do you know how long that drive from Atlanta would be? I can only drive at night! You couldn't find anything closer?"

I stared at her, confused. "Why wouldn't you fly?"

She rolled her eyes. "You know why."

I opened my mouth to ask because I had no idea why, but then shook my head. How she got to Colorado didn't matter.

"Unbunch your panties," I said instead. "I can't have a job offer. I haven't applied for anything new in ages. And definitely not in Colorado."

She glared at me for another long moment, and she must have seen the truth in my eyes because her baby blues began to soften and she started fiddling with the contents of her apron pocket. "Yeah, well, you shouldn't leave your shit out and open if you don't want me to know. But if you care at all about my opinion, I think it's pretty perfect for you. You should take it." She broke our eye contact as she glanced around the restaurant. "My shift's about to start. Where are you tonight?"

"Nowhere. I have the rare night off."

"Then get your ass home, and if you don't take that job, find another—a real one."

"Hey! You bartend and wait, too. You can't get any more real than those."

"*Those*. Multiple. When was your last day off? Three weeks ago? You really want to hold down two jobs for the rest of your very long life? And at a 24-hour, hole-in-the-wall diner and meat-market nightclub? You're too smart for this, Kae. Go use your degree, for Christ's sake." She turned and headed for the kitchen.

"Yeah, well, easier said than done. Not too many companies have night shifts for their PR teams."

I stood up and threw some money on the table, although I hadn't eaten anything. I *could* eat food. Blood sustained me, but I still loved food. Just not while watching the Ryan & Heather Sappy Love Show starring the two people who'd been my favorite souls in the world at one time. They still kind of were. Sindi had nudged them into second and third place, but I still loved them both. It wasn't their fault they'd fallen for each other. That was all on me.

"Sindi," I called out to her back as she retreated. She turned halfway and threw me an impatient look. It was all a cover, I knew. She'd never tell me I was one of *her* favorite people—she'd never open up enough to admit to that anyone—but she'd basically just shown it. "I'm not going anywhere. Relax."

"Don't worry about me, doll face. You do what you need to do. I will be fine. Always am." Her mouth curved up in a smirk before she tossed her red ponytail over her shoulder and disappeared between the swinging doors to the kitchen.

I headed down the corridor toward the bathrooms—and the back door. Although I hadn't permanently left the area in the two years since the night that changed my entire life, I'd been successful in avoiding running into *them*, and I didn't want to change that now. I might have sometimes (frequently) watched (stalked) from a distance, but the thought of actually coming anywhere close to Ryan or Heather sent me into panic mode. Sindi had compelled them both to forget me and everything that had happened between us, but unfortunately her vampire power didn't work on me, fellow vampire and all. I remembered it all—the good, the bad, and the very gruesome ugly.

The cool night air of winter in the South was a welcome relief as I slipped into the dark alley and headed home, thinking about how Sindi had been my saving grace when I'd been a newborn vampire. She'd found me in this very alley covered in blood. My fiancé's blood. Hence, the "ex" part of our relationship. I'd nearly killed him when I ripped half his throat out. Hey, I didn't know what I was doing. Seriously. We'd gone to sleep after making love, and I awoke a couple of hours later with a throat-searing thirst. Water just didn't cut it. I'd been overcome with bloodlust, although I didn't know that's what it was at the time.

Yep. I'd nearly murdered my fiancé. The night he'd proposed.

After taking care of him with the healing qualities of her own blood, Sindi whisked me away from civilization before I could kill anyone and taught me how to control the thirst. It took a while—and a lot of fights with Sindi and many nights locked up in her storage room to keep me from becoming a murderer—but I eventually grew to the point where animal blood sustained my body and actual human food satisfied my hunger. Once I knew I'd be okay, I thought I'd give the Ryan and Kaela Show another chance. But I was too late. He'd already moved on, of course. He'd moved right on top of my best friend. I couldn't blame either of them, though. After all, they didn't even know I existed. How could they know the betrayal I felt?

Once inside the townhouse Sindi and I shared—well, she shared with me since it was hers long before she met me—I found my laptop open on the coffee table in the living room. A swipe of the trackpad proved the truth of her story: on the screen was an open email. Weird. I hadn't seen it this morning. I dropped down onto the couch to read.

Dear Ms. Peters,

After reviewing your history and qualifications, we believe you are a perfect fit for the Night Manager position at Whisper Falls Inn in the beautiful mountains of Colorado, and we're excited to offer you the job. We have outlined the terms of employment, including compensation, below. If you agree with our conclusion, we would like you to start as soon as possible. We understand you may need time to consider our offer, but we hope you will respond quickly so we may start making preparations for your arrival.

Yours truly,

The rest of the email outlined a modest salary enhanced by free lodging and meals but failed to provide any other details, such as an address or even city.

"Spam is getting weirder by the day," I muttered as I closed the email, cursing spammers and hackers. I wondered what this joker's end-game was. What did they get out of a fake job offer?

Not two seconds later, another message popped up, opening itself.

Ms. Peters,

We apologize that in our excitement of offering you the job, we failed to provide necessary details. Our inn is located in what we like to think of as the prettiest and most charming small town in the world. We are surrounded by majestic mountains and forestland with a larger variety of wildlife than anywhere else in the state, perhaps the country. While the area offers much to do, from skiing to hunting to art classes, we have safeguards in place that ensure our hometown remains a lovely place to live, not just to visit. We've attached a few pictures so you can see for yourself why we believe you will quickly learn to call it home and the people family.

Yours truly (again),
M. Luiza

A slideshow began to play at the bottom of the message, featuring gorgeous photos of a small town nestled in a cradle of purple mountains with snowcapped peaks.

"Awesome," I muttered as my hand moved the cursor to X out of the window. "Virus must already be installed."

My finger lowered over the trackpad and was about to press down when the slideshow displayed a photo that made my breath catch, and not because of its beauty. A large Victorian manor, complete with turrets and gingerbread trim, forced my pause. *How do I know that place?* The sense of familiarity poked angrily at the back of my mind. The photo changed, focused in on the plaque by the manor's front door: Whisper Falls Inn, Est. 1854.

Home.

The word floated through my mind, not as a premonition or wishful thinking as the letter promised, but heavily laced with nostalgia. The townhome's living room in front of me disappeared as other, seemingly random images hijacked my vision. Images of what could have been the rooms inside the inn, followed by portraits and snapshots of people. Faces that I felt deep down I should know. A close-up of a woman with long, dark hair like mine . . . gray-green eyes, the same shade and shape as mine.

Home.

"What the hell?" I slammed my finger down on the pad, closing out the message, and shut the laptop before jumping back in my seat, as though the message could hurt me. My heart raced, and I struggled to breathe. I curled into a ball on the couch and glared at the offensive machine on the coffee table. After several moments, my heart settled and everything returned to normal. Another few moments and I couldn't remember what had caused such a visceral reaction. "I'm losing my damn mind."

Sindi had warned me about vampires losing their sanity, but always in relation to being starved of blood. I was not starved of blood, nor of food. Well, I didn't eat earlier. I unfolded myself from the sofa and headed for the kitchen to find something for . . . I glanced at the clock on the stove. 11:48 p.m. Something for brunch.

As I cooked and ate, my mind wandered back to Sindi's orders and the fake job offer. Maybe it wasn't real, but it got me to thinking. Hotel night manager wasn't exactly what I'd had in mind when I switched my major from pre-med to business after I'd turned and then continued with night classes to earn my event planning certification, thinking event planners worked at night. They did, but, turned out, not *only* at night. But maybe there was potential here. After all, hotels hosted events and many at night. I'd taken the bartending job to grow into a special events planner at the club, but it'd been more than a year and that had gone nowhere. And this was a full-time, salaried position with benefits in a place so far away, it didn't get reception for the Ryan & Heather Super Sappy Love Show.

The small-town part, though . . . I'd come to Atlanta in the first place to escape the small-town life of my childhood. I'd done quite well in putting that misery behind me, never thinking about home and the family that had taken me in only because they had to, but didn't really want me. I'd escaped that life once. Did I really want to go back? Of course, the pictures of the mountain village looked nothing like the dusty Texas town where I'd grown up. Maybe Colorado small towns were different.

"Yeah, right." I dropped my plate in the dishwasher and cleaned up the rest of the kitchen before sitting down to clean up my computer.

After the virus scan came back clean, I went on an online hunt for a new job—hotel night manager. Every single listing I found on every single job site was the same one: Whisper Falls Inn.

CHAPTER 2

"*S*leep well?" Sindi asked me the next night when I came into the kitchen, a teasing glint in her eye and smirk on her lips.

I groaned with embarrassment. "Did I . . . make noises?"

She shrugged. "How would I know? I sleep like the dead."

Bada-bing. It was one of her favorite lines, but it grew old two years ago. I rolled my eyes.

"But I can smell it." Her smirk grew.

My cheeks flushed. Sometimes, I wished my vampirism was more like hers. She couldn't blush.

"All sweet and sexy at the same time," she added.

"Ugh. Sindi! Stop."

She placed a glass of blood in front of me—our version of the protein smoothie. "But it's such a delightful way to wake up —horny as hell. Starts the night off right."

"Not when it's the only action you're getting," I muttered.

"Speak for yourself." She swatted me on the ass before heading back upstairs to get ready for work.

I lifted the glass to my mouth and forced the cool liquid down. Stored blood compared to fresh blood like fat-free cheese compared to the real deal—it just flat-out didn't. I should have left the city last night to hunt out in the country, but I'd promised Sindi I'd wait for her to make the trip on our next shared night off. *Whenever that might be.* It'd been weeks since we'd hunted, and the blood we'd collected then was running low. The thought of living in a small town surrounded by forest and wildlife admittedly sounded more and more appealing. *I could drink fresh every night . . .*

If only I could find a job in a place that actually existed. I was letting the fictional Whisper Falls Inn get to me—and it had to be fictional, because all the weirdness last night just couldn't be real. *That reminds me. I need to take my computer in to Joe tonight.*

After finishing my blood, I downed a cup of coffee before jumping into the shower. Visions from my dream floated lazily behind my closed lids as I stood under the flowing water—full lips traveling over my neck and shoulder . . . large hands skimming down my side . . . my tongue playing over the birthmark on his muscular chest . . . gray-green eyes, darker than my own, piercing all the way into me, touching my soul . . .

I'd never admitted that last part to Sindi, not really even to myself. Because those eyes—I felt like I knew them, except I didn't. The rest was all Ryan, I was sure of it. I'd been dreaming of him since the day I met him freshman year at Emory University. But for some reason, all my dreams had those eyes that looked nothing like Ryan's warm brown ones. The intense feeling that came with those eyes, what they did to my heart and soul, could only mean they'd belonged to my ex back in Texas. The one whose memory I'd chosen to bury, but my subconscious thought we should bring out on a regular basis, like whenever I was horny.

"I need to get laid," I muttered as I towel-dried my hair.

"Yes, you do!" Sindi called from her own bathroom. She didn't have to yell. I could hear her as well as she could hear me. As though realizing this, she dropped her voice to normal tones.

"I bet Colorado lumberjacks are great in bed. What else do they have to do with their free time?"

"I'm pretty sure not everyone in Colorado is a lumberjack."

"Maybe not, but they sure are sexy. You're gonna get so lucky."

"I'm not even going. Just stop it already."

"Yes, you are."

"It wasn't real."

"If you say so. Or maybe it's very real and they really want you and you just can't admit that to yourself."

"How would they even know what skills or experience I have?" Or didn't have, as it was.

She appeared in my doorway, her head tilted as she secured her earing while watching me with a raised brow. "Are you telling me not once after graduation or since did you put your résumé on the internet? And if you say no, I'll have to kick your ass." She barely paused, not letting me answer, because she already knew I had. "So someone obviously, *finally* found it, and they want you. Don't look a gift horse in the mouth, Kaela. Take the damn job."

"If I didn't know any better, I'd say you're trying to get rid of me," I said between breaths as I did the necessary dance to tug on my tight black jeans. "Something you want to tell me?"

When she didn't answer immediately, I glanced up to find something dark flicker across her blue eyes, but they cleared instantly. "Yeah. Start your career. Get your own place. And then *I'm* coming to stay with *you* this time. Maybe I can meet a sexy lumberjack who doesn't mind sharing his bed and his blood every night."

She threw me a wink before spinning and sauntering back to her room.

∼

"I HAVE to make a stop on the way to work, okay?" I said a half-hour later as we left home, indicating my laptop bag on my shoulder. "I just need to drop it off with Joe. It'll be quick, I promise."

Sindi lifted a perfectly shaped brow. "We can't be late again."

"We won't. I swear." I held up my pinky as we began walking down the residential street toward Peachtree Road and the nightclub we both bartended at tonight. We didn't actually do the whole pinky-swear thing—the finger lift was enough in our book.

"I'm pretty sure we're both out of warnings," she reminded me.

"We'll be fine. It'll only take a second. And if you want to go on, you can."

"Yeah, sure, because if *you* get fired, you already have another job waiting for you."

I ignored the comment. She refused to believe the job offer was a fake, and I couldn't prove it until my computer was professionally scanned and remedied. So it was a moot point to argue any further about it.

Joe's computer repair shop was right around the corner from home and a few blocks from the club, on the second floor over one of the many restaurants and bars lining the street. I'd insisted Sindi go on without me because we both knew she was a lot closer to losing her job than I was. So I couldn't believe it when I came out of Joe's and saw her crimson head bobbing in a small crowd in front of one of the restaurants. I pushed by a few people and tapped on her shoulder.

"What the hell are you doing?" I demanded, unable to see what she could considering she stood taller than most of the crowd, while I stared at people's backs. "I thought you didn't want to get fired."

She glanced down at me before looking forward again. Then as though something spooked her, she looked at me again with wide eyes. She grabbed my upper arm and started tugging me back out of the crowd.

"Hey!" I said. "What's going on?"

"Nothing. Come on. We have to go, right?"

The crowd gasped as we began to make our way around it without stepping into the busy street.

"There's the ring," someone squealed excitedly.

I looked over with curiosity. Did I mention how much I enjoyed sappy love stories? That's when I noticed exactly which restaurant everyone had gathered in front of. I shouldn't have been surprised. The Bird Cage, a fancy, romantic gig famous for the number of proposals that took place on the little metal gazebo out front. The place where Ryan had proposed to me. I usually avoided it, crossing the road to walk on the other side ever since. I hadn't been paying attention when I'd come out of Joe's.

"You think she'll say yes?" someone asked.

"So romantic!" another sighed.

I stopped, unable to help myself. I was drawn in along with everyone else. I peeked through a small gap in the crowd to see what looked like men's legs bent down on one knee.

"Kaekae, come on!" Sindi insisted.

"You go on if you want. I just want to see."

"No. You don't."

I shook my arm free from her grip and threw her a harsh look. "I'm fine. It's not like I can avoid this place or public proposals the rest of my life. In fact, they make me happy."

"You do *not* want to see this one. It won't make you happy. Trust me."

"Why n—" As I looked in her eyes, realization dawned on me.

Go. Just move along, get to work, and go on with your night. I tried to convince myself, but did I mention what a masochist I was? My feet carried me closer, and I pressed into the crowd, ignoring the jabs and comments about my rudeness. I was a woman possessed, by what I didn't know, but I couldn't stop myself until I was at the front of the crowd. And I couldn't stop the sob when I saw them.

Ryan on one knee, just like he'd been that terrible night.

Ryan holding a small, black box up, just like he'd been that terrible night.

Ryan smiling with that nervous tic where his dark hair touched his temple, just like he'd been that terrible night.

And Heather, her curly hair bouncing as she jumped up and down in her slinky dress and heels, which she'd also been doing that terrible night.

But she hadn't been the one squealing, "YES!"

She'd been out here, right where I stood, excited for me.

I'd been the one saying, "Yes!"

I couldn't say what overcame me. Every possible emotion known to man, or vampire, whatever. At least, all of the negative ones, exploding with the intensified force of my kind. Tears burned my eyes. Sobs choked me, making me gasp for air. Hurt, denial, sadness, anger—they all swirled together inside me.

People started screaming. And running. And I didn't know why.

Heather cried out. Ryan ducked and tried to push her behind him. She grabbed onto him as she tripped, ripping his dress shirt open as they both went down, him on top of her. He held his arms up, as though trying to stop something from hitting them.

"Kaela." Sindi's voice came from a great distance, muffled by the whir of blood rushing through my ears.

I couldn't turn to look at her. My vision tunneled onto the scene in front of me, through a thick, red haze. Heather splayed out on the ground, Ryan on top of her, his shirt hanging open, baring his chest. The gazebo, shaped like a bird cage, appeared to be collapsing over them. Several support bars snapped free, and the ends twisted inward, all pointing at Ryan, closing in on him.

"Kaela!" Sindi's voice came more urgently now. A vice

grabbed my upper arm and jerked at me. "Kaela, stop this! Now!"

She tugged me again, harder now, twisting me away. I looked at her and blinked with disorientation.

"Stop," she said much more calmly, her blue eyes locked on mine. I tried to look back, but she moved her face, blocking my line of sight. "No more, Kaekae. No more."

I blinked again. My head cleared. My lungs seized. "Oh my god! What did I do?"

She tried to stop me from looking again, but I had to know. I shifted to see around her and threw my hand over my mouth. Heather and Ryan were crawling out of a gap in the metal bars of the gazebo, which looked like a large hand had squeezed the top of it like a beer can. Except, some of the bars appeared to be partially melted. *Metal* bars. *Melted.*

"Come on. We need to get out of here." Sindi took my hand and tugged me along behind her. I stumbled in my heeled boots at first, but caught myself and followed without paying attention to where we went. We walked in silence for a while, how long I didn't know, as I was lost in my own mind. We finally stopped, and Sindi turned to me. "Are you going to make it through your shift?"

I realized we stood at the back door of the club, a metal door in a brick building. My hand lifted to the door, but nothing happened. It didn't melt or crumple under my touch. I inhaled a deep breath and nodded. "I'm okay. I'll be okay."

She studied my face for a moment and nodded, although she didn't look entirely convinced. She shouldn't have been. I was far from okay. I was a mess at work, making the wrong drinks, dropping glasses, giving incorrect change. My mind was still stuck on the proposal. On the deformed bird cage gazebo. On Ryan's bare chest.

That didn't have a birthmark.

For some reason, that's what my mind obsessed on the most.

If he didn't have a birthmark, then he wasn't the one in my dreams. And if he wasn't, who the hell was?

"You need to take that job and get far away from here," Sindi said once we were home.

I sat on the couch in a ball with my legs drawn in and a blanket wrapped around me. I stared at her blankly.

"You could have killed him, Kaela. Again."

My eyes squeezed shut, and I nodded. "I know," I whispered.

"It must happen when you lose control of your emotions," she said, referring to the deformed metal. "Or when you're angry or hurt or something."

I nodded again. Something similar had happened before. Only once, the first time I'd seen Ryan and Heather together, through the window of the apartment he and I used to share, both naked in our bed. The entire metal fire escape bent and melted before I turned away and ran. Sindi had followed me there, just in case things went bad with Ryan and me as I was making the first move to try to start over with him. She'd witnessed the whole thing.

"And as long as you're here and they're here . . . well, it's not good for you. And it sure as hell isn't good for them."

She was right. I couldn't deny it anymore. I had to shed my masochistic tendencies and do what I should have done a long time ago. Otherwise, I'd never be able to move on. And if I killed one of them, I'd never be able to live with myself.

"What about you?" I asked her, my voice thin.

She gave me a warm smile and patted my knee. "I keep telling you. I'm a big girl. I'll be fine. You helped me through a rough time, too, gave me a distraction from my own shitty life. But I'm good now." Her smile broadened. "You and me, we had a lot of fun together. We got through some fucked-up shit, but we had a lot of fun, too, right?"

I smiled weakly and nodded.

"So we're good. And now it's time for you to spread your wings and fly, baby bird." She leaned over and gave me a quick hug. Something she didn't do very often. She was much more of a badass vampire chick than I was. "Besides, I'm not kidding. Once you're settled, my ass is so out there to visit. It'll be a long drive, so you better make it worth it."

She handed me my phone and a piece of paper with the number for Whisper Falls Inn. Why was I not surprised she'd written it down from the email? She stared at me expectantly. She'd never give up until I proved to her the inn was a hoax. So I dialed the number and tapped the green send icon.

"Whisper Falls Inn," the sweet female voice on the other end answered, surprising me.

Sindi laughed at my shocked expression, then nodded with encouragement.

"Um . . . hi. This is Kaela Peters. I'm calling for M. Luiza. About a job offer."

CHAPTER 3

*A*fter spending the day in a nearby motel waiting for night to fall, I pulled into the McDonald's parking lot in Durango, Colorado, exactly two weeks later. As Ms. Luiza had promised, I couldn't have missed the shuttle bus parked in back that I was supposed to meet. A huge wrap around the entire vehicle advertised the beauty and fun to be had in Havenwood Falls, my soon-to-be hometown. Several people were boarding the bus. I parked my car nearby and glanced at the clock. 7:14. I had just enough time to pee and grab something to eat before we hit the road again.

"Holy fuck, it's freezing!" I yelped when I opened my car door. I grabbed the thick, white coat from the passenger seat and wrapped myself up before climbing out.

"Michaela Petran?" a deep and raspy voice said from behind me, and I turned to face an old man with gray, shaggy hair and a long beard to match, wearing a thick flannel shirt, jeans, and boots. I had to bite back a smirk, thinking of Sindi's lumberjack dreams.

"Um . . . Kaela Peters," I corrected as I pulled on my coat. How was he not freezing?

His gray, furry brows pinched together before laughter twinkled in his blue eyes. "Of course! Silly me! Gettin' forgetful in my old age. Anyway, good on you for meetin' us here. The drive from here on in can get confusin' and treacherous. You sure you want to drive it?"

"I'm sure. I'll be fine," I promised. It wasn't like I really had a choice. I needed my car.

He eyed said car. "In that thing?" He chuckled. "Good thing the roads are clear right now. But winter ain't over yet up in the mountains. You better be gettin' a four-wheel-drive A-S-A-P."

"Um . . . thanks for the advice," I said. I supposed most of my savings would be going to a new vehicle soon. "I'll be fine for now, right?"

"For now," he said with a nod. "Alrighty then, Ms. Petra—I mean, Ms. Peters. I'm waitin' on a few more arrivals, but we leave in ten minutes with or without them and with or without you."

"Understood." I gave him a smile, then hurried inside to take care of my personal business, worried about being left behind.

For some odd reason, I couldn't find Havenwood Falls anywhere on any map, not even Google's. I had coordinates, but Ms. Luiza warned me that GPS often led people down the wrong roads, taking them hours out of their way. After being on the road for three nights, I really didn't want to add hours if I didn't have to, especially if it risked me being outside at sunrise. So I made sure to be back in my car and ready to go by the time the bus, decorated with ski slopes and restaurant facades, pulled out. To my surprise, I wasn't the only car following. A five-vehicle caravan made its way up and around the mountains.

The roads were steep, twisty, and pitch black except where the beams of our headlights bounced off rock walls on one side and plunging cliffs on the other, with plenty of thick-trunked trees that would split a car in two with one wrong turn. My old Ford Fiesta fell behind at one point, and I rounded a bend and almost slammed into a herd of elk starting to cross the road. I swore they stood at least three feet taller than my car because all I saw at first were legs.

Once I saw the sign welcoming me to Havenwood Falls, I could finally loosen my white-knuckled grip on the steering wheel, damned glad I was part of the caravan, because Ms. Luiza and the old man were right—I'd have never found this place on my own, especially in the dark.

A spotlight lit up the welcome sign, made of layered stone with beautifully made black metal lettering. At once, it was both charming and sinister, as I imagined living in a small mountain town surrounded by the wild would be. My stomach began to flutter with butterflies as the giddiness of my new adventure overcame me for the hundredth time in the last two weeks. Yet, at the same time, a feeling of comfort slid over my shoulders and down my back, like a warm blanket, a comforting hug, a lovingly whispered *welcome home*.

We drove on several miles past the welcome sign, curved another bend, climbed a little higher, and even before I saw them, I knew there'd be lights as soon as we crested the ridge ahead. And there were. A smattering of lights lit up the town below with silhouettes of the looming mountains inky black against the night sky, their white caps appearing to glow. Even in the dark, I felt their intimidating yet wondrous presence. Realization that I'd never see them in the daylight hit me like a punch in the gut. Maybe once I hung my blackout curtains and took certain precautions, I could take a quick peek.

We passed Creekwood, a housing development on the left, then the road forked, but I already knew to stay to the right. And not just because Ms. Luiza had given me directions to the inn from here. I could somehow see in my mind's eye each landmark even before I came to it: Havenstone, a townhouse and villa development built in a wooden ski-lodge style, on the right; the high school's two-story brick building on the left; a shopping center and an apartment complex (Havenwood

Village, I somehow knew) on the right; and then I'd reach the town square. Staying on the same road along the south side of the square, I passed by a two-story row of darkened shops and what I assumed to be apartments above them, considering the lights glowing in a couple windows. Then finally I came to the large Victorian manor that was the inn, sitting at an angle on the corner so it faced the square, a dim light glowing through the glass door. But the inn wasn't exactly as the pictures had promised and what I'd envisioned. Even in the dark, it looked as though it had seen better days—more than a few years ago.

A little old woman wearing an old-fashioned dressing gown stood in the driveway flapping her arms, waving me down although I was already turning toward her. She motioned me along as she scrambled as fast as her little legs could carry her down the drive toward the back of the inn. She could move surprisingly fast considering her age and plump stature. She waved me into a parking space next to the last of five cottages lining the back of the property. Exactly like I'd seen in my mind a few weeks ago.

The woman clapped her hands together under her chin, and a big smile filled her sweet face when I climbed out of the car, making her gray eyes twinkle. "Oh, honey, I'm so glad you're here!"

Her arms opened, and she took a step toward me as though she wanted to hug me, but stopped herself. "I'm sorry! It's just so exciting to have you finally back. I mean, finally here. Back here, in your cottage, yes, that's what I mean. This is your place, dear." She bustled up the steps of the front porch, stood by the front door, and gestured at it. "I'll let you do the honors."

She moved to the side and waited for me to ascend the porch and enter.

"You must be Ms. Luiza," I said as I mounted the steps and held my gloved hand out to her. Damn was I thankful I let Sindi talk me into buying a bunch of winter clothes before I left, all on end-of-the-season sale in Atlanta.

"Madame Luiza, dear. The M has always been for Madame. I'm too old to be a Ms." She patted her gray mop of hair and again motioned at the knob while completely ignoring my outstretched hand. "You should have everything you need for now, and I'll help you get situated for good over the next few days before your first day at work."

I gave her a wary smile before opening the door and crossing the threshold into a small living room that couldn't have been more perfectly decorated for me if I'd done it myself. The cozy room's walls were painted a light neutral color with white trim and was furnished with a plump-cushioned taupe couch and a dark brown chaise lounge set between a large bookcase and a fireplace. Blankets and quilts draped over the sofa and chaise, and flames licked the logs inside the hearth.

"Thought you might like a warm fire to greet you. It's a bit colder here than Georgia, I imagine," Madame Luiza said from behind me.

I snickered. "Just a bit. I'm surprised I can't see my breath."

"Well, that's silly. It's forty-one degrees out. That's a heat wave for this time of year." She emphasized her statement by fanning her face with her hand and letting out a chortle. "That's supposed to change by the end of the week, and we'll be back to cold for a bit longer. But don't you worry. You'll get used to it one of these days." She babbled on as I moved farther into the cottage, glancing around at what I could see through the doorways—a kitchen and a small hallway that led to a bedroom and bathroom. "In a year or two from now, you'll be hitting the swimming hole in June with the rest of the young'uns. I'd go, but ain't nobody want to see this old lady in a bathing suit!"

She chortled again, the sound warming my heart. Rather than annoying me, as it normally would have done, her babbling came as a comfort.

"Well, I'll let you get on then. Sun'll be up in no time, which means our guests will be, too. You get some rest, and I'll see you soon enough."

I stood in the doorway to the kitchen and turned toward her. "It probably won't be until later tomorrow, probably in the evening. I've been driving for days and . . ."

She waved her hand in dismissal. "Oh, I know, honey. No worries. We'll get that all taken care of tomorrow night. Get your tattoo and everything. Or I could probably get Adelaide to come here, make it easier—"

I cut her off. "Um . . . *tattoo?*"

Her eyes widened as she clapped her hands over her mouth. "Did I say that out loud? I'm sorry. I'm trying so hard not to throw everything on you at once. Go on now. There are refreshments in the refrigerator. Bedroom is that way, and blackout curtains throughout. Sleep well!"

She gestured toward the back of the cottage, then hurried out the front door before I could say another word. I followed her, but she was already completely out of sight when I stepped onto the porch.

"What in the hell?" I muttered out loud as I went back out to my car to grab the necessities. I'd unpack the rest tomorrow night.

After dropping my suitcase in my room and kicking my shoes off to replace them with socks and slippers, I padded into the kitchen for something to drink. And nearly squealed when I opened the refrigerator door and saw the bottle on the top shelf.

"Yes! Wine!" The next best thing to blood, but without knowing my way around yet and with sunrise less than two hours away, I wasn't about to go out and hunt tonight. I found a set of wine glasses in the cabinet and a bottle opener in the drawer. This place really was stocked perfectly for me. And when I opened the bottle and took a whiff, I realized just how perfectly.

Too perfectly.

My hands began to shake.

"Blood."

How the hell did they know?

I paced the lovely cottage for hours, unable to settle down and sleep even when the sun rose, which was only barely noticeable behind the total black-out curtains on every window, keeping the interior dark and comfortable. My gut instinct swung erratically between being completely freaked out that my new employers were apparently aware of my state of unusual existence and feeling completely comforted and welcomed by their considerate gestures. I obviously knew other vampires existed in this world because, well, Sindi, and the small handful of others she'd introduced me to. And not to mention whoever had turned me—we'd never figured that out. Whoever they were was a total dick, leaving me to turn and adapt all on my own. It could have been a bloody disaster with a high body count if not for Sindi. We'd heard rumors of other types of supernatural beings as well, although nobody we knew had ever actually met any others. But what were the chances that the owners of Whisper Falls Inn not only understood that vampires existed, but knew that I was one?

Probably the same chances that every hotel night manager job on the internet was at the same place. And the same chances that you'd seen in your mind the very grounds you drove up to tonight, the very cottage you're in now. The same chances that you feel like you've been here before when you've never even stepped foot in the state of Colorado.

So maybe the owners were also vampires, and they'd heard of me through the vampy grapevine. That was plausible, I supposed. But the rest didn't add up. This place wasn't right. Or maybe I wasn't. Maybe I had gone insane after all.

I stood at the front window, next to the front door, aching to go outside and prove to myself that I did not know that there was a coffee shop three doors down to the west and another on the far side of the square, right across from the chamber of commerce. That there was no way I knew that four blocks to the east of town square and two blocks north, at the end of a cul-de-sac, sat a large log cabin with a green tin roof and a stream running along the back of the property. These kinds of details weren't on the Havenwood Falls website I'd skimmed through after taking the job. So there was no way I knew these things. I had to be wrong.

My legs carried me across the living room, into the kitchen, and back again, trying to expel the nervous energy that had been coursing through my veins since I discovered bottled blood in my fridge. I cursed my vampirism for holding me hostage in here—but, in truth, my avoidance of severe pain was my true captor. I wouldn't die if I went outside. At least, not immediately. But it would sure hurt like hell and leave me all blistery and fucked-up for days. However, I *could* look out the window, at least for a few moments, with no painful repercussions.

I hurried to the bedroom and fished in my suitcase for the sunglasses I held onto for those times when I just needed a peek to remember what the world was like in the light of day. I'd almost trashed the shaded specs while packing, because I'd learned long ago to stop indulging in those little glimpses. They only depressed me. It was better to try to forget life as a normal person and embrace my new existence as a creature of the night. Now I was glad I'd thrown them into the suitcase at the last minute.

After pulling on a hoodie and gloves to cover as much skin as possible, I put on the shades and pushed the front curtain back a few inches. My heart pulsed with longing at the bright world out there . . . except I couldn't really see much. The roof over the front porch blocked out almost everything. I could see my car and the white trunks of aspen trees on the other side of it, an expanse of brown lawn that stretched out from the cottages to the wrap-around porch of the extremely large Victorian-era main building of the inn, and a portion of said porch with its peeling paint that might have been white at one time. Flower beds surrounded the porch, but only a few scraggly vines stuck out of them. I tilted my head and adjusted my angle to catch a glimpse of a brick building across the street, but that was about it.

Fuck.

I was about to let go of the curtain when a blue, late model pickup truck parked about halfway up the drive that led back to the cottages. A moment later, a man walked across the lawn toward the main house, a tool belt hanging low on his hips over his perfectly fitting jeans cladding his perfectly sculpted ass. My breath became lodged in my throat as I drank him in. Tall, broad-shouldered, arms thick with muscles that strained the sleeves of his green Henley. He wore a knit cap, sunglasses, and a closely trimmed beard, preventing me from seeing his face. With my eyes, anyway. Because in my mind, I could see him clearly. He glanced over his shoulder, directly toward me, and I let the curtain fall. Not that he could have possibly seen me from that distance and behind the window under the shadow of the roof . . . but it was a compulsive reaction.

The lump in my throat grew, making it difficult to breathe. *I . . . know . . . him. In all the ways a woman could know a man.*

CHAPTER 4

I shook my head and then the rest of my body, shaking off the impossible feeling. The exhaustion of the move, the drive, and everything else finally slammed into me. My body must have pumped through the last of the adrenaline from discovering the blood bottle and now I was crashing. *I just need sleep. This will all make sense after I've had some rest.*

After a quick shower to wash off the travel stink, my head hit the pillow, and I was out.

Full lips skate over my jaw and up to the corner of my mouth. His tongue flicks out, over my bottom lip, before he sucks it in between his. I moan and press my body against his, digging my fingers into the skin of his shoulders as his mouth assaults mine. His hand splays on my lower back, pulling me in tighter against his thigh that's between my legs. I whimper from the friction as my breasts swell and tighten against his bare chest. Needing a breath, I pull away for a moment. My finger traces the birthmark over his heart as my gaze slowly slides upward to meet his. Beautiful gray eyes flecked with green stare back at me.

"You shouldn't be here," he says, *although his voice calls me home.*

I awoke with a start, my heart pounding a hard rhythm against my ribs. My eyes swept around the unfamiliar room as my mind tried to remember where I was. Oh, right. Freakwood Falls. *Home.* I drifted back to sleep almost immediately.

A light knock on the door brought me out of a deep, dreamless slumber, and I was relieved to see night had fallen. *Now I can get answers.* I threw on a robe before hurrying for the door as another knock sounded. When I pulled it open, Madame Luiza was about to descend the stairs off the porch.

She turned around, and a bright smile lit up her face. "Oh, you *are* up! I was beginning to think I came too early. You're probably exhausted from all that driving. I can come back later, if you'd like, and we can get you all set up with the important stuff then."

She made to turn again, but I stopped her. "No! Wait! I need answers. Now."

A frown momentarily marred her sweet features. "Oh, dear, you are all worked up, aren't you? I should have known. Tsk tsk. I'm so sorry. Here you were, stuck here all day, too. But we'll get that taken care of in a jiffy. The Court is expecting you."

I blinked as my still sleep-fogged mind tried to catch up. "The court? Why?"

Was it really necessary to change my driver's license and car registration my first night here? And how would the court even be open now?

"Well, you have to sign into the Registry and get your mark." She said this as though I should have known what she spoke about.

I lifted a brow. "My mark? As in the tattoo you mentioned last night?"

Realization dawned on her wrinkled face. "Oh, there I go again, getting ahead of myself. You have no idea what I'm talking about, do you?"

I shook my head.

"No worries. Adelaide will explain everything and take good

care of you. As long as you follow the rules and laws, you'll be fine."

"This Adelaide will explain everything?" I asked, and she nodded. "Then take me to her. Now."

Madame Luiza gave me a once-over. "Don't you want to put on something a little . . . um . . . *warmer?*"

I glanced down at my nearly naked body clothed in only a short, terrycloth robe barely covering the important parts. I'd been too concerned about answers to even notice the cold. "Oh my god. Of course."

I turned to rush inside and change, but Madame Luiza stopped me. "As soon as you're dressed, you can head on over to the Court. It's across the town square, at the back of City Hall. You can't miss it. There's an emblem with a sun and a moon over the door."

"You're not taking me?"

She smiled warmly. "Oh, no, honey. I have guests to take care of. Doing your job—and everyone else's—for now."

"Do you need help?"

"Yes, but that's what you're here for, right? I can manage another day or two while you get settled. It's important you take care of everything with the Court first. Don't want to get in their bad graces already."

Thirty minutes later, I hurried down my porch steps, bundled in my new coat, hat, and gloves, and focused on finding this court, whatever it was, but more importantly, this Adelaide, who could give me answers. When I set foot on the inn's lawn, though, I had to stop for a moment and close my eyes to take it all in. I inhaled the cold air deeply—or tried to. My lungs struggled to pull as hard as I wanted to, and it took me a moment to remember the thinner air at this altitude. I'd been warned about that.

Still, I sucked in enough to savor the clean, crisp fragrance in my nose and taste on my tongue. Freezing cold, but all natural, the earthiness of aspen, pine, and dirt. Several different food aromas lingered from neighbors' dinners, combining with the smoky warmth of burning wood. Barely a hint of gas fumes, oil, asphalt, or even concrete.

I listened to small animals scurrying into their nests for the night along with the muted chatter of people in their homes and the low hum of television shows. From somewhere not too far away came the sound of people in a bar and nearby there, patrons in restaurants and coffee shops. The sound of tires on roads was definitely present, but not like the nonstop whooshing of the big city. There was still a cacophony of sound here for my vampire ears, but one that was actually calming rather than irritating.

A light breeze kissed my face, chilling my skin, and I was brought out of the moment. My eyes opened, but I hesitated, and for the first time since arriving, I really looked around. The three story inn with its turrets, many bay windows, and gingerbread trim stood ahead at an angle to the corner, its back to me. To my left and slightly behind me was the row of cottages that provided five of the eighteen guest rooms—well, minus one for me now—and beyond them, near the street going north and south, was a small and noticeably empty parking lot. To my right was the driveway that led to the cottages, each one with its own space behind me. All but mine was also empty. Were all the guests Madame Luiza had to tend to still at dinner? And nobody stayed at the inn to eat? I thought I remembered it having its own dining room, supposedly with rave reviews.

The thoughts about the state of the inn drifted away as my gaze lifted to the mountains beyond the structure, soaring thousands of feet high. In awe, I turned in a slow, complete circle, and they were everywhere, boxing this little town in. I guessed that's why they called it a box canyon. Up to the tree line, the mountainsides were dark with forest, and the jagged edges of their white peaks seemed to scrape the stars in the sky. And those stars . . .

"Holy. Shit," I whispered. I'd always half-believed pictures of the night sky with this many stars—and so close!—were fakes. I gasped as I turned in a circle again, now while staring at the sky. "That's the fucking Milky Way!"

I lifted my arms and waved my fingers in the air as though I could actually touch it.

"It's so magical." The words came out softly, barely audible to my own sensitive ears, but they were followed by what sounded like a snort from the direction of the inn's wraparound porch.

I dropped my head, and my gaze swept across the porch, but I saw nobody there. Chills rose anew over my skin, and I tightened my coat around me as I began to walk again when a scream and a crash came from inside the main house. I immediately bolted to it, across the lawn and at the door in less than a second before remembering myself. Not that any witnesses were around, considering all the empty parking spaces.

"Madame Luiza?" I called as I rushed through one set of French doors and into a parlor room. I heard a whimper and a faint heartbeat a level above me. I hurried through the parlor, past the empty and dark dining room, and into the lobby before turning for the curving staircase, taking two steps at a time. Not until I stopped at the end of the hallway, where Madame Luiza lay, did I realize I'd known exactly where to find her and how to get here.

"I'm . . . okay." The old woman's gasp came from the floor, and I dropped to my knees by her side. What appeared to have been a tea set lay in pieces on the floor, the tea mixing with blood gushing out of a gash in her forearm.

"Oh, no. Here." I peeled off my coat and gloves and lifted my wrist to my mouth to pierce my skin and give her my healing blood, but she gave a minute shake of her head.

"No, no. That . . . won't work," she gasped out. "Just . . . get me . . . to bed." Her voice faded, and her eyelids drooped before closing completely.

I grabbed the tea towel and pressed it to her wound before

picking up the little old lady and carrying her into the room that I instinctively knew was hers.

"What happened?" I asked as I lay her down.

Her eyes fluttered open for a moment. "Old . . . lady. Accident."

She fell silent again as her eyes closed.

"What the hell happened? What did you do to her?" The girl's voice demanded in that accusatory tone teenagers always seemed to speak in. She pushed past me and dropped to the old woman's bed, glancing at me long enough to show her disgust before giving Madame Luiza all of her attention.

"What's going on?" a deep voice asked from the doorway, making the hairs on the back of my neck raise. "Oh, fuck. Is she okay?"

The large body pushed past me as well, nearly knocking me over. He knelt down next to the girl, his broad shoulders blocking me from seeing anything else. I took several steps backward before turning to leave the room. I assumed they were her family and would take care of her, so I stood in the dark hallway, not knowing what to do besides wait. Oh, and clean up the mess. Just as I bent down to start picking up the ceramic pieces, the man's body filled the doorway again before he strode right on by me, again without a glance.

"I have to find Isabella," he growled over his shoulder.

"Wait! Don't leave me with her!" the girl shouted, her voice filled with annoyance.

"She's your family, Aurelia. Get over yourself." He disappeared down the stairs then, although I could hear him stomping around the lower level as though looking for something. A moment later, I heard a door open and close.

"Asshole," the girl huffed as she stomped out of the room, also right past me. "I notice *you're* not staying."

She kept talking, although he was long gone. A moment later, she too left through the same door.

I stood there stupidly for a long moment, until Madame Luiza's faint voice called out to me.

"What do you need? What can I do?" I asked as I rushed inside and knelt by her bed.

"Arm," she croaked. I looked down to find the towel, now stained crimson, still pressed against her wound.

"Oh, god, of course! Are you . . . sure?" I held my wrist out.

She gave me a weak smile. "I'm sure, dear. I'm far beyond healing. A bandage will do. Keep me from messing up the bedding any more than I already have."

"Anything else?" I asked. "Water?"

"That would be good."

I hurried back down the stairs and to the kitchen. The first aid kit was exactly where I knew it would be and so were the glasses. I tried not to think about that too much, forcing myself to focus on Madame Luiza. She drifted off while I bandaged her arm, and I couldn't help but notice the odd odor—her blood was not of a healthy human. I tried not to think about that too much either.

When I finished, I lifted her unconscious body into the chaise lounge, the only other piece of furniture in the room besides the bed and a dresser between them. I easily found the closet of linens and changed her bedding, then I studied her, wondering if I should change her, too, or if that would be crossing the line. After all, she was my boss. Undressing her might be going too far.

As I looked more closely at her, I noticed in more detail the lines and curves of her face. I hadn't noticed so many wrinkles last night. I'd thought her hair was a steel-gray then, but now it seemed lighter, with more white strands than I'd realized. She was even older than I'd first thought. And she was running this place by herself? No wonder she'd been so desperate to hire someone! I wondered if she knew how to spam the internet by herself, or if her grandchildren had helped.

Speaking of whom, what the hell happened to them? Did

they really just take off and leave her here with a near stranger? I thought they'd gone to get help, but more than an hour had already passed, and still nobody had come.

"Help me?" The little old lady's soft voice jerked my attention from the doorway and back to her. "I'd like to change. Purple dress in the closet."

My eyes squinted as I looked at her. "I don't think you should go out. You need to rest."

She let out a long, sad sigh. "Yes, I know, dear."

"Then wouldn't you be more comfortable in a nightgown?"

She reached up and patted my hand as she gave me yet another weak smile, this one reaching her eyes with a faint twinkle. "Please, dear. I don't want to die in my night clothes."

I returned her smile as I held her hand in mine. "You're not going to die, Madame Luiza. Not on my watch. It's just a cut. The bleeding's already stopped."

She squeezed my hand weakly. "Oh, no, not from that. Look at me and tell me death's not coming. Maybe not tonight, but soon. It's simply my time. I'm the last hold-out. At least you're here, though, honey. That's all I wanted. Now help me put on my favorite dress, will you?"

I gazed at her for a moment, and she was right. I could practically see her aging in front of me. My heart suddenly felt like it weighed three tons. My emotions confused me. I barely knew this woman, but I couldn't deny the deep sadness filling me. Swallowing down the lump in my throat, I nodded.

After changing her into the purple gown that looked as though it had been in fashion at the turn of the *last* century, I helped her lay back down.

"Who can I call?" I asked.

Her eyes fluttered closed. "Nobody, dear."

"But your family—"

"They won't come if you call, but Aurelia and Gabe might come on their own. You're here, honey. That's enough."

I won't let you die alone. She obviously didn't want that if

44

having me here was enough for her. The poor woman was nearly as bad off as I was in the family department. Although it wasn't something I'd say aloud, regardless of how well she seemed to be accepting her imminent death.

She fell asleep almost immediately, although it was a fitful sleep. Afraid to leave her side and not knowing what else to do, I sat on the bed, then paced, then sat on the chaise for a while, then paced some more. Hours passed. The earlier sounds of town square had fallen fairly silent. Aurelia never returned. Neither did the guy, who I assumed to be Gabe. So much for going to court and finding Adelaide. They'd have to wait until tomorrow night. Sunrise was only a few hours away. At least the curtains appeared to be blackouts, so I could stay if nobody came. I stood at the window after inspecting them, watching the moon as it began to set behind the mountain. The sound of a door downstairs barely registered in my mind.

"Adelaide's here for you." The deep voice once again sent a shiver down my spine.

I turned to meet a very familiar pair of eyes that even in the dim light I knew were gray with green flecks.

CHAPTER 5

e both stood frozen, staring at each other for seconds that stretched into eons. His face was turned down, causing a lock of his dark hair, combed back from his face, to fall forward by his temple. His narrowed eyes gazed up at me, almost accusingly, through thick, black lashes. His dark brows were pinched together, forming two vertical lines between them and several creases across his forehead. My fingers twitched with the desire to smooth them out, to relieve the pain he was obviously in.

The longer we stared, the more I felt like he was trying to reach into my soul and claim it. Or maybe that he already had. My heart beat erratically, and my mouth and throat went dry. The room suddenly became too small for the both of us. For him. And not just because he was far over six feet tall and built like an Olympian. His very presence filled the room completely . . . started to fill me.

"I'll, uh, let you—" I stammered at the same time as he said, "You need to go . . ."

His angry tone made me flinch, and he sounded like he wanted to say more, but then looked like he couldn't be bothered. Another long, awkward moment passed before I could finally will my feet to move. I shuffled forward, and he stepped to the side, and things became even more awkward as we did some strange dance to move around each other in the small space without daring to touch. As though that would scar us for life. Maybe it would.

Somehow I made it out of that room without even brushing against his arm or, you know, accidentally falling on top of his very nicely formed body.

Finally out of the room, I felt like the temperature dropped ten degrees. I had to pause to take a few breaths and settle my speeding heart. Before heading down the hallway to the stairs, I looked over my shoulder to see the god-like figure bending over and planting a kiss on Madame Luiza's forehead. For a fleeting moment, I felt jealousy for her. *Get a grip, Kae. You know nothing about him.*

Except, something way in the back, dark corners of my mind niggled at me, saying I did.

Once I finally gathered my wits back about me, I went down the stairs to meet the mysterious Adelaide who supposedly could answer all my questions. Because of the way Madame Luiza had spoken of her, and maybe also because of her name, I expected to find an older woman, smartly dressed and full of wisdom. Even if it was a ridiculous time of night, or early morning, for such a woman to be out making house calls. What I found was a young woman about my age, wearing a dark purple sweater, ripped up jeans, and knee-high boots. Her light brown hair was pulled back into a messy bun, she wore a diamond stone in her nose, and black-framed glasses added a studious touch to her otherwise edgy appearance. Several rings decorated her fingers.

"Michaela!" she gasped as a hand flew to her mouth. She let out another squeal, this one muffled. "I mean, Kaela, right?"

I blinked. That was the second time someone in this town had called me Michaela. What was wrong with them?

"Um, yeah, Kaela. You must be Adelaide?"

47

Her mouth twitched as though she fought a frown. "Addie. Please." Her voice dropped and filled with sorrow. "How is Mammie?"

My head cocked to the side.

"Madame Luiza?" she corrected.

I bit my lip. "Not well. I don't know what happened. I think she collapsed from exhaustion, but she's fading so quickly . . . Gabe is up there with her."

Addie's brows jumped up to her hairline. "Gabe is here? I thought he was at my house. The poor kid. What did he do when he saw you? And what about Aurelia? They've been through so much. It's good that you're here . . . Hey, what happened to Xandru? I thought he went up there to get you."

I tried to follow her questions, but they confused me. "Wait. Gabe's a kid?"

Now it was her turn to cock her head and blink at me. "Uh, yeah, he's twelve. I thought you said—"

I pressed my fingers to my temples. "I'm sorry. I don't know anybody here yet. I thought that was Gabe. He was here earlier with Aurelia, but they both took off, looking for an Isabella . . . I'm so confused."

Addie crossed the room to stand in front of me and placed a hand on my shoulder. "It's okay, Mich—I mean, Kaela. You'll get it soon, I'm sure of it."

"So who's up there with Madame Luiza now?" A blush crept across my skin just at the thought of him.

One side of her face pulled up in a knowing smirk. "Judging by the look on your face, that was definitely Xandru. Alexandru Roca, but we call him Xandru or Xan. I'm surprised you don't . . ."

She trailed off, and I waited for her to continue, but she shook her head before gesturing me into the nearby seating area.

"Never mind. Let's get you all taken care of before the sun rises so you can do what you need to do and not have to worry about those pesky UV rays."

She produced an old leather satchel I hadn't noticed before and set it on the floor next to a large cushioned chair that she motioned for me to sit on. I stood in place as she disappeared through a doorway behind the front desk and returned a moment later pushing an office chair on wheels. She sat on it and proceeded to pull what looked like a tattoo kit out of her bag.

"Come on," she said, once again gesturing at the bigger chair. "Don't tell me you're afraid of needles."

"No, and I'm not against tattoos or anything, but, um . . . are you freaking *serious*? I just got to town, just met you people, and you expect me to sit down and say, 'Okay, sure, ink me up. I don't give a shit what you to do my body. That I have to live with for . . . *forever*. Literally! And let's do it right now, even though your new boss is upstairs dying, and who knows what will happen to this place if she does, so you might not even stay, so here, this will give you something to remember your very short visit with us."

"Nobody remembers Havenwood Falls," she muttered.

"*What?*" That was her response to my rant?

She blew out a sigh. "Calm down, Kaela. It's not what you think. You can tell me whatever design you want, where you want it. Anywhere. I've done it all. If you feel more comfortable in a private room, we can go upstairs."

I let out a humorless laugh and threw up my hands. "Unbelievable! You don't get it. What in the *fuck* makes you think I want a damn tattoo?"

She looked up at me and said flatly, "Because it'll allow you to walk in the daylight."

I froze and stared at her, my mouth partially open. She gazed back at me with a brow lifted and her arms crossed, as though challenging me. In less than a heartbeat, I stood right in front of her and snarled, fangs out.

"If you know what I am, then you know you shouldn't fuck with me."

She stood, her face right in front of mine, and her eyes narrowed as her fingers flicked. I was suddenly on my knees, doubled over in pain as though I'd been stabbed in the gut. Then as quickly as it came, the sensation was gone. I slowly stood up and glared at her.

"Did you do that?" I whispered.

"Yeah, and I'll do a lot worse if you ever threaten me again. We're friends, Kaela. I'm on your side." She sat back down and picked up a bottle of ink. "Now, are we going to do this or not?"

"Not."

She looked up in surprise. "You don't want to be able to walk outside in the sun? See the world again in the light of day? Live a little more normally?"

"More than anything," I admitted. "But not until you explain how."

"How what?"

"How . . . everything. How you know what I am. How you did that to me. How your tattoo can allow me to walk in the sun. Oh, and maybe how I feel like I know weird, random things about this town."

She exhaled a long breath. "Fine, I will. As long as you sit down and give me some kind of idea of what you want your tattoo to look like so I can come up with a design."

When she obviously wouldn't say anything else yet, my head tilted to the side. "It'll really allow me to go outside in the day?"

"Yes, and your skin won't burn up or anything. You'll be just like a human in that regard."

"And you know this because . . ."

"Because we give these things out almost every week."

My eyes widened. "There are that many vampires? Here?"

She shrugged. "Well, not all vampires. Other supernaturals, too. They all get marked when they come to town. Everyone gets a benefit from it, but that's how you sign into the Registry so the Court knows who's in town. If they're only visiting, they get temporary ink."

"What's this Court? Madame Luiza kept talking about it."

"I'll explain, I promise. Just sit down already."

After another moment, I dropped into the lumpy chair. "So why can't I get temporary ink?"

Her eyes narrowed. "I guess you can if that's what you want, but you'll just have to get it redone in a couple of weeks."

I considered for this moment, then nodded. "Okay, then, that's what I want. Just in case."

"In case of what?"

My turn to shrug. "In case you're lying." I frowned. "Or in case she doesn't make it and I don't have a job."

"Pft. You have a job as long as you want one."

"You don't know that."

"Trust me. I do."

"Yeah, well, I don't trust you."

"You will. Now, can we do this?"

I gnawed on the inside of my cheek for a long moment as I stared out the picture window behind her. It was dark now, but how beautiful would that view be in the morning?

"Fine. Temporary ink only," I said out of bull-headedness. "Give me a sun, since that's what this is all about." I paused. "No, wait. A moon. Because I've come to love it."

"How about both?" She pulled a small pad out of her bag and a pencil and quickly sketched out a beautiful image of half a sun and half a moon with a swirly design around it.

"Wow. You're very talented."

"Thanks. I do a lot with suns and moons, because they're such a big part of our lives, you know? With how they affect so many of us, especially here in Havenwood Falls."

I didn't miss her use of "us." She wasn't human, either. But what was she?

She traced over the image with a purple pen, then tore the page off the pad. "Where do you want it?"

I pulled my sweater off, revealing a tank top underneath, and tapped on the back of my right shoulder. "So I'm doing this. Now tell me more. How does this work?"

She sprayed the paper with what I presumed to be water before pressing it against my skin. "The ink is infused with magic."

"Excuse me?" I twisted to stare at her, my mouth again partially open.

"Be still!" She pulled the paper off, wiped my skin, then tried again. I stayed still so it wouldn't smudge this time. "Yes, I said magic. I'm a witch. That's how I brought you to your knees."

"Whoa," I breathed out. "For real?"

"For real. I'm a Beaumont, one of the founding families of the Luna Coven, the main one here in Havenwood Falls." She started setting up her tools and bottles. The black ink shimmered with silver streaks.

"There's more than one coven?"

"Oh, yes. Not everyone wants to do what we have to do, considering our role with the town and the Court." She pushed her sleeves up, revealing tattoos on both forearms, stretched and wiggled her fingers, and then picked up her tool and dipped it in the shimmery ink. "It can get so political. I hate that part, too, but I can't really leave it."

"Why not?"

"I'm being groomed for the High Council. Some day. In probably a few hundred years."

I snickered, thinking she was joking.

"I'm not quite next in line, thank goddess. There's a couple of generations to get through, and we live extremely long lives."

Wow. My questions paused as I considered that. Were there really others, besides Sindi, whom I could possibly be friends with and not have to worry about them growing old when I didn't? Speaking of Sindi, I couldn't wait to call her! She was going to freak. And then be out here in a heartbeat. I knew she should have just come with me. Although, she'd be all over Xandru, and I couldn't let that happen. Maybe I wouldn't tell her right away. At least give myself a chance to be humiliated with rejection before she came out and dug her claws in. Of course, he seemed to be more her type anyway—kind of an asshole.

"So," I continued as the needle worked the ink into my skin, "you're a witch. And there are other supernaturals in this town? Such as . . . ?"

"Mmm . . . such as pretty much all kinds of species and sub-species. Shifters, vampires, mages, fae, sirens, gargoyles, various kinds of magically touched . . . Even hunters."

"And they're all here? In this little town? Are there *any* humans?"

She nodded. "About half the population. But we seem to be a magnet for the non-humans. We do everything we can to keep the town secret, but too many still find us all on their own. The town's always been that way, according to legend." She paused, and I sensed there was more, something she didn't want to, or maybe couldn't, say. "Hence, the reason for having to sign into the Registry. The Court wants to know who—and what—we have in town."

"And everyone gets along? Even with hunters?"

"Ha! Now that's funny." She fell silent for a moment, and the hum of the tattoo needle filled the silence. "We're *supposed* to. That's what the Court of the Sun and the Moon is for—to make sure everyone plays nicely together. But, as you can imagine, that doesn't always happen."

"Sounds like the sun has become the least of my worries. Hunters? Really?"

She chuckled. "Unless you lose control of your thirst, you don't need to worry about them. It really isn't so bad here. In fact, it's nice to be surrounded by some of your own. Maybe not everyone's exactly like you, but we *get* you. You'll see."

"A whole town of supernaturals. Wow." I shook my head as I tried to absorb it all. "This . . . this is kind of insane."

"This is Havenwood Falls. Welcome home."

CHAPTER 6

"So do the humans know?" I asked as Addie dabbed at my tattoo with a tissue.

"Not most of them, but some do. Keeping the secret is paramount to our existence and the town's."

I nodded. "Same number one rule I learned when I first turned: protect the secret."

"Well, actually, around here, law number one is don't kill the humans." She stopped working and leaned over to look at me. "But that should have always been *your* number one rule."

I grimaced. "Um . . . not that I have, I almost did but was able to stop myself and it's most definitely a rule for myself, but, well, where I come from . . . some of the vampires just didn't give a shit. Said it was their right as a superior race. Not that I agreed with them or anything," I quickly added.

She rolled her eyes and snorted. "Damn vampires and their fucking arrogance."

"Hey!"

"Sorry. Not you. I know you wouldn't. Your kind *can't*. But some types are just . . . ugh. Some I just can't stand." She inhaled a deep breath, then said, "Okay, I need a moment."

She placed her palm against the fresh ink and closed her eyes as her lips moved. A warm tingling sensation entered my skin through the tattoo and spread into my blood and throughout my body.

She dropped her hand and opened her eyes. She smiled with an excited twinkle in her brown eyes. "It's done. And just in time."

She nodded toward the same set of French doors I'd come through at the back of the inn. The pitch black outside was no longer pitch black. I jumped up and rushed to the glass. The sky over the top of the eastern mountain was beginning to lighten.

"Oh, my god!" I threw open the doors and ran outside but barely stopped myself at the top of the porch steps, still under the cover of the roof, as I looked up.

Slowly the lighter blue bled into the darker hue of the night sky, and the few clouds glowed deep pinks and reds. It was beautiful, colorful, and full of promise of a fresh beginning. A second chance. A new day.

In a heartbeat, I was back inside.

How could I have been so stupid? So trusting? So naïve? I *knew* better! But I'd let my guard down, so eager to live in the daytime again.

"It's okay. It really works," Addie urged.

I spun and glared at her. "How stupid do you think I am? I don't even know you, what kind of person you are, or how you get your shits and grins. How do I know you're not trying to kill me?"

She flinched as though I'd slapped her, but watched me with steady eyes. "One day you will apologize for that. One day you'll see that it's like we've known each other forever. For now, you just have to trust me."

"Like that's gonna happen," I muttered. "Look, I have no idea what games you're playing and why, but I do know if there was a way for vamps to become day-walkers, they'd be all over this place. I don't care what your laws are. Vampires aren't exactly

56

law-abiding citizens. There's no way in hell this would stay a secret."

I eyed my cottage through the glass doors and wondered if I could make it there without losing too many layers of skin. I had to get to safety and far away from this chick and her psychotic lies. Either she was delusional or she was a heartless bitch. But I was the fool, the dumbass who believed her childish stories of magic.

The back of my shoulder prickled and stung, a reminder of the tattoo, and heat coursed through my veins. A reminder of the magic? I shook my head. I couldn't fall for it. Again. Maybe that was the true secret ingredient of the ink—hallucinogens. This was Colorado, after all. Could have been cannabis oil in that bottle.

"You'll find out the truth soon enough," she said. "So just get it done with. Test it with a hand. Or, hell, even a finger. Surely you can recuperate from that if I'm lying?"

Nope. Not gonna happen.

"Oh, for shit's sake." She grabbed my arm and yanked me toward the doors. When I tried to fight back, an electric charge traveled through my body. I had no choice but to stumble along her side. "This is really stupid of me, but you've always preferred showing over telling, haven't you? Did you know there are only a few ways to kill a witch? And do you know what one of them is?"

"I'd sure like to find out," I snarled.

"A pissed off vampire," she said, and I tripped over my feet, startled that she'd tell me her weakness. Then I straightened, realizing what she meant, as we passed through the doors. "Of course, you have to be super fast, faster than I can cast off a spell, but it's been known to happen." She tugged me across the porch. "So, I've already provoked you and now I'm about to throw your ass out into the sun, which will hurt, and probably piss you off, right? But I know your specific type doesn't explode into flames right away, so I know there's time for you to do your worst on me. Yet, here I am. *Trusting* you. Because I know you won't do anything but thank me."

And with that, she shoved me down the stairs.

I stumbled a few steps onto the dormant lawn before catching myself. I was about to spin and attack—how the hell did she know so much and who did she think she was? But the light of dawn paralyzed me. As the realization that I wasn't sizzling and smoking settled in, I slowly lifted my gaze to the sky. My breath caught, trapped in my lungs, and I wasn't sure if I'd ever breathe again. *Is this really happening?*

The bright hues over the mountains lightened, and my heart rate went from 0 to 180 in an instant. A lump formed in my throat as tears welled in my eyes. Then, there it was. A bright yellow ball climbing over the jagged peaks, spilling its light down the mountainside and over the town like liquid gold. I gasped. My whole body trembled. And the tears spilled over. *This is really happening!*

I couldn't remember the last time I'd seen the sun rise. I'd rarely woken up early enough before, and by the time I knew what I was missing, it was too late. I clapped a hand over my mouth and the other over my still-racing heart as disbelief and awe for such beauty filled me.

When the orb finally made its full appearance over the ridge, I ran farther out on the lawn, threw my head back, and soaked in the sun as I spun in circles like a child. I thought I'd never again feel the kiss of the sun's rays without immediately blistering. I thought I'd live forever, yet never again be able to see the various blue shades above and the fluffiness of the clouds except through a window, peeking from behind the security of a blackout curtain. My heart swelled. The tears fell relentlessly, but laughter bubbled up and out as I continued spinning. Then I fell to my back on the grass and laughed hysterically while never taking my gaze from the sky.

I knew I was being watched, but assumed it was Addie. After another long moment, I reluctantly pulled my eyes from the sky and turned my head to see a large male body in the shadows. He leaned on his forearms against the railing as though he'd been there for a while. Had he been watching me? Our gazes locked, and I swore I could see something appreciative in his. A shiver ran through me, although I couldn't say if he caused it or the cold air did.

He cleared his throat. "She's asking for you."

Before I could respond, he turned and went back inside. Well, turned out he was just as cold as the air.

I didn't have to ask who "she" was. Addie sat on the porch steps, and there was only one other "she" who'd want to see me. I glanced up at the sky one more time and pinched myself. I'd spent years indoors or out only in the dark. I didn't want to go in yet. What if the spell broke? What if this temporary ink was really, *really* temporary? What if I'd been a fool treating Addie like I had and she rescinded her magic? What if this was my last chance to feel the sun caressing my skin? I didn't know it last time. This time I wanted to make the most of it.

"You can come outside any time you like," Addie said. "Now, do you have something to tell me?"

I sat up and looked at her, giving her a sheepish grin. "Thank you! Thank you, thank you, thank you!"

She nodded and grinned back. "And?"

"I'm sorry."

She shrugged and waved her ring-covered fingers, as though she hadn't practically demanded the apology. "Don't worry about it. You're not the first to call me a liar when it comes to this. In fact, I'd wondered what kind of stupid you were when you almost charged right out into the sun the moment you saw it. Now, come inside and take care of business, and I promise we can go to the park later as long as you wear a coat."

"I can't wait to tell Sindi," I nearly squealed as I sprang to my feet, partially out of excitement and partially in response to the way she'd spoken that last phrase, as though I was a small child with a new toy. That's exactly how I felt.

59

Addie's tone immediately flipped, becoming dark and harsh. "You have to wait."

I stopped at the bottom of the steps. "But—"

"Number two rule, remember?"

"But she's my best friend!" I didn't even mean to sound like a child now, but I heard the whine in my own voice.

Addie didn't respond at first, and I looked up at her expectantly. Sadness filled her expression. Her lips pressed together.

"She'll keep the secret," I promised. "I trust her more than anyone. She helped me when I needed her most. I can't possibly *not* tell her!"

Addie's throat worked as she swallowed. "Just . . . we have to follow certain protocol when we invite people to town. Even the tourists are handled a certain way. Otherwise . . . could you imagine all the supernaturals who'd swarm our town? And all the human lookie-loos? And then the carnage that would follow?"

The visions came clearly. I hadn't been making shit up before —every vampire in the world would be here if it meant seeing the sun again. And she'd said every supe gets inked, so they all gained something from it. I couldn't imagine how the others benefitted that could be as good as being a day-walking vampire, but it must have been just as life-changing.

I suddenly understood all of the secrecy and strangeness of the job offer, the scarce information available on the internet about Havenwood Falls, and the inconvenience of traveling here. They purposely made the town difficult to find.

"So why can't they all come, get the tattoo and leave? Or why don't you tell other witches about the spell or potion or whatever it is you use? There are other witches outside this town, right? Do you know how *valuable* this is?"

"Of course we do! And the reasons are nearly endless for not sharing, starting with the survival of humanity. There are wards on the town. Precautions in place. Limitations," Addie said as we headed inside.

"Such as?"

"Such as, the protection from the sun is only good while you're within the town's wards. If you go outside of town more than twenty-five miles, the tattoo vanishes and so does the magic."

"Well, that's good to know. No leaving town in the day or I fry."

"You can leave town. Just not the immediate area."

"Okay. 25 miles. Got it." We reached the lobby and began climbing the steps. "What else?"

My name came softly from Madame Luiza's room, and whatever else there was would have to wait.

"Michaela, dear," Madame Luiza whispered when I entered her room. My jaw ticked at hearing the wrong name again, but this time it was laced with a heavy accent, sounding more like Me-HAY-la. As I chose to not make a big deal of it as this elderly woman lay on her deathbed, it occurred to me that I must have reminded them all of someone named Michaela and having a similar name didn't help matters. Maybe she'd even worked here before, making it easy to slip up. Regardless, I sat on the bed next to her and took her outreached hand. "Listen to me, dear."

I nodded. "Of course. What can I do for you?"

"Just that. You can listen. Listen and not react. Because . . . I have much . . . to tell you." Her words paused as she struggled to simply breathe. I reached for her glass of water, but she shook her head. "Water won't help me now."

"It could make you more comfortable."

"I don't . . . have time . . . to be comfortable." She paused again to catch her breath, and I noticed little beads of sweat on her forehead. "You have a home here. You . . . always . . . have a home."

I gave her a small smile. "Please don't waste another ounce of energy worrying about me. I'll find another job. Another place to live."

"I *always* worry about you. You've always had a . . . special place." I thought she was losing her bearings again, but then she became completely lucid as her gray eyes hardened. "I mean it, Mehayla. This place . . . is yours. Take care . . . of it." Her voice faded, and her eyes began to drift closed, but she jerked herself out of it to pierce me with another hard look. "Take care of *them*. They don't know it, but they need you. And you need . . . them." Her gaze slid toward the door, as though she thought *they* might be standing there. Her voice came out softer when she spoke again. "You be careful . . . with those . . . Rocas. I know your heart . . . I know what it wants . . . but be wary, dear. They've gone . . . far . . . this time. But you . . . you are strong . . . you can change . . . everything."

I studied her face, trying to decipher anything of what she'd just said as her eyes fluttered closed and stayed that way. With her small hand still held between mine, I watched and waited for her to wake up again. A definitive peace spread over her face, slackening it, causing her mouth to curve into what appeared to be a secretive smile.

With soft steps, Addie came in and stood over us. She placed her palm against Madame Luiza's cheek and closed her eyes. When she reopened them a few moments later, they glistened. She bent over and kissed the old lady's forehead.

"Good night, Mammie," she whispered. "See you on the other side."

Addie must have heard the little gasp in my throat. She turned to me with a sad smile and gave my shoulder a squeeze. "It'll be soon, I'm sure. She's been hanging on for a long time, but now that you're here, she can go with peace. I need to go inform the Court. And don't worry. She's right. You always have a home here."

I returned her sad smile and nodded, then she left. Left me alone with a dying woman I barely knew and none of her own family around. Left me in an inn with nobody else to take care of it.

Left me to pick up the pieces, but to what I didn't know.

Madame Luiza never awoke. She drifted away peacefully the next night. I'd stayed by her side almost the entire time except to tend to guests—it turned out we did have a few—and to shower. When I'd returned from cleaning myself up, I could tell visitors had been in to see her. I'd only "met" Aurelia in passing that once, but I recognized her scent. Addie came and sat with us and was there when the old lady passed. I sensed Xandru nearby, too, lurking in the shadows. Others weren't far, but for some reason never came in.

Not until she was gone and Addie informed the Court.

Then suddenly people seemed to flood through the doors. Not knowing any of them and not wanting to deal with the awkwardness of being a stranger in such a personal situation, I slipped out to my cottage. I thought I heard my name whispered as I left, but figured they'd come get me if they needed my help. Nobody did for two days, and at first, I'd planned to stay holed up in my cottage until the commotion died down and I could slip away for good. But then I remembered the gift Addie had given me—the one Madame Luiza had insisted I receive right away—and I spent as much time outdoors during the day as I could.

I thought I'd explore the entire town, but simply standing at the inn's corner, the town square a diamond at this angle, sent tingles down my spine every time I saw something that felt familiar—which was pretty much everywhere I looked. Stores, restaurants, and bars lined three sides of the square, streets with parking separating them from the park setting at the center of town. A gazebo stood in the square's corner nearest to me, large and wooden with a round roof, nothing like the Bird Cage gazebo in Atlanta, but nonetheless I felt emotionally tied to it. A large, brick building lined the north side of the square, across from me, its clock tower pointing to the blue sky. It was clearly City Hall, but from here, tall pine trees blocked both buildings flanking it, yet I knew they were the Chamber of Commerce and the police station. *But how do I know?*

Forcing myself to keep going, I'd barely made it down one side of the square when the feelings became too much. The eerie sensations. The visions that popped in my head when I saw the Coffee Haven sign and the Shelf Indulgence storefront with a scene from *The Secret Garden* artfully displayed in the window. The ache of nostalgia in my heart when I stopped across from the middle of the square, staring down its bench-lined walkway to the fountain in the center. I somehow knew its sparkling interior came from real gold flakes in the paint, and I knew just as well that something significant had happened there. *But what?* And then there were the stares of people, strangers, as I passed by. Being out here no longer felt like freedom as the world seemed to be closing in on me.

I turned on my heel and hurried back toward the inn and the warmth and refuge of my cottage.

The next day I went east instead of west, away from the square, and found a large park in the corner of town, at the base of two mountains. It brought images of warmer days with music fests and movies in the park. At the far end was a trailhead that I followed a little ways up the mountain. But even in the middle of nature, with white aspen trunks and pine trees surrounding me and when I stood on the bank of the partially frozen river, I couldn't rid my mind of the visions. Couldn't dismiss the odd feeling that they weren't fiction created by imagination, but memories I hadn't known I'd possessed.

"This place is seriously fucking with me," I muttered to myself when I walked back into my cottage. "I should probably get out of here before I lose my insanity."

I restarted my fire and was warming my backside when there was a knock on my door. I found Addie on the other side.

"I don't know if you want to go or not, but the funeral is tomorrow," she said. "They're trying to beat this storm that's coming. I think she would have wanted you to be there."

Not until my feet carried me across town did I know if I was going or not. I followed a procession through a pretty cemetery to the back, then up a hill and through a stone-pillared passageway into another, separate and secluded area that appeared to be much older than the main section. We stopped in front of a stone building, where a man in a black suit placed an urn on a podium. I felt the bristle of Aurelia and the boy by her side who I assumed was Gabe, so I stayed back, huddled next to a large tree with my hat pulled tightly down over my ears. I could feel the colder air and smell the approaching storm Addie had mentioned. When the crowd cleared, I said my goodbyes silently as the funeral director took the urn inside what I presumed to be a columbarium.

As I walked back to the inn only a few blocks away, I solidified my plans to figure out what needed to be done before I could pack up and return to Atlanta. I hoped Sindi wouldn't mind. I hadn't even been able to talk to her yet, once unable to find a good signal and the next time connecting to her voicemail. No internet at my cottage meant no email. I'd sent her a couple of texts, but she hadn't replied. Maybe she'd gone on with life, already forgetting about me. Maybe I wouldn't return to Atlanta with all of its memories and pain, after all, but would find a new place for a fresh start.

Which Havenwood Falls was supposed to have been.

But the longer I stayed here, the more I began to believe that it too contained many memories and much more pain. And even as I planned to leave, I also felt compelled to stay. One reason was to figure out the mystery of why Madame Luiza had taken to me so quickly and what she'd been trying to tell me with her last words. Were they irrational statements of a dying woman, or did she expend the last of her energy trying to tell me something?

And, hello, day-walking. I'd lose that as soon as I left.

Then there was the greatest pull keeping me here: the lone figure standing in front of my cottage when I returned, casually leaning against the post in a thick army-green coat over his formal funeral attire, with a look that made me want to undress right there and then. Fuck the cold.

"Everybody else thinks you're fragile and will break with what you need to know, but I know you better," Xandru said, and I could only nod because he was right. I didn't yet know how, but I couldn't deny the truth ringing through my soul: He knew me better than anyone.

CHAPTER 7

I couldn't breathe under the scrutiny of Xandru's piercing gray gaze as we stood motionless staring at each other. Everything about him was mesmerizing, from his high cheekbones and almond-shaped eyes to his square jaw and chin. Beautiful, yet too rugged to be called a pretty boy. The light color of his eyes was a bright contrast to his dark hair, dark brows and lashes, and olive skin tone. He looked like he hadn't shaved in days, considering the full beard growing in. And while his body was sculpted and chiseled perfectly, his posture always showed a confidence that could be perceived as threatening. Challenging.

But it wasn't the intense physicality that had seized me heart and soul.

Because the physical being in front of me was not quite what my heart and soul remembered, deep down, the memories, so faint I could barely grasp them, of a younger, less chiseled version. Except for the eyes. They were the giveaway. Especially now as they delved deep, reaching for those vague memories floating way back in the dark, and touching my soul. Showing me his. One I knew. Better than anyone.

He cleared his throat, breaking the connection. "Okay, then. I have a lot to show you. Come with me."

Blood flushed my face as I took that last phrase in more than one way, especially as he walked past me. I couldn't help but follow, if only to watch his powerful gait, the way his shoulders moved, his back muscles rippling under his white dress shirt . . . and that ass. Holy guacamole, what a fine ass. Jeans suited him better, but I didn't think I'd ever seen anyone make black dress pants look so good.

I followed him up the back steps and through the back doors of the inn. We headed toward the front, but instead of going all the way to the lobby, he opened a door and turned into the offices behind the front desk. We passed by a couple of free-standing desks and into the only closed-off room, in the back. I presumed it to be the owner's or manager's office.

"Here you go." He gestured toward the large, wood desk, which was covered with photos, some quite old and others recent, as well as a slew of papers.

My gaze immediately landed on a photo of me—albeit a younger version, dressed in snow pants and ski boots, goggles pushed up on my head and poles in my hand. There were others of me, as well, including one of a woman who looked like a slightly older version of myself, although that was impossible unless this town's weirdness also included time travel. I walked around the desk for a better look, picked it up and studied it, feeling an unexpected pang of longing for her.

"This must be Michaela," I murmured. No wonder people mixed me up with her. Similar names and nearly identical appearances. Only the coloring was a little different—her hair darker, her skin tone much lighter.

"Um, no," Xandru said. "That's Irina Petran."

I lifted my gaze to him, confused. "Why do I look so much like her?"

"She's your mother."

My eyes swept around the room, but not really seeing

anything at all, my focus inward on the facts of my life. "Um . . . come again?"

"Irina Petran is your mother. That—" He pointed to a picture of a somewhat familiar looking man in another photo. "That's Mihail Petran, your father."

I shook my head. "I don't understand. These are the people who gave me up? Who left me in a dirty little town in Texas with complete strangers who didn't want me either?"

Xandru's brows scrunched together, forming two vertical lines between them. They smoothed out almost immediately. "Ah. I think that was the story they told you."

"Story? Who?"

"Irina and Mihail. Or, more accurately, whoever in the Luna Coven did the amnesia spell."

I threw the picture back down and cocked my head. "What the fuck are you talking about?"

He gnawed on his bottom lip and for a very brief moment, I was quite jealous of that lip. Or the teeth gnawing on it. I wasn't sure which. Then I came to my senses. I dropped my hands to my hips and tapped my foot.

"Nobody left you in Texas. You're not Kaela Peters. You're Michaela Petran, and you've always been here in Havenwood Falls, with your parents who loved you very much. So much that they gave up everything so you could go live a normal life and become the great doctor everyone believed you would be. The town's memory ward wipes away everyone's memories of Havenwood Falls once they leave—immediately for visitors and after a moon's cycle for residents—but they wanted to make sure your loss was thorough, that you forgot everything . . . every*one*." His voice caught, and he paused for a moment. "They gave you a history. A sad one, very far from here, that would keep you from ever wanting or even thinking about coming back here."

"In other words, they didn't want me," I whispered as I

69

dropped into the chair behind the desk, my eyes roaming over all the pictures.

"That's not—"

I looked up at him. "Then why? Why would they send me away to never return and make me forget about them? I was just a child!"

"Because you're so fucking *special*." The sarcasm and anger dripped on the girl's last word as Aurelia showed herself in the doorway, her dark hair pulled up in a formal twist to go along with the black dress, sheer stockings, and heels she wore, making her look older than her behavior showed. Her brown eyes shot daggers at me. "And you weren't a child. You were a grown-ass adult."

"Aurelia," Xandru said as a warning.

She huffed out an annoyed breath with the expertise of a teenager and shifted her glare to him. "What is she even doing here, Xan? She shouldn't be here, and neither should you!"

"Someone has to do it," Xandru said. "And who else would it be? The coven's all tied up. My parents have no interest, and it's probably best to keep them away anyway. And you and Gabe are just kids. You can't take care of this."

"I'm not a kid!" she said petulantly as she crossed her arms over her chest and stuck her bottom lip out. I wondered if she'd stomp her foot next. "Everyone needs to stop treating me like one!"

Xandru turned, giving her the full force of his glare and that powerful stance. "We will when you stop acting like one. But you're sixteen, Aurelia. Don't rush it. Trust me. Being an adult isn't all that." He lifted his chin. "Now, if you care at all about your family, you'll stop acting like a brat and do what needs to be done. Otherwise, go back to the wake."

"Mingling with a bunch of adults giving me looks of pity and asking me how I'm holding up got old in the first five minutes."

"Get lost, Aurelia," Xandru said, in almost a growl.

She narrowed her dark eyes at him as her nostrils flared with each heavy breath she took. This girl had balls. I couldn't imagine standing up to Xandru at her age. Her eyes finally broke away and slipped to me before she spun on her heel.

"Fuck off, Xandru," she said under her breath, but I'd heard her. Xandru chuffed, clearly hearing her, too.

As he began to turn around, I had to brace myself, inhaling a slow breath, preparing for the inevitable shock-and-awe that always hit me when I saw his face. His eyes. They still pierced into me with the force of a laser—right to all my girl parts. I tried not to moan on my exhale.

"What did she mean?" I asked once I refocused.

His gaze found mine, and he immediately glanced away again as he pushed a hand through his hair, then rubbed it over his face. As though I unnerved him as much as he did me. His Adam's apple bobbed as he swallowed.

"You had just turned eighteen and graduated from high school," he said. "You'd been accepted to Emory University, which you'd been dreaming about attending since you were ten and read about one of their medical research studies. Considering who—*what*—you are, your parents had two choices: force you to give up the dream and stay here as part of the family and community, or allow you to go, reach your full potential, and live a normal life, but with no memory of them, of anything about your past."

"What do you mean, what I am? I wasn't *this* until a couple of years ago."

His stunning eyes slammed into me, nailed me to my seat. "Michaela, you've always been *this*."

"Uh, no. Regardless of what you say about my previous memories, I know the exact day I became a vampire. That is something I will *never* forget."

He nodded. "Trust me, I know. But you've always been moroi. At least, you've always had it in your blood."

My brows pulled together. "Moroi?"

71

"You really don't know any of this? Nobody told you about the moroi?" He blew out a breath when I shook my head. "It's the type of vampire we are—a mortal vampire. Have you ever met other vamps? You've noticed you're different?"

I hesitated before nodding.

"There are various kinds of what the mundane society, hell, even the covert world, refer to as vampires. We share similarities, but we also have differences. We, for example, are mortal. We're born human, but with a dominant vampire gene. If our gene is triggered and we turn, we live for hundreds of years, but we're not immortal. We can die of old age. Our hearts still beat, and if they stop, we die. And we can have children." He paused for effect. "The human way."

I flushed at his implication. He smirked.

"And you can still do that," he murmured with appreciation, and I felt like there was more meaning than I knew in that statement.

"Wait," I said. "Hold on. You're saying we and us. You're a moroi, too?"

He nodded. "A mature one, which means I've been turned."

My gaze dropped to the pictures. "And my parents?"

"They gave you the gene. It has to be triggered before age twenty-one."

"How?"

"You don't know how you were turned?" I shook my head again. "You don't know *who* turned you?"

"I know nothing. I didn't even know I was turned until I woke up with a killer thirst and almost killed my fiancé."

Something flickered in his eyes, but I couldn't determine what. A darkness. Perhaps a sadness or regret. He scratched his cheek before answering my question. "A moroi is turned by drinking the blood of another, mature moroi. Usually the parents provide their blood in a family ceremony because it strengthens the bond of the bloodline. The blood also passes extra powers and abilities from the source to the recipient."

"Powers and abilities?" I glanced back up at him and was immediately distracted, so I returned my gaze to the photos.

"The Romanian moroi originated from a sorcerer whose black magic backfired into him and his family. Ever since, the magic manifests in different ways when the gene is triggered. Usually something with the elements. It's basically a family trait, although there are stories of parents sometimes allowing another's blood to be given to their child if the source of that blood had a unique power or extra strong ability."

My brows dipped down as I studied one photo in particular, of the man and woman who were supposedly my parents. Who noticeably hadn't been around here. The question came out in barely more than a whisper. "And if it's not triggered by twenty-one?"

"The child goes on to live a completely normal, human life, able to marry a human, have children whose genes are dormant and don't need to be triggered, and grow old with their mates. And the moroi parents and the entire bloodline behind them . . . they die. As though their bodies slowly return to human, and their true age catches up, eventually killing them over time."

Unexpected tears blurred my vision, and I blinked several times to keep them at bay. "They're . . . gone?"

He didn't answer at first. He strode around the side of the desk, turned my chair, and dropped into a squat in front of me so he could look me in the eye. Trepidation filled his expression. "Your father passed a few years ago. Your mother a little over a year ago. And Mammie . . ."

"Madame Luiza?" I gasped.

"Your aunt."

My hand clamped over my mouth as my head shook. "No. This can't be true. It doesn't make sense. I don't even remember them!"

"Are you sure?"

My eyes closed as I inhaled a jagged breath. The visions I'd been trying so hard to repress since arriving in this town started pushing through. The sob escaped me.

"I wasn't turned in time! Why? *Why* would they do that?"

"They all wanted the best life for you, even knowing it would kill them."

I choked on another repressed sob. "Why couldn't I have that here? With them?"

He paused, and when I looked up at him, the trepidation was gone, now filled with sadness. "They believed Havenwood Falls, and the people here, were not the best life for you."

"I don't understand. This was *our* life. *My* life. Right? How could they think sending me away, forcing me to go off completely on my own, embedded with memories of a false past . . . how was that the best life for me? No family, no friends. If they wanted me to stay human, why couldn't I do that here? Or at least be able to come back, memories intact? *Life* intact?"

His eyes darkened, and he looked away. "They said it was too risky. You were more likely to be turned here. You'd *want* to be turned."

I didn't understand the problem. I mean, I wished I wasn't a vampire, but being a moroi sounded not quite as horrible—I could still have children, a dream I'd given up—especially if this really was my heritage. My family. And, more importantly, they'd still be alive. On the other hand, I knew too well that I'd never choose this life and the insatiable, murderous thirst that came with it, no matter how well controlled.

"Why would I do that?" I asked. "I mean, besides to save them, but obviously that was never a choice given to me. So why else would I choose to turn and give up the normal life they wanted for me? That I must have wanted so badly?"

His gaze came back to me, and our eyes collided. "For me."

I had no response. I could hardly think, especially the more intense his stare became. Capturing me. Swallowing me. Claiming me. My lungs began to burn and scream for air because I couldn't breathe, so lost in his gaze and his words and their meaning.

I gasped and broke the connection, turning away, looking everywhere but at him. A wave of emotions began to build—emotions I wasn't ready to take on yet. This was too much. All of it too much.

"I . . . I can't," I finally said on a soft breath as I stared at the desk in front of me. But the rest of the words, of what I wanted to say, failed to form, to come out. *I can't* applied to just about everything at the moment. I couldn't think, speak, and while I could probably feel, I really didn't want to.

Xandru blew out a harsh breath and stood. He walked back around the desk and turned. "Well, then, I can't either."

And with that, he strode out and away.

Finally able to breathe again, I sagged over with my elbows on the desk and my head in my hands. *What just happened?*

"Xandru?" Addie's voice came from the door that led back out to the lobby.

"I can't do this," he growled before the sound of his heavy footsteps carried across the wood floor of the lobby and out the door.

My fingers curled into my hair and rubbed into my temples as I drew in several breaths. Addie entered the room, but I didn't look up. Instead I stared at the contents of the desk under my elbows. A piece of bank stationery caught my eye, and my focus narrowed in on the letter.

"What the hell?" I straightened up and pulled the piece of paper out from under the photos, then read the full letter. Addie silently took off her coat, seeming not to mind that I hadn't acknowledged her yet. When I finished, I looked up as she tugged at her black miniskirt before sitting in the chair in front of me. She was sans glasses today, and her light brown hair was down, spread out over the shoulders of her gray blouse. I held the piece of paper up. "Do you know anything about this? Particularly this part right here?"

I pointed to the name Michaela Petran, which supposedly was mine. Which part of me had already come to accept was mine—the part that dared to acknowledge the visions that had been floating around my head for days as actual memories. My memories. Buried but returning from the grave.

"Hello to you, too." Addie gave the letter a quick read and shrugged. "It's a transfer of ownership of the inn to you."

"Obviously. But why?

Her caramel brows lifted. "Because it's been in your family forever. You're the next in line. Why do you think Mammie worked so hard to get you back here? Aurelia and Gabe are certainly too young."

"Wait. What?"

"How much did Xan tell you?"

I blinked, then shook my head and waved a hand in the air, as though I could shoo away those last few minutes between him and me. "Obviously not everything. He told me who my parents were. That they're gone. That Madame Luiza was my aunt. That they didn't want to trigger my gene, even when it meant they'd die."

She nodded. "Your parents owned the inn. Mammie's been taking caring of it since they passed. As best as she could, anyway. Aurelia and Gabe, too . . . as best as she could. I think she'd been hanging on to wait for your return."

My chest tightened at the thought of Madame Luiza trying to do so much. Then Addie's meaning really sunk in. *And the hits keep on comin'.*

"Aurelia and Gabe . . . ?"

"Your sister and brother."

I sat back in my chair and blew out a long breath. That bratty little bitch was my sister? But I began to understand. "She hates me. And I can't blame her."

"She's a teenager. Remember when we were that age—oh, no, I guess you don't." She smiled sadly. "You will soon. For some people, the memories return as soon as they're back within the town's ward. For others, it takes time. And the spell they put on you was so strong. It may be a while."

"We were friends," I blurted. Although no memories of that had surfaced, I knew we had some kind of connection.

Her smile brightened a little. "Practically sisters. Besties forever." She sighed. "Until your parents decided forever was over for us. For you. And—" She looked over her shoulder, toward the door, and she didn't have to finish her thought.

"I'm not ready for that. For him." My eyes once again traveled over the desk. "There's just . . . so much."

I began sorting the photos into piles and the papers into a stack. Another letter from the bank caught my attention. And seriously. The shocks really wouldn't stop.

"Foreclosure?" I read the letter again, then let out a sad laugh. "Well, I guess I don't have to worry so much about the inn being mine. It won't be much longer."

My fingers released their hold on the letter and let it drift back to the desk. Addie snatched it up.

"This isn't right," she said as she read it. "We'll take care of this, Kales. They can't take this place from you, from your family. Something's going on here . . ."

I barely paid attention to the rest as the nickname made the tips of my ears tingle. Nobody in my recent past had ever called me that. It had always been Kae for short, or Sindi's occasional Kaekae. But I *remembered* that nickname. I remembered standing by the fountain in the square, gold flakes sparkling in the sun as Addie gave me a hug, and said, "Besties forever, Kales. Try not to forget me, okay?" And Xandru stood next to us, his hand on my lower back. And—

The sound of heavy and purposeful footsteps coming up the walk to the front door knifed into my recollection, severing it. I blinked and cocked my head.

"Oh, right. I came over to warn you," Addie said. "The wolves are descending."

"I'm sorry?"

"Sheriff Kasun and his deputies were on their way over to question you."

"For what?"

The front door opened.

"Um . . . for murder?"

CHAPTER 8

Kaboom. The biggest bombshell of them all.

The little bell on the front desk dinged.

"*What?*" I gasped.

Addie cringed. "They found a body outside of town, in the woods. Looks like a vampire attack."

"And of course they immediately come to the new girl in town."

"You're not exactly new."

"Maybe not, but I wasn't a vampire the last time I was here, was I?"

The bell dinged again, several impatient times. I stood and exhaled a sharp breath. Like I needed this right now. My brain was spinning with information overload. I didn't even know if I could form a coherent answer to the simplest question, let alone ones that could put my freedom at risk—possibly my life. As I headed out of the office and toward the lobby, I realized I didn't have an alibi for much of my time here. In fact, most of it had been spent with a woman who's also now dead. Fabulous.

"Careful," Addie whispered as she walked behind me. "Wolves aren't exactly vampires' best friends."

I stopped in mid-step and hissed, "What does that mean?"

She bumped into me before catching herself. Her mouth was right by my ear as she explained in a low whisper. "They're wolf shifters. They always showed outward respect toward your father because of his seat on the Court, but the natural instinct to hate your kind runs deep."

Awesome.

Two men stood in the lobby, one in a khaki uniform with a deputy badge pinned to his chest and a brown felt hat in his hands, the older one in flannel and jeans. Both standing well over six-foot tall and with the same silvery-blue eyes and facial structure, they *had* to be related. Brothers, maybe.

The younger one bristled when he looked next to me, at Addie. "Came to warn her, did you?"

Addie gave him a warm grin, and her tone came out sickly sweet. "I came to make sure you do this properly, Deputy Kasun. She's entitled to a representative from the coven."

A noise almost like a growl rumbled in his throat, barely audible except to my keen ears.

"Ms. Petran," said the one who appeared to be in his mid-forties based on the laugh lines near his eyes and the speckles of gray around his temples and in the scruff along his jaw. While the cop seemed uptight and ready to pounce, this guy was more relaxed, his tone softer around the edges. "We're sorry about your aunt."

"Peters," I corrected. The deputy stiffened and peered at me with narrowed eyes. "That's what's on my ID, which I'm sure you want to see, right?"

"We already know it's fake," he said rather curtly, accusingly. As if *I'd* known it was fake. The older guy gave him a sideways look of warning.

"And thank you," I said to the older one. "Although, I just learned she was my aunt."

He nodded. "I'm Sheriff Ric Kasun. This is one of my

deputies and son, Conall. We're aware of your background and understand this all must be rather strange for you."

"Strange would be putting it mildly."

"Doesn't matter what you remember from the past," Conall said, his demeanor in contrast with the sheriff's. Like they had a good cop–bad cop thing going on. Although, on closer inspection, while Ric's posture appeared more relaxed, his muscles were tense and his gaze swept subtly around the lobby, likely taking in every detail, ready to spring if he saw something he didn't like. "We need to know about last night. Where were you?"

"Care to be a little more specific with the time there, deputy?" Addie asked, her voice still dripping syrup, but with an underlying warning.

His upper lip twitched. "Between 4:25 and 5:12 a.m.," he bit out.

Addie snickered. "That's *very* specific. Russell's lap time?"

"Something like that," Sheriff Kasun said. "He found the body on his final run of the night out near Wylie's gulch."

"So where were you?" Conall snarled at me.

I pretended to think about it. "Pretty sure I was sleeping."

"At night?" he scoffed.

I couldn't help the small smile. "I've been working toward a more normal schedule, now that I can."

"When do you hunt?" he asked. "If you're on animal blood, as we've been told, best hunting is at night."

"You would know," Addie muttered. He ignored her.

"Madame Luiza provided me with more than a week's worth of bottled blood. I haven't needed to hunt yet. I don't know when I will, either. The bottled stuff here isn't too horrible, much better than anything I'd had before. And I kind of like animals. I don't like having to kill them." I paused. "Most anyway. The ones that don't wish me harm."

Conall cocked his head, sensing the challenge I might have been making.

"You have somebody to vouch for your whereabouts at that time?" the sheriff asked.

"That you were in bed," Conall clarified quite rudely.

And there was the question I knew would come. I tried not to take offense at the implication, although I'd been here less than a week. What kind of girl did he think I was? Oh, yeah. Murderer.

"I sleep alone," I said as nicely and calmly as I could muster.

"No need to be a dick, Conall," Addie said.

"We need to know if she has an alibi, Adelaide," Sheriff Kasun said to her. "That's well within procedure."

"Are you questioning all of the vampires?" she demanded.

"We will be. If we need to."

I blew out a breath, trying to release some of the tension that only continued to build. "Look, I get it. You have a dead body, and I'm the newbie here. You want to believe you know me, except you don't, because I'm not the old Michaela. But I'm not a murderer, either. I've never killed a human. I take pride in how well I control my needs. I swear I'm not the vampire you're looking for."

"In other words, you're barking up the wrong tree," Addie sniped, and I had to bite the inside of my cheek to keep from laughing.

"We do have empaths here in town," Conall said. "They'll know if you're lying."

I shrugged. "Bring them on."

"She's not lying," said a deep voice from behind me, sending stupid tingles down my spine. I couldn't even see him, but my whole body came on alert as he approached. "I'll vouch for her."

Oh, shit. What the hell was he doing? Barely more than an hour ago he was stomping away, acting like he wanted nothing to do with me. Now he was willing to lie on my behalf?

Conall looked over my shoulder, the disgust he felt obvious. "You were with her?" His nose wrinkled. "At least I know why she'd lie about it."

Xandru growled behind me. Seriously growled. The sound a vampire makes in warning. His hand suddenly appeared in my peripheral vision, pointing a finger at the deputy. "Show some respect, asshole."

Conall lifted a brow.

"To *her*," Xandru yelled, making me jump.

"Calm down," the sheriff quickly said, sensing the testosterone and who knew what other pheromones skyrocketing. "Both of you. Answer the question, Mr. Roca. Were you with her?"

I felt him bristle as he moved next to me.

"Not exactly," he said. "I was on her porch the whole night, though."

The sheriff squinted his eyes and cocked his head. "You were what?"

Xandru shifted next to me, sending heat over my skin. "I was watching her place."

"Watching or stalking?" Conall muttered, and the next thing I knew, Sheriff Kasun was breaking up a fight of an inhuman sort.

He stood between the two younger men, both of their chests heaving, more likely from adrenaline than needing to catch their breaths. Conall's eyes glowed a golden color, and Xandru's fangs were out. The sheriff stood there for a long moment, his arms out to keep them separated. When they seemed to have calmed down and gained control, he put his hands on his hips and turned to face Xandru.

"Why were you watching her place?" he asked.

The muscle of Xandru's jaw ticked. "You know why."

They stared hard at each other for a long moment. Something passed between them, but the sheriff seemed to let it go.

"Anyone see *you* out there?" Conall demanded.

Xandru turned his glare on him. "Russell did. And you also know why to that."

The two law officers continued their staring contest with Xandru. Another silent communication seemed to pass.

"Is this nonsense over?" Addie finally asked from my other side.

"Yes," Xandru said at the same time the other two said, "No."

"What else do you need from me, then?" I asked. "It's been a hell of a day, and I need a drink." Both pairs of silver-blue eyes cut over to me. "*Wine.* A glass of wine. Or a bottle. Sheesh."

"One more question," Conall said as he continued staring at me now. "What happened to Luiza Petran?"

Addie stepped forward. "All right, that's it. Now you really are just being a dick."

Xandru moved to her side, both of them in front of me now. "It's time for you to leave."

"Go on," Addie added. "Before I have to file an incident report to the Court."

"No worries, Adelaide," Sheriff Kasun said. "I think we'll be going over there ourselves."

With a final glare at all three of us, the men turned for the exit.

"I'd better go with them," Addie muttered quietly. She threw me a look over her shoulder before following them out the front door. And it wasn't until they were out of sight that I realized Xandru and I were alone.

He turned to face me, dropping his hands to his hips as his gaze traveled down my body and back up. I could hear his heartbeat change as he did so. Slowing at first, but then spiking again as his eyes studied my mouth.

"Why did you lie for me?" I asked.

His tongue swept over his lips, and I nearly forgot my own question, consumed by the desire to be that tongue. Those lips. "I didn't lie."

My gaze flew up to his eyes. I lifted a brow. "You were seriously on my porch all night? And I didn't know it?"

Those delicious lips curved into a smirk. "Vampire stealth."

I pointed to my ear. "Vampire hearing."

He lifted his chin. "You don't live in a town like this without learning a few extra tricks."

We stared at each other in silence, both of our hearts pounding. "Why then?"

He shrugged. "Maybe I like the view."

"So you were watching the inn?"

"Maybe."

I blew out a frustrated breath. "Can you give me a fucking straight answer? Finding out you were sitting on my porch all night last night without me knowing is a little damn unnerving."

"Every night. Since you've been here."

I pulled back. "What?"

"I've been around every night since you've been here."

"Watching the inn?"

"Yes. And your cottage."

"Why? And don't give me a vague non-answer about the view."

He hesitated, his eyes again doing that appreciative journey over my whole body. "Protecting you, Kales. Protecting the inn."

"From what?"

He chuckled. "All kinds of things. Them—the law. The Court. The bank. And the one committing those murders. I knew they'd come to you first, try to use you as a scapegoat."

"Whoa. Whoa. Whoa. You said murderssss. As in plural. They only mentioned one." I watched as Xandru pressed his lips together and rocked back on his heels. "You know something, don't you?"

"I *suspect* something. Yes."

"That you're not going to tell me?"

"Nope."

"Even though I could be in danger."

"You're not in danger as long as I'm around."

"Hmph. Well, that's the problem. You walked out today. How can I know or trust that you'll be around?"

He took two strides toward me, until we stood toe to toe. I had to tilt my head back to look up at him. He leaned down until his forehead nearly touched mine. His eyes locked onto mine, piercing into me, delving down, down, down, and I found myself leaning closer to him.

"I'm not the one who left," he said, his voice low, his breath fanning over my lips. The smell and the taste and the feel of him so close overcame my senses, making my body tremble and my knees weak. And my panties wet. But I held on to barely enough wherewithal to understand what he meant.

"It wasn't up to me," I said, and as soon as the words spilled from my lips, the memory of 18-year-old me in a fight with my parents rose to the forefront of my mind. I hadn't been given a choice to leave. I hadn't been asked what I really wanted—what I was really willing to sacrifice. Because it wasn't them. Not this life. Not Xandru. Memories of us growing up together, from when we were toddlers to our first kiss when I was in the fifth grade to how we were virtually inseparable throughout high school, even when he graduated two years before me. A clear vision of seeing him for the first time with gray-green eyes instead of blue, after being gone for a couple of weeks. And how, right after, my parents told me about my acceptance to Emory and that I'd be leaving in two days. "You were right. I would have chosen to be turned. And to stay. With you."

Our eyes held each other's, and old feelings began to push against the barriers, what I could feel was about to become an avalanche. Before they overwhelmed me, sucked me under, buried me, I pushed up and against him and crashed my mouth against his.

His hands immediately came to my face, cradling it and holding tight. Mine slipped up, into thick, soft hair. The kiss deepened, our lips parted, our tongues met. And not for the first time, I knew. In fact, the moment mixed with the memory of the last time. The urgency, the passion, the desperation of saying goodbye, but now we were saying hello again. I missed you. I want and need you now more than ever. With just as much urgency and passion and desperation.

His mouth was delightful. His kisses delicious, sending a ping straight through my core. I sucked on his bottom lip, and he returned the favor, eliciting a whimper from me. He groaned in response, then suddenly pulled way. I nearly fell forward at his sudden absence, and I gasped for more while staring at him halfway across the room.

"What?" I asked.

"There's something I don't get, Kales." Xandru's gray-green eyes suddenly turned hard. Angry. Accusing.

"What?" I repeated.

"How could you forget me so easily? Forget us? After everything we'd been through?"

CHAPTER 9

$\mathcal{I}$ stared at him, panting, my brain muddled.

"You promised our love would conquer the amnesia spell," he said.

"You promised you'd follow me to the ends of the earth," I countered. I didn't know I knew that until I said it, but then the memory of our last moments together floated through my mind.

"And I did."

"Uh, pretty sure you didn't. I was there. You're still here . . ."

He ran a hand through his hair, causing the top to fall forward over his temples. "I did go to Atlanta. I wasn't supposed to. I'd sworn to the Court I wouldn't interfere. But fuck, Kales. I couldn't do it anymore. It hurt too much. I was fucking up all over the place, contributing to the Roca reputation when I'd promised you I never would. I had to find you."

My heart pounded at this revelation. "Did . . . you? Find me?"

Pain filled his eyes, overflowed into his entire expression and stature. But only for a moment. He quickly straightened up to his full height, lifted his chin, and hardened his eyes again.

"Yeah, I did. And you were so fucking happy. Taking your classes. Making friends. Dating some pretty-boy asshole."

I sucked in a breath, imagining him seeing me with Ryan and Heather, when they were both mine, not each other's. "When was this?"

He threw his hands up. "A few times over the years. I don't know what I was thinking. I was a fucking masochist, I guess. Because the first time was hard. You'd only been gone a few months. And I was nothing to you. Not even a vague memory. You looked right at me that time, and not a hint of recognition. I realized they were right. That was the best life for you, and I needed to leave you alone."

Pain filled his voice, mixed with resolve.

"But for some dumb ass reason," he continued, "I went back again. And again. Hoping maybe something changed with you, especially after you turned. I would have taken just a flicker of familiarity in your eyes. But there was still none. I finally had no choice but to accept that you were truly gone. That you really had forgotten me, everything we'd been through, the life we'd had planned. That you'd moved on to a better one. And while it killed me, I was happy that you were happy."

Silence fell over us as we stared at each other. I knew exactly how he'd felt—the same way I'd felt with Ryan and Heather. Except not quite. For one, what Xandru and I had was so much more intense than Ryan's and my relationship. So much more real. Although I couldn't remember every detail of our relationship, I could feel that fact in my bones. In my soul. The relationship Ryan and I had, the one I'd thought was my epic, forever love, was superficial in comparison. And for two . . .

"I didn't forget you," I whispered. His brow shot up. I took a few slow steps closer to him. "Some part of me didn't let go. I was confused. Maybe because of the spell or whatever. But there were things I'd attached to Ryan that didn't belong. And, I don't know, maybe that's why I attacked him, because the very basal part of me knew he wasn't mine. I wasn't his. Because I already belonged to someone else. Someone my subconscious has never completely let go."

He cocked his head. I moved a few more steps toward him, close enough to lift my hand to his face. He leaned into my palm as my thumb swept over his cheekbone.

"These eyes, for example," I said quietly. "They've haunted my dreams for years."

His hand grabbed mine, but I took control and brought his knuckles across my lips, along my jaw.

"These hands," I continued. "They touched me almost every night."

He exhaled heavily, slowly. "Could have been anyone's hands. You could have been dreaming about anyone. Pretty boy, for example."

I tilted my head. "Did I mention the eyes? You do know nobody has eyes like yours."

He dropped his chin and looked at me through his lashes. "They're moroi eyes. *You* have eyes like mine."

"Nope. Not exactly the same. Similar, but . . . I know your eyes, Xandru. Maybe I couldn't grasp the memory of who they belonged to, but I lost myself in them every night. And besides." I undid the top buttons of his dress shirt and slid my hand underneath it, slowly pulling it to the side while cherishing the feel of the heat of his skin against my palm. "I have never forgotten this."

"My birthmark? You remembered that?"

"Who could forget a birthmark shaped like a duck?" I smiled as I glanced down at the skin over his heart. My fingertip traced over the mark as I slowly looked back up at him.

"Dragon. How many times have I told you, it looks like a dragon?"

"Nope. I still see a duck." Both of our lips curled up for a moment as we gazed at each other. "I'm sorry—"

My apology was cut off when his mouth slammed down on mine.

The kiss started as though he searched for something, his eyes open, piercing deep into mine while his lips and tongue explored. I held his gaze while kissing him back, and he must have found what he wanted, needed. With a growl, he lifted me, and as he started walking, I had no choice but to wrap my legs around his waist. He carried me up the stairs and to an empty guest room, kicking the door shut behind us, our lips never separating the entire time.

But now he let go, setting me back on my feet. His eyes raked over me, sending a shiver down my spine with their heat.

"Are you sure about this?" he asked, his voice husky. "Because I've been waiting a fucking long time for it. But I need to know you want this. That you're in. For good this time."

"I'm in, Xandru. My heart, my soul, they've always been in. My brain just didn't know it."

He studied my face as he stalked toward me, forcing me to back up until my knees hit the bed. But just before I was about to plop on my ass, he swooped me up, spun us, and sat on the edge of the bed with me straddling him, my skirt bunched up around my hips. And with only my cotton panties and his dress pants between us, I could feel with all certainty just how much he wanted this. His hand slid up my back and into my hair, cradling my head, while the other splayed out over my lower back and pulled me against him. I grasped his shoulders as my breasts pressed into his chest, my hips rocked, and the friction brought out moans from both of us.

Our mouths moved together in perfect sync, pressing and sucking, parting and tasting. When his left mine, I whimpered, but then he pulled on my hair, tugging my head back, lifting my throat to his lips. His open mouth skated over my jaw and down my neck, his tongue swirling against my skin, sending webs of pleasure everywhere. He paused at my carotid, first licking the thick, pulsing vein, then sucking on it. Pleasure shot all the way to my core.

"Oh my god," I breathed as I pushed down on his lap and

rocked again, needing to feel the pressure between my legs. "Do that again."

He paused, and his eyes rolled up to look at me through those thick, dark lashes. "You've never fucked a vampire before?"

I scowled. "I never fuck anyone and tell."

He smirked, knowing my answer already. "Get ready then. I'm about to—"

"If you say rock my world, I am so out of here."

His eyes darkened for a brief moment, but then he laughed. Who knew that sound would be a total turn on? When I reacted with another shift of my hips, rubbing my center against his erection, his eyes darkened in a very different way.

"I was going to say," he said huskily, "I'm about to show you one of the best parts of what we are."

His fangs let out right before he leaned into my throat again, licking and sucking at my vein, the tips of his fangs scraping across my skin. At the same time, his hand slid from my back, over my ribs, and to my breast. He cupped it for a moment, the heat of his palm making my shirt and bra feel nonexistent. His hand expertly teased my breast, the friction causing my nipple to pebble against his palm while his mouth never left that spot on my throat. I arched back more, rocking in a quickening rhythm, rubbing my clit against his hard-on at the same pace his tongue assaulted me. He rolled my nipple between his thumb and forefinger before giving it a hard pinch, making me cry out with pleasurable pain. Then his hand traveled southward, over my stomach, down in between us, slipping into my panties.

"Oh, fuck, you're so wet," he said against my throat. His fingers stroked my folds before finding the swollen bundle of nerves aching for his touch. He barely grazed it, and I cried out again. His thumb pressed into it, swirled over it as his fingers slid to my opening. "Get ready, Kales. It's like nothing else."

His lips clamped onto my throat and sucked, then his fangs dug in at the same time his fingers slid into me. I came undone. Completely. Fucking. Undone. And I couldn't stop coming undone as his fingers stroked and his mouth sucked. I lost all control as my back arched and my hips rolled on their own, fucking his fingers while he drank my blood. And just when I didn't think I could climb any further, his thumb pressed against my clit, my entire body clenched around him, and I screamed his name as I soared.

"Oh god," I finally breathed as I started to come down.

"Not the first time I've been called that."

The deep voice, as sexy as it was, cut into my bliss. His tongue slid over his bottom lip, licking my blood off it. I touched a finger to my throat, but of course the wounds had already healed. The smell of myself all over him, the way I'd just lost control . . . heat exploded in my cheeks. He smirked.

"You're fucking beautiful," he said as his hand slipped out from me. He lifted it to his mouth and sucked on his fingers. "I'm not sure what tastes better, though—your blood or your pussy."

I might have come again just from his dirty words.

"Should I get a better taste?" he asked. Before I could respond, he flipped us over, and I found myself on my back, my ass on the edge of the bed, and Xandru between my legs. He leaned his head down.

"No," I gasped.

He froze. "No?"

"I want you inside me. *You.*"

He gave me a sexy grin. "Say what you really want, Kales. Talk dirty to me."

I shook my head. "Not now, Xan. I don't want to fuck. I want to make love. It's . . . it's been so long."

He stared at me for a long moment, then his beautiful eyes fell closed. He exhaled a long, slow breath. But otherwise didn't move. I leaned up on my elbows, waiting. Then he stood up.

"You're right," he said as he started pulling my skirt down over my thighs.

"Um . . . I'm not sure if you heard me right. I *want* you. Now. But *all* of you. Your whole being, not just your cock."

He leaned in and pressed his lips to my ear. "I know. I do understand. And this is not how it should be. Not our first time . . . our new first time. You deserve better."

His mouth moved to my mine and delivered a delicious but tame kiss.

"You misunderstand," I said against his lips.

"No, but you have to stop." His fingers wrapped around my wrist as I moved my hand down his stomach. "Or I won't be able to."

"Then don't. I don't want to stop."

"I do."

I stilled in his grasp, only inches from stroking him. "Let me take care of you at least."

"Ah, Michaela, you already did. Watching you come like that . . . something I never thought I'd do again. And drinking your blood while you did—it was my own personal heaven." He tugged on my wrist, pulling me to my feet. "There will be lots of time to take care of me, yeah?"

I straightened out my clothes. "Yeah. Plenty of time for us both."

"You're staying then?"

I glanced around the guest room, my gaze pausing at the window and the view of the mountains, before coming to his face, nearly as impressive. "Where else would I go?"

He leaned toward me as though to kiss me, but his pocket buzzed. He retrieved his phone, glanced at the screen, and swore under his breath. His entire demeanor changed.

"I have to go, but I'll be back later. We have a lot to talk about."

When he didn't come back, I began to wonder what kind of fool I was, thinking I wouldn't be given a taste of my own medicine.

CHAPTER 10

The snowstorm hit, forcing me to spend a few days inside. I spent a lot of time admiring the beauty of the freshly fallen snow on the mountains and the trees, and the rest learning about the business side of the inn. I seemed to know the inn itself quite well, as though I'd grown up in it, which, I began to recall, I basically had. Checking guests in and out also came as second nature, and apparently nothing had changed since I'd worked the front desk all through high school. I only had a few guests come and go, and once I learned how to use the ancient reservation system, I understood why the inn was in such disrepair and being threatened with foreclosure. The low revenues couldn't possibly pay the utility bills for this huge manor, let alone any other expenses.

"There's just no way," I said on a sad sigh as I sat behind the desk in the back office. I'd cleaned it off, set the photos to the side, and organized all of the papers that had been covering it. Then I studied everything I could find in the files. None of it good news.

"No way what?" a female asked from the doorway.

I looked up to find Addie standing there in jeans and a black hoodie with a big silver eye on it, her coat folded over her arm.

"No way this place can stay in business." I gestured toward the bills and bank statements spread out in front of me. "From my calculations, we need at least a fifty-percent occupancy rate to break even, and we haven't had that in over a year."

"Probably not since your mother died." Addie came in and took a seat in one of the chairs on the opposite side of the desk. "Mammie didn't really know much about managing this inn. Business was never her forte. She was spectacular at making people feel at home, but she didn't know how to get them here in the first place."

I frowned at the papers in front of me. "It got worse with her, but honestly, it started years ago. Five years ago this fall, to be exact." I looked up at her. "My father was the businessman, right? Is that when he . . . passed?"

She tilted her head as she briefly thought about it. "Erm, he wouldn't have even started aging yet. You wouldn't have passed the age of maturity, so he would have been fine." She gnawed on her lip for a moment. "I think I know why, though. A couple things, actually. First, your mom was pretty depressed after you left. She'd been part of the decision, as far as I know, but that didn't mean she liked it. Everyone noticed a change in her. So your dad was dealing with a lot. And then, well . . ."

"Well, what?" I asked when she didn't continue.

"You might get mad."

"Why?"

"Well, that's about the time Tase Roca bought the ski resort and started expanding it."

I folded my hands on the desk. "I don't get it. Why would I be mad?"

"His first phase of expansion was adding a few cabins right at the bottom of the mountain. Ski-in/ski-out kind of places."

At the mention of skiing, all sorts of memories flooded my mind. Visions of us on the slopes, skiing when we were younger and then snowboarding. Racing each other because most of the guys our age couldn't keep up or didn't dare do the moguls like we did.

"Do you still ski?" I asked excitedly.

She blinked at the unexpected change in conversation. "Uh, yeah. Love to. So did you—wait. Do you remember something?"

"I do! You and me killing it on the slopes. I can't wait to go again!" I nearly squealed.

She laughed. "We had a lot of fun out there."

Her expression fell, though.

"What?" I asked. "Please don't tell me it's not the same."

"Well, it's not that. I mean, it's not quite the same because we have more tourists coming in than we used to."

I glanced at the papers on the desk. "More tourists, but fewer guests?"

"That's the thing. Like I said, Tase bought the resort and started expanding it."

"With a few cabins."

"At first, yeah. Then over the next few years, he added a second ski lift, a couple of new trails, more cabins . . . The growth was slow at first, but then it kind of exploded two years ago. The Court wasn't happy about it, but they do like the extra money flowing in."

"Obviously not to here. Isn't the Whisper Falls Inn the largest hotel in town?"

She nodded.

"But the least busy." That wasn't a question.

"Besides the cabins at the resort, there have been other places popping up. A couple of B&Bs. The Green Coven even bought up a bunch of the townhomes and condos and rent them out by the week. We've been working overtime, the Luna Coven that is, to ensure the wards stay intact and everything remains under control. They had to pull the reins in on Tase. He's been flipping out lately because of it."

"Tase? You said Roca?"

She picked at her sleeve. "Yeah. Xandru's older brother."

Something was off in her tone. My eyes widened as I remembered.

"You still have a crush on him! Oh my god. Are you *with* him now?"

"Uh, *no*. Not really, anyway. I don't think anyone will ever nail that man down." Her rings glinted in the light as she waved her hand in the air as though dismissing him. "I don't want to talk about that. He's an ass most of the time. Especially lately."

I dropped my chin in my hand. "So Tase's business ventures are responsible for the Whisper Falls' demise."

"Bottom line? I think so."

I gnawed on my lip. "Does Xandru have anything to do with it?"

She became completely engrossed with her sleeve again.

"Ah. This is where I get mad," I said as realization set in. After everything he'd said about protecting the inn and me, come to find out he'd played some kind of role in the inn's sad state. "He did, didn't he?"

"They keep everything close to the vest, but I think it's a family affair. I don't really know how deep for Xan, though. He's always done his own thing, but when you left . . . he pretty much lost it, Kales. Adrian, Andrei, and Tase were all he had."

My mind conjured forth vague recollections of faces obviously related to Xandru as she ticked off the names. His brothers. The entire family had somewhat of a bad reputation in town, but I'd always thought if given the chance, they'd do the right thing. I supposed I'd expected them to live up to Xandru's standards. Apparently, they'd brought him down to theirs.

Then something else occurred to me.

"Holy shit. Maybe Xandru's so damn interested in keeping an eye on the inn because they plan to buy it! Have the Rocas ever mentioned that?"

She pulled a face and squirmed in her chair. "Well . . . they *have* held a grudge against your family for a very long time. I don't know all the reasoning behind it, but I do know everyone in town practically worshipped your father and your family, while the Rocas were always treated differently."

"Maybe because they have a bad reputation?"

"Or maybe they earned the reputation because they got tired of being treated like shit for a hundred or so years."

"And now they found a way to screw my family over. I can't believe I let him—" I cut myself off.

Addie's eyes sparked with curiosity as she leaned forward. "Let him what, Kales? What did you let Xandru do to you?"

She said it as though she knew exactly what he'd done to me, causing blood to rush to my cheeks. Which made me even madder.

"I can't believe I let him play me! He totally fucking played me."

Realizing I wouldn't dish out any more details than that, she sat back in her seat. "Don't jump to conclusions yet. The Rocas . . . they're complicated. If you remembered everything, you'd know that. And Xandru most of all."

I nodded. "I do remember that. But at least you had a pretty good idea of what you were getting into with Tase. You *wanted* the bad boy. I'd always thought Xan was different, though. But I guess he changed. Or maybe I was wrong from the beginning. Maybe he and I were wrong, together."

"Kales, you don't really believe that, do you?"

I shrugged. I didn't know what to believe anymore. Not when it came to Xandru.

"At least give him a chance to explain. Talk to him."

"That'd be a lot easier if he didn't disappear right after . . . *playing* me."

She giggled at the innuendo, and my anger diffused.

"Like a fiddle?" she teased.

"More like an electric guitar," I quipped. "And I sang like a damn rock star."

Her eyes popped open wide, and we both fell into a fit of laughter.

"Well," I said once I regained control. I lifted my chin and squared my shoulders. "I'm not giving in yet. I don't know how, but I'll find a way to save this inn. The Rocas—or anyone else who's trying to get their hands on it—can fuck off."

She grinned. "That's the spirit! But can you start tomorrow?"

I pointed at the letter from the bank. "I have 32 days to come up with a payment plan."

"Good. So you can start tomorrow. Come on. I have some time off." She stood up. "You've been avoiding a few things—some important people—and I think it's time you got reacquainted."

"I don't know," I said slowly.

She was right. I'd been avoiding everything and everyone as much as possible. I hadn't exactly been welcomed back with open arms, but there had been a lot of staring. I guess I couldn't blame anyone, considering I wasn't supposed to ever come back and especially not with a blood thirst, there was a death in my family the third night after I returned, and shortly after, I was accused of murdering someone else.

"The longer you stay holed up in here, the more they're going to stare when you do finally come out. Just rip the Band-Aid off already."

"Ugh!" She was right. I glared at her with her smug grin. "I hate you, Bratty Addie."

She laughed and then rushed at me with her arms open, slamming into me with a hug. "There's my girl! I've missed you."

Feeling her arms around me, smelling her so very familiar scent, I sighed with content. Everything I felt about Xandru was all mixed up now, but Addie truly did feel like home.

The bright sun and blue sky were deceiving, because the air remained cold. The snow had been cleared from the roads and sidewalks, but still blanketed the grass and rooftops. Bundled in coats, knit hats, and gloves, we walked to the town square, getting as far as Coffee Haven before we stopped for hot coffee and a late breakfast. The scent of freshly baked pastries and java beans immediately cued my memories, and I noticed the shop had changed somewhat from what I vaguely remembered about it, with more plants and paintings and drawings hanging on the walls. Addie credited Aster McCabe, who caught us up on the local rumors about the recent murders.

Aster was a couple of years younger than us, always quiet and a bit of a loner, while her sister Reeve, who'd been in our class, had been the perfect little doll that Addie and I not-so-secretly made fun of. Mostly because Reeve and I were always pitted against each other in every possible way—GPAs and test scores, homecoming and prom royalty, cheerleading . . . she especially hated me on the slopes because I was as good as her although I was human then and she never was. I'd love to race her now. But she'd left town, and here was Aster, managing the coffee shop like a boss. And dude, could she make an amazing blueberry scone.

"See? That wasn't so bad, was it?" Addie asked as we crossed the street to the park area of town square.

A blue pickup on the far side caught my attention. "Hey, isn't that Xandru's truck?"

Addie followed my gaze. "Yeah, it is."

Xandru and another guy who looked remarkably similar to him—Tase, I thought—walked up to it and opened the doors. He looked over at us, obviously hearing his name. I waved for him to wait. He shook his head before they both slid in the truck and took off.

"Well, what the hell was that?" I asked.

Addie waved her gloved hand in the air. "That was typical Roca. They're always like that."

My coat pocket buzzed with a text message notification. Hoping it was Sindi, I retrieved my phone, only to find a curt message from Xandru: "Talk later. Promise."

Maybe I don't want to talk to you, I thought with a scowl as I shoved my phone back in my pocket and continued strolling with Addie.

I stopped us at the fountain, remembering my last day here and saying goodbye to Addie and Xandru. Although I'd known what was about to happen—whatever the town's memory ward didn't wipe out when I left, the coven's spell would make sure I forgot forever—but I hadn't believed it'd be as thorough as they'd promised. I'd held onto the hope that some part of me would remember, that I couldn't possibly forget the lifelong friendship Addie and I had or the epic, deep love Xandru and I shared. They'd called it puppy love, young love, a high school crush. He and I had always known it was so much more than that. And my parents had, too. He was one of the reasons they'd wanted me to leave.

Maybe they'd been right all along.

"You're getting sad on me," Addie said. "Come on."

She slipped her arm around mine and tugged me past benches and old-fashioned lamp posts toward the south side of the square as the clock on City Hall's tower began to dong in the next hour. Children ran around us, laughing and screaming as they threw snowballs at each other.

"Let's stop for a visit with Madame Tahini so you can access the residents part of the website," Addie said as we approached a storefront with Euro-Asian style writing on it. As soon as I saw her, I remembered the strange little woman known around town as Teeny Weeny Tahini. Besides giving readings and whatever else she did in her weird little shop that smelled like a complex concoction of herbs, she was the keeper of the website's password.

"Make sure you have her number and know her hours," Addie said once we left. "She changes the password like every 26 ¾ hours. I think just to mess with us."

"Why is she the one in charge of it? She's not even affiliated with the website. Does she even know how to use the internet?"

Addie laughed. "Who knows? This is Havenwood Falls. Not a lot makes sense."

We left town square and the main business district, passed City Hall, and entered the residential area as we headed north up Eighth Street. As the street began to slope steeply upward, we came to a gate that crossed the road, with a fancy metal sign that said Havenwood Heights.

"The sign looks different than I remember," I commented.

"The Rocas redid it," Addie said. Right. Mr. Roca had a metalworking shop. My memories were slowly returning in the weirdest ways.

Addie flicked her fingers and murmured something, and the gate began to roll open. I could hear the waterfalls nearby, a whisper of a sound in town on a quiet night, but a muffled roar out here. Something dark poked my mind as we passed through the gate.

I grabbed Addie's arm. "I don't know about this."

"It's time, Kales. Band-Aid, remember?"

I exhaled sharply and followed her up the steep incline. We passed an enormous house on the right, then a road on the left. Addie's family owned two of the mansions at the end of that cul-de-sac, but we weren't going to Addie's house. We kept on up the mountain road, passing by woods of aspen and evergreens that separated the large estates, tendrils of mist from the falls rising above them. The late winter sun beat down on us, and for the first time since I'd arrived, I could actually feel its warmth. If I were human, my legs would have been rubber by now from the climb. As it was, I struggled to breathe properly, still adapting to the thin atmosphere. But the closer we came, the more I was drawn to the estate like a magnet. I smelled home. I tasted it. I felt it.

When it finally came into view, though, my heart dropped.

What had once been a magnificent manor on the right side of the upper cul-de-sac was now not much better off than the inn. While the inn was a Victorian style built during the first days of the town in the 1850s, our house was quite newer but with an older, gothic style to it. Mom had said it made her feel more at home—as in Romania home. I swallowed against the lump that formed in my throat when I realized I'd just thought of her as *Mom*.

We walked up the long sidewalk to the front door, where loud rap music blared behind it. Addie gave me a surprised look as she threw open the door with a twist of her hand. The music cut off immediately. We walked inside, into a grand foyer with marble floors and a double curving staircase of wood and intricately detailed wrought iron. More Roca handiwork. A layer of dust covered the bannister and the table that sat in the middle (I remembered fresh-cut flowers in vases were usually there in the spring and summer), and wallpaper that had once been elegant and luxurious curled and lifted at the edges.

"Aurelia!" Addie yelled, her voice echoing off the marble floors. The girl ran from one of the upstairs hallways to the balcony above us. "You're supposed to be at home at my place. Or at Lena's. What the hell are you doing here?"

"Lena had shit to do. And *this* is my home, not yours! What the hell is *she* doing here?"

The boy I'd seen with her at the cemetery came out from the same direction she'd come from. From their rooms, I recalled. My bedroom had also been down that hallway, at the end of the wing. He had the same color hair as mine, not quite as dark as Mom's and Aurelia's, but with the same brown eyes as our sister —the same brown mine had been before I'd turned. He was thin and awkward looking, like all twelve-year-old boys. He simply scowled at me, but didn't say a word.

"She has every right to be here," Addie said.

"She has *no* right!" Aurelia screamed.

"Her name is now on the deed," Addie countered.

Aurelia seethed, her nostrils flaring as she glared at me. "That is so unfair! Two more years and it would have been mine." Her eyes narrowed, shooting daggers at me. "What did you *do* to them? They weren't supposed to go so soon!"

"Aurelia," Addie warned with a kind voice.

"Just leave me alone!" She ran off, back to her room.

Gabe still stood there, staring at me. "You shouldn't have come back," he said flatly before turning and disappearing down the hallway.

"They blame me," I said, my shoulders dropping.

"They were too young to understand."

"Why would our parents do that to them, though? To all of us? The hell with being too young. *I* don't understand."

"Well, she's right. They did go too soon. It wasn't supposed to be that quick. They should have had at least another ten years, maybe longer. Long enough for those two to grow up and begin their own lives."

"Away from here?"

"I think that was the plan."

"But everything got messed up."

"Yep. Goddess always has Her own plans."

I crossed the foyer to the formal living room to our left, where all of the furniture was draped with protective covers, and walked over to the big picture windows lining two walls. Out one side was the spectacular view of the town spreading out below, looking like it belonged on the front of a Christmas card. The City Hall's clock tower and a couple of church steeples stood up like sentinels over the town. The sun was nearly straight overhead, its rays blinding as they bounced off the snowy roofs and lawns. Across town, the ski lifts climbed the mountainside, and skiers carved their way down the slopes.

"Maybe we'll get another snow this season to go," Addie said from my side. "We can go up in the summer now, too. There's a lookout with a snack shop at the top of the mountain over there. One of Tase's new additions. He's planning to add a slide and other things for the summer tourists next year. Eventually a restaurant."

"Good for him," I muttered as I turned to the other wall.

Although the view of town was beautiful, this one was breathtaking. Another mansion sat across the cul-de-sac, most of it blocked by evergreens. But beyond it was an upper portion of the falls. From here, they appeared to shoot out the side of a rock wall and free fall into the trees below. Right now, they were partially frozen over, cascades of ice that created an incredible work of art by Mother Nature herself. That explained why the roar had been muffled. In summer and close-up, the sound was nearly deafening.

I couldn't see it from here, but I remembered what looked like a large log cabin at the top of the falls, but was a tavern owned by the Alversons. Lena Alverson was one of Aurelia's good friends. I also recalled a pool at the bottom of the mountain that the falls poured into, surrounded by boulders and trees. During the warmer months, a great mist rose from the pool enshrouding the area with a magical feel. And if memory served me right— which it was starting to do—the pool fed a stream that crossed town and fed into Mathews River, which carved its way along the base of the south mountain. Tears stung my eyes as I remembered standing here with Mom, who loved those falls so much.

"So, uh, what do you want to do?" Addie asked from behind me.

I swiped at my eyes with the backs of my hands before turning, and then I looked around the room before my gaze rested on her face. I shrugged.

"I don't know. It's home, but it's weird."

She gave me a sad smile. "I figured it would be, but thought it'd help with the memories."

"It has." I glanced around again. "It just feels different. Without them."

"I'm sure the covered furniture doesn't help. We've had the house closed up for months on Mammie's orders. Well, I thought we had. I don't know how long those two have been coming here. They'd wanted nothing to do with the place until very recently. Aurelia said it was too painful, yet here she is."

I trailed my fingers over the dusty cover on the sofa. "People deal with grief in different ways."

"Maybe Mammie's death changed their minds."

"Or my arrival."

"They'll come around. This could be home for all of you some day."

I shrugged as I looked around and let the memories in. "Yeah, maybe. I don't think any of us are ready for that yet. I think I'm good at the inn."

Addie nodded, then gestured toward the back of the house. "Before we go, then, I thought you should go through some things in your dad's old study. Your mom left it virtually untouched, but maybe there's something there that can help with the inn."

"Like insurance or secret accounts nobody knows about?"

"Who knows? You don't until you look, right?"

I started heading that way. "Yeah, I guess it won't hurt. Well . . . it will, but it's okay."

"While you do that, I'll go see if I can get anything out of Aurelia."

As I entered my father's formal study with its large mahogany desk and many bookshelves, all filled with leather-bound books, I took note of the mixed feelings I had for both of my parents. I was at once angry at them for what they had done to me, to all of us, yet I missed them so much and ached to see them just one more time. I hated and loved them at the same time. I supposed I wasn't the only child who felt that way toward their parents, but it was new to me. A few weeks ago, I'd thought I had no parents, no family at all.

I pulled the covers off the furniture and sat in Daddy's chair and spun it around, taking his office in. Heavy drapes blacked out the windows, and although my vampire eyes could still see, I turned on the desk lamp. After another glance around, I began going through the drawers, finding interesting tidbits here and there. At some point during my rummaging, music began playing again, but not rap and not quite as loud as before. Low enough that I could hear Aurelia and Addie singing and even laughing, and I smiled to myself.

Mom and Mammie must have been through everything, because I didn't find a single item relevant to insurance, bank accounts, or anything of the like that didn't have a copy I'd already seen at the inn. However, I did find some photo albums. I sat on the leather loveseat by the shelves and paged through them, allowing the pictures to begin filling in the holes in my memory. As I studied the photos of the three of us kids growing older, I could see in Aurelia's face what I'd often seen in Aster McCabe's, and a sadness filled me. She'd grown up in my shadow. And then our parents had shipped me off to have a perfect life without them, leaving them here to die and Aurelia and Gabe to pick up the pieces. Because I'd been turned, I hadn't even been able to become the doctor that had been all of our dreams. Tears streamed down my cheeks by the time I closed the back cover.

"No more photos for now," I muttered as I replaced the album on the book shelf and wiped my tears dry.

My gaze fell on one of the leather-bound books that looked to be different from the others. I pulled it off the shelf, and it wasn't a press-printed piece of literature like the others. It was very old, soft, supple leather, tied with a leather strap. I carefully untied it and opened the cover to find yellowed paper with swirly handwriting. I'd found a journal. More specifically, I'd found my mom's journal. Dated in the 1840s.

"Whoa," I breathed as I dropped back into the loveseat.

Turning the delicate pages carefully, I became immersed in Mom's notes of a time long gone by, in a place far away. She wrote about her life in a small village in Romania, the ritual ceremony of when her parents triggered her moroi gene, meeting my father and marrying him. How they'd planned to use their gifts of giving people comfort and setting them at ease combined with manipulating earth and stone to build and run their own inn in Romania. I read about their life together as husband and wife, living near their families, including Luiza, who'd been married to my dad's brother.

And then about the births of four children. One was Madame Luiza's. And the other three were mom's.

"What on earth?" I muttered under my breath as I reread the entries. I looked up, although not really seeing the office around me. "Mom and Dad had previous children. So did Luiza. What happened to them? Did I know about this?"

I don't know how long I sat there wondering about these older siblings we had but was pretty sure we'd never known about. The office was only lit by the lamp, but the light in the hallway had changed. And then I realized how quiet the house had fallen. No music or dancing or laughing or talking. No breathing or heartbeats.

I tied the journal up to protect the pages and hurried into the main part of the house, out to the foyer. Night had fallen while I'd been engrossed in photos and journal entries, moonlight pouring through the soaring windows over the front door. "Addie? Aurelia? Gabe?"

Nobody answered me. Where had they gone? Why had they taken off, leaving me alone? I called for them again. Dead silence.

Then a large shadow swept overhead. I looked up. And screamed.

CHAPTER 11

A white bat hung from the ceiling. A bat the size of a man. I blurred for the front door, but it beat me there, dropping in front of me just as I was about to grab the handle. I jerked my hand back before I touched the hideous monster. It had the body of a man, naked and muscular, with large wings spread out from its outstretched arms to below the knee. Its bald head was also that of a man's, but with pointed ears, sharp-edged cheekbones, and fangs. Its irises were pitch black, but a green light shone in the pupils. Grayish-white, leathery looking skin covered it from head to toe, not a single hair to be seen.

"Like what you see, puppet?" it asked me, and I gasped with surprise that it spoke. *Teased.*

I spun and ran, blurring for the back door. But the thing was faster than me, soaring over me, and swooping me up into talon-like fingers. I kicked and thrashed and tried to wriggle myself free from its hold, but it was so much stronger than me, even with my vampire strength. We crashed through the two-story Palladian windows at the back of the house and immediately climbed higher in the sky, veering to the right to avoid the mountainside. I opened my mouth to scream, but I suddenly felt like a hand had clapped over it, something invisible silencing me. No matter how hard I arched and thrashed, the beast kept its grip, its claws digging into my shoulders as we soared over town. The icy air bit at my face and hands.

Town square passed under us, to our right, and the lights of emergency vehicles sped below, headed in the opposite direction. I tried yelling at them to turn around, but couldn't. The acrid odor of fire and smoke came faint on the air as we traveled away from the source.

We began descending on the far side of town as we approached the east mountain. The thing expertly avoided crashing through the tree branches before coming in for a landing at the back of a log cabin at the end of a cul-de-sac. I knew this house. I'd remembered it one of my first days here, although I hadn't known why then. But now I did. I'd been here many times.

This was the Rocas' home.

The thing released me several feet from the ground, and my feet had barely touched the wooden deck in front of the back door before I lunged for the edge. But a powerful hand grabbed me by the back of the neck and jerked me inside. Another hand gripped my upper arm hard enough to bruise it, and the person behind me shoved me forward, making me stumble. They kept me upright, though, pushing me until I started walking, through the familiar kitchen and headed for the basement door. They practically carried me by the neck and arm down the stairs into the dark cellar, unrelenting regardless of how hard I bucked and kicked, always missing my mark.

A second pair of hands wrapped around my wrists and lifted my arms above my head and out. I snarled and snapped at them, but they remained out of reach. Cold metal replaced the long, bony fingers, clamping around my wrists. The sound of metal grated against metal as my arms were lifted higher until my feet left the ground. More metal cuffed my ankles, and my legs were also pulled apart. I jerked against the bindings to no avail. A bright light was suddenly turned on, momentarily blinding my sensitive eyes. Once they adjusted, I found Mrs. Roca, wearing black dress pants and a yellow silk blouse, standing in front of me, and I was surprised I even recognized her.

I remembered thinking she was beautiful, just as beautiful as my own mom, but that wasn't quite the word I'd use now. She was vamped out—her eyes bloodshot, her skin blanched and veiny looking, her fangs protruding between her lips—but her beauty could still be seen. Only now, her pale skin pulled taut over the sharper edges of her bones. Her lashes weren't as long and thick as they'd been before, something I'd always envied a little of all the Rocas. Her hair wasn't as thick and glossy as I remembered either. Not the jet-black it used to be. What happened to her?

A whimper from the corner beyond her caught my attention. My eyes bugged when they saw my sister and brother chained up just like me on the other side of the room. Blood dripped from Gabe's lower lip, and Aurelia's clothes were shredded. Fear shone in their wide eyes. I thrashed and fought against the metal cuffs, but they only dug in deeper. I tried to scream, but the invisible muffle remained.

A movement to my left brought the man-bat into view as it moved closer to my siblings. I tried to scream and fight again, ignoring the pain of the cuff's bite into my skin. I just needed to get to them, free them before that monster hurt them even more.

"Where's the witch?" Mrs. Roca demanded.

"She wasn't there," the creature said, and before my eyes, its wings disappeared and it morphed into Mr. Roca. Except a thinner, much more muscular and younger Mr. Roca than I remembered. He could almost be mistaken for any of his sons, if not for the glowing irises, now a lime green instead of black.

Mrs. Roca's green eyes narrowed as she glared at me, but spoke to her husband, and as her vamp traits faded, I noted another difference in her. Her eyes used to be grayer. Moroi eyes, as Xandru had said. Now they were a brighter green. Almost as bright as her husband's. "Did Adelaide see you?"

"No. She was gone before I got there," he answered as he pulled a pair of black jeans off a work bench scattered with various tools and, I couldn't help but notice, some mighty long, sharp-looking knives. I immediately averted my eyes to not give away that I'd seen them while I tried to figure out how to break out of these cuffs and reach the knives before they caught me. My vampire abilities were not an advantage with them. *Come on, Kales, think!*

"You damn well better hope so," Mrs. Roca replied to her husband, "or she'll have the Court here in no time. I will not watch them put you down."

Mr. Roca buttoned his jeans, then pulled on a dark gray button-down shirt. He stared at me as he began buttoning it. "Nor I you. We'll take care of this, Isabella. Just like I promised. Now, get the girl."

Aurelia's eyes widened with fear, her body thrashing against the restraints, her cries muffled like mine. I once again tried to fight my way to freedom as Mrs. Roca approached my sister, and tears filled my eyes. But then she passed Aurelia and Gabe and disappeared around a corner, a smirk on her face. *Bitch!*

A moment later she returned, gently leading a young woman about my age dressed in only a satin teddy. Her glassy blue eyes wandered around the room as her finger twirled in a long, blond lock. Mrs. Roca walked over to me and beckoned at the girl.

"Over here, dear," she said with a kind voice, and the blonde followed until she stood in front of me. Mrs. Roca gave me a tight grin. "We brought you a present, *Michaela*." She said it like Mammie had, dropping the hard K. "How long has it been since you've had human blood straight from the vein?"

My eyes widened, and I shook my head. *No!* I tried to scream. It'd been more than two years, when I'd first been turned.

"Come now, dear, just a taste." She placed her hand on the

girl's head and tilted it to the side, exposing her throat. The older woman blew across the girl's skin, engulfing me with her delicious scent. My tongue automatically swept over my lips as my gaze fell on her prominent carotid. The throbbing artery called to my thirst.

But I knew what just a taste did. I knew there was no such thing as "just a taste," not when direct from the vein. I'd almost killed last time I'd wanted just a taste of the fresh, warm blood. My mouth watered, and I was nearly panting.

"Here, I'll start," Mrs. Roca said, and she vamped out before bending over the girl's throat and latching on.

The woman flinched but otherwise didn't respond. She was under compulsion.

Mrs. Roca came up and licked the blood off her lips, but left the wound gushing. "Hurry, or I might take her all for myself."

She shoved the woman up against me, her bleeding throat level with my nose and mouth. I turned my head, refusing. Mr. Roca suddenly stood behind me, his large hand on my head, pressing me toward the girl. My lips touched her throat, the deliciousness filled me, and I couldn't help it. *Just a taste.* I licked the warm, thick liquid from my lips, my eyes fell closed, and for a moment, I thought I'd died and gone to heaven. I needed more. *Now.*

I lunged forward with a sudden thirst that felt like fire in my throat. My lips closed over her wound, my fangs sank into her skin to widen it, and I sucked her delicious, sweet and salty life force, my eyes rolling back with bliss.

"That's our girl. Drink up. Then only a couple more to go," Mr. Roca cooed, and at first, the sound was soothing, encouraging, but then something flipped inside me.

I jerked back. *No!*

"Drink!" Mrs. Roca spat as she shoved the girl in my face again. I shook my head violently, refusing. Her eyes glowed green, and she growled at me. Then she went in for the kill herself.

"No, darling," Mr. Roca said as he pulled the blonde out of his wife's embrace as though she were a ragdoll. Mrs. Roca hissed at him, and I thought she was about to pounce. He held up a hand and shook a finger at her. "This one's Michaela's. Remember the plan. You can have yours later. After we take care of this for the kids."

Mrs. Roca growled lowly, but backed off.

"Now come on, Michaela, drink up," he said to me, once again holding the girl in front of me. I pressed my lips together and turned my head. "Well, I'll just leave her right here. You won't be able to resist for long."

He let go of the girl, and she collapsed to the floor. Her eyes fluttered closed as she fell into a deep sleep. Her wound still seeped, and flames licked up my throat at the smell. He eyed me for a long moment.

"Let's have a talk, why don't we?" he said, and he made a gesture in front of me. The strange muffled feeling disappeared. The whimper I couldn't control because of the burn finally could be heard.

"Why are you doing this?" My voice was choked, raspy, as everything within me yearned for the girl at my feet. For her blood. "What did I do to you?"

He laughed, but no humor filled the creepy sound. "You mean, what did you to do *us*. All of us. My whole damn family, if I don't put a stop to it."

"I don't know what you're talking about. I haven't done anything!"

He growled in my face. "You fucking exist!"

I flinched as though he'd slapped me.

"You went and turned yourself when you weren't supposed to, not giving a fuck what you were doing to the rest of us. Not just your family, but mine, too." His facial features began to morph back into the beast. "You did this!"

"I . . . I have no idea what you're talking about."

He glared at me with green eyes. "You're making us go

strigoi. That curse on you, on your family—it's ruining us, too. But I won't let it. Mrs. Roca and I will deal with it, but I won't let you get our kids killed by the Court. I'll make sure it's you instead."

"Now drink," Mrs. Roca ordered, gesturing at the woman at my feet.

"I will not."

She laughed. "And you pretend not to understand. You know exactly what will happen."

"Why the hell do you want me to kill her? What did *she* do?"

Mrs. Roca shrugged. "*She* existed. She was convenient, left in one of our cabins while her boyfriend went out skiing. We have him, too. He'll be your next kill."

"What? No!"

"Oh, yes, dear. You will. You will start to go strigoi, the Court will kill you, and this damned curse will be over with. *Before* it takes our children."

"What the fuck is strigoi?" I yelled.

They both fell silent and stared at me. Mrs. Roca tilted her head. "You really don't know?"

I didn't answer, thinking it was pretty damn obvious.

"It's what happens to moroi when they kill one too many humans," Mr. Roca said with a thrill in his voice. "It's what's happening to me, to Mrs. Roca. You saw what I turn into. But that's barely the beginning. Moroi are mortals. Fully turned strigoi are immortal. Stronger, faster, more abilities, indestructible, unstoppable."

"Each kill makes you even thirstier," Mrs. Roca added, and I could hear the thirst in her own voice. "Leaves you burning for the next one until you can't fight it any longer. But each kill stains your soul, until it turns so black, you simply don't care anymore. You become a monster, and not even the Coven can end you."

"Why the *hell* would you want me to be like that?" The

thought of becoming what they described scared the shit out of me, but it made no sense.

"We don't," Mr. Roca said, and now I was even more lost. "We just want you on your way to becoming strigoi, where it's too late to turn back. Far enough that the Court has no choice but to put you down before you get out of control."

"Like you are?" I spat.

"I'm not quite there, but will be soon enough," he said with a sickening smile. "Someone fast enough with a blade might still be able to take my head. But I'm not worried about that anymore. The missus and I will be long gone before the Court knows about us. They'll be too focused on you. And once they end you, the curse breaks, and our family won't have to know what this is like."

"What curse?" I asked.

"That's enough questions. Now drink!"

"If you're going to make me do this, you owe me a full explanation. What curse?"

"Tell her," Mrs. Roca said. "It might motivate her, if she cares about her brother and sister at all."

My gaze flew to Aurelia and Gabe hanging by their wrists, watching us. Both of their bodies trembled. I looked back at the Rocas. "Tell. Me."

Mr. Roca rubbed his chin. "The curse against your family after their first offspring went strigoi."

I blinked as I remembered the journal that I'd read just today. I must have dropped it when Mr. Roca's bat-form kidnapped me.

"Nobody knows why, but your older brothers and cousin weren't quite right. Never were. As soon as they were matured, they gave in to the bloodlust. They went on a murderous rampage throughout the countryside back in our Old Country. They killed dozens in only a few nights, trying to quicken the process of becoming strigoi. They *wanted* to be monsters, and they knew if they didn't force the transformation fast enough, they'd only need to be decapitated to be stopped. But if they were fully changed, they thought nothing could stop them. Witches and sorcerers had to be hailed to contain them before they killed any more. It took much magic, but they were eventually eliminated. Your uncle was killed in the mayhem."

I stared open-mouthed as my brain processed all of this. Once it did, I looked over at Aurelia and Gabe. She shook her head. She hadn't known either. Gabe only stared, his eyes glassed over with fear. They shouldn't be hearing this.

"Your parents and your aunt had to pay. Losing their children, and your uncle, wasn't enough. So the magic wielders cursed them."

"Cursed all of us," Mrs. Roca corrected.

Her husband nodded. "Our punishment was minimal. We didn't have children yet, so we'd had no part in the murders. But since the Rocas served the Petrans, the mages said our ties were too close. They cursed all of us to not be able to bear children for seven generations of the families who'd been massacred. And then, if your parents or your aunt had any more children, their moroi genes could not be triggered, or the whole family bloodline would die. They wanted to ensure the intense bloodlust didn't repeat itself."

I squinted at him. "But if the gene's not triggered, they would die anyway."

"The matured eventually would, but not as fast. The curse took them quickly." He nodded toward Aurelia and Gabe. "And the curse takes the *entire* family."

My breath caught. I shook my head. "No. I don't believe you. This has nothing to do with you going strigoi. You're just trying to distract me."

He chuckled. "It really doesn't have anything to do with it, does it? It shouldn't. *We* didn't do anything wrong. But then, shortly after you turned, my brother changed. We had to put him down before the Court found out. Then his wife. And now us. I don't believe in coincidences, Michaela, but when I found out about you, the pieces came together. Your father did this somehow, but I *will* end it. By ending you. Now kill. The. Fucking. *Woman!*"

The blonde flew up off the floor in a blur, and he shoved her in my face again.

"Fuck you!" I spit out.

"She needs motivation," Mrs. Roca said, and in a heartbeat, she stood behind Aurelia, her fangs at my sister's throat.

"No!" I screamed. The metal cuffs tightened on my wrists and ankles, and the chains cranked on their own, pulling me tighter. I fell still. Recalling what Xandru had said, I realized why the Rocas were such good metalworkers. And something else clicked in my mind. My heart squeezed painfully, then shattered into pieces, but I couldn't dwell on that now. I needed to protect my siblings, and I knew what I had to do. "Okay!" I yelled. "Just leave them alone. I'll drink."

"Good answer," Mr. Roca said. "After all, you'll be saving their lives, too. The curse will be lifted from them, as well."

I nodded, sagging with defeat. "I get it. My parents . . . Mammie ..." I shook my head as tears spilled. "They died too soon because of me."

"That's right," Mr. Roca soothed. "But you can stop it all. You have the power to protect our children *and* your siblings."

The fear in their faces gave me the motivation the Rocas had hoped for. But not for what they'd expected. As I leaned in toward the girl's bloody throat, I redirected my bloodlust, focusing everything within me on the metal bands wrapped around my wrists and ankles. And it worked. As much as I hated what it meant, I was right. My jaw clenched against the burn, not in my throat now, but on the skin of my extremities as the metal began to melt. The moment I was free, I sprang for Aurelia and Gabe, while retargeting my energy to the knives on the work bench. They flew through the air, one toward Mr. Roca and the other toward his wife.

"What you failed to consider," I seethed, "is that *your* son turned me. And he gave me your power to manipulate metal."

Before they could react, I swished my finger, and the knives sliced across their throats.

I spun and freed Aurelia and Gabe with a simple touch to the metal, releasing the clasps. Wish I'd thought of that when I'd done my own. We ignored the thumps of falling bodies behind us and rushed for the stairs.

To find a whole family of Rocas lined up on them.

CHAPTER 12

Several large bodies and a couple of smaller ones pushed past us as I tried to usher Aurelia and Gabe to safety.

"Aw, fuck," a low voice came from behind us.

"Shit," said a girl's voice. "Tase and Xandru were right."

"Go," I urged my sister and brother toward the stairs, needing them gone before shit went bad again. "Get out of here."

"But—" Aurelia looked over her shoulder at me.

"Just go," I hissed, but before I could stop her she turned and threw her arms around me. I gave her a quick return hug, then rushed her and Gabe up the stairs.

They weren't out of sight five seconds when more figures came to the top of the stairs.

"Michaela," Addie gasped as she flew down the steps.

"Are you okay?" Xandru asked me at the same time, his hands on my shoulders, turning me toward him. He raised a hand to my face, but I pulled away.

"Don't touch me," I seethed. "You have no right."

His eyes darkened with confusion.

"Kales, are you okay?" Now Addie turned me around.

I fell into her arms. "I . . . I don't know."

She squeezed me harder. "Well, you will be."

I chuckled humorlessly. "I don't think you've seen that mess over there. I don't think I'll be okay."

She tried to soothe me, but more people came down the stairs. As large as the full basement was, it suddenly felt like an overcrowded tomb.

"What happened down here?" asked a woman dressed in a business suit, her silvery white hair pulled into a fancy twist. A few lines etched her face around her brown eyes as their gaze traveled over the backs of the Rocas gathered around their parents. Then they landed on me. "Michaela?"

As soon as she addressed me, her face clicked in my memory. This was Adelaide's grandmother, Saundra Beaumont, one of the Luna Coven's high council members. One of the most powerful witches in town. The one who both served, and from what I remembered my dad saying, led the Court of the Sun and the Moon. Basically, the person who would decide my fate—if the Rocas didn't first.

"Mr. and Mrs. Roca . . ." Several pairs of eyes suddenly focused in on me. I swallowed the lump in my throat. "They abducted Aurelia and Gabe, and then me."

"Hey, there's a human girl over here," one of the Roca brothers—not Xandru, he still stood there staring at me—said from the place where I'd been shackled. He looked up and tugged on the chains until what was left of the melted cuffs fell in his hands. "What the hell?"

"I think there's a guy somewhere, too," I said. "Another human."

Saundra Beaumont nodded her head to the others behind her, and two began moving about, searching the house. "Why do they have humans here? The girl looks like she's been nearly drained."

"She's alive," another Roca brother said, nearly growled.

"Michaela?" Saundra looked at me again with a white brow raised.

"They wanted me to go strigoi."

Once again, everybody froze and directed their full attention to me. I gave a quick rundown of what had happened, except the part about the curse. I mentioned it and that they believed if I went strigoi it'd be broken, but I said no more about it.

"I don't know if there really was a curse," I said. "Maybe they were just trying to finish the job of framing me for those murders."

Saundra studied me for a moment, probably wondering if she should stay on point or interrogate me about what I knew about the murders.

"It had to have been them," I continued. "I just learned about this strigoi thing, but if they were lying about that, they were definitely *something* different. They would have killed Aurelia and Gabe if they had to. Definitely would have killed that girl and her boyfriend."

"They were definitely going strigoi." One of the Roca brothers strode over to us. Tase, the oldest. He and Xandru exchanged a meaningful look. Addie squirmed next to me. "Their eyes are bright green even in death."

"Tase and I confronted them a couple of weeks ago," Xandru added, "but they denied knowing anything about the first murder. Then there was the second one…" He looked over at me. "We hadn't been able to find either of our parents, though. Until now."

At least now I knew why he'd disappeared right after professing his undying love for me. *Undying* taking on a whole new kind of meaning.

"The curse is truth," Saundra said. "Mihail Petran had come to us years ago, begging for a way to break it. We tried, but we could not find its weak point. There's always a loophole in magic, but this one's is tiny. After you turned, though,

123

something interesting happened with the Rocas. Something that would only happen under a specific circumstance."

"They began going strigoi," I said. "Starting with Mr. Roca's brother."

Saundra nodded. "Yes, and according to Mihail and Irina, that would only happen if someone forced you or your siblings to turn. If someone triggered your gene without your consent, the curse would also jump to that bloodline, but with even more dire consequences."

"That's exactly what happened," I said as my gaze locked with Xandru's. "*Why*, Xandru? Why would you do this?"

"I didn't," he said.

I blew out a breath. "You're going to stand there and flat-out lie to me after all this? Unbelievable!"

"Michaela, please believe me."

"How can I? You admitted to coming to Atlanta. You admitted to wanting more than anything for me to remember you. So you *turned* me? Against my will? And now look what's happened! The repercussions of such selfishness!"

He shook his head while still holding my gaze. "That's not what happened, Kales. I couldn't ever—"

"You killed my parents, Xandru! You killed Mammie! Maybe not directly, but you made it happen. And now *your* parents!"

His whole expression filled with pain. "Michaela—"

I held up my hand and cut him off. "I don't want to hear more lies. Do you know how I knew? Look at those metal cuffs. I did that. It's not the first time I've controlled metal. Where do you think that ability came from, considering it's a *Roca* trait?"

All of the Roca siblings reacted at once, filling the room with a loud din.

"Enough," Saundra said with a firmness that hinted at her power, silencing everyone. "We haven't found a way to break the curse, but we do have a way to contain it. To ensure this strigoi business doesn't continue."

I stood up straighter in front of her and lifted my chin. "I'll do it."

She peered at me with Addie on one side of her and her other people gathered behind her. "You don't know what's required."

"I assume you take care of the source of the problem. Me. I'll do it, but not for the Rocas. For Aurelia and Gabe. Whatever it takes to give them some kind of normal life."

She nodded. "You're partially right. It will sever the curse from them. But you're not the true source, are you?"

I swallowed as she looked beyond me at Xandru and the rest of the Rocas.

"We can contain the curse to the one who turned Michaela against her will. The blood thirst will take hold, whether immediately or in weeks or months, we do not know, but it will come, and it will come on strong. Everyone here is aware of what happens when a moroi goes strigoi. It's not tolerated in Havenwood Falls, and we will not allow it to escape our town either. We will end the life before it's transformed into a monster."

The Rocas all burst out in protest, yelling at each other, at me, at Saundra. But then they suddenly fell still and silent as the witches moved around the room and into formation, encircling the family, chanting as they lifted their arms above their heads. My hair began to stand on end as the volume increased and energy sparked in the air. They continued circling, the energy built higher, and the urgency of their words increased. Then they stopped their movement, and each of them pushed their hands toward one of the Roca siblings, then pulled. A green light followed their movements, as though flowing out of the Rocas' bodies. Then they gathered the light above all their heads, swirling in a streak until it tightened and formed into a ball. As the ball began to shrink, my lungs seized.

A sob flew up into my throat, and I clapped my hand over my mouth to hold it in. Reality came crashing down on me.

Xandru was about to be given a death sentence. I felt so much anger toward him for all that he'd done, but the thought of him no longer existing in this world . . . it was unfathomable. He was the love of my life. The love that had never truly reached its potential because so much had been against us. And maybe what he did was wrong, but could I blame him? If the situation was reversed, would I have done the same? It's not like he knew about the curse and the consequences. And I'd thought about making Sindi reverse Ryan's compulsion numerous times, and what we had was nothing compared to Xan and me.

My whole body curled inward as the green ball traveled over the group's heads, circling slower and slower as though searching for the one it now belonged to. Xandru had been staring at me the whole time, and I fell into his beautiful gaze now as the ball hovered over his head. Tears streamed down my cheeks.

I love you, I mouthed as the ball wobbled, then dropped.

Everybody gasped. The sob I'd been holding in choked me. *Oh. My. God. Oh my god, oh my god, oh my god. What just happened?*

Addie cried out. "Tase? NO!"

All eyes stared as the green light filled the man standing next to Xandru.

Seconds ticked by in total silence. The light faded, settling into him. Then Addie's sobs broke through as she lunged for Xandru's brother.

"No, no, no," she cried as she held onto him and they fell to the floor. "What the fuck did you do?"

I stood glued to the spot as everyone else seemed to process everything much faster than me. A multitude of emotions battled inside me, and I didn't know how to feel.

But then that big, powerful body moved toward me, those stunning eyes locked on me, and I knew exactly what I felt. I lunged into Xandru's open arms and wrapped my entire body around his. I never wanted to let go. With great reluctance, I eventually pulled back and cradled his face in my hands.

"It wasn't you," I said.

He gave me a small smile. "Don't you understand? More than anything, all I want is for you to live the life *you* want, not what others choose. All I want is for you to be happy. Even if it's without me."

I shook my head as I returned his smile. "It will never be without you."

NONE of us wanting to stay in the big mansion yet, Aurelia, Gabe, and I walked into the inn, each of them holding my hand. As soon as we passed through the double doors, I gasped, Aurelia screamed, and Gabe simply froze.

"My babies," said the figure standing behind the front desk with a big smile on her face. "Did you miss me?"

"Do you see and hear that?" Aurelia whispered.

"You, too?" I asked.

"Uh-huh." Gabe nodded.

"How?" Aurelia asked.

"It's Havenwood Falls, dear." The woman moved toward us, eliciting another gasp and a scream. "Nothing makes sense here."

"Oh. My. God. She just walked *through* the fucking desk," Aurelia said.

"Language, love," the ghostly figure warned.

Gabe blanched and began to turn around. "I'm out of here."

"No way," I hissed, clasping his shoulder. "We stick together now. Man up."

"Oh, dear. I didn't mean to frighten you." She clapped her hands under her chin. "I'm just so happy to see you. All of you, together."

"Um . . . I don't mean to be rude," I said, "but, well, we just buried you, Mammie!"

She squealed with delight. "You called me Mammie!"

"It's really you, isn't it?" Aurelia asked. She stepped forward and tried to touch Madame Luiza, but her hand went right through her.

The old woman giggled like a child. "That tickled!"

Whether from giddiness or exhaustion, the three of us all broke down in a fit of laughter. Mammie clapped her hands and danced around us.

"What are you doing here?" I asked, then I frowned. "Are you okay? Are you stuck between planes or something? Does someone need to guide you into the light?"

Mammie laughed. "You have sure come to accept things, haven't you? Even the most bizarre. You must have had an eventful time while I was gone."

"You don't want to know," I muttered. To a ghost. We were talking to a freaking ghost.

"Why *are* you here, Mammie?" Aurelia asked.

"Well, someone has to keep an eye on you kids," she said with a wink. Then she looked at me. "And I thought I could help you out around here."

I cocked my head. "How exactly would you do that?"

"I admit I am no genius when it comes to marketing, but I've watched enough TV. I'm pretty sure haunted hotels tend to stay booked up."

"Mammie! You're a genius!" I threw my arms open, but then dropped them. "I'd hug you, but . . . well . . . this is awkward."

"It's okay, dear. I feel your energy." She smiled. "It's good energy, too. I'm so happy for you. Welcome, home, Michaela."

I grinned back. "It's good to be here."

After the shock of finding a ghost in our lobby wore off, it didn't take long for everyone to settle down for the night. Over the next couple of days, though, we planned how to make the most of Mammie's paranormal visits, as well as brainstormed ideas for the changing season and all of the festivals coming up in the spring and summer. As new guests arrived or townspeople stopped by for one reason or another, Mammie tipped me off as to who was human and who was supernatural, shocking me every time. Well, except for the creepy old dude with shifty eyes who came in. He had weasel-shifter written all over him, and Mammie and I worked together to scare him away.

Addie didn't come by for several days, even after I told her about Mammie, caught up in Coven business. The smoke I'd smelled while in Mr. Roca's clutches had been a fire at the library, which was where she'd disappeared to right before the Rocas kidnapped Aurelia and Gabe. As the Court's business manager and Coven liaison, she was required to monitor the scene for any suspicious supernatural activity. Since then, she and the rest of the Coven and Court have been busy trying to quell rumors about the Rocas and the fire.

Xandru was held away, too, unsurprisingly with family issues. Such as nearly killing his brother for what Tase had done. The police were even called and would have been happy to kill two vampires, especially Rocas. So the brothers made up, but still had much to work out, with their family and each other.

Tonight, however, was ours. We had a date at the Fallview Tavern at the top of the falls. Aurelia helped me get ready for the evening in my cottage before she went to spend the night with her friend Lena. Gabe was already at a friend's house for a sleepover. They were making the most of their last non-school night after their bereavement, and I planned to, as well.

A knock at the door had Aurelia and me exchanging a happy glance. I looked in the full-length mirror one more time.

"You look amazing," my sister appraised, and I felt amazing in the silky black dress and black suede stilettos. I rarely dressed up, because it just wasn't my style, but when I did, I felt all the more beautiful.

"Someone's getting laid tonight," Aurelia sing-songed.

"Shut *up*," I muttered as I headed for the door, sure the vampire ears on the other side heard her.

But they weren't the vampire ears I was expecting. I opened the door to find Addie and Tase on the porch, both looking quite nervous. I stepped outside, rubbing my bare arms against the cold bite of the night that promised another snowstorm. We stood in awkward silence for several beats.

"Um . . . how are you?" I asked Addie, noting the stress and sadness etched into her face.

"Tase has something to tell you."

I looked at him with a brow lifted, mixed emotions swirling within. He'd caused so much heartache for my family and now for his own, but I wasn't sure if a death sentence was quite fair. His forlorn expression tugged at my heart strings.

"I want to apologize," he said as his green gaze, similar to Xandru's but more green than gray now, held mine. "I did it partly for the money, but I didn't know the truth of the consequences."

My brows pinched. "I'm sorry?"

He blew out a sigh. "I was bribed to turn you."

I pulled back and blinked. "By who?"

"It's Coven business," Addie said.

"I think it's *my* business," I countered.

"I promise to tell you when the investigation is final," she replied.

"It was a witch?"

They both nodded.

"She'll be banished," Addie said, "but that's why I can't say who yet."

I nodded. "Fine. But for money, Tase? Really?"

He shoved his fists into his jeans pockets and gnawed on his lip like Xandru did. "Not completely. I thought I was doing Xandru a favor. I went with him on one of his trips to Atlanta, and I saw how fucking miserable he was. The bitch didn't tell me about the curse, so I thought triggering your gene would be a win for everyone—you and Xandru, your family, me. I knew you'd passed the age of maturity, but it was worth a shot. She offered enough money to do the expansions to the ski resort like I wanted, so, well, I did it. I know it sounds like greed. I know it sounds like a Roca thing to do." He looked at Addie and back at me. "But I really was trying to do the right fucking thing for once. Now I'm paying for it."

Addie gave him a look.

"I know. I know. It is what it is," he said. He pulled something out of his back pocket and held an envelope out to me. "I want you to have this. Dad did all kinds of shit to take business from the inn and give it to the resort, and I know you need it."

I took the envelope and looked inside. I held it back out to him. "I can't take this."

"You deserve compensation of some sort."

I shook my head. "It feels too much like blood money."

"Kales," Addie said, "don't be stupid. This goes back to before any blood was spilled. It's money they took from your family. And maybe it'll lead to forgiveness."

"I'm sorry. I can't."

"Think of Aurelia and Gabe."

"We'll be fine. I said I can't take it." I shoved the envelope against Tase's chest. He finally took it back.

"It's okay," he said with a smirk. "The bank note's already been paid off, and you can't give that back."

He turned and walked off, sauntering back to his truck as another drove up the driveway. My body immediately sensed Xandru.

"Jerk," I muttered as I watched Tase's retreating body.

"He's trying to make amends."

"Feeling guilty on his deathbed?" As soon as the words came out, I regretted them. Addie's face looked crestfallen. "I'm sorry. That was mean. Are you holding up okay?"

She shrugged. "As best as I can. Saundra's been trying for years to come up with a way to counter the strigoi transformation. I've been spending every waking minute researching. I'll find a way. I can't lose him, Kales."

I watched as Xandru poured out of his truck and strode toward us, sexy as ever. "I know what you mean." I turned and gave her a hug. "I believe in you, Bratty Addie. Just, you know, don't squander away the time you do have with him."

She nodded against my shoulder before pulling away. "Now you go have a song-worthy time." She winked before traipsing off the porch.

My eyes fixated on Xandru as his large, powerful body climbed the steps, his breath-taking gaze traveling from my head to my feet and very slowly back up, pausing at places that immediately heated. "Mmm . . . you make me want to skip the dinner date part and dive straight into dessert."

"Alexandru Roca," I said with my best Southern drawl picked up from my time in Atlanta, "what kind of lady do you think I am?"

He wrapped one strong arm around me and pulled me up against him. His breath tickled my ear. "You're mine. That's what kind."

I couldn't argue with that. But I did have an addition. "And you're mine."

"Never to be forgotten."

"Never," I breathed before his mouth claimed mine.

WE HOPE you enjoyed this story in the Havenwood Falls series of novellas featuring a variety of supernatural creatures. The series is a collaborative effort by multiple authors. Each book is generally a stand-alone, so you can read them in any order, although some authors will be writing sequels to their own stories. Please be aware when you choose your next read.

Other books in the main Havenwood Falls series:

Fate, Love & Loyalty by E.J. Fechenda

Old Wounds by Susan Burdorf

Covetousness by Randi Cooley Wilson

Coming soon are books by Lila Felix, R.K. Ryals, Belinda Boring, Heather Hildenbrand, Stacey Rourke, and more.

WATCH FOR HAVENWOOD FALLS HIGH, a Young Adult series launching in October 2017.

IMMERSE yourself in the world of Havenwood Falls and stay up to date on news and announcements at www.HavenwoodFalls.com. Join our reader group, Havenwood Falls Book Club, on Facebook at https://www.facebook.com/groups/HavenwoodFallsBookClub/

ABOUT THE AUTHOR

Kristie Cook is a lifelong, award-winning writer in various genres, primarily New Adult paranormal romance and contemporary fantasy. Her internationally bestselling Soul Savers Series includes seven books, as well as several companion novellas. Over 1.2 million Soul Savers books have been downloaded, hitting Amazon's, B&N.com's, and Apple's Top 100 Paid lists.

She has also written The Book of Phoenix trilogy, a New Adult paranormal romance series that includes The Space Between, The Space Beyond, and The Space Within. The full trilogy is available now.

Besides writing, Kristie enjoys reading, cooking, traveling, getting her hippie on, and feeding her addictions to coffee, chocolate, cheese, The Walking Dead, Game of Thrones, and Supernatural. She has lived in ten states, but currently calls Florida home.

Email: kristie@kristiecook.com
Author's Website & Blog: http://www.KristieCook.com
Facebook: http://www.facebook.com/AuthorKristieCook
Twitter: http://twitter.com/kristiecookauth
Goodreads: https://www.goodreads.com/KristieCook
Instagram: http://instagram.com/kristiecookauth

ACKNOWLEDGMENTS

Thank you to my Maker who stayed with me always, even when my faith wobbled and wavered.

Thank you to my sons, Zakary, Austin, and Nathan, for all that you have taught me about unconditional love and family bonds.

And a very special thank you to all of you who never gave up on me—my parents, my aunt, my writer friends, my readers— even when nobody would blame you if you did.

This collaborative world started as a flicker in my mind several years ago, and finally grew into something more over the last several months. I didn't know exactly what it would become —and I still don't—but I believe wholeheartedly in the idea and its purpose. It could not have happened without the help and support of my aunt and uncle, and the insight and wisdom of Meredith Frank Mendez, the intellectual property attorney who took the time to understand what I wanted to accomplish and created a contract that could make that happen. I also give a shout-out to my Dynamis sisters, Kallie Ross, Morgan Wylie, and Lila Felix, for giving me feedback and cheering me on when I began throwing out this crazy idea. Also to Rick & Amy Miles and their Red Coat PR team, who have been great supporters of me as a writer, as a friend, and as a publisher. And to my betas, Julie Bromley and Stacey Nixon; to Randi Cooley Wilson for the critique; and to Liz Ferry at Per Se Editing for making my words shine.

Finally, I thank the creative souls so far involved in this constantly growing and evolving project. Regina Wamba, Art Director, and the authors who've created the characters and settings of Havenwood Falls: Susan Burdorf, E.J. Fechenda, Randi Cooley Wilson, Kallie Ross, Morgan Wylie, Kristen Yard, T.V. Hahn, Amy Hale, Lila Felix, R.K. Ryals, Michele G. Miller, Belinda Boring, and Stacey Rourke. You've made this project everything I dreamed it would be and so much more. I can't wait to see what happens next!

OLD WOUNDS

BY SUSAN BURDORF

~ A Havenwood Falls New Adult Novella ~

HavenWood Falls

OLD WOUNDS

SUSAN BURDORF

ABOUT THIS BOOK

Welcome to Havenwood Falls, a small town in the majestic mountains of Colorado. A town where legacies began centuries ago, bloodlines run deep, and dark secrets abound. A town where nobody is what you think, where truths pose as lies, and where myths blend with reality. A place where everyone has a story. This is only but one . . .

Betrayed by love, Sherry Grimes flees the city, seeking solace in an unfamiliar place that calls to her from deep in the mountains. But her search for comfort goes awry when she's chased by a wolf through the forest, falls, and blacks out. She awakens in a strange room with a mysterious and forbidding—yet undeniably sexy—man by her side. So much for finding solitude. But despite the craziness that brings her to the small eccentric town, she discovers herself drawn into the magic that is Havenwood Falls.

Russell Higgins had long ago given up the idea of finding the one he could trust his secrets to—until he met Sherry. One look at the feisty woman with a broken heart has him defying his pack and rethinking his own ideas of his perfect mate. What he can't deny is the wolf inside, claiming the human as his.

Bradley Monahan wants Sherry back, and he would do anything to make that happen. Even fight the mysteries of a town that doesn't forgive transgressions.

While love may heal old wounds, it's the fresh ones that Sherry must overcome to find her way back home. Wherever that may be.

BOOKS BY SUSAN BURDORF

A Cygnet's Tale

Breaking Fences

I would like to dedicate this book to the readers who are about to discover the magic of Havenwood Falls.

CHAPTER 1

$\mathcal{S}$herry threw her Ford Focus into gear, wishing she was driving Brad's Viper instead of her old clunker. She ignored the vehicle's hesitation and the grinding sounds that came from underneath as she sped backwards out of the driveway without looking. Banging into the garbage can, she winced, knowing the heavy rubber container likely dented the side of the car, but not really caring.

She just needed to be gone, and to be gone as quickly as possible. As she spun the car to face the other end of the cul-de-sac, momentarily stopping to shift gears once more, Brad ran up and pounded on the window, startling her. He was bare-chested, his ripped muscles bulging with effort as he tried to force her to look at him. He wore a pair of gray sweatpants and little else. Normally the sight of his hard, athletic body would cause her to pause and stare at him with hunger, but today she only felt disgust and anger.

"Sherry, come on!" Brad's muted plea came through the closed window. Her fiancé—correction, *former* fiancé—raced barefoot alongside the slowly moving vehicle as she attempted to leave. He had one hand on the locked door handle and the other on the window as he tried to keep her from moving forward.

Sherry's heart beat out a rhythm that begged her to flatten him, but she waited for him to retreat back a step before she glared at him.

Rolling down the window, she said, "Get away from the car, or I'm gonna run over your toes."

Brad wisely stepped farther back, hands raised in surrender. His face turneda bright shade of red. He tossed his black hair out of his eyes. Pointing a finger at her, he said, "Go ahead, run off like a baby. You never were a good lay. I don't need you anyway."

"You will when the rent comes due next week," Sherry spat out before she sped off down the street. In the rearview mirror, which Sherry mentally kicked herself for looking into, she saw the blonde draped around him, rubbing his chest and consoling him in the only way a strumpet like her knew how to.

The girl was dressed in the silk robe Brad had given Sherry on her last birthday. Her favorite silk robe. The one Brad said brought out the blue in her eyes and the sexy in her toned and petite body. She was half-tempted to whip the car around and rip the silk off the woman's slender, tanned form, but decided to forgo that pleasure in favor of getting the heck away from there. Flipping her dark hair over her shoulders, she forced herself to keep her eyes on the road.

A short while later, blinded by tears, she nearly sideswiped a delivery truck and city bus before her pounding heart calmed down and she could breathe normally again. After several hours, with the radio blasting rock music loud enough to melt her eardrums, Sherry pulled over to the side of the road into a small rest area. She had no idea where she was, or where she was going, but something had told her to keep driving, so she followedher gut instinct.

The brisk spring air, chilled with the promise of more winter this close to the mountains of Colorado, greeted her as she emerged from the car. Stepping into a slushy puddle, she groaned in frustration. These were her favorite black heels, their leather now ruined forever in the salty, half-melted snow that encased her foot up to the ankle.

Sherry grabbed her cape from the passenger side and wrapped the thin material around her cream-colored silk blouse. Neither article of clothing was any protection from the cold air that whipped around her. Her dark hair had fallen from the loose bun she'd put it in earlier while driving to keep it out of her eyes. She shivered.

The sound of laughter drew her eyes to a family walking toward the entrance to the building that housed the bathrooms and snack machines. The little girl held tightly to her father's hand, while the boy—in his mother's arms as he was just a toddler—hugged the woman tightly. Looking over her shoulder at her husband who walked slightly behind them, the woman smiled at something he'd said with a look of complete adoration, which he returned with an easy smile of his own, and Sherry felt her throat tighten in jealousy.

Would she ever see anyone look at her like that?

She'd thought Brad would be that one, the one who would make her heart sing with passion that could last forever, but he obviously played their love song out of tune. What was so wrong with her that she couldn't find anyone to love her for longer than it took to cash her paycheck?

She'd met Brad in church, for Christ's sake. How could he have turned out to be such a snake? Was this bimbo the first, as he'd claimed while throwing on his pants to chase after her when she fled? Or was this one just the first he'd been caught with? If she hadn't come home from work early today due to a gas leak near the therapy office at the middle school, she never would have known anything about what he was up to when she was gone each day. Who knows how long this had been going on without her knowledge? Brad certainly wasn't going to tell her, and the bimbo was barely able to string a sentence together, so no help there.

Shivering in the cold, Sherry already regretted her hasty decision to run away. She should have made him, and the bimbo, of course, leave. She considered turning around and driving home, but the last thing she wanted to do was have another argument with him or, worse yet, admit she was wrong to leave so quickly. Even though she knew she wasn't.

That love nest of his was *her* apartment, dammit. She should have made *him* leave. Her face darkened as she remembered the sounds that greeted her when she'd opened the door, sounds she was all too familiar with making herself after a few glasses of good wine and great jazz.

Pinching her lips, she closed her eyes, willing the tears not to fall.

"Lady?" said a small voice to her right. "Are you okay? Do you need a sucker?"

Slowly opening her eyes, Sherry said, "No, thank you." Under her breath she muttered, "I *am* the sucker," which came out louder than she intended.

Sherry looked down to see a tiny blonde girl holding up a bright red sucker, the kind the dentist used to give her back when she was young, if she was a good girl and didn't squirm too much in the seat while they drilled her teeth. She'd always thought it ironic that a dentist would give sugar on a stick to a kid whose teeth he'd just worked on, but she hadn't complained too loudly. And it *had* seemed to ease the pain, at least for a little while.

"Thank you," Sherry said, reconsidering. She took the sucker the little girl offered and smiled, hoping her mouth made the appropriate shape and wouldn't scare the child. Sherry wasn't sure what to do next, as the girl didn't seem to want to leave.

"I am so sorry. I hope Destiny wasn't bothering you too much." The little girl's mother took her daughter by the hand and gently tugged her away.

Sherry smiled crookedly. "Destiny? Perfect name for the first person I speak to right after the disaster of my current life. Almost like a sign."

A sign? Of course it was a sign. Sherry was a firm believer that if you stood still long enough, the universe would find a way to connect with you. Watching the tiny girl and her mother walk with hands clasped tightly, she wasn't surprised when the girl turned, locked eyes with her, and gave Sherry a solemn wink before getting in the car with her family and driving off.

Sherry entered, then stood in the middle of the information building as she looked around. She was surrounded by maps marking the nearest hiking trails, along with brochures advertising tourist traps, which were neatly lined up on the wall in metal racks. The slick, curved, white walls and cheap marble flooring somehow both soothed and unsettled her. Sherry felt the walls closing in on her, although nothing was moving. She felt something happening—changing—inside her. She breathed deeply, eyes closed, and waited to see if the universe had another sign for her.

But nothing came. At least not right away.

No one said, "Go home, patch things up with your skanky boyfriend, and forget that he tends to like other women once in a while." Conversely, nothing else said, "Forget that jerk, keep driving."

Then she heard the soft *swish-swish* of leather-soled shoes on the floor.

"Can I help you, miss?" A kind dark-skinned man, with eyes like chips of coal in his lined and weathered face, looked at her in concern. "Are you lost?" He wore a dark green uniform with a slim silver badge that announced him as BRAD.

Sherry wanted to laugh out loud at the irony of meeting someone with her ex-boyfriend's name, but swallowed back the mirthless sound instead. Sometimes the universe could be cruel. She shook her head, but her watery eyes gave away her true emotional state. The man patted her arm and then squeezed it as he led her over to where the brightly colored and labeled maps rested.

"Perhaps you're looking for a nice place to visit?"

Sherry felt herself gently propelled closer toward the maps. She took the one he proffered to her, barely glancing at it. The second she touched it, she felt a tingle, gentle and insistent, travel up her arm. Nothing uncomfortable or painful—it was more like the pins-and-needles feeling when your arm fell asleep after resting your head on it for a while.

"This is a brochure for a lovely town not far from here called Havenwood Falls. A lot of folks find the town quite pleasant to visit, and I'm sure you will, too."

Sherry raised an eyebrow as she looked at the one-page, double-sided flyer he'd handed to her. The old man stood in front of her, slightly stooped and expectant, as if her decision mattered a great deal to him.

Sherry's eye was caught by the promise of a "cabin in paradise," and she was sold before she even knew what else to say.

Chuckling as if he knew the answer before he asked, the old man said, "You have a plan now?"

"Why, yes," Sherry said, answering his twinkling eyes with a shy smile of her own. "I think I do. These cabins sound wonderful. I see a number down here. I'm going to call and see if they have anything available."

"Good idea. You'd better move on now. There's a storm heading this way soon, and it wouldn't do to get caught in it. Those late spring squalls can be quite temperamental in the mountains. Oh, and miss," the old man said as she started to turn away, "the town is a bit difficult to find. You can take the shuttle outside, or if you prefer to drive your own vehicle, you are welcome to follow the bus for the best way to get there. I strongly urge you to do that. The shuttle bus will be leaving in about ten minutes, though, so you'd better hurry."

Sherry looked where he pointed and saw a large bus idling

in the section reserved for buses and trucks to park. She couldn't see through the tinted windows, so wasn't sure if it was full already or not. Since there was so little time to get on the bus if she wanted to take it, and since she was planning to rent a cabin and would need her car, she decided not to take the bus. But she would definitely follow it. She had a feeling the old man was not lying about it being a difficult town to find and wondered why. Mountain roads could be tricky sometimes, with quick turns and perhaps that was the reason why. Either way, she was getting excited at the thought of having a plan.

Sherry nodded. Chuckling once she walked outside, she grinned at the kindness of the old man. He'd been pushy, but pretty darn cute in spite of it. She liked him. Looking back through the glass doors, she was surprised not to see him standing in the doorway watching her. Instead, she could make out a tall, stocky woman behind the desk, shuffling papers and talking to an elderly couple who had just walked up.

After calling the number on the flyer, Sherry was relieved to find there was one cabin left. Because it was higher up on the mountain than she would have liked, she hesitated before committing to the idea of the cabin. *I'm just planning to hike the area for a few days until things have a little time to cool off at home,* she reasoned, justifying both the expense and the remoteness of the cabin.

"That will be three hundred dollars for the week," the woman on the other end of the line said.

Sherry gasped in surprise. "Are you sure? That seems pretty cheap."

"Oh yes, ma'am. Your cabin is very rustic, therefore a little cheaper," the woman replied. Her voice sounded pleasant and certain, exactly the way a customer service person should sound.

Sherry gave the woman her card number and then, just as the woman hung up, thought of a question she needed to ask. When she tried to call back, the number was busy. Hanging up,

Sherry decided to go back inside and thank the old man for his help and try the number later.

Moving inside, Sherry waited a minute until the woman behind the counter was free. Sheila's name badge was slightly crooked and not as shiny, but still lettered the same. When Sheila looked up, Sherry smiled sweetly and said, "I wonder if you might give that sweet old guy, Brad, a message for me?"

"Brad?" Sheila's expression was puzzled and annoyed, like she had plenty of better things to do than play secretary.

"Yes, the nice man who helped me a few minutes ago."

"How did he help you?" the woman asked. Her expression had changed from annoyed to cautious, as if afraid of what Sherry might answer.

"Well, he gave me this flyer, the one about Havenwood Falls and renting a cabin. Let him know that's what I've decided to do. And I owe it all to him. So please, tell him thank you."

Sheila hesitated. Biting her lip, she folded her hands together on the desk and stared Sherry squarely in the face. "I'm not sure what game you are playing at here, young lady, but we have no one working here named Brad. And I have never heard of Havenwood Falls. What are you trying to pull?"

Sherry, totally shocked by the woman's attitude—which she felt was totally uncalled for and very hostile—stepped away from the desk. Holding the flyer in front of her, she spoke slowly as if making sure the woman behind the desk would understand the words she was saying. "I just met one of your employees, a nice old man named Brad—it said so on his badge—and he recommended I check into a cabin listed on this flyer."

Sherry flashed the flyer in front of the other woman's face for emphasis and was shocked to discover it did not say "Havenwood Falls" in bold black lettering, but instead encouraged visitors to visit a ghost town about forty miles down the road in the opposite direction.

"Whhhhat???" Sherry dropped the flyer on the desk as if it burned her hand, her face bright pink, and slowly backed away as a young man wearing a backpack walked up to the desk for assistance.

Sherry practically ran from the building and jumped in the car, not surprised to see her hands shaking. *What is going on? I know I had the flyer for Havenwood Falls in my hand. How else could I have called that place for a cabin? Now how will I ever find my way there?*

Sherry looked over at the passenger side of the car, and her eyes widened in shock. On the seat next to her lay the flyer she was sure she'd just dropped on the counter in front of Sheila. And there, written in bold black print, were the words, "HAVENWOOD FALLS. DISCOVER THE MAGIC."

What an odd town motto, she thought as she set the GPS for the location of the cabin rental office where the woman had said they would leave her a key.

"Strange," she said as she tapped the GPS. "What is wrong with this thing? Why won't it pull up the address?"

Sherry shook the device, but nothing changed. She turned it off, and then on again, and still nothing changed. The address was not pulling up at all.

"Now what?" Sherry slumped back in the seat, trying not to cry. This was just too much.

Ahead of her she saw the large bus pulling away from its parking spot. On the side of the bus were the words Havenwood Falls in large lettering with picturesque scenes of the mountains. Without thinking about it too much, Sherry decided she would have to follow the bus like the old man suggested. It looked like the kind of bus you might charter, the kind tourists would use.

Putting the car in gear, once again ignoring the grinding sound, she backed slowly out of her parking spot and pointed the nose of the car toward the highway. Something weird was going on, and she felt like she was in an episode of The Twilight Zone, one of her favorite shows. The grainy black-and-white program had been a staple in her household, much preferred over the banal sitcoms that passed for quality television these days.

As she drove, her phone buzzed, a bright blue-white light signaling an incoming call. She'd turned the ringer off earlier to avoid Brad's many attempts to contact her, so she heard nothing but the buzzing.

Humming to a song on the radio as she ignored the phone, she focused on the road ahead of her. Keeping the bus in sight was pretty easy, since it was so large. She felt the excitement building at the prospect of spending time alone. This was the start of a great adventure. There was no doubt of that in her mind.

Sherry hoped there was a town along the way with a store where she could purchase some clothing appropriate for an extended stay in a cabin, or that the town would be able to supply her with what she needed. She was certain her hastily packed suitcase had nothing she could wear in the woods, and she would need to purchase some food, too. The rumbling of her stomach was a reminder she hadn't eaten in several hours, and the trauma of her situation was starting to take its toll on her. She was starving.

As she drove, she caught sight of a sign on the side of the road noting that Havenwood Falls was just six miles down the road. Not understanding why, she felt almost giddy at the prospect of spending time in the mountains near what she was sure would be a quaint tourist town, if the flyer was a truthful representation of its appearance, that is. After nearly six hours on the road, she was ready to stop for the night. She didn't realize how far this place was from Albuquerque until she glanced at her phone. But she didn't regret one minute of the drive. It had been beautiful driving through the mountains. She hadn't been this spontaneous in years, and it felt good to be free. She hadn't realized how being with Brad had held her back from doing things she enjoyed. He hated the woods, bugs were not his friends, and he swelled up like a dirigible anytime he got bit by something as inconsequential as a mosquito.

She chuckled as she remembered his reaction the one time she'd suggested going weekend camping. He'd just about fainted at the thought of his model-perfect body deformed by nature, a place he referred to as "Alcatraz with trees," since he felt imprisoned if not near civilization, otherwise known as his local craft-beer brewery. "The only nature I ever want to be in, baby," he'd said in perfect seriousness, "is the kind where they have an infinity pool and girls in skimpy white outfits bringing you those drinks with umbrellas in them."

She'd thought he was adorable then. She knew the truth now.

But she'd gone along with it, feeling that being in love meant making sacrifices so the other would feel appreciated. Now she wondered what he'd ever given up for her. She couldn't think of a single thing he'd sacrificed for her good. It had always been her doing the compromising.

She pinched her lips tightly as she thanked her lucky stars they hadn't married yet. It was bad enough imagining the untangling they would have to do when it came time for him to leave now. A marriage would have meant a split of everything right down the middle, and she had a lot of memories tied up in the things in her apartment, not something she was willing to share with someone who treated her so badly. There were photo albums and valuable pieces of decorative art and small treasures that had belonged to her now-deceased parents. Most of the items had been in her family for a long time, and she was not willing to let him take anything just because he'd warmed her bed for a while.

Sherry attempted the phone number once more and sighed in frustration when there was no answer. She paused a moment, considering her options. Should she go forward, or back? Thinking of Brad, his expression smug and sure of himself if she went back, she pinched her lips and decided back was not a place on her GPS.She would only be able to go forward. So, Havenwood Falls it would be. She hoped the old man was right, that she would find in Havenwood Falls the answer to her prayers.

"Yep," she said softly. "This might turn out to be the stupidest idea I have ever had, but—" She paused as the bus increased the distance between them and she stepped on the accelerator to keep it in sight. "Havenwood Falls sounds like exactly what I need right now."

CHAPTER 2

*R*ussell—"Rusty" to his friends—Higgins looked out over the forest and sniffed. The wind brought the smell of something unexpected. Rain? Or something else? He could smell the coming storm. It was still a little while away, but it was definitely going to bring some kind of moisture.

Shaking his shoulders free of his shirt, he shivered in the sudden cold air that struck his bare skin. His muscles contracted across his ripped chest as he stretched his arms toward the sky. It was nearly time for him to take his wolf form and roam the woods on his nightly patrol.

He folded his shirt, shaking it free of leaves from where he'd been laying on the ground just moments before. His thoughts were jumbled, not just by the feelings of unease that permeated his mind, but by a conversation he'd had earlier that day with his distant cousin, Sheriff Kasun.

Rusty hated being boxed into a corner, and his cousin had just given Rusty an ultimatum he wasn't willing to accept. He liked the freedom of being in the forest, with no demands greater than those necessary for survival in the woods. The needs and wants of the human world exhausted him. If he had a choice, he would never leave his beloved woods. But that might not be an option for him much longer.

While Rusty prepared himself for the change, he replayed the brief conversation he'd had with his cousin in the store that morning.

"Choices," the sheriff had said, "aren't always of our choosing. Sometimes the choices are made for us. You know we would like you to return to the pack. I wish you would think about it. The choice is yours, of course. But we would welcome you back."

The memory of that conversation resurfaced as he watched the sun give way to the night in a sky flushed pink and gold, chased by the deeper blue of gathering dusk.

"Curse you, cousin," Rusty said softly to the night air. "I like my life just the way it is." And he did. He was happy being alone.

Like a petulant boy, told he couldn't have that extra cookie, Rusty stuck out his chin in defiance. Why did he have to disturb his way of life? Why did he have to make a choice? All he wanted to do was roam his beloved woods, keep to himself in his cabin, and not interact much with the people of the town unless he had to. That was how it had been for too many years to count, so why did he have to change his life?

Havenwood Falls had existed on the edge of discovery for generations too numerous for him to count. He didn't like the idea of having to join the Kasun pack again. Just because he was a wolf-shifter didn't mean he had to be in a pack, at least not in his mind. Rusty understood how some might like that feeling of camaraderie and unity that a pack brought to a group of the supernaturals, but he had always been a loner, and he wasn't about to change that, no matter what his cousin wanted.

His woods, his trees, and the animals that occupied the environs of the kingdom he protected were all he needed to survive. He was most content here, on this land. Something about these woods calmed him, soothed his soul, and he wasn't willing to give it up for a house in town complete with the wife and 2.2 children the rest of the pack seemed to find satisfying.

For him, the confines of four walls would be like a prison, no matter the pretty trappings. His forest was the only home he needed. His cabin was sparse, barely furnished with only the pieces he'd made from the offerings the forest gave him. His own two hands had constructed the cabin years before. He had a generator to run the electricity that powered the lights. Although he preferred the romance of firelight for the most part, he conceded that a good electric lamp was a blessing when reading after dark.

His cabin was a tight little building with a sleeping loft above the main floor, and wide beams in a dark wood lined the ceiling. His bedroom was on the ground floor, with a rough bathroom just off it. The kitchen, which held a refrigerator and a table with two chairs, was cozy. He rarely used the second chair, though, as he discouraged visitors. There were no pictures on the walls, and no curtains were necessary on the windows, as his cabin was secluded in the woods.

He was not an ugly man, his body kept fit by his nightly patrols in the forest, his hair a rusty brownish-red that gave him his nickname, which was also a variation of his given name. His eyes, a deep chocolate brown, seemed to appeal to the women he sought for comfort, none of whom had ever been to his home. He preferred to meet them away from his cabin.

So far, none had roused his mating desire, merely his body's need for momentary comfort. He wasn't a cruel man, though. He always let the women know it was not their attractions, or lack thereof, that couldn't hold him, but rather his need to roam was too strong. He never gave out false hope. While a woman might turn his attentions down based on those terms, there was always someone else willing to take her place.

Sometimes he worried he was too careful, that he would have no one to pass on his legacy to, but when those doubts crept in, Rusty usually brushed them aside, knowing in his heart that the right woman would come along. He had decided a long time ago he would not settle for less than his perfect mate.

"Time to go," he whispered to himself, surprised at how he was suddenly so melancholy. What had set off this strange mood? He quickly took off the rest of his clothes, sliding pants down strong lean thighs, already furring with his signature rusty color. His boots had already been kicked off, his socks placed neatly inside the boots.

He slipped off his remaining clothes and stood naked in the waning light of the sun. He stretched to his full height, straightening his spine, reveling in the feel of the night's chill wind on his bare skin.

That brief moment before he became the wolf was fraught with so many questions. Would it hurt this time? Would he survive the night and return to his human form with the sunrise, or would he forget the rules and end up a wolf forever? He had only once come close to remaining in wolf form, and it was not an experience he wanted to repeat. The way his mind had gone from human to wolf and refused to return to his intelligent thinking had been a fluke—at least he'd thought so at the time. But now, with many changes gone past that nearly tragic day, he'd come to understand the true consequence of allowing the wolf full control of his mind and body, and he knew he'd never allow it to happen again.

The tingling that signaled the beginning of the change intensified, and he turned toward the distant horizon to watch where the sun sank lower in the sky as it slipped away from view.

Where the setting sun touched his body, he glowed with a highlight of red that set fire to his skin. He closed his eyes, face raised upward to welcome the moon, his mistress. What need had he of a woman, when he could be anything he wanted by the silvery light of the white orb that welcomed his change with such hunger each night?

Bending down, he stuffed his clothes and boots into the backpack that lay next to them. He quickly placed the backpack in his hiding place; when he changed back into his human form, he would need those clothes once more. The discomfort that signaled the change was growing stronger, and he knew his time in this human form was growing shorter. It wouldn't do to begin the transformation without taking care of his clothes first. He'd forgotten once to do that, and the end result had been a walk home without any, not something he wanted to make a practice of, not that anyone saw him this deep in the woods. Still, one never knew who might be hiking or wandering the woods these days. He breathed a sigh of relief when all was ready.

In moments, he felt the familiar stirrings of his body's shift. The pain had long ago become something less than euphoric, but he still shivered with the anticipation of what would come next.

He crouched down as his body began the transformation into its supernatural wolf form. His teeth elongated and his limbs shortened and thickened, their muscles popping and snapping as they reshaped.

He howled, unable to stop the primal reaction to his new form, and shook his fur into place. Lifting his head, he looked around and howled at the moon once more. It was a long, extended howl, one meant to announce his arrival to both the forest and himself. He liked giving fair warning.

His mouth curved into a fierce smile, one that might frighten children, although he was a gentle wolf, not like some of his brethren who liked to rip out the throats of their victims. He rarely fed while in this shape, though the restraint took all his willpower, but his teacher, the one who'd long ago taught him about being a wolf shape, had warned him that if you forgot your humanity and became the beast, you could never go back. Human blood was the surest way to cross that line. No matter how angry he became, he never allowed himself to reach the point of no return. There had been times over the years when his willpower had been tested by poachers, or butchers as he liked to refer to them, who thought the forest was their supermarket. He'd met some such hunters not long ago, but since that encounter, they'd pretty much stayed away from his forest.

He'd heard rumors when he was in town of a couple guys in the bar talking about doing the town a favor by ridding them of "that beast," but they'd been convinced by Sheriff Kasun to leave the woods alone and to stay away if they knew what was good for them.

That was what had brought his cousin out to see him in the first place, but the battle to bring Rusty into the pack had been an ongoing one for quite a while. While his attempts to coerce Rusty to the fold were half-hearted, his reasons were not. Rusty was aware of the difficulties facing the supernaturals as the human world crept closer to their secrets, but he wasn't yet ready to give up his freedom. This forest was his home—end of story. Warnings about the humans and to be wary of them had been part of his life for a long time. Not encroaching on their world too much was a constant dance of vigilance he was willing to choreograph as long as it meant he could remain free to go where he pleased. So eating a human, even ones who deserved it, were not on his to-do list.

Fear of that permanent change, and how it would keep his human side from being in greater control, was something he kept in his mind always. He might feed if a small animal happened to cross his path while he was running, but most in the forest now knew him and stayed in their homes until he'd passed by. He ignored them, and they had all learned to exist together.

As his mind slowly became the mind of the wolf, his alter ego's intelligence almost as great as Rusty's, the man stretched his wolf legs and began his nightly prowl.

Sniffing the air, he caught whiff of an unfamiliar scent and turned his nose in that direction. His super-sensitive ears caught the sound of a car, and fearing it might be more poachers, he headed in that direction, his pads making soft footfalls on the forest floor as he hurried toward the road.

CHAPTER 3

A short distance later, Sherry's confidence was shattered when her car began making a very distinct sound of distress. As it rattled to a stop, a small puff of steam rising from beneath the hood, she cursed. Why, oh why, hadn't she taken Brad's car instead? At least his was kept in tip-top shape so he would have transportation to his auditions. In her haste to leave, she'd grabbed the first set of keys she could find and that had been hers, even though she knew her car was in need of a trip to the garage.

Sherry leaned forward until she bumped her head on the steering wheel and tried not to cry. *Not now*, she thought, biting her lip to control her frustration. She turned the key, hoping the car was just being its usual temperamental self, but not surprised when the loud click told her her worst fears had come true. The car was momentarily toast.

"Great, just great," she said, trying to remain calm. The sky was full dark now, adding to her unease at being alone. The road was bordered on both sides by thick forest, and she hadn't passed, or been passed by, a single vehicle since losing sight of the Havenwood Falls bus.

Reaching for her cell phone, she groaned when she saw there was no reception here. She couldn't even call for a tow or a ride. She didn't think they would have Uber out here in the sticks, but she'd never know since she couldn't use her phone. In this age of technology crowding into every corner of the world, how could this place not have reception? Perhaps the mountains were disrupting the signal because not even a single bar was lit.

"That figures," she said bitterly, tears threatening to fall. She sniffed. Closing her eyes, she leaned back in her seat. *Now what? I suppose I can walk to the town. It's only around six miles. I used to do that in the city all the time. But at least in the city I had sidewalks, interesting things to look at on the way, and it's a concrete jungle, not a forest with wild animals or worse waiting to jump out at me.*

She breathed in and out slowly a few times, gathering her thoughts and considering her options. Since the traffic was nonexistent, there was no rescue coming from that direction. Maybe if she walked a bit farther down the road, the forest would thin out, and she could find a place to make a call. That would have to do. She felt better already, having a plan in mind.

Then she remembered the flimsy shoes she had on, and she groaned again. She would never be able to walk half a mile in those shoes, let alone six if she had to walk the whole distance to town. She thought back to what she'd packed and shook her head at her foolishness. She hadn't packed any extra shoes at all, not even a pair of flip flops. She'd been in such a hurry, she didn't remember even packing extra underwear.

"Stupid, stupid," she cursed out loud.

After a couple minutes of swearing at herself, she took a deep breath. Trying the key in the ignition one last time, she wasn't surprised when it didn't work, but she hit the steering wheel anyway, ignoring the sting of pain.

Darkness had now completely taken over, the last rays of sunlight disappearing behind the mountain peaks. She shivered in the chilly air. If she stayed where she was, waiting for a car that may or may not pass, she might freeze to death. Best to start moving and do it soon.

Opening her car door, she stepped out and shivered again as a blast of cold air struck her through the thin blouse. She walked to the back of the car and opened the trunk.

Reaching in, she pulled the suitcase to her and nearly jumped for joy when she found a sweatshirt, which she immediately threw on over her blouse. The only thing that would have made her happier would have been to find a better pair of shoes for walking, but unfortunately, she didn't find a single pair.

She debated taking the suitcase with her, but decided it would be too hard to walk and drag the case behind her even though it had wheels. Surely the town would have a store where she could purchase clothes and shoes? And she'd be back with the tow truck soon, so stay it would.

Decision made, she zipped the case back up and closed the trunk. Slapping her hands together, she was surprised at how the sound comforted her. She hadn't realized until just now how alone she was out here on this road. She listened to the sounds of the night around her. From the trees on either side, she heard creatures stirring in the underbrush. She shivered, wondering what creatures were going about their night hunts.

In the distance, an owl hooted softly, followed by the sound of wings as the bird took flight. At least, she hoped it was the owl. She shook her head and grinned wryly at her overactive imagination. Honestly, what did she expect to find in the woods —a ghost, or vampires, or werewolves? She cursed those late night horror flicks she'd watched as a child for giving her the idea that creatures lurked around every corner or behind every tree.

Overhead, the stars that dotted the night sky gave off a faint light. The moon, what she called a fingernail moon, was still low enough in the sky that its sliver of silver gave off little more than a glow, but clouds were gathering overhead, and she wasn't sure how much longer she would have that limited light.

Sherry opened the door to the passenger side, grabbed her purse, and pulled it over her shoulder. She then opened the glove box and rifled through the papers and other items until she finally found the flashlight she knew was there. She found a pack of cigarettes and a lighter shoved in the back of the glove box and frowned. Brad must have hidden them in there, although he'd told her he quit. Just one more lie to tally against him. How stupid of him to hide them in her car. While this was a small transgression on his part compared to what had driven her to this deserted stretch of road, it was still a mark in the glad-I-am-not-with-him-anymore column.

She pulled the flashlight out, but threw the cigarettes back inside. Turning on the flashlight, she sighed in relief when its silver beam shot out. She'd been half afraid, the way her luck was running tonight, that the flashlight would be dead. On this darkened road, with who knew what kinds of creatures lurking about, she didn't want to have to walk by starlight alone.

"Okay, girl," she spoke to the night air in an effort to keep herself from being afraid, "no time like the present to get moving."

Straightening her shoulders and shining the light in front of her, Sherry started walking, hoping the next six miles would pass quickly. Keeping her eyes on the road, she ignored the feeling of night creatures watching her. Her heels, totally inappropriate for walking, clicked loudly on the asphalt. She hunched her shoulders inside her sweatshirt and quickened her pace, trying to keep herself warm. The night air had dropped at least ten degrees since she'd left the warmth of the vehicle, and she knew it was only going to grow colder as the clouds gathered in the sky, intermittently blocking the moon and stars.

As she walked, she tried to think what she would do once she reached the cabin, *if* she made it to the cabin, she corrected herself. If her luck didn't turn, who knew if she would make it to the refuge of the cabin before the next day? Hopefully the car was repairable, and she could be on her way quickly.

She focused on the walk, ignoring the rustling of the leaves and sigh of wind through the trees, and the sounds of soft padded footsteps.

Wait. Footsteps?

She whirled around, flashlight beam pointed behind and around her in a wild arc as she tried to identify the source of the sounds she'd heard. There. She pointed the flashlight in the direction of the sound and thought she caught the flash of something red in the beam.

But the closer she walked toward the shoulder of the road that rimmed the edge of the forest, the more she thought she was just being ridiculous.

"Come on, girl," she chided herself as she walked slowly forward, toward the thick brush and tree line at the shoulder's graveled edge, "don't make trouble for yourself. There's nothing there. Even if there were, it was probably just a raccoon or something like that. There couldn't possibly be anything more dangerous out here. Oh Lord," she whispered as she turned back toward the road, "if you get me out of this alive, I promise to stop making fun of those church shows on TV."

The only answer to her prayer was a gust that chilled her to the bones. Was that agreement? Or just the cold night air reminding her she was alone on a dark and nearly deserted road? She narrowed her eyes as her flashlight caught the glint of something silver in the brush lining the road. She pointed the beam where she'd seen the flash of silver but saw nothing else. Shivering, she tugged the sweatshirt tighter around her body as she backed away from the edge of the road.

She straightened her shoulders, turned herself in the direction the sign had indicated for Havenwood Falls, and walked into the fog that now covered the road in front of her.

CHAPTER 4

*R*usty watched her go, a strange tingling singing in his blood. She wasn't remarkably beautiful, but in the sudden patch of moonlight that had fallen on her before she turned away from where he was hiding, she'd looked ethereal. Haunting. Ghostly, almost. A woman, he knew immediately, with steel in her blood.

A woman he wanted to know more about.

He followed her, carefully picking his way among the underbrush as he kept hidden while paralleling her path. There was something about her that drew him. Obviously, she was human—he scented only her light flowery perfume. Jasmine, he thought. There wasn't a hint of anything supernatural about her, and yet . . . and yet there was something drawing him to her and her to the town.

He had thought for just a moment that she'd spotted him. The way she'd walked toward the forest's edge as if she sought something, perhaps him, had him holding his breath until she hesitated and moved back and then down the road.

Her car must have been the one he'd heard earlier. He watched as she headed toward town. If she intended to walk the six miles, he would have to follow her the whole way. There were creatures in the woods tonight, creatures that she shouldn't come across. Her disappearance might be hard to explain.

He padded softly ahead of her, making sure nothing crossed her path. Most of the forest creatures, sensing his presence, had already gone to ground, but it wasn't the usual beasts he worried about. It was the unusual. The kind the town might have a hard time explaining if something happened to her.

He sent out a silent prayer that no one but him would be out tonight. He hadn't sensed anyone, but one never knew who might decide this was a good time to go out and about in the woods on their way to a feeding or other assignation. Sometimes the high school shifter kids were brought out here for lessons on their crafts and legacies. He hadn't seen any of the witches, vampires, other shifters, or their children out in the woods in quite a while, but that meant nothing.

So lost in thought was he that he missed when the woman he followed stopped in the road. She was adjusting a shoe that seemed to have come loose. He grinned, noting that her shoes were definitely not the kind you wore for a long walk, and wondered why she hadn't changed them when she'd put on her sweatshirt.

Watching the moon's shadow as it disappeared behind the gathering clouds, Rusty silently cursed. Lifting his nose, he whimpered slightly at the change in the smell of the wind. The storm was not far off now.

This woman had better hurry, or she would be on the road when the bad weather hit. The wind smelled of cold air and bitter snow. This was not going to be a quick storm. He had a feeling it would hit hard when it came.

He watched the woman shiver. Maybe she felt the storm coming, too? She looked up, and a few seconds later, she began walking again, this time a little quicker.

Without realizing he was doing it, he quickened his steps to keep close to her and stepped on a branch. The crack of the broken twig reverberated through the woods like a gunshot, and the woman whirled around, the flashlight's beam brushing over the top of the bush under which he had taken shelter.

He narrowed his eyes until they were nearly closed to keep their gleam from lighting when the flashlight crossed over and around the bush. The woman did not move any closer, but he could tell she was nervous by the way she kept jabbing the beam of light here and there in a scattershot attempt to see if anything was there.

He crouched down, barely breathing, opening his eyes just a slit to see when she moved on. As she moved away, her scent grew fainter and he found himself increasing his movements to match hers.

After a few moments of pacing closer and then away from the forest's edge, the woman began walking toward town again, this time faster than before. He cursed himself for his carelessness. The last thing he wanted to do was alarm her.

He sped up to keep pace with her, bounding over fallen logs and landing soft-footed on the path. This went on for at least a mile before the woman slowed. Her exhaustion was showing. He wished he could change back, reassure her she was doing the right thing in heading into town, but if she was afraid of an invisible creature in the dark, he was certain his naked form would scare her even more, and he had no clothes hidden in this part of the woods to change into if he shifted back to his human shape.

No, he would have to continue to watch her, at least until he could change to more suitable attire than his birthday suit to greet her.

He observed her as she walked. She was cautious, glancing left and right as she kept up a pace that might have exhausted others, but seemed to keep her invigorated. He grinned in spite of himself. She was feisty, he would give her that.

It was obvious she was afraid, but she wasn't giving in to it. Other women in her situation might have cried or carried on, or made comments about their plight, but she never uttered a word. She kept moving at a pace that would require a predator to reveal themselves, in shoes that were most likely uncomfortable in the office, and on this surface, must be killing her.

He chuckled, which in his wolf form came out more as a thin growl, as she stopped to check her shoe. She jerked her head up when a long thin howl caused her to freeze.

Drat! Rusty thought, whipping his head around. *Who is out here in the woods playing games?* He didn't recognize the howl or the one that answered it. His first duty was to the forest, but he knew, looking over at the woman who was frozen in place, that he couldn't abandon her, either.

Had someone seen her? Was someone going to cause her harm? Not in his woods. But where had that sound come from? He raised his head above the underbrush, instinct to protect the forest overcoming his need for secrecy, and sniffed. He moved onto the road to get a clear view of the forest and down the road, forgetting momentarily that she was also in the road and now had a clear view of him.

Nothing. He couldn't smell a thing out of the ordinary. The rich loam of the forest filled his nostrils, mixed with vegetation, the faint odors of animals, and the girl's strong flowery scent.

The scream from behind shocked him.

He whirled around, his teeth bared, ready for battle to defend his property, when the beam of light struck him in the face. The girl screamed again and threw the flashlight in his direction, hitting him on the edge of his nose.

He howled in pain. The most sensitive part of his body was his nose after all, and her aim had been perfect. He howled again, and she screamed, then ran for the edge of the forest and disappeared into the thick brush.

He heard her screaming as she crashed through the vegetation at a speed not safe for the darkness of the night, and he cursed silently.

By the Moon! He howled. *Instead of running into the woods, why didn't she keep running down the road? And why did she throw her flashlight instead of keeping it? Foolish, foolish, foolish.*

Even as he thought it, he was giving chase. Just as he rounded a large boulder, he found her on the faint path made by deer crossing the valley. The trail was barely more than a thin ribbon of dirt bordering the side of a hill, but the human girl stood in it, pointing a large stick at him. On one side of her was a rise of land that came up to her shoulders; on the other was air as the land dropped off into a small tree- and rock-lined trench. In rainy weather, there was a stream that rushed through that trench, but right now there was nothing but debris in it. He'd crossed it earlier in his nightly rounds.

"Stay back, you beast," she threatened, stabbing at him with the stick for emphasis. "I might be little, but I know how to use this."

He chuckled again at the sight of the disheveled woman standing before him, holding the stick for all the world as if it would stop him.

She blanched at the sound of his chuckle, which to her ears must sound like a growl, and he saw the stick falter.

He wasn't sure what to do now. If he advanced toward her, he was pretty sure one of two things would happen. She would either stab him, or she would faint. Neither was an appealing prospect.

He decided the best course of action was to slowly back away, pretend his wolf pride hadn't been hurt by this little slip of a trembling woman with the big stick, and continue to follow her until she arrived safely in town. He could find out who the transgressing wolf was later on. His priority was her safety.

He realized suddenly that even if the first priority wasn't to ensure her safety, that was what he would do. The townhad wanted her here—he was certain of it. He didn't know why, but Havenwood Falls periodically drew people in for reasons of its own.

He started backing up, his soft brown eyes meeting her terrified blue ones, and for just an instant, he saw a reaction in them that wasn't fear, but rather something indefinable like recognition. He felt the same flash of familiarity as if he knew her. But how could he? Where would he have met her before?

His heart pounded being this close to her. He was overpowered by her scent masked by her fear. He felt he knew her on a level that went beyond mere sight. She was his. His paw stopped mid-step. That was it. She was his.

This was his mate?

This was the woman he'd been waiting for?

A human?

How was this possible? Yes, he'd asked the moon goddess for his mate, but . . . her?

Overhead, a crack of thunder sounded as if to agree with his realization. Then the rain came, cold, wet, and full of the promise of thicker moisture later. The girl, startled by the sudden onslaught, slipped.

With a delicate *Oh* of surprise, she disappeared over the side of the trail.

Rusty stared in shock for just a second, then bounded to the edge she'd fallen over.

She was nowhere to be seen.

The storm had swallowed her.

CHAPTER 5

*S*herry stared at the wolf, his teeth bared, the stick pointed at him. She knew it was a foolish gesture on her part. That weapon was hardly going to keep the large animal from charging at her, but she had to do something to protect herself. His brown eyes locked on hers, his teeth were huge and white in his snout, and she jabbed toward him with the stick in warning. She fully expected him to charge, but he didn't. To her great surprise, he backed up, as if considering what to do next. For just a second, Sherry felt like she had a chance to survive this encounter. What a great story that would be for the grandchildren.

Sherry wasn't sure what to do next, either. Trapped on that thin trail, she cursed herself for running into the woods, not sure what instinct had sent her into the underbrush instead of running down the road. Worse yet, without a flashlight since she'd foolishly thrown it at the animal.

Now what? Sherry felt the electricity in the air around her, surprised at the intensity of the tingling that set her nerve endings on fire. Glancing up, she saw the clouds scurrying across the sky, covering the moon and stars and obliterating almost all light. She narrowed her eyes, trying to see the wolf's shape in the total darkness. She still held the stick pointed in its direction, and she was certain it would leap at any second.

But nothing happened. Her breathing became rapid with fear, and her knees and arms trembled as she sought to remain calm in the face of this threat to her person.

Then, out of nowhere, the sky erupted into a thunderstorm of such intensity that, before she could react, Sherry felt the thin trail giving way. Reacting by instinct, she leapt to the side as the dirt under her feet began to crumble, but she was too late. She clawed nothing but air as her body fell into nothingness.

She crashed on rocks and trees and felt herself falling, end over end, down the side of the hill she'd been poised so precariously on. Her body crashed into another rock, head whipping back and cracking onto a thick tree. Still she continued to tumble down, rocks and dirt falling with her. Unable to grab onto anything to slow the fall, she cried out as she slammed into another rock hard enough that she blacked out.

So this is how it ends, she thought before darkness took her, *on the side of a hill in a place I never heard of before, with a wolf the only witness to my end.*

SHIT! Rusty shouted, his voice a howl of displeasure as he followed the woman over the edge of the trail and down the hill.

There was an eerie stillness as he followed her smell until he found her, bleeding from a deep head wound, at the bottom of the hill.

He whined and whimpered as he nuzzled her, trying to see if she still breathed. He was reassured she was still alive when she stirred slightly at the touch of his cold nose on her cheek.

Alive.

Breathing.

Now what? He couldn't run for help. Leaving her here would mean she would be without protection, and if the rain kept up with the intensity it was falling right now, she would drown. She'd slid under a pile of logs and old trees that had followed her down the side of the hill to land piled up at the bottom with her in the middle of the tangle of logs and dirt.

He tried to pull her from under the logs by grabbing the collar of her sweatshirt in his teeth and tugging her out, but all that did, now that the ground was so damp, was cause the logs to shift, burying her deeper underneath them. Already the water was beginning to fill the trench. He let her go, careful to ensure her head was protected from the rainwater that crept closer to her body.

He would have to transform into his human form, but he had no clothes nearby. If she woke . . . well, that might be hard to explain.

For a few precious seconds, he considered his options. One, stay and continue, in his wolf form, to try to free her, dragging her out of harm's way until he could get to a stash of his clothes and return to "find" her and bring her to safety. Or two, transform and then bring her to safety without a stitch of clothes on and hope she didn't wake.

Whimpering at the cold water that crept up his paws to his knees, he realized there was nothing else he could do.

His decision made, Rusty closed his eyes. Forcing the change too quickly was always more painful than letting it happen naturally. Praying to the moon goddess, he felt the familiar surge of pain and tingling take over his body. He groaned as his body lost its protective coating of fur and the cold air rushed over his skin, searing him with icy pellets of rain and sleet as the storm slammed into him.

He stood, stretched, and cried in his humanness at the loss of his furred body. Looking through the rivulets of rain that ran down his face and body, he stared at the woman at his feet. She was still unconscious, and the water now reached up to her waist. The rain pelted down as he worked to shift her from her prison, the water now climbing with icy fingers up her body to cover her up to her armpits.

He realized he had only minutes before the water would cover her completely, and he worked feverishly to free her, finally breathing a sigh of relief when, with a loud sucking noise, the trees released her form to his grip.

Groaning, he pulled her, his muscles aching and sore from his efforts to free her, stretched to their limits. He lifted her from the mud and pulled her to his chest where her head landed with a soft *thump*. He breathed in the scents of earth, dead leaves, jasmine, and the humanness of her.

That was what undid him. Her humanness overwhelmed him, and for an instant, he just wanted to hold her, his body protecting her from the worst of the rain as he pulled her away from the place that had almost become her tomb. As he crab-crawled with her up the hill, away from the encroaching water, he dug his heels in and held her to him tightly. Breathing heavily, he calmed his body, adrenaline from the near disaster and rescue making him weak at the knees. He needed to rest for a minute before continuing the climb to the top of the hill. Along the way, he found her purse, which he slipped around his neck to ensure it wouldn't be lost again. He imagined, like most women, she'd be devastated if it'd been lost.

He held her close, her form stretched down the length of his body. Holding her this way, he hoped to give her some of his body warmth and stop her from shaking. At least, that was the reason he used to convince himself that his contact with her held some necessity, and he wasn't just doing it because he liked the feel of her against his naked skin. Rusty concentrated to his slow his breathing and his racing heart that seemed to speed up with her proximity. Just when he thought he had his body under control, she did the worst possible thing she could do.

She opened her eyes.

She stared at him in confusion, her hand traveling up his

bare chest to rest near his pounding heart, and he felt an unfamiliar shiver of pleasure at her touch. For just a second, he wanted to lay her down and take her in the woods, just like this, in an animal way he'd never wanted a woman before. It took all his strength not to follow thought with deed.

Unfocused, pain evident in their depths, her eyes met his gaze, and she whispered a soft, "Are you an angel?" before closing them again. She moaned, whether in pain or not he wasn't sure, as he picked her up and carried her up the hill and back onto the trail.

An angel? Well, I suppose there are worse things she could have called me, Rusty thought as he quickly traveled toward his hidden clothes.

CHAPTER 6

*C*arrying her to where his clothes were hidden proved to not be as easy as he'd thought it would be. Whether because he was exhausted from his night prowls, or because he was battling the emotions that being near her roused in him, Rusty was trembling by the time he reached his destination.

He laid her down gently, checking once again to make sure her breathing was regular, and was relieved to find it was. He noticed the cut on her head still oozed blood, but not as badly as it had at the beginning. Overhead, the storm still raged, but here, the canopy of trees was thick enough that it protected them from the worst of the rain that was now turning to sleet and would soon become snow. He shivered in the chill damp air, wishing once again he were wearing his wolf pelt.

He quickly brushed away the layer of leaves and twigs that covered his waterproof backpack and unzipped it. He pulled out his clothes, dressing quickly with furtive glances at the woman, making sure she was still unconscious. He really didn't want to have to explain that she'd been carried through the woods by a naked man who had been the wolf who'd caused all the trouble in the first place. Oh, and then there was that bump on her head.

But now, he thought as he squatted down next to her, *what am I to do with her?*

His phone, retrieved from the bag, was not showing any reception, which was odd in itself, as he had often made calls from this part of the woods without difficulty. He had to believe that the storm probably interferedwith the reception out here, even though weather had never affected it before.

Instead of panicking, though, Rusty considered what he should do next. Obviously, he needed to get her some help. She might have a concussion, or at the very least, a really bad headache when she woke. He was closer to his cabin than to the town, but would she suffer too badly if he took her there first and gave her first aid there? He could take her to town in his truck once she regained consciousness or he finished his rudimentary first aid on her wound. His hesitation to turn her care over to the doctor in town played at the edge of his thoughts, but he put aside the deeper consideration of his reasons for wanting to keep her with him.

Then he had a startling thought. *If she were not who she was, would I still want to bring her to my cabin?* He decided that was a thought best left for later.

Before Rusty could ponder any longer, the air around him dropped another few degrees. Snow fell, slipping like icy fingers down the collar of his shirt in an ever thickening cloud of whiteness.

He reached down and gently picked her up. Taking her to his cabin it would be. At least there they would be out of the elements, and he could call for help from Havenwood Falls. Getting her warm was his first priority. The head wound looked to have finally stopped bleeding, but her unconscious state still had him worried about the possibility of a concussion.

Carrying her was somehow easier now. He curled her body into his for warmth, and within a half hour, they'd traversed the distance to his cabin. In that short span of time, the intermittent flakes that had first fallen had become a mini-blizzard that had him wiping snow from his eyes as he walked, not an easy proposition as he carried her. Snow had accumulated along the path, and he left footprints behind him as he walked.

Hard to believe it was spring, but that was Colorado for you. Wait a few hours and the weather would change, the locals said. Today was definitely proof of the vagaries of Mother Nature's mind.

When he reached the cabin, he sighed in relief. The wood was stacked to the left of the door, and he noticed the rack was half full. He made a mental note to cut more. His front porch, holding two rocking chairs and a few half-hearted attempts at greenery that were just twigs in dirt right now, was the most welcome sight he'd seen in a while.

As he passed, he noticed his truck—a beat-up Ford issued by the park for his use as a ranger, the job he occupied in his human form—listing to one side.

"What?" he asked no one, inspecting it as he walked. One of the tires was flat. "Oh, that's great. How did that happen?" This would put a monkey wrench in his plans to take the woman into town.

They might just have to stay here for a few days after all. At least until he could get Joshua out here with either a tow truck or a new tire.

Once they entered the cabin, Rusty walked to the far end where his bedroom was and set her on the bed. After wrapping two layers of quilts around her, he left the room to find his first aid kit.

When he returned a few minutes later, he found her snuggled into the covers, snoring lightly. She looked adorable, and he couldn't resist reaching out and smoothing her hair off her face. She moaned at his touch, and he drew his hand back, afraid he'd hurt her. She muttered something under her breath, and he thought he heard the words "my angel" before she fell back into a fitful sleep. Watching her for a few minutes more, he felt a strong desire to join her under the covers. The thought of her body against his bare skin roused him once again to desire.

He treated her head wound as best as he could and bandaged it. She never moved under his touch. He rubbed her cheek, the feel of her silky smooth skin overwhelming him, and he had to draw back several times to maintain control over his body. He could still feel the wolf inside him.

Once her wounds were treated, he stepped from the room and closed the door, leaving it slightly open so he could hear if she stirred.

He shrugged into his coat and went outside to retrieve some wood for the fireplace. The storm had picked up in intensity. There was no way anyone was getting to his cabin tonight in this weather. His arms full of wood, he leaned down to the fireplace and settled the fire into a rush of flames. He tried to stop thinking about what might have happened had the woman continued to walk toward town in this storm, dressed inappropriately for the weather as she had been.

He set about preparing some leftover stew for dinner, hoping she might wake soon and knowing she would be hungry when she did. While he waited for the stew to cook, he checked his phone and noticed there was still no service. Now what was he to do?

This woman appeared to be on the mend, so once she woke up, he could check her for a concussion, but until then, he had to pray she was okay.

His thoughts turned to whom she might be as he settled into a chair near the fireplace. He picked up a book and read three pages without remembering a word. Keeping his thoughts off the woman and his strange reaction to her presence was not going to happen if this book couldn't hold his attention.

He stared into the flames and pondered this development.

Who was this woman? Why was she occupying so much of his thoughts? What had his strange need for her meant? Was he losing himself to his wolf side? Was his need for companionship as a human translating itself into animal desire when he was a wolf?

What would have happened if he'd given into those desires on the hillside when he'd held her in his arms? He shivered at the thought of the consequences of his actions if he hadn't been able to control himself.

What if she was his perfect mate?

There were consequences to that, too. Consequences that could do her more harm than good. Being with someone like him wasn't as simple as going to a justice of the peace to get married.

His eyes traveled to the room where she slept and widened in surprise.

She stood in the doorway, holding one of his guns, and it was pointed at him.

"Who are you?" she said in a soft voice, her hand trembling. "And what have you done to me?"

CHAPTER 7

*R*usty's first reaction was to hold up his hands. His second was to determine how many seconds it would take him to close the distance between them and disarm her. His third thought, and the best one he could come up with under the circumstances, was to play dumb.

"Ma'am?" he asked, trying to reassure her with his confused expression and non-threatening manner that he had no idea what she was talking about.

He studied the gun she held and then smiled slightly, knowing it wasn't loaded. But she didn't know that, and he had a feeling if he told her, she would be less than believing. He decided to let her think she had the upper hand.

"What. Am. I. Doing. Here?" she asked.

Her hand trembled, and her voice, brave though it was, was weak, indicating she was not fully back to her strength yet. He could overpower her in an instant if he needed to. He chose not to.

"Here, why don't you sit? I'll get us some stew. I think it's ready now."

"Where am I?" she persisted. She raised the gun, using two hands to hold it steady.

He ignored the weapon, pointing again to the chair. Rising, he carefully went to the stove and put the stew into two bowls. He set one on the table next to the empty chair and one next to his seat. Returning to the kitchen island, he cut a couple slabs of bread and put butter onto two plates, which also held a few strawberries and grapes he'd pulled from the fridge.

Once he was seated, he began eating, blowing on the food and taking a bite to let her know it was safe to eat. She eyed the stew, then him, and then the stew again.

"It's okay," Rusty reassured her.

The woman finally sat, shifting the gun to her other hand while keeping it pointed at him, and picking up the spoon for a taste of the stew. The moan that erupted from her lips surprised them both. She giggled, embarrassment pinking her face.

Rusty reached over and took the gun from her hand, and she gave it up without resistance.

"It's not loaded," he told her quietly.

"Oh," she said, looking at him with wide eyes. Rusty noticed they were a light blue ringed by a dark velvety blue like the twilight sky before true night fell. He liked them. These were eyes a man could get lost in, and find himself again.

"I . . . what happened to me?" she asked, as she buttered her bread.

"You were injured in a fall in the woods. I'm a park ranger for this forest. I was out on foot patrol and came upon you under some logs. I managed to pull you free and get you back here to my cabin before the full force of the storm hit."

"There was a wolf . . ." she said, her brow furrowing at the memory. "I remember seeing a wolf." She touched her forehead, her spoon clattering into the empty stew bowl. "And I remember . . . you?" She said that last as if it was a question.

He didn't answer, pretending to have a mouth full of stew instead.

"Was it you?" She looked at him with an intensity that made him blush.

"I suppose it was . . ." he finally admitted. "I did rescue you, after all."

"Thank you . . ." She hesitated. "But my rescuer was . . . different."

"How do you mean 'different'?" Rusty asked, wondering how much she did remember.

"Why did you bring me here?" she asked, changing the subject. She blushed, and Rusty silently cursed. How much did she remember?

"The storm," he explained. "I was walking in the woods, you see." Taking her bowl, he went to the kitchen and refilled them. "When I found you, I had to carry you someplace to get your wound treated. I decided it was faster to bring you here than try to take you to town since my phone wasn't workingand calling for help wasn't possible. This was both a good thing and a not-so-good thing."

"Oh? Why's that?"

"Well, this storm for one thing. I had no clue it was going to hit with this kind of ferocity. It's already several inches thick in some spots and getting deeper, and my truck has a flat tire with no spare. Probably can't get anyone out here tonight just for a flat. We have plenty of food, so if your condition wasn't too bad, I thought we could just hunker down here and wait it out. I expect it will only last through tonight, maybe tomorrow. Then we can get you to town and have someone look at your wound. Although, I think it is okay."

"My phone isn't working either," she said. "My car died on the way to Havenwood Falls. I thought if I walked down the road a bit, I might find an area that was clear, and I could get reception and make a call. But it didn't...clear, that is."

Rusty grunted at her explanation.

～

SHERRY TOOK a moment to look around the cabin. The walls were uncovered, with not even a picture anywhere on the shelves. There was nothing personal at all in here that she could see. Its rustic walls were logs stacked on top of each other, reminding her of those Lincoln Log houses she'd built as a kid. She wondered if he'd built the cabin himself. It had the feel of the tender touch of someone's hands on it.

He did, however, have books scattered everywhere. Some were by popular authors she read herself, and others by people she remembered from her college days. There was a guitar in one corner, its surface oiled and gleaming. Obviously, he played it often. The bed she'd left had been covered by layers of quilts; obviously he spent a lot of time here in weather that was less than ideal.

Two kerosene lamps hung beside the door. There was also an axe, its blade down, resting against the wall.

The fire blazed and popped merrily in front of her, and Sherry felt herself relaxing as its warmth enveloped her. She had stopped shivering, the stew and inviting fire working wonders on her psyche. She blushed at the thought that she'd nearly shot him, thinking he had kidnapped her with evil intent, and then remembered the gun hadn't even been loaded. How foolish she'd been. If he'd wanted to harm her, he could have done so when she was unconscious, and who would've been the wiser? She had to stop comparing all men to her former fiancé. Not all men had secrets and ulterior motives.

"Who are you?" she asked, taking the second bowl of stew from him. She was so comfortable with him, now that she wasn't worried he was a murderer or worse, that she'd forgotten to ask for his name. How silly of her.

"Rusty...sorry, everyone calls me Rusty because of my red hair. My given name is Russell Higgins. Like I told you, I'm a park ranger, and this is my forest. And you?"

He looked at her out of the corner of his eye, as if her name didn't matter to him.

Sherry hesitated, dipping her bread into the stew before answering. How much should she tell him? Yes, he'd rescued her, but she only had his word that he was who he said he was. What if he really was a sick guy who lived in the woods kidnapping unsuspecting tourists? What if he'd brought her here for . . . for what, exactly? Even though she was oddly comfortable around him, what did she really know about him? Nothing. Not a darn thing.

She glanced around the cabin, once again reassured by the fact that there was nothing more dangerous here than an unloaded gun and an axe that was used to chop wood.

"Sherry Grimes. I'm a teacher—therapist really—in a school with children who have special needs. I work with children with disabilities. You know, like autism or Asperger's syndrome. I teach them how to cope with real-life situations before they are mainstreamed into a regular school."

"Around here?" Rusty asked.

"No," said Sherry. She took a long sip of water before continuing. "I work in a school out of state." She gave no further information.

"So, what brings you to our state? To Havenwood Falls?"

She laughed. "Chance?"

"Chance?" Rusty repeated.

"Yes, I was driving with no particular destination in mind. My school is on spring break right now, and I stopped at this information place, you know the kind where you pick up maps, go the bathroom, or get snacks?"

He nodded.

"Well, while I was there, this nice old man suggested I visit Havenwood Falls. He gave me a flyer, and it had a number to rent cabins."

"Old man? Who was he?" Rusty's tone was curious.

"I'm not sure. He looked like he worked at the rest area, but when I tried to thank him, the woman working there acted like I was crazy. She said she didn't know who I was talking about.

Now that I think about it, the whole thing was a little strange. But I did call the number on the flyer to rent a cabin. That much was normal."

"A cabin at the ski resort? Or at the vineyards?"

"No, it didn't sound like those. She said it was rustic, in the middle of the woods, up the mountain."

"Must be Melissa Richter's place, then. She owns a few cabins up the mountain. Was it her?"

"I guess so. She was very nice. I rented one for the next week. Well, I guess I need to cancel that, since I seem to be stuck here for a bit. Of course, I have no phone reception."

Sherry buried her head in her hands, releasing small sobs as her situation suddenly overwhelmed her. A few moments later, having cried herself out, he reached a hand toward her and said, "Whatever is bothering you, do you want to talk about it?"

Sherry shook her head. Getting up, she walked to the kitchen and rinsed out her dishes. Cleaning the counters took her mind off her thoughts. She wondered—and instantly hated herself for it—what Brad was doing right now. After scrubbing furiously at an invisible spot on the counter's surface, she finally threw the scouring sponge into the sink and stalked off toward the chair.

Rusty looked at her, but said nothing. For that she was grateful.

Unbidden, the image of the russet-skinned man entered her thoughts. She closed her eyes, willing the image of her angel from her mind. It was her imagination that a wolf changed into a man in front of her—a glorious man. *That is not possible.* The bump on her head had addled her brains, that was all it was. This was the real world, not a fantasy one.

How in the world could she possibly have been lifted up and carried in the arms of an angel back from death? Honestly, she needed therapy. Shaking her head, she stood and walked toward the bedroom.

Turning at the door, she asked, "Is there a bathroom in here, or do I need to go outside?"

He laughed. "Rustic as my cabin is, I, too, like some comforts. There's a small bathroom with a shower in the back of the bedroom."

He walked with her into the bedroom and pointed to the closed door at the far end of the room.

Eyeing the shower, Sherry sighed in pleasure. She felt horrible, covered in mud and debris from her time under the logs. It would be nice to be clean again.

"Can I . . .?" she pointed in the direction of the bathroom.

"Oh, of course." Rusty colored in embarrassment. "I'm sorry. I should have offered that to you as soon as you woke." Neither mentioned that she'd been pointing a gun at him at that time.

"I . . . have no clothes," Sherry said in sudden embarrassment. Which was true. All her spare clothing was in her abandoned car.

"No problem. I'll see what I have that you can wear," Rusty said. "I have a washer and dryer, so if you'll leave your clothes outside the door, I'll throw them in while you shower."

"My blouse is silk." Sherry sighed. "It's probably ruined. Just throw it away. Cannot be washed, but the rest of my clothes can be."

"Okay. Just leave them outside the door."

Sherry slipped her clothes off, setting them outside the door as requested. She stepped into the shower, grateful for the spray of hot water that greeted her. She found soap and a washcloth inside the tub, along with a generic brand of shampoo that smelled delightfully of herbs, not too manly, and that surprised her. He struck her as a Head and Shoulders kind of guy. Just goes to show you how wrong you can be.

Fifteen minutes later, she stepped out of the shower and grabbed a white towel that she wrapped around her body, and another, smaller one that she wrapped around her hair. Sighing in contentment, amazed at what a shower could do to revitalize a person, she stepped into the bedroom to find a pair of sweatpants, at least two sizes too big, fortunately with a drawstring, and an oversized T-shirt waiting for her. He'd also thoughtfully provided her with a thick sweater to wear over her shirt.

Sherry pulled them close to her, not surprised they smelled delightfully like him, woodsy and a bit musty, like a fur coat that had stayed in the closet too long. She decided she liked that smell. It smelled real. Not like Brad's cologne that smelled of stuffy boardrooms or what he liked to call "old money." Thinking of Brad made her mad again, and she stomped over to the far side of the bedroom to look out the window when she heard the sound of chopping.

She could see Rusty's trim figure in the squall that was still going full force outside. He was wearing a sweatshirt, and every time he raised his arms to bring the axe down, the fabric stretched across his back. She liked the view; Rusty's backside looked like it'd been molded into those jeans. His model-like good looks were obviously natural, not like Brad's, which were the product of expensive monthly trips to the spa that she paid for.

She chuckled as she wondered what Brad was going to do now that she was no longer footing the bill for his primping. He was a struggling actor—the struggling part coming from her juggling their bills to afford his wardrobe and mani-pedis, all of which had only garnered him a toothpaste commercial and walk-on part in a play—without a speaking role, mind you. It had been an off-off-Broadway play at best and had closed on the road after its stint in her town. Not that the play's closing could be attributed directly to Brad's part in the play, but still . . . she liked to think his bumbling entrance and exit as Bellboy #3 had had some small part in its disastrous run.

She calculated how much not having to pay those bills anymore would mean to her bank account and smiled as she realized she would finally be able to afford to travel at least once a year, something she'd been aching to do for ages. She'd put it off at Brad's insistence they stay close to home in case he got a call for an audition. Even though they didn't live in a place like Los Angeles, there was a thriving theater community in Albuquerque, and Brad's good looks were often needed for a role. Of course, now she wondered if his refusal to leave had to do with his bimbo. Not that it mattered anymore. She had never felt so free in her whole life.

Grinning widely, she waved at Rusty, who'd turned and waved to her.

She might be in the cabin of a stranger, but at least she was going to have some fun while she was here. When this weather cleared, she would go to Havenwood Falls and not regret one thing that might happen in between.

She almost skipped her way into the other room. She'd never felt this right about any decision in her life.

CHAPTER 8

When Rusty came back inside with an armful of wood, which he laid in the box next to the fireplace, Sherry was sitting in the living room again, freshly clean and a little distracting in his clothes. She'd somehow managed to find some popcorn he didn't remember having. She pointed to the television, but when they turned it on, hoping to watch a movie, only snow greeted them. He thought that was rather ironic—snow outside and snow inside. Not to be disappointed, Sherry suggested they play a game. He couldn't find anything that appealed to her.

Sighing, Sherry collapsed back into the chair, her disappointment and boredom evident in the droop of her shoulders.

Rusty couldn't stop staring at her. She was fascinating. From the way her hands moved, so delicate, like they were conducting the very air around her, to the way her eyes sparkled when she smiled. She wore her emotions on her sleeve, and he could smell them as if they were flowers. His house was full of so many interesting textures, butuntil she'd arrived, he'd never known he was missing out on any of it. No other woman had ever excited or awakened his senses like she did.

Her dark hair, a rich brown with golden highlights, drew his eyes to her every time she turned her head. The way her hair fanned out gently, like angel wings resting on her shoulders, made him want to reach out and touch the ends to feel how soft they were.

He wanted to explore every one of the hollows at the base of her neck. He wanted to bury his face in her skin, taste the magic that was her. He pulled his eyes away from her before he revealed his desire. He'd only just met her, and her first impression of him had been fear that he was going to harm her. He couldn't make that fear come true.

His eyes fell on his guitar, and he said, "How about some music?"

He wasn't' sure what drew him to do this, as he rarely played in front of friends, let alone a woman he was desperate to impress, but without her permission, he walked over, picked up his guitar, and brought it back to his seat.

"So, I'm not a professional," he said with a nervous chuckle, "but I will give it my best shot. Any requests?"

Sherry pulled her legs up under her and rested her elbows on her knees as she set her chin in her hands.

"Surprise me," was all she said.

He ran through his repertoire and tossed out a couple of the rowdier songs Joshua Breem, the local mechanic, and he liked to play together. Those were best left to days filled with beer and touch-football games. He tuned the guitar while he considered the options remaining to him.

Finally, he thought of the song he'd written a few years ago when, in a fit of loneliness, he'd first sent his wish up to the moon goddess. Strumming a few chords, he found the key and began.

"Here's one I wrote a little while ago," he said. "It's called, 'Before I Ever Met You.'"

Before I ever met you, the sky wasn't blue
The grass wasn't green, and my heart wasn't true
Before I ever met you, the oceans didn't come to shore
The waves crashed unheard, and the gulls cried no more
Before I ever met you, the night was dreary and dark
The day held no sun, my world was cold and stark
I was waiting for the possibility
Against all improbability
That you would find me
Your love would set me free
Before I ever met you, I cried myself to sleep
Prayers unanswered, dreams a wish my heart could keep
Before I ever met you, I was haunted by desires
Secrets unrealized, wishes tossed upon a funeral pyre
Before I ever met you, I waited for life to wake me
Then I met you and all doubts deserted me

As HE STRUMMED the last chord, Rusty looked over, curious to see what Sherry thought of it. He was surprised to see her wiping tears from her eyes on the sleeves of the sweater.

"Sorry," she said in a voice thick with emotion. "That was beautiful."

"Thanks," he said. He continued strumming the strings, grateful for the distraction from his own emotions. He realized, casting another sidelong glance in her direction, that he wanted her to like that song. He *needed* her to like that song.

"Whom did you write it for?" she asked. She leaned forward, and the sweater, two sizes too big, fell open slightly at the neck, revealing her collarbone and the top swell of her breasts. He wanted to reach out and touch the smoothness of her skin right where it throbbed at the base of her throat and let his hand travel further down.

It took all his willpower to look away from her. Getting up from his chair abruptly, he set the guitar back in its stand, giving himself time to think how to answer that simple question. Whom did he write it for? He wrote it for a love he had never known. He wrote it for a love he was waiting for. He wrote it for . . . her.

And he realized that was true. She was the answer to his entreaty to the moon. But how would she take it if he told her that their meeting had been arranged by the supernatural, and not by a fall down a hill?

How would she feel about being chosen as his mate? If she would even have him, that was.

There was always the fear that mingling human and supernatural blood might cause problems in the future. There were people on both sides who were strongly against such unions and would not allow it, or at the very least would make their marriage difficult, but the fact remained that he was given very little choice in the matter. His wolf blood had chosen her, and he was bound as securely as a golden ring to her.

Surely the moon goddess had sent her to him. Why else would he be there at the exact moment she needed him most? Why else would she be here now, in his cabin, in the middle of a snow squall no one had expected or predicted? Surely this was fate, the answer to his prayer? But how could he tell her this? She was a human after all, and not one who likely knew of the existence of supernatural beings. She wouldn't understand. She would hate him. She would be repulsed by what he was. He couldn't put her through that. He couldn't put himself through that. No, no secrets would be revealed tonight. If she was to know his secret, he would have to move cautiously, bring her around to their fate slowly and with finesse.

Whom did he write this song for, after all? He wrote it for the one who would complete his life. He wrote it for the one who was to share his world.

She was the desire of his heart. She was his mate.

So how did he answer her question?

She stared at him with the calmest of expressions, as if she was innocent in all of this. And she was. She was very innocent. And yet, she was totally captivating and alluring.

So he said the only thing he could think of to say.

"I wrote it for someone I haven't met yet."

The disappointment in her face almost made him change his mind.

Almost.

CHAPTER 9

Sherry knew he was lying. She couldn't have said why she knew it, but she was certain he had written that song for someone who mattered a great deal to him. She respected his right to privacy, but she felt oddly disappointed that he hadn't trusted her enough to tell her who it was.

And then she mentally kicked herself. Who was she, after all, to demand he bare his soul? They'd only just met. Of course, their meeting had been a bit unusual, and in a way, she felt strangely drawn to this taciturn man with so many layers. But in a few days, she would be on her way back to her old life far away, so why should she expect him to tell her anything that mattered as much as the woman he'd written such a beautiful song for?

The air in the room seemed charged with secrets, and it made her uncomfortable. Yawning, she decided it was time for her to go to bed.

"Um . . . where shall I sleep?" she asked, not sure he wanted her in his bed, but not seeing any other options in the small cabin. She supposed she could sleep in one of the chairs. They were big and comfortable, and she was fairly small. She hated the thought of Rusty, with his long legs and body, having to try to sleep in the chair, when it was her unexpected arrival that would put him out of his bed.

"Oh, you can have the bed," he assured her. "Let me just change the sheets. I'm afraid I wasn't comfortable changing you out of your clothes when you arrived, and there's some mud on the sheets."

Sherry blushed at the idea of this man removing her clothes and was relieved he had remained a gentleman. Then she remembered she'd accused him of intending her harm when she'd awoken and blushed even deeper.

Her eyes met his, and she saw a twinkle in their brown depths and a dimple in his cheek from a barely suppressed smile, letting her know he'd read her thoughts. Turning away, she said, "I can do that."

"It's no trouble, but we can get it done in no time if you help."

Nodding, Sherry followed him into the bedroom. He removed a set of sheets from the chest at the foot of the bed and set them aside as he began removing the quilts. Sherry took the top quilt from him and folded it, setting it on top of the chest. She did the same with the second quilt. Running her hand over them, she admired the tight stitching and beautiful patterns on each of them. She could tell they'd been hand-stitched by someone who took pride in their work, and she remarked on it in a voice full of admiration.

"These are beautiful. Who made them?"

Rusty hesitated, then finally said, "A friend from town. She was worried I might be cold out here all on my own."

"She did a wonderful job on these. I would love to get one. Does she sell them?"

Rusty paused again before answering. "She passed away."

"Oh, I'm sorry, I didn't mean . . ."

"It's okay. You couldn't have known. She was a dear friend. The wife of a dear friend. She had cancer."

"Oh, sorry." Sherry hated repeating herself, but she couldn't think of anything else to say. It was obvious this person had been someone dear to him, and she wanted to console Rusty.

Without realizing she was doing it, Sherry reached out and touched Rusty on the arm. His muscle tightened under her hand, sending tingles under her skin. What was it about him that excited her so? Sherry was confused, removing her hand almost immediately, and she stepped away. There was something deep in his eyes, something that drew her back to him.

Standing next to him, she looked up, reaching out to touch his arm again. Ignoring the tingling, she watched her hand slide up his arm as if her hand wasn't attached to her body. She felt him tense up. She looked at him as she moved closer until her body was almost pressed against his.

She saw a muscle twitch in his jaw, and her fingers touched the spot, warmth traveling up her body as his heat enveloped her. He smelled of musk and wood smoke, and she was suddenly aware of how little space separated them.

"I'm sorry . . ." She cursed herself again for saying that over and over. What did she have to be sorry about? She kept apologizing, not knowing why.

"Can you move slightly to the left so I can get the old sheets off?" His voice sounded so calm, but she had a feeling he was anything but. She smiled nervously and stepped away to give him more room, moving to the right instead of the left in her nervousness, bringing her up against his rock hard chest.

"Sorry . . ." she started to say again and then bit back the words.

He didn't move.

She didn't move.

They stared at each other, and she felt herself leaning into him even more, craving the warmth of his body. There was something primal in this need, something she didn't understand. Something she needed, wanted, and yet feared was about to happen. She knew she should step away, leave that room—that cabin—or she would never leave.

She couldn't move, though. Her feet felt rooted to the floor. She waited.

Finally, he groaned, and leaning down, he took her mouth with his, pushing into her with his tongue in a way she'd never been kissed before. She slipped her arms up around his neck, welcoming him into her embrace.

He ended the kiss after a blissful minute that she wanted to go on forever.

Looking at her, his eyes boring into hers, he said in a strangled voice filled with repressed emotion, "Are you sure this is what you want? You don't know what you are asking of me."

Sherry, eyes locked with his, nodded, not trusting herself to speak.

He lowered his head to hers, pushing her back onto the bed as he did so, his long form hot against her own.

Before she lost herself in his kisses, Sherry felt they had rather satisfactorily solved the dilemma of who would be sleeping in the bed.

CHAPTER 10

*L*ater, as the night lightened into day, Rusty woke to find his arm asleep under the still form of the woman he'd just marked as his own. He traced a finger along her jaw and down her throat, careful not to wake her. He wanted to remember her like this always. She was beautiful.

But her beauty was more than skin deep. Her dark hair was spread out on the pillow like a fan, framing her tiny face with its delicate cheekbones. He was amazed at how fragile she appeared, for her lovemaking had been fierce.

In spite of his wanting not to hurt her, she'd become ferocious in bed, begging him to love her with every fiber of his being. He tried to hold back, tried to keep from marking her as his own, but he couldn't. Her touch had set him afire, and her kisses had seared him to his soul.

While there was no outward change in either of them, he knew that she was marked now and would always be his, even if they never made love again. If he couldn't convince her to stay with him and accept his transformation into the wolf, he would never love another woman.

She was his.

More importantly, he was hers.

Forever.

There would never be another who could take him to the heights of love that the two of them had experienced last night. Their bodies, both naked and glowing from lovemaking, were cooling. He feared she might catch ill, so he started to move from the embrace of their bodies to get a blanket. That slight movement caused Sherry to rouse.

"Don't leave me," she murmured in a soft whisper, pulling his body back to hers with a possessiveness he found endearing.

She ran her fingers along his bare hip, her leg sliding between his, her body rising to meet his desire as she pulled him tighter to her.

He kissed her shoulder and whispered in her ear, "I need to get a quilt before we both freeze."

She laughed, her eyes still closed, her breath raising goose bumps on his skin that had nothing to do with the cold.

"Hurry, lover," she said as she caressed his chest with a finger. Her body promised more, and he quickly jerked a quilt over them, pulling her into its warmth as his mouth reached hers.

He sent a silent prayer of thanks to the moon goddess, because he had a feeling that all their tomorrows would bring nothing to match this night, and that all the nights that followed would pale in comparison.

Rusty woke later to the glare of sunlight through the window, an empty bed, and the smell of coffee. For just a minute, he was disoriented.

"Hello, sleepyhead," said a voice from the doorway.

Rusty turned over to see Sherry, wearing nothing but his overlarge sweater and carrying a tray on which she had placed two plates heaped high with eggs and toast, and two cups of steaming coffee.

He wasn't sure which he was happier to see.

He smiled seductively at her. "What's all this?"

"This," Sherry said, setting the tray down carefully on the

chest at the foot of the bed, "is a thank you breakfast for my rescuer."

"Oh?" Rusty took the coffee cup she offered him. The sweater lifted up slightly as she leaned over, revealing her very pert backside. He admired the view without apology. He remembered the feel of that flesh as he'd cupped it in his hand the night before, his lips curling in a satisfied smile.

"Do you often make thank you breakfasts?" he said to distract himself from wanting her again.

"Nope, this is the first one," Sherry admitted as she tapped her coffee cup against his in a silent toast. Taking a sip, they looked at each other with unabashed hunger.

"The storm has nearly stopped," Rusty said, looking out the window. He tried to keep his voice light. "I think there might be reception on our phones now. I can call for someone to come for you, if you would like me to."

"In that much of a hurry to have me leave, are you?" Sherry quipped. She turned her face away, so he had to pull her around by the chin to regain her attention.

"That's not it at all. I just thought you might like to continue with your vacation. This," he pointed around the room, "might be a part of your trip you might not want to remember in the light of day." He kept his tone light, even though his heart was breaking. He couldn't let her know. He'd decided that revealing his secret to her might not be the best idea right now.

SHERRY NODDED. Handing him the rest of the breakfast she had prepared, she considered his comments. She had come here to get away from romantic entanglements, and what had she done the very first chance she'd had? Jumped in bed with a very sexy park ranger. In what way had that solved anything?

She realized Rusty was just a rebound guy and that their encounter had no lasting consequences or expectations for either of them, but she felt oddly disappointed that he could dismiss her so easily. She touched her head. The wound was sore, but not too painful, and she'd had no headache to speak of, so thankfully she'd been spared a concussion, but Sherry found herself trying to think up excuses to stay here a little longer. She could pretend she was still too ill to travel, but her lovemaking last night made that lie a little thin. She blushed, remembering how enthusiastic she'd been in bed. She'd never been that free with Brad, and perhaps that was why he'd felt the need to seek comfort in the beds of other women. She immediately dismissed that self-deprecating thought. Brad's infidelities were not her fault, and she would stop blaming herself.

"I suppose I do need to call someone. At least to cancel the cabin up the mountain. I have a feeling the road will be impassable."

Rusty nodded, taking a sip of coffee. "With my truck out of commission, I have to call my friend Joshua, so I think he can give you a ride to town after picking up your car. He's the town mechanic as well as the tow truck driver. He can take you to the Whisper Falls Inn, which I think would be the best place for you to stay in town. The inn has fallen on hard times, but is still a beautiful Victorian manor with a lot of character, and its new owner, Michaela, is working hard to put it back to its original condition. You'll like it very much."

"Okay," Sherry said, hating how flat her voice sounded. She was disappointed he wasn't fighting to keep her here, but oddly understood. He was a man who liked living alone. She got that.

"I'll get my clothes if you'll call your friend?"

"Sure," Rusty agreed. He seemed to want to say something else, and Sherry held her breath, hoping he'd say what she wanted to hear, but he didn't. He offered her the shower first, slipping out of bed.

His nakedness in the light of day caused Sherry to gasp. He was magnificent, an Adonis of the forest, and she would forever be comparing future boyfriends to his lean, muscular form and finding them lacking.

If he felt her admiration, Rusty made no mention of it. He slipped on a pair of sweatpants and walked into the other room. She appreciated his kindness in giving her time to pull herself together. A minute later, he returned with her clothes, neatly folded, which he handed to her before taking the tray and cups to the other room.

As the door closed behind him, Sherry let the tears fall that had been prickling at the back of her eyes. She sobbed in the shower, letting the warm water run over her body, hoping it would wash away her desire as easily as it washed away his touch.

CHAPTER 11

*R*usty listened to the shower and tried to keep his emotions in check. All he could imagine was the feel of her body against his. He cursed the moon goddess for sending him the one woman he could never keep. Putting her in his bed had been the cruelest of jokes.

He found his cell phone. Relieved to see several bars lit up, he called Joshua and in a few words, explained to his friend what was needed. Joshua agreed to attempt the trip to his cabin to help with the tire.

"The roads are still a bit treacherous," Joshua said cautiously, "but I'll set out in about an hour."

Rusty hung up and was just finishing the call to Melissa Richter when Sherry came into the kitchen. Dressed, she looked less like the woman who'd warmed his bed and more like the stranger he'd met in the woods. He felt their separation keenly. But outwardly, Rusty gave no sign of his broken heart.

He supposed it was a good thing she'd changed back into her own clothes, because if he'd had to send her out in his sweater, he wasn't sure he could control his actions. He was already fighting to keep his desires in check.

"I'm ready. When will your friend arrive?" She played with the strap of her purse in her nervousness.

"Joshua said it would be about an hour. He'll come here first, and we'll fix the tire. After that, he'll drive to your car, and then take you to town. I was just getting ready to call over to the inn to reserve you a room."

He picked up his phone and pulled up the inn's number. In a few minutes, he'd secured Sherry a room. Nothing else needed to be said, and the silence between the two grew louder than a jet airplane. Sherry went to the living room and sat down while she waited.

When Joshua pulled up, his truck loud in the stillness of a snow-blanketed world, Sherry nearly jumped up. At the sound of his footsteps on the porch, she met Rusty's gaze and then lowered her eyes. She wasn't sure what to say, so said nothing.

Joshua knocked, entering when Rusty called out to come in. Stepping inside the room, the other man looked between the two, eyebrow raised, and stomped his boots to remove the snow.

"Well, I reckon we can get that tire taken care of first. I brought a replacement. You got the jack?" He glanced over at Rusty, who nodded.

"You must be Miss . . .?" Joshua said, extending a hand to Sherry.

"Sherry Grimes," she said, introducing herself to the mechanic.

Sherry found his handshake firm and brief. He looked like a man who liked to keep things simple, and the silent exchanges between the two men were a little disconcerting. It was as if they had a secret language, one she had no clue how to speak, let alone understand.

"Okay, well, let's get that tire fixed. Then I will take the little lady into town."

He was out the door as soon as the words were out of his mouth.

Sherry looked at Rusty, who was shrugging into his coat.

Pulling gloves from his pocket, he nodded toward the kitchen. "There's fresh coffee if you want a cup before you go. This shouldn't take long, and then you can be on the road."

Sherry raised her hand as if wanting to reach out to him, but nodded instead. Turning away, she walked toward the kitchen. Closing her eyes, she forced unshed tears back. Letting Rusty see her regret to be leaving would serve no good purpose.

A short while later, both men returned to the house. Sherry offered Joshua a cup of coffee, which he declined.

"Never touch the stuff," he said gruffly, "but I thank you kindly for the offer. You ready to go? The storm's coming back, I think. Best we get your car and get you to the inn."

Sherry nodded. Stepping past Rusty, she was careful not to touch him, but the urge to squeeze his arm was strong. A kiss in parting wouldn't have been out of order, but he didn't offer, and she wouldn't beg.

As she stepped up into the truck, she resisted the urge to look back.

Joshua backed out the truck, his gears grinding as he moved the large truck down the rutted drive. The air was growing cold again. Just before they rounded the corner to turn onto the main road, Sherry caught sight of Rusty out of the corner of her eye.

He stood on the porch, leaning against the post as he watched them disappear.

"He's a good . . . man, our Rusty," Joshua said, glancing over at her. "You can trust him. You can always trust him with . . . whatever needs trusting."

Sherry shot him a quick glance. Was her broken heart that obvious?

"My wife trusted him. She was dying of cancer when they met. They became instant friends. Best decision we ever made was to move to Havenwood Falls. Best decision I ever made was to marry my Evelyn in spite of...well, in spite of our differences, I guess you could say. I wouldn't trade a minute of the time we had together to be with anyone else."

Sherry nodded at him, confused about what he was really telling her. What did he mean by "differences?"

Before she could ask him for an explanation, they came to her car. It was covered in snow, but otherwise just as she'd left it. Could it only have been last night? So much had happened since that fateful decision to drive down a deserted road in a less-than-perfect car.

"You stay in here where it's warm, miss. I'll get the car in gear. May I have your keys?"

Sherry dug around in her purse, pulling out the keys and handing them to him. His gloved hand gripped hers for a second, forcing her to look at him.

"It'll all be okay, miss. If there's one thing my Evelyn was always right about, it was that the moon takes care of her own."

Sherry looked at him in confusion. What in the world was he talking about?

In a little over half an hour, they were back on the road and headed toward town. He'd first tried to start the car, but it was still not running, so he'd pulled her bag from the trunk before loading her car onto the truck's bed, and the bag now rested at her feet.

Joshua dropped Sherry off at the Whisper Falls Inn and told her he'd call her with the verdict on her car. "Don't you worry, miss," he said before closing the door, "we'll have you back on the road and out of Havenwood Falls in no time. That is, if that's what you truly want."

Nodding to her, he continued on down the road.

"What an odd thing to say," Sherry muttered as she watched him go, her car traveling away from her. She hoped the damage wouldn't be too much, and at the same time, she hoped the repairs would take a few more days.

"Hello, are you coming in?"

Sherry turned at the sound and smiled at the young woman who stood on the porch. Glancing around the town, Sherry was struck by how much she liked its quaint shops and houses. This was the kind of town she'd always wanted to live in. It felt like it could be home.

Pulling her suitcase behind her, she walked up the steps and into the inn.

The smell inside the building was warm. The yeasty scents of freshly baked breads mixed with the smells of fresh wood and paint from the remodeling work in the lobby, and she felt instantly comfortable here. She wasn't disappointed in the room, either. It was occupied by a bed, a dresser, a desk with a phone on it, and a comfortable chair with a lamp nearby. There was a large window at one end of the room that looked out over a small garden.

She set her bag on the floor at the end of the bed and sat on the bed. In seconds, she had laid her head on the pillow, pulled up another beautifully quilted blanket, and let loose the tears she had been holding back all day.

Wrapped in the warm quilt, she cried away all her hurts. Old wounds had a way of creeping up at the worst of times. This was one of them.

CHAPTER 12

*B*rad looked at the woman asleep in the bed next to him and sighed. It was time for her to go, but he wasn't sure exactly how to get the bitch out of his house. She'd practically moved in once Sherry had left in such a tizzy. He knew she assumed she would take Sherry's place, but he found that idea less appealing than he once might have.

He'd met her in a strip club after another failed audition. At a low point, he'd invited her back to his house after they'd spent the night doing it in the back of his car. He'd taken her to breakfast, and then, knowing Sherry would be at work, brought her back to their house.

Well, Sherry's place actually, since she paid the rent on the small apartment they'd been living in together for the last six months.

He assumed she'd drive around and come back like a dog with its tail between its legs. But she hadn't, and now he was beginning to worry. It didn't help that he was stuck with this chick—Stephanie? Doris? Amanda? He couldn't remember her name, didn't even try. These days he just called them all "baby," and so far none had complained.

He usually only dated women he knew wouldn't want more than his body, which he was happy to donate to the cause of making women happy, but this one seemed to want the whole package. Not likely.

He needed his space; he'd thought Sherry understood that. In his roles as a model and sometimes actor, he needed to be footloose and fancy free. He'd thought Sherry was just a fling, something to fill the time in between jobs. She was fun, and smart, and seemed to really care about him, but his need for a walk on the wild side had doomed them.

Now he regretted it. The idea that the grass wasn't always greener on the other side was true. He needed to get her back.

Looking at the woman in the bed next to him in the cold, harsh light of day, he realized her boob job was sagging, her legs had been subjected to lipo so many times the cellulite had pock marks, and her wrinkles were not as appealing as they were in the darkness.

He slapped her hip harder than he intended and shoved her to wake her up.

"What's wrong, baby?" she asked him with what she probably thought was an adorable sexy pout, but which disgusted him now.

"Nothing's wrong. You need to get up. Get out of here. I got stuff to do. Come on, move it."

She sat up, calling him every name in the book in words of four letters and more. He ignored her. He walked like a cat stalking its prey toward the living room where he kept a pack of cigarettes hidden in a vase. Finding them, he lit up, even though he knew Sherry hated the smell of cigarettes in the house.

He'd told her he quit, but it was a lie.

Like so many other lies he'd told her. They all blended together into a jumble in his mind.

"Bitch," he whispered in the empty room.

"Hey, baby, when can I see you again?" the bimbo stood in the bedroom door, her blond hair disheveled from sleep, her lips pouty and full. He thought about taking her there, on the floor, before she left, but quickly dismissed the idea.

No sense giving her the idea she had a chance of getting back with him.

Instead he pointed to the door and silently sent her on her way.

She turned angry eyes in his direction, giving him the finger before the door closed on her.

She was already a memory to him, though.

Watching through the window as she left, his thoughts turned to Sherry. Where was she? Why hadn't she come crawling back yet? How was he going to find her?

Then he had a flash of brilliance. At his last audition, he'd sat next to a private investigator, someone with the ability to trace vehicles. What if he reported Sherry's car as stolen and had him trace it? Now, where did he put that guy's card?

A short while later he'd found the card and was chortling with glee to think of the surprise on her face when he showed up to surprise her. He imagined the reunion, which would involve a lot of time under the sheets, because the insult he'd thrown at her about being a bad lay was a complete lie. She was definitely *not* a bad lay. She was probably the best lover he'd ever had, and it had taken her running away to prove that to him.

In twenty minutes, he was connected to the private investigator and detailed his problem.

"It'll take a little time," the PI told him. "I'll get back to you when I know something. That'll be $200 for a motor vehicle trace. Fifty up front, and the rest when the information is found. Agreed?"

Brad hesitated—he had exactly $350 in the bank—but he was certain Sherry would be happy to repay him once he'd won her back. He could tell her it was "research" for his next role.

"Yep, that would be great."

A little while later, dressed in a pair of running shorts and a shirt in his signature black, Brad stretched before heading out for a jog. Keeping his body in great shape was important, and no matter what else was going on, he was not going to miss out on his run.

As he was undressing for his shower, his phone rang.

"Hello?"

"Got that information for you," the voice on the other end of the line said. "Car is at a place called Havenwood Falls. It's in Colorado. There seems to be no address for the garage, just some vague directions to it. I think they have a bus that you pick up at a place nearby. Here's where you can pick up the shuttle."

Brad wrote down the address. "Got it, thanks."

Per the agreement, Brad paid the bill, wincing at the depletion of his bank account.

"Well, well," said Brad with a huge grin, "gotcha. See you soon, Sherry, my girl."

Time for a road trip.

CHAPTER 13

*R*usty felt the emptiness in the cabin as soon as the door closed behind Sherry. He stripped the bed, but as he stood in front of the washer, he couldn't bring himself to put the blankets into the machine.

Instead, he pulled them closer to his face and breathed in the deep rich smell of their lovemaking, reliving it all over again like a movie.

The feel of her skin, soft and fragrant with their friction, was almost more than he could bear to relive, but he needed to, wanted to. Wanting her was an ache in his soul so deep that it struck him in his bones. It was both pain and pleasure, joy and agony.

Knowing she was his mate, and knowing he could never force her to be with him, was driving him insane. He paced the cabin like one possessed, and when he had time to think about it rationally, he kicked himself for his hesitance in telling her the truth.

She was human, he rationalized. She wouldn't understand; she would have thought he was a freak. She wouldn't have wanted him, not the way he needed her to. He wouldn't take her pity. He wanted her wholly, body and soul.

Why had the town brought her here?

He wanted to talk to someone about it, and when Joshua had arrived, it had seemed the perfect chance to let down his guard. He'd known Joshua for a long time. Joshua had been married to Evelyn, a shifter like Rusty, even though Joshua was a human. Until the cancer had taken her, the two had been inseparable upon meeting. Joshua had been able to accept Evelyn's uniqueness without question, his love for her deep and forgiving.

The two had never kept secrets from each other, their love in the open for all to see. Their union had, while producing no children, been a very satisfying one, the kind of relationship Rusty hoped to have one day with his own mate.

But Sherry was special. She was a human who had no experience with supernatural or shifter beings. She was probably not even aware supernaturals existed, and had he revealed his true nature, it would have been a great shock. They'd only just met. He couldn't dump that on her.

Rusty knew this was true, but it still didn't take the pain away. He needed to shift, to run in the woods, to become the wolf. He could feel the need driving him mad with desire to race, to rend something apart. His emotions were so raw, so on edge, that he feared what might happen if he did change.

"Don't give in to it, Rusty," Joshua had cautioned him. "If you do, you'll regret it. You cannot let it control you. You must control it. You are too dangerous right now. Raw emotion leads to poor decisions."

Rusty had nodded, realizing his friend was trying to help him, but still hating the need for caution when his heart and body wanted him to do the most irrational thing he could think of, convince Sherry to stay with him…forever. But was love ever rational? Add to that the urgency of a mating denied, and you have the recipe for a disaster.

"I want to tell her how I feel," Rusty confessed. "But I sense she is raw from something emotional in her own life, and I'm afraid it will destroy her if I tell her what I am."

Joshua paused before speaking again. "When Evelyn and I talked about her change, the way she had to separate her two lives to be with me, the one thing we agreed on was that we would always be truthful. Secrets cause pain. Truth, while it may cause pain, too, is much kinder in the end."

"But my truth is the kind that people—those who are not supernaturals—don't understand. Their view of us is warped by television, movies, and books that depict us as killers with no control over our emotions and needs."

"That's true," Joshua had agreed. "In the end, I guess it all comes down to trust. Do you trust her to keep your secret? To understand *who* you are? Not *what* you are?"

"How did you and Evelyn reconcile this?"

Joshua smiled crookedly, the pain of Evelyn's death still written in his friend's face, and Rusty regretted mentioning her name.

"I loved her. That's all I needed to know. The rest was just window dressing. I wanted to be with her, and who she was inside mattered more to me than anything else. Give Sherry that chance, that choice, to make the decision. You won't regret it."

Rusty was still thinking about that as night fell and he prepared to go out on his nightly prowl.

Going to the end of the drive, he set off into the woods with thoughts of Sherry on his mind. The moon was high and bright tonight. Reflecting off the snow, the moonlight lit his way on his rounds.

He found himself on the edge of town, not a normal part of his route, and he knew why. Unable to stop himself, he crept along until he was at the back of the Whisper Falls Inn. Standing in the shadows, he looked up at the large, Victorian manor, wondering which window was the one to Sherry's room.

He saw one room at the far end overlooking the garden with

its light on. Was that where she was? Was she unable to sleep, too? Was she thinking of him? He sent a silent message to her, hoping she was comfortable and would soon be asleep. And then, as if thinking about her had conjured her up, she was standing at the window.

He stared, willing her to see him, and fearing that if she did see him, she would guess his secret. He stepped from the shadows for just a brief second and then slipped back into darkness, heading toward the woods.

The night was uneventful, for which he was grateful. After the recent library fire, which was suspected to be arson, and the body he'ddiscovered in the woods near Wylie's Gulch a few weeks ago, he was glad to have found nothing out of the ordinary tonight. He turned back toward home, feeling better just being out in his beloved woods. As he loped along the side of the road, he heard the sound of a motor. Leaping quickly from the road, he crouched down as the shuttle passed and behind it, a car.

He saw a man, hunched over the wheel, his blond hair spiked in a style that was fashionable in movie stars and other celebrities. He was driving slowly, weaving slightly as if tired, and Rusty paused, something about the guy setting off warning bells in his mind.

Following him a short distance to make sure he didn't have trouble on the road, Rusty watched as the man rounded another corner and disappeared into the lights at the edge of town.

What was this fellow doing in Havenwood Falls?

CHAPTER 14

Sherry tossed and turned in bed, unable to get comfortable. Nothing she did made her sleepy. She tried reading one of the books Michaela had loaned her, but she couldn't concentrate. She tried a warm shower, but that just made her think of Rusty and his cabin.

She tried warm milk and a chocolate chip cookie, which Michaela had brought to her room, but that just made her less tired, not more.

Finally she stood up, her restlessness a surprise to her. She was exhausted. She should have been asleep hours ago, but here she was, pacing her room. She finally felt herself drawn to the window.

Looking down, she saw the garden, still and silent in the night. Her eyes were caught by movement at the edge of her vision. A large dog, or possibly a wolf, sat on its haunches watching the inn. She felt a shiver, but not of fear. Rather, she felt a familiarity with the wolf.

Raising a hand to her forehead, she touched the small bandage she'd replaced earlier that night and then watched as the animal slipped back into the shadows and she lost sight of it.

Was it a dog? Or was it something else?

She continued to stare out the window for several minutes, but the creature never returned.

Finally, exhausted, she fell into bed and slept the night through, her dreams populated by a wolf that became at various times and an angel and a man.

CHAPTER 15

*D*riving into town so late, Brad's options for lodging were limited. The lights of the Whisper Falls Inn were dark, indicating they were not welcoming guests at this hour, so Brad drove to the nearest motel where he got a room for the night.

The clerk grumbled and made pointed remarks to the time, but Brad ignored him. Paying with a credit card, he had to think if he still had any room left on it. Sighing in relief when the card went through, he took the key and went to his room.

Throwing his bag on the bed, he lay down, careful to stay on top of the covers. He didn't need to catch anything while here, and who knew who had been in this room—and doing what—before he'd arrived. He hoped Sherry would appreciate the effort he made to get them back together.

Falling asleep, he dreamed of the reunion the two would share when they met again. He was sure she was staying someplace better than the rathole his limited funds provided him.

CHAPTER 16

*T*he next morning, Sherry woke up and headed downstairs. The first thing she needed to do was buy some new clothes. She couldn't wear half of what she'd grabbed when she had run from her fiancé's indiscretion. She definitely needed some new shoes.

She liked Michaela, the young woman who managed the inn. If she were to stay around, Sherry had a feeling the two women would become great friends. Michaela was always busy running the inn, and with all its remodeling needs, it made her time to visit pretty limited. Sherry felt guilty keeping Michaela from what she needed to do, so she curtailed her interruptions as best she could.

Pointed in the right direction by Michaela, she found herself at Backwoods Sport & Ski, the local outdoor shop where she picked up some jeans, sweaters, and a new sweatshirt with "Havenwood Falls" emblazoned across the front and a ski jump and ski slope in the background. Complete with thick socks and hiking boots, she felt like a new woman in her new clothes. She had also picked up some mittens, a hat, and a scarf in her favorite shade of blue. She almost felt like dancing down the street.

She made her way past the shops that wrapped around three sides of the town square's park. The area appeared to be vibrant and thriving. Everything smelled fresh and clean, the storm having added an edge of pine-scented air to the normal smells of coffee and fresh baked goods that captured her attention. She turned toward the smell of coffee, intending to purchase a cup, but stopped to admire the view of the street first.

Nodding to a few early morning risers like herself, she was surprised when they smiled and waved back before moving on to their activities. It made her feel welcome. A woman, jogging by in a bright purple track suit, waved and smiled like the others, as if greeting an old friend. Sherry waved back, a smile turning up the corners of her mouth.

As she wandered the streets, she marveled at how the brightly painted shops blanketed with freshly fallen snow from last night's storm added to the Currier & Ives appeal of the town. After a short time, she found herself in front of the Havenwood Falls Garage and decided to check on the progress of repairs to her car.

"Hey, Joshua," she greeted the mechanic. "Any word on my baby?"

Joshua turned, caught sight of her, and waved before walking toward her. He wiped his hands on a rag. Shaking her hand, he gestured for her to join him in his office.

"I was just starting on your car, so no definite word yet, but I think part of the problem is some loose wiring. For sure you have a busted hose, which I have replaced. I'll know more later today."

"Great," Sherry said with a smile. She sent up a silent prayer to whatever gods looked out for cars that the damage to her bank account wouldn't be too serious.

"Sherry," Joshua said, stopping her from leaving the shop, "I wonder if I might have a word with you?"

"Sure," said Sherry. "Is it about the car?"

"No, it's about our conversation last night."

"Oh." Sherry wanted to say that she would not discuss Rusty, but she had a feeling Joshua needed to say something important to her, and her therapy training kicked in.

Sitting back down in the bright red plastic chair, she faced him. This time it was Joshua who looked uncomfortable. She kept silent, waiting for him to open the conversation.

"I may have overstepped my boundaries, and for that I apologize. Sometimes I cannot help but interfere. It's my curse, Evelyn used to say."

Sherry smiled, waving a hand as if to say it was okay, but Joshua continued.

"This town has its secrets, and it's not my place to tell them, but I think you need to talk with Rusty. I think you need to know . . ."

"Know what?" asked Sherry, her tone sharper than she'd intended. She'd managed not to think of the sexy park ranger for the last hour, and here Joshua was, dragging her back down that road again.

"Just . . . talk to him."

And that was all the mechanic would say. He promised to call her as soon as he knew what was wrong with her car, and then he walked her to the door.

As the door closed behind her, she shook her head. Joshua was an odd one. She had no intention of following his advice. Rusty had had his chance to explain himself before she left, and he'd chosen not to. She had nothing more to say to him.

Walking back to the inn, distracted by her thoughts and not paying attention to where she was going, Sherry bumped into someone. Raising her eyes, an apology on her lips, she stared in shock.

"Well, hello, stranger," Brad said. He held her by the arms and gazed intently into her eyes, gauging her reaction.

"Brad?" she said, recovering her voice.

A truck passing by stopped quickly, before pulling up next to her. She heard the door open and close, but didn't take her eyes off Brad to see who it was.

"Sherry, is this man bothering you?" Rusty's voice penetrated her shocked mind.

"Mind your own business, stranger. This is my fiancée." Brad gripped her arms tighter.

"Sherry, is this true?" The hurt in Rusty's voice cut into her like a knife.

Glancing over at him, she hesitated then nodded. "Yes . . . I mean, no . . ."

Brad glared triumphantly at Rusty and then stared at her in consternation.

Rusty stared pointedly at Brad with his arms crossed and stepped closer to the pair.

Both men stood there, glowering at each other. Sherry felt like the pickle in the game of pickle in the middle.

"Is he or isn't he your fiancé?" Rusty pressed her, not taking his eyes from Brad.

"He was, but now he's not," Sherry said, ignoring Brad's strangled cry of anger.

"Yes, I am. I've come to ask you for your forgiveness," Brad insisted. He hadn't released her arms yet.

"Let her go," Rusty said softly, the threat of bodily harm implied in his tone of voice.

Brad released her.

Sherry stepped around both men, unable to stand the proprietary, testosterone-fueledglares that passed between them. She wasn't sure which one was more dangerous, and she didn't intend to find out.

Brad, seeing her leave, made as if to follow, but she heard Rusty warning him to stay away.

"Not sure who you are, cowboy," Brad said through clenched teeth, "but you'd better back off. That's *my* woman there. And I intend to take her home with me."

Before Sherry could protest his unjustifiable, territorial alpha attitude, Rusty moved toward Brad with clenched fists. His expression dark, Rusty said, "Don't you think you should ask her what *she* wants?"

Sherry reached out, her hand on Rusty's arm, stilling his anger for the moment. He shot her a quick glance, then returned his expression to Brad. Sherry pulled her arm away, but not before Brad noticed it.

Brad, awareness dawning in his eyes, darted a quick look between Sherry and Rusty and smirked. "I see. Sherry, is there something you need to tell me, sweetheart?"

Sherry threw up her hands in annoyance. "Stop it, Brad. Stop it, Rusty. Both of you, just stop being children. I belong to no one, Brad."

Rusty moved toward Brad, every muscle tight with the effort of holding back from physical violence. Sherry reached out. Touching Rusty on the arm once more, she felt his muscles relax, and she pulled her hand away again. Rusty's glare remained focused on Brad.

With a disgusted sound, Sherry walked away from the two men. They paid her no attention, neither man reacting to her leaving.

When she reached the gate to the inn, she turned and saw Brad and Rusty arguing. Rusty, facing her, locked eyes with her, and she was surprised to see longing and regret in them.

She quickly turned away and walked up the stairs to the inn, closing the door firmly behind her.

Two hours later, Brad showed up at the inn to take her out to dinner. Sherry wanted to decline, but she was starving and dinner at the inn wouldn't be served for at least another hour. She knew Brad would just follow her anywhere she went, so against her better judgment, Sherry left with him. Throughout dinner, he kept trying to convince her he'd changed, that he wouldn't cheat on her anymore, that he loved her.

"Come on, baby," he'd said, taking her hand and raising it to his lips. "You know I mean it. I love you. I truly do."

Sherry was disgusted by his attempts to woo her. He was clumsy, and all she kept thinking about was how Rusty had never lied to her, that his emotions were always out in the open. She knew he could be trusted.

"Brad, it isn't just the blonde, or even the cheating, that has me thinking it is time to end our engagement. You barely pay anything toward our bills, and I pay all your bills, too. I cannot keep doing this. We are too different. You lie, and think everything is okay if you say you're sorry, but it's not okay."

"All right, I get it, you're hurt. But honey, what other choice do you have? I'm here, I'm what you need. You know this."

"No, Brad, it won't work. I want you out of the house when I get back. I won't do it anymore."

He stared at her with narrowed eyes. "It's that ranger, isn't it?"

Sherry looked away, her blush revealing everything.

"You slept with him, didn't you? And you talk about me being easy," he said bitterly.

Sherry stared at him with cold eyes. "It's over, Brad. I won't discuss it with you any further. I'll be home in three days. I want everything you own out of the house when I get back. And if you dare take anything of mine, I'll have you in court so fast, your head will spin."

"He'll never love you like I love you," Brad spat out as he stood up.

"I hope not," Sherry muttered under her breath. She wasn't even embarrassed by the temper tantrum Brad was causing as he stomped from the restaurant, promising revenge.

"You okay, miss?" the waiter asked when he brought her the check.

Sherry appreciated the waiter's concern, but wanted to leave as quickly as possible. Stepping outside, she remembered too late that Brad had driven them to the restaurant, since her car was in the shop one more day.

"Damn," she said, fumbling in her purse for her phone. She wondered if they had Uber in this neck of the woods, but doubted it.

"Need a ride?"

Sherry's head jerked up at the sound of Rusty's voice.

Was he following her? How had he known she was stranded?

"I was passing by on my way home," Rusty explained as he settled her in the truck, "and I saw you standing there, looking a little lost."

"Yes, well, Brad isn't too happy right now. Stranding me is the least of what he would like to do to me."

Rusty chuckled, and suddenly Brad's childish temper tantrum struck her as funny, too.

The two of them were laughing loudly when they arrived back at the inn. Sherry, uncomfortable now that Rusty had turned off the engine, glanced toward the inn with some trepidation. What was the protocol here? Should she kiss him good night as a thank you for being her knight in shining armor, or should she shake his hand, or just get out of the truck with a thank you and not touch him at all?

She wanted to touch him, though. That was the problem. She knew, instinctively, that if she offered to spend the night with him again, he wouldn't say no, but she also knew that would be the worst thing she could do right now.

She was too fragile emotionally, and another night with this man who haunted her dreams would drive her over the brink. So, without another thought, she opened the door and hopped down.

"Thank you for rescuing me again," she said before she closed the door and ran up the steps to go inside.

Rusty, watching her go, muttered, "By the moon." He put the truck in gear and headed home.

Sherry, leaning against the door, listened to the fading sounds of his truck and sobbed.

CHAPTER 17

*A*fter leaving Sherry in the restaurant, Brad drove around until he found a bar. Its rustic interior wasn't his usual type of place, but he needed something to slake his thirst, and this would fit the bill.

The place was occupied by a handful of tables scattered about the dirty floor, at which were seated some couples and groups of drinkers. Three rough-looking characters in plaid shirts were bellied up to the bar, and several couples and a few rowdy men in matching bowling shirts were drinking and talking.

The dark interior of the bar smelled of stale beer and sweat, staple odors for a place like this. Wrinkling his nose, Brad made his way toward the bartender. As he sat down, he gestured for the man's attention, ignoring the slurred comments from three men who sat nearby. Ordering his drink, he stared at the large moose head that occupied the place of honor on the back wall. Several other heads were mounted in various positions around the room.

"Where you from, mister?" asked a voice at his elbow.

Brad thanked the bartender who'd brought his drink and

tried to ignore the men who were now sitting on either side of him and the one standing behind him, pressing close enough he could smell the man's cigarettes in their package.

Smelling them made him hunger for one, but he took another sip of his drink instead.

"What brings you here, mister?" asked one of the other men.

"You too good to talk to us?" asked the third. There was a threat in his voice. Brad looked down the bar, but the bartender ignored his plight.

"I'm just visiting your fine state," he said as he took another sip. He figured about ten more sips, and he could slip on out of here.

"Yeah, where you staying?"

"A place nearby."

"You one of them?" asked the first one who'd spoken.

"Them?" Brad asked, confused. He took another sip. Nine to go.

"The strange ones," said the second man. His breath was stale, and Brad tried hard not to gag. Another sip. Eight more to go.

"Strange ones?" he asked, then cursed himself. He hated that he was encouraging them, but they seemed to want to talk, and talking was better than robbing him. He didn't trust any of them as far as he could throw them. Another sip. Seven more to go.

"Yeah, some of the folk around here ain't quite right. You need to watch out. There are rumors."

Brad took another sip, then a second one. Five more to go.

The men warmed up to their tale and told Brad stories, but not the normal small-town kind of gossip he expected. More like the kind you told children when you wanted them to behave, about wolves and other animals that were not just animals.

"You should probably stay out of the woods," the third one repeated for the fifth time, his voice slurring more now that his glass was empty.

Brad gulped down the rest of the drink and thanked the men for their stories. He hurried from the bar.

On the way back to his motel, Brad considered what those men had said. What if they weren't just rumors? What if there really was something weird going on in that town? What if that ranger was part of it? Wolves, huh?

CHAPTER 18

*R*usty, preparing for his nightly prowl, felt a need for speed tonight. He decided to do another perimeter run around the town at the end of the night, his fears for Sherry overcoming his common sense. He could call Sheriff Kasun and let him know he suspected something might happen with her ex-fiancé, but he selfishly wanted to be the one to watch out for her. And really, he had nothing concrete he could point to for the sheriff to get involved at this point.

Roaming the mountainsides and trails around the town, he found nothing out of the ordinary. Nearing the back of the inn, he once again stayed in the shadows. His wolf form sensing no unusual scents or sounds, he finally turned away.

As he roamed about on his patrol, Rusty caught a whiff of Brad's odor. He stopped, and lifting his nose to the air, he turned, trying to discern where it came from and how long ago, but the smell was too faint, disappearing on the wind. While it unsettled him, he couldn't go after the man simply for smelling bad, so he dismissed it.

A little while later, Rusty reached his stash of clothes and transformed back into his natural shape. His nakedness highlighted silver by the moon, he dressed quickly and returned to his home where he went to bed, falling into a deep, exhausted sleep.

◠

SHERRY ROSE the next morning with a new attitude. She ate in the small dining room of the inn and walked outside. Just as she reached the gate, Brad met her. He wore a huge grin on his face, and groaning, she began to turn back around, but he grabbed her arm.

"How are you this morning, darling? Going anywhere special?"

"No," Sherry said, trying to shake off his grip. He didn't remove his hand, but instead increased the pressure of his hold. "Brad, stop it. You're hurting me."

As if on cue, Rusty drove up in his truck. Pulling over, he stepped in front of the two and motioned for Brad to let her go.

Brad laughed. Pulling out his phone, he turned and confronted Rusty.

"You might want to back off, ranger," he said, waving his phone like some kind of flag, "or I just might have to reveal your little secret."

Rusty looked at him with a wary expression while Sherry jumped to his defense.

"What are you talking about? You're the one with secrets!"

"Am I? Why don't you ask your lover here what he does at night?" Brad turned to Rusty with a smug look.

"What do you mean?" Sherry exploded. Grabbing Brad's arm, she spun him around to face her. "What are you up to? I told you already. It's over. We're over!"

Brad leaned closer to her. His voice lowered, and his eyes stared deeply into hers. "Baby, I love you, can't you see that?"

"You love me, and every other woman you can get your . . . hands on." Sherry glared back at him.

"I know. I'm not perfect." Brad looked humbled, ashamed even, as he begged her to reconsider her decision. "But I love you. I really do."

"Sometimes love is not enough, Brad." Sherry said.

"But it used to be all we needed." He reached out and touched the side of her face. Encouraged when Sherry didn't flinch or slap his hand away, he continued, "We are perfect for each other. We have plans," he whispered.

For just a moment, Sherry's heart wavered at the mention of their plans and the thought of the life full of love she'd always wanted. She could see in his eyes that he thought his ploy was working, but she knew it was just that—a ploy. He could never give her that love, that life.

"No," said Sherry, her tone cold. "There isn't room for me *and* all your secrets in our relationship."

"So it's secrets you don't like, is it?" Brad said, his voice hardening.

"Yes," Sherry agreed. She stepped away from him, closer to Rusty.

"At least I'm not a freak," Brad snarled.

"Don't be a jerk, Brad!" Sherry grew angrier by the minute.

"What if I told you your lover wasn't natural? What if I told you he was a werewolf? Would you still prefer him over me?" Brad clicked on his phone, and the video played.

Sherry watched, fascinated, as a beautiful russet-colored wolf changed into a man, naked and unmistakably sexy in the moonlight.

Unmistakably Rusty.

Sherry's eyes widened as her gaze went from the video to Rusty.

"What? What is that?" Sherry said, her expression confused, and then, "It was you. You're the wolf, and the angel, and the man all wrapped up in one package, aren't you?" Her voice came out in a strangled whisper, as if the truth was suddenly clear.

Rusty didn't deny it, but the look he tossed at Brad was murderous.

"This isn't how I wanted you to find out…" he started to say. His eyes begged her to let him explain, but she backed away.

Brad, triumphant, restarted the video and said, "Yep, I'd say that wolf thing is a secret. Kind of a big secret, right, Sherry?"

"This changes nothing between us, Brad. I still want you to leave me alone. I want nothing more to do with you. Especially not now. I'm not sure what I ever saw in you, but I see you clearly now."

Rusty reached out for her, but she deftly avoided his hands, waving him away, too.

And with that, she turned to run down the sidewalk toward the garage.

"But Sherry, baby, you can't be serious. I'm not a freak at least!" Brad shouted to her receding back, but she ignored him, focused on the garage and the hope that her car was ready so she could get out of this place.

RUSTY, watching her go, wasn't sure whether he wanted to follow her or throttle her former boyfriend. He wasn't worried about Brad spreading rumors about him. Once he left town, the video would disappear and the memory of this place would be wiped from Brad's memory by the town's magical wards, but the damage to his relationship with Sherry was irreparable, and for that, he wanted to kill Brad.

Rusty, fists clenched at his sides and his face darkening with the promise of bodily harm, faced Brad, who had turned a lovely shade of white as if afraid and backed up a few steps.

Holding his hands up, Brad said, "Okay, man, don't rip my throat out. I don't want to be a werewolf."

Rusty, through gritted teeth, said, "I'm not a werewolf, you idiot. But I could rip your throat out and wouldn't regret it for an instant. If you don't leave town right now, I might just forget my oath to not harm humans."

Brad, realizing he'd finally crossed the line, quickly turned and ran to his car. He peeled out, and Rusty watched him speed down Main Street, barely stopping for lights as he headed out of town.

Rusty slowly walked toward Joshua's. He had to explain. But he wasn't exactly sure how to do it. How did you tell the woman you had just met—and rescued from a situation that *you* caused —that she was meant to be with you? Oh, and by the way, you were a man who could shift into a wolf?

He frowned when he found Sherry in Joshua's office, sobbing in his friend's arms. The quiet man looked up when Rusty entered with eyes that begged for help. Strong emotions were hard for the man. He'd usually left that up to Evelyn, who'd been a strong empath as well as being a shifter.

"Sherry," Rusty said quietly.

She looked at him and then quickly buried her face in Joshua's chest.

"Sherry," Rusty said again.

Finally, with a great sob that wracked her body into shivers, Sherry turned and faced him. Her eyes blazing, she spat out, "You lied to me."

"No," he said with calm certainty, "I didn't lie to you. I just didn't tell you the whole truth."

"You were the wolf that caused me to nearly die," she said.

"It was the storm that caused you to fall," he defended himself. Rusty took another step closer to her. "But, yes, I was the wolf you saw in the woods."

"You were the naked angel who saved me," she whispered.

"Sort of. I was naked, but I'm no angel."

Her gaze traveled up and down his body. "You were the man I made love to, or was that a lie, too?"

"No, that was not a lie." He stood as she watched him

through tear-filled eyes, like she was trying to gauge the sincerity of his words.

"*Why* did you make love to me?" she asked, her tone beseeching him to explain.

"Because . . . because you are the one. You are my mate. You are my world." He paused, but pressed on. "That song . . . it was written for you."

"You wrote that song ages ago. How could it be about me?" Sherry's tears stopped flowing. She watched him with hungry eyes, and he knew he had to couch his words carefully or he would lose her forever.

"My kind love only once and forever. We wait lifetimes for a mate who will be our equal. And sometimes, sometimes the mate is not our kind. But that does not make the bond any less strong. You were sent to me by the moon goddess. I am yours, and you are mine. You were mine before I knew you." He spoke simply, sensing that her tumultuous emotions would not be able to accept the harsh truth of what loving someone like him would bring to her. Both the highs and the lows.

If she could accept him, accept *them*, he would gladly deal with any backlash when the time came.

Sherry looked at Joshua and said in a near whisper, "This is what it was like for you and Evelyn, wasn't it? This feeling of not being good enough, or of just not being *enough*, isn't it?"

Joshua nodded. "You are a child to one such as him, an infant, but you will grow old together. This I promise you."

Turning to Rusty, Joshua said, "If I can do anything to help you two, at any time, you only need ask."

Then, nodding to the two of them, he slapped Rusty on the shoulder.

Rusty nodded in gratitude and then turned to Sherry. Everything rested on her decision, after all.

Sherry, eyes bright with tears, turned back to Rusty and said simply, "I love you. I loved you the second you touched me. I don't know how I know that, but I believe you are my fate."

Rusty, hardly daring to believe her honesty, said, "You're sure?"

"Yes, my love." She moved toward Rusty, holding out her hand. "I'm sure. You are mine, and I am yours. Old wounds be damned. We will face what comes next together."

"Oh, Sherry, my darling. I cannot promise you our journey together will be easy, but I can promise you it will always be filled with love. Although our love might be . . . unique . . . it will never be normal or dull."

Sherry laughed a deep, throaty laugh that sent shivers down his spine. "Normalcy is highly overrated. Unique is much better when it comes to pleasing the heart."

Lowering his lips until they almost touched hers, he whispered, "Then get ready for some of the most heart-pleasing times of your life."

He leaned slightly away, taking the time to brush a hand across her cheek, sending shivers of need racing through her.

Sherry knew, glancing up into his soft brown eyes, that nothing could hold her heart more truly than the man whose desires turned him into a beast.

She pulled Rusty's face closer to hers, lips meeting his with all the confidence that comes from knowing, without a doubt, that you have met your equal.

We hope you enjoyed this story in the Havenwood Falls series of novellas featuring a variety of supernatural creatures. The series is a collaborative effort by multiple authors. Each book is generally a stand-alone, so you can read them in any order, although some authors will be writing sequels to their own stories. Please be aware when you choose your next read.

Other books in the main Havenwood Falls series:

Forget You Not by Kristie Cook

Fate, Love & Loyalty by E.J. Fechenda

Covetousness by Randi Cooley Wilson

Coming soon are books by Lila Felix, R.K. Ryals, Belinda Boring, Heather Hildenbrand, Stacey Rourke, and more.

WATCH FOR HAVENWOOD FALLS HIGH, a Young Adult series launching in October 2017.

IMMERSE yourself in the world of Havenwood Falls and stay up to date on news and announcements at www.HavenwoodFalls.com. Join our reader group, Havenwood Falls Book Club, on Facebook at https://www.facebook.com/groups/HavenwoodFallsBookClub/

ABOUT THE AUTHOR

Susan Burdorf is the author of several YA Contemporary novels as well as numerous short stories in a variety of anthologies. She is thrilled to be part of the shared world stories of Havenwood Falls and looks forward to many more adventures within its magical boundaries. A resident of Tennessee, she is often found hiking the trails on the hunt for waterfalls. Susan can be reached on her Facebook page at www.facebook.com/susanburdorfauthor and on Twitter at @sburdorf.

ACKNOWLEDGMENTS

A book is a collaborative effort even when written by a single author. In this case, *Old Wounds* is a work of collaborative teamwork of the highest degree, and I want to thank Kallie Ross Mathews for the loan of her character, Sheriff Kasun, and Kristie Cook for the loan of Michaela, the owner of Whisper Falls Inn, and also for the invitation to join the growing world of Havenwood Falls.

Thank you also to Regina Wamba of MaeIDesign for the amazing cover that brought Rusty to life; and to Liz Ferry of Per Se Editing for her work making this project so fantastic to view. If I have forgotten anyone, I apologize, but know how much your knowledge and expertise is appreciated by this humble author.

FATE, LOVE & LOYALTY

BY E.J. FECHENDA

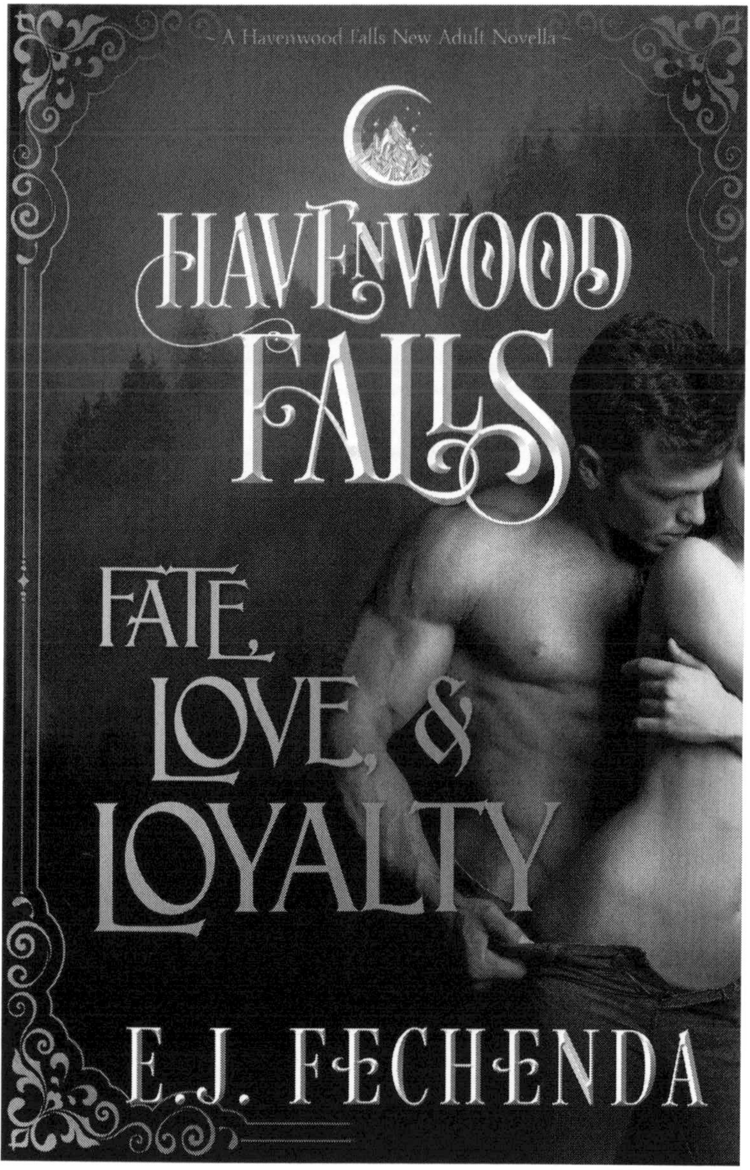
~ A Havenwood Falls New Adult Novella ~
HAVENWOOD FALLS
FATE, LOVE, & LOYALTY
E.J. FECHENDA

Welcome to Havenwood Falls, a small town in the majestic mountains of Colorado. A town where legacies began centuries ago, bloodlines run deep, and dark secrets abound. A town where nobody is what you think, where truths pose as lies, and where myths blend with reality. A place where everyone has a story. This is only but one . . .

Aster McCabe couldn't be happier with her job managing Coffee Haven and baking blueberry scones the whole town raves about, especially her sweet and sexy boyfriend Patrick. She loves her simple, small-town life in Havenwood Falls. At least, until her sister suddenly shows up with trouble not far behind.

The sisters' relationship has always been volatile, especially with the pressure of being the alpha's daughters and the expectation to be perfect. Reeve never failed in that department, and Aster grew up in the shadow of her sister's success. But when Reeve left for college, Aster blossomed. So she's dealt a painful blow the moment her sister walks in the door and meets Patrick —a mountain lion's call to its mate couldn't be any more obvious. Neither can it be controlled or refused.

When an unstable alpha from another den claims Reeve as his mate, Aster, bitter over the recent betrayal, practically draws the guy a map to Reeve's location, unknowingly putting her entire family and den in danger. Aster must figure out how to right her wrong and save her family. But loyalty and love are further tested when a stranger appears with the potential to forever change Aster's fate.

BOOKS BY E.J. FECHENDA

The New Mafia Trilogy

The Beautiful People

Clean Slate

Endings & Beginnings

Enforcer (a prequel novella)

The Ghost Stories Trilogy

End of the Road

Havoc

This book is dedicated to Annette and Carrie. You may have lost your battles this year, but you fought until the end. You taught me to not take anything for granted and to persist, no matter what.

CHAPTER 1

The bell above the front door chimed, and Aster McCabe looked up from the espresso machine, anticipating her boyfriend since she'd been counting down the minutes all morning. They were going away to celebrate their six-month anniversary with a long overdue trip to her family's cabin located in a remote area in the mountains. There they'd be able to shift and run and hunt together, away from the watchful eyes of the community. With Patrick being new to the den and new to Havenwood Falls, there were some who viewed his attachment to Aster as more of a strategic political move. Being the alpha's daughter placed Aster and anyone she became involved with under more scrutiny—a fact that she hated. She always felt she was being held to a higher standard than the other members of their den, and her perfect sister, Reeve, had raised the standards even higher. At the thought of her sister, Aster scowled. The last time Reeve had been home was for Christmas, right before Patrick had shown up in town, and they'd fought constantly.

Instead of Patrick, Aster's boss, Willow Fairchild, walked in cradling her swollen belly—the reason why she'd been showing up later and later for work. A gust of wind followed her in, carrying the sweet fragrance from catalpa trees that were in full bloom. The town square across the street was home to several of these towering trees, which had more fluffy white blossoms than leaves.

"How are you feeling?" Aster asked, deftly steaming milk without even looking at the machine.

"Good. Tired. The baby kicked up a storm last night." Willow eased into a chair at one of the few empty tables near the front counter.

"I can cancel my weekend away if you're not up to running the shop," Aster offered as she handed a latte to a waiting customer.

"No, no. You and Patrick have been planning this. I'll be fine, and Paisley is able to work some extra hours." Willow dismissed Aster with a wave of her hand before resting it back on top of her baby bump. With her white-blonde hair and pixie features, Willow looked barely old enough to be pregnant. While her fae heritage gifted her with a youthful appearance, she was really six years older than Aster. After Aster graduated from college in December, Willow promoted her to manager—a timely decision, since Willow found out a month later that she was pregnant.

Shadows under Willow's eyes, more noticeable because of her porcelain skin, made Aster worry. What if she left and something bad happened? Willow had become more like the sister she wanted, and Aster suddenly felt guilty about leaving. Was it selfish of her to go? She attempted to shrug off the negative thoughts, but it was too late. Willow had already received them. It was hard to hide anything from her boss, one of Havenwood Falls' most powerful empaths. She sensed emotions from miles away.

"Stop it, Aster," Willow said. "You worry too much about what other people think. You need to get out of here and let loose—it will do you some good."

Aster smiled and smoothed her apron, wiping at a clump of flour from a batch of her blueberry scones that won Best of Havenwood Falls two years in a row. Streaks of white powder stood out against the black fabric. "I know."

Willow's command was easier said than done. Having grown up in Reeve's shadow, Aster had years of feeling insecure holding her back. Reeve had moved to Denver and had been gone for more than six years, but the comparisons never stopped. Reeve was high school class valedictorian, she was Miss Teen Havenwood Falls, and she practically walked on water. Guys of all species salivated in her wake. Back then, Aster had been an awkward teenager, and puberty hadn't been kind. All knobby knees and elbows with carrot-orange hair that stuck out in a riot of uncontrollable curls, she was a far cry from beautiful Reeve. She was even envious that her sister was able to leave Havenwood Falls to move to the city, where she lived a glamorous life. Of course, the Court of the Sun and the Moon, the governing body for supes in town, made an exception for her and lifted the spell that usually made other supes and humans forget their time spent in Havenwood Falls.

"You're doing it again." Willow's voice broke through Aster's thoughts. "Have you heard from Reeve?"

"Not lately. She's probably busy planning some extravagant event for some celebrity." Aster turned around to open the oven door. Heat blasted her skin, and the sweet aroma of blueberries and cinnamon assaulted her nostrils. She grabbed an oven mitt and pulled out a tray of golden-brown scones, setting them on the marble counter to cool. She loved the old-fashioned counter and that she didn't have to worry about using a cooling rack or hot pad.

"Aster, you have carved out your own life here and landed an awesome job with the coolest boss ever. Oh, and you have a hot piece of man meat. Who knows, soon you could be sporting one of these." Willow patted her baby bump dramatically, making Aster laugh.

"No! Hell no! I'm not ready for that." Aster shook her head in denial, her ponytail swishing along her back with the movement. Her once carrot-orange hair had darkened to a light auburn, and the longer she grew it, the more the curls relaxed. These days she had grown to appreciate her locks, but had to keep them pulled back. No one appreciated hair in their scones. While she disagreed with Willow on babies, she did agree with her about having an awesome job.

Aster surveyed the shop, taking a moment to admire all of her hard work over the past year. Paintings from local artists hung on the red brick walls, adding color to the space. At Aster's suggestion, Willow had added flower boxes to the large front picture window, and the wildflowers that bloomed were a cheerful greeting to anyone walking by outside. Several hanging plants inside, along with Willow's crystal collection, added a quirky vibe. Overall, the effect was relaxing and inviting. Combined with the good coffee and food, Coffee Haven was a favorite among locals and visitors.

"Well, it's going to happen one of these days, because you're a catch. Why do you think eighty-five percent of our customers are male?" Willow winked, because at that moment Patrick walked in the door. "And all of them are hot for you. Feelings . . . I pick up on these things, you know," she said and tapped her temple.

"Who's hot for you, besides me?" Patrick said with a growl. He stalked across the shop and around the counter, pulling Aster into his arms. She sank into his warmth and breathed in his musk. He rubbed his cheeks against her hair, an instinctual way of marking her with his scent. She tilted her head up, and he slanted his mouth over hers, sending the message to any male in the coffee shop that she was taken. This sent a shiver through her, though she never would have admitted the whole display of male dominance turned her on. Of course, Willow picked up on it and started to giggle. Aster flipped her off behind Patrick's back, which made Willow laugh even harder.

"You ready to go, babe?" Patrick asked when they separated.

"Yes," she responded breathlessly. "My bag is upstairs."

One of the perks of being manager of the coffee shop was the apartment upstairs, which Willow rented to her at a reduced rate, since having a mountain lion shifter living upstairs was added security. Aster untied her apron and tossed it in the hamper under the sink.

Just as they were preparing to leave, the bell above the door chimed. Aster turned to see who was coming in and froze in place. *What the hell was Reeve doing here?* There her sister stood, wearing simple jeans and a black T-shirt, but still managing to showcase every curve. Her hair looked like she had just had it professionally styled; auburn waves framed her heart-shaped face. While Aster was momentarily stunned, Patrick was not, and she watched in disbelief as he prowled toward Reeve.

"Patrick?" Aster called, and she reached for his arm, but he shrugged her off. "Patrick!" she said louder, and he looked back at her briefly with a dazed look in his eyes.

He blinked once, slowly, before focusing on Reeve again. Aster stared in disbelief as she noticed Reeve's dreamy expression and how her sister tracked Patrick's every move. Then she realized what was happening, and her stomach dropped to her toes. She'd seen this before, when their brother Braden met his wife, Kaitlyn.

"Oh, shit," Willow said from behind the counter, and Aster looked at her. "I'm so sorry, honey." Her bright blue eyes shone with sympathy.

Willow's confirmation hit Aster like a punch in the gut, and she bent over as if in physical pain. She couldn't breathe and couldn't process what was happening. Reeve wasn't even supposed to be there in the first place.

"Unbelievable!" she screamed. "You always get everything. Why?"

She couldn't bear to look at them anymore as they scented each other and began touching every inch of exposed skin, oblivious to anyone else around them. With a sob, Aster stormed out through the back of the shop. As soon as she was in the alley behind Coffee Haven, she stripped off her clothes, shifted into her cat form, and took off for the woods on the outskirts of town. She didn't care that running through town as a mountain lion was frowned upon or that there would be consequences. All she cared about was running far away from her sister before she did something stupid, like gouge her eyes out with her claws . . . or kill her.

CHAPTER 2

For Reeve McCabe, meeting her true mate couldn't have come at a worst time. She wanted to fight it, but was powerless against the attraction. She felt inexplicably drawn to the handsome stranger in the coffee shop, and he became her only focus. She smelled her sister's scent all over him, and it made her want to pounce on him to claim him right then and there. Aster. The only reason she stopped by the coffee shop to begin with. She broke away from her mate's gaze when her sister cried out and winced when she saw the hurt on Aster's flushed face, her red cheeks stained with tears. When Aster took off, Reeve ran after her.

She called out for Aster to come back, but by the time she reached the alley, Aster was gone, her clothes a discarded heap on the pavement. Reeve started to call her cat forward so she could pursue her sister, but her cat had nothing but mating on her mind and refused to cooperate. She was unable to leave her mate. She didn't even know his name or where he came from, but that didn't matter. Now that they'd crossed paths, she knew she'd never stray far from his side.

She had come to tell Aster she was home for an indefinite

amount of time. Life had gone sideways in Denver, and she needed the security, the protection, of the den and her family. Trouble had followed Reeve lately, and sadness weighed heavy on her heart when she realized the source of her sister's anguish. Her mate was Aster's boyfriend. Shit. Without even meaning to, she had once again caused her sister pain. With a sigh, Reeve picked up her sister's clothes and folded them. She brought them inside and left them in a neat stack on top of a cardboard box before returning to her mate.

"I feel just as shitty, too. Aster doesn't deserve this. She's a good person. I've seen you in the pictures she has in her apartment. You're Reeve?" her mate asked in a deep voice that echoed within her soul. He brushed a tear off of her cheek before his hands came to rest on her hips, and she felt the strength they possessed. His eyes were a warm brown, framed with thick lashes. His light brown hair was long on top and tousled. A straight nose brought her attention to his full lips.

"Yes," she replied and stepped closer so their bodies were a breath apart. "And you are?" His heart pounded a strong, steady beat, and she was shocked to discover her heartbeat had already aligned with his.

"Patrick O'Shea." A hand left her hip and ghosted up her side, lightly brushing against her right breast before cupping her cheek. She leaned into his touch and purred. All thoughts of anything except Patrick disappeared when he touched her. She knew they had an audience in the coffee shop, but she didn't care. The instinct to fully mate with Patrick clouded her brain. "Please tell me you have your own place, because I'm staying with my parents."

Patrick smiled, his canines already grown longer, and his eyes flashed golden. "I do. Let's go."

They quickly left Coffee Haven, a boatload of pheromones following them out the door.

Patrick lived in Havenwood Village, an apartment complex located a block away from downtown Main Street. At the speed they ran, they reached his apartment within minutes. He opened the front door, and that's as far as they got. Patrick pressed her up against the wall and lowered his head to capture her lips. She tilted to meet him and growled in appreciation when they connected. His lips were soft, but the kiss was hard with urgency. She parted her mouth and welcomed his tongue while burying her hands in his thick hair and tugging on it, encouraging him to deepen the kiss. Reeve moved her hips forward, and as if in sync, Patrick did too. His arousal pressed against her belly, and she broke off the kiss.

"I can't believe this is really happening," she panted.

"Me either," Patrick said between kisses that he traced from the corner of her mouth and along her neck. She tilted her head back, giving him more access. He brushed her long auburn hair behind her shoulder and gently bit down on at the juncture of her neck and shoulder. His canines just barely broke the skin. The act of dominance triggered waves of lust.

"Wait, I don't even know you, and what about Aster?" she asked, trying to retain a grip on reality and not be consumed by her emotions. Reeve's voice shook as she struggled to form the words.

Patrick groaned, but raised his head to meet her gaze with glowing eyes, his irises darker slits, echoing her struggle for control as his cat called to hers. "Trust me, Aster needs her space, and honestly, I don't think I can stop. We will get to know each other—we have our entire lives to learn everything there is to know and so much more."

He kissed her again, and Reeve allowed her cat closer to the surface. She shifted enough to allow her hands to transform into paws tipped with sharp claws, and she shredded Patrick's shirt. He growled with approval, his eyes flashing golden again right before he sliced her shirt open with an equally sharp set of claws. Soon their shredded clothes lay in a pile on the floor, and they stood naked before each other without any shyness.

Reeve admired her mate, running a hand down his muscular

chest and stomach. He had a few scars on his side—faint claw marks that had faded to white—which she guessed were from an old injury. Leaning forward, she gently licked the scars, then placed a soft kiss on his skin. His scent filled her nose, and her whole body pulsed with a powerful wave of arousal. She gasped and stood up straight, almost dizzy with need. Patrick looked her over appreciatively, and her skin flushed under his gaze. His nostrils flared, and his eyes glowed amber right before he spun Reeve around so she faced the wall.

"I don't have the patience to be gentle or slow, but I promise the next time . . ." He ran his nose along her neck and cupped her breasts from behind. She arched her back and pressed into his hands. With every touch, she felt her hold on reality slipping, her conscience suppressed by the call to mate. Every nerve in her body hummed with promise and came alive with each caress.

She whimpered as she stopped resisting. "Take me. I'm yours."

The moment he entered her, Reeve knew there would never be another man for her. Their souls merged, and she felt his need as acutely as her own. His hard, muscular body pressed her against the wall, and she pushed back against him, causing him to drive deeper.

"Oh my God," Reeve cried out, and her knees threatened to go soft.

Patrick brushed her hair aside and bit down on her neck. This time his teeth pierced her skin, completing his claim on her. An overwhelming sense of peace and pleasure consumed her as she felt her blood surging into his mouth. With a final thrust and grunt, Patrick stilled and rode out her orgasm while licking the bite mark clean. They stayed pressed against each other, their pulses pounding, for a few moments, catching their breaths. Reeve slowly turned around to face her mate. His hair stuck out in all directions, and his cheeks were flushed from exertion. Reeve wrapped her arms around his neck and stood on her tiptoes, pulling him to her for a kiss. Now that the initial itch had been scratched, the urgency had waned, but after a few strokes of her tongue, Patrick was ready again.

This time they faced each other. She raised a leg and hooked it over his hip, and he slid inside. They moved in sync, creating a rhythm that quickly rose to a crescendo. Patrick lifted her up, so she wrapped her legs around him. From this angle, she was at the right height to stake her claim. She licked the spot on his neck first, and the vein pulsed underneath her tongue. Her canines dropped, and she struck, drawing his blood into her mouth. The iron-rich warmth bubbled up, and she drank deeply until Patrick released with a muffled groan. Then she retracted her teeth and licked the wound. She was his, and he was hers. The mating bond was officially complete, and there was no going back.

After they collapsed in Patrick's bed, sated and drowsy, the guilt set in.

"I don't regret finding you, my mate," Patrick said as they lay in his dark bedroom. "But I just hate that Aster is hurt. I do care for her, but now, you're all I can see."

"I know. I tried to resist, but the mating call . . . I've never experienced anything so powerful before. Poor Aster." Reeve sighed and rolled over onto her side to face Patrick. He moved so she could settle against him with his arm tucked in behind her, holding her close. "It's not like I planned this. Trust me, I have enough complications in my life, and I just added another reason for my sister to hate me forever."

CHAPTER 3

*A*ster stayed in her cat form all weekend and lost herself in the woods. At first, she ran to the waterfalls, but because it was June and a gorgeous, sunny day, there were too many people around, so she went high up into the mountains. She almost reached the peak, and at 13,000 feet elevation, a significant snow pack from the harsh winter remained on the ground, which meant fewer people. Aster made sure to stay within the 25-mile radius of town, the boundary for the memory ward, one of the protective measures put into place to protect Havenwood Falls' secrets.

Here she roamed along jagged rocks, and when she paused to rest, she stared down at her hometown nestled in the box canyon. Lights twinkled like stars below, and from above, Havenwood Falls appeared even smaller, almost fake, like a diorama. Aster found her escape in the mountains, away from the sometimes suffocating routine of small-town life. Patrick had provided a break from the mundane. He had been new and different and exciting. Before she could dwell on her loss, Aster caught the scent of a deer on the wind.

Going back to nature and giving in to her animal instincts

helped to take her mind off of Reeve and Patrick's betrayal, but it didn't take the hurt away. She returned to her apartment early Monday morning. The sky was still dark, but the chorus of birds that silenced as she slinked through the town's quiet streets let her know dawn was coming. She had followed Mathews River that ran south of Havenwood Falls. Once she passed the ski resort, she cut up Ninth Street, which led right to the shops on Main Street. She stuck to the shadows, where the illumination of street lamps didn't reach, and she ducked behind parked cars or bushes whenever her acute hearing detected somebody nearby.

When she reached the privacy of the alley between Coffee Haven and Callie's Consignments, only then did she shift. Focusing on her human form, she willed her cat to let go and shifted back. She had to stay crouched down until her body adjusted to the transformation. The longer she spent in her cat form, the harder it was to transition. Her animal nature wanted to dominate, and the euphoria from hunting lingered. She shook it off and slowly stood up, adjusting to being bipedal before hurrying up the stairs.

Since she was naked and left her keys inside Coffee Haven, she bent down and lifted up the doormat to retrieve her spare, but it wasn't there. Sniffing the air and doorknob, she figured out who last had entered her apartment, and the visitor was still inside.

Aster opened the door and stepped into the kitchen. Her apartment was dark, but her enhanced vision enabled her to see everything clearly. Her bedroom was just past the kitchen to the left of the hallway, so she stopped there first to put on the pajama pants and camisole top that were still draped on the foot of her bed.

Anne McCabe sat on the futon in the living room, waiting for her. Wordlessly, Aster crossed the room and sunk down next to her mom. She grabbed a throw pillow and hugged it to her chest.

"Willow told me what happened," Anne said. "I'm so sorry, sweetie."

Aster curled her legs up and leaned into the comforting warmth of her mother. Her familiar scent, a combination of sweet honeysuckle and jasmine, helped soothe the ache of Aster's wounded heart. She let out a sob that was quickly followed by another. Soon a full-on crying jag consumed her. Her mom held her close and combed her fingers through Aster's tangled curls while she poured out her bottled-up emotions.

"The hurt will fade, sweetie. Don't be angry at your sister or Patrick. They're powerless against the bond. You know that is something that can't be controlled." Aster sniffed and nodded, hating to acknowledge that her mom spoke the truth. "Someday you'll find your true mate and experience how powerful the connection is, then you'll truly understand."

"I'll never find my mate in Havenwood Falls, or I would have already."

"Hush. You can't know that. Who's to say your mate won't find his way to you?"

This made Aster remember the tales she'd heard growing up, about how mates were pulled toward each other. That didn't explain Patrick's appearance, though, since Reeve didn't live in Havenwood Falls, and she said so to her mom.

"Patrick showed up in January, right?" her mom asked, and Aster confirmed. "Not too long after Reeve left after being home for the holidays. Maybe he was close and felt the pull. It's possible Patrick felt drawn to you since you have similar DNA— a close match, but not a true match. It's happened before."

"Really?" Aster sat up, wiping her tearstained cheeks, and twisted to face her mom.

"You haven't heard about Great Aunt Cordelia?"

"No, I don't think so."

"Great Aunt Cordelia, who you remind me a lot of, had been out for a run up on Pike's Peak when she came across another mountain lion shifter, but he was a stranger. Apparently they had quite the romp in the woods, and he followed Cordelia back to Havenwood Falls. There was a great bonfire party that night by the waterfalls—what we now call the Carnival at the Falls—and practically the whole town was there when Cordelia showed up with her date. Unfortunately, the moment she introduced him to her twin sister, Great Aunt Courtney, well, that's when the true mate bond took hold. Not even a year later, Cordelia was working as a waitress at the Fallview Tavern when a shifter who was on vacation was seated in her section. The handsome stranger turned out to be her true mate."

"Uncle Paul?"

"Yup, and if you ask him, he'll tell you he had never heard of Havenwood Falls before, but the bus he was taking to California from Missouri drove through Grand Junction, and he felt the call of his mate tugging at him from over a hundred miles away, like he had a rope tied around his waist. He ordered the bus driver to let him off and followed his instinct right to the tavern."

"Wow! I had no idea."

"The pull can be very strong. So don't give up hope. Aunt Cordelia didn't talk to her sister for weeks after, and the sting of humiliation lasted longer. It's not just the McCabes who are stubborn," she said with a wink, referring to her mom's side of the family, the Fitzpatricks. "But Cordelia eventually got over it."

Learning about her great aunt's history did provide a spark of hope. All Aster wanted was a close relationship with her sister, and maybe someday it would be possible.

"Thanks for being here, Mom." Aster leaned over and kissed her mom's cheek.

"No problem, sweetie. Now you're probably ready to crash. Go get some rest."

At the mention of sleep, Aster yawned and felt the fatigue from her weekend exertions bearing down on her. Her tired eyes were even scratchier since her crying fit. She walked her mom to the door, and after a hug goodbye, she climbed into bed and immediately fell asleep.

Aster woke a little bit before noon, but not until she showered, brushed her teeth and drank two glasses of water did she start to feel human again. She checked her phone and saw the text from Willow telling her to take the day off. There was a text from her brother as well as some friends, all of them expressing concern for her. Gossip spread fast in Havenwood Falls. She ate a bowl of cereal while checking her email to see if Reeve or Patrick had tried reaching out that way, but they hadn't, and this made her lose her appetite. *Do they not care about me at all that they don't have the decency to check on me after three days?* She dumped the soggy remains of her cereal in the trash and set her bowl in the sink.

Only an hour had passed since she had showered, and boredom was quickly setting in. Aster walked back into her bedroom to grab a book when she noticed the bag she had packed for the weekend getaway sitting on the floor by the door. Seeing it triggered a powerful wave of anger and sadness, and she kicked it, sending it skidding across the hardwood floor. Knowing she needed a distraction, she went downstairs to throw herself into work.

There were a few people sitting at tables. She said hello to Harlow, a friend and witch who was a member of the Luna Coven. She waved at Caleb, a bear shifter who had just graduated high school. He sat with Nikki and Serena, friends of Willow's cousin, Paisley. The teen girls were twirling their hair and sitting to display their assets. Aster recognized the flirting techniques, and Caleb's rapt expression indicated he wasn't immune to their charms. The poor boy was outnumbered and didn't stand a chance. A couple of dragon shifters sat in the corner with iced coffees dripping condensation on the table. She located Willow behind the counter, taking inventory of baked goods. A few months ago she would have done this task while standing, but now she sat on a stool.

She paused to read a poster taped to the front of the counter by the register that Willow must have put up over the weekend. The poster advertised a book drive fundraiser to help rebuild the library that had burned down.

"Can I help? I can make more blueberry scones," Aster offered, since they were sold out.

Willow looked up at her with a scowl. "Yeah, you can help by taking the day off and getting your head together. I could sense your emo angst from across the room."

"Emo angst?" Aster replied with a laugh. "I think only guys can be emo."

"Well, whatever. Just go away. Take advantage, because once this baby comes you'll be working more."

Aster leaned against the counter and crossed her arms, taking in Willow's appearance. Her fair skin was flushed, and her brows were furrowed together, creating a crease in an otherwise flawless face.

"What's wrong?"

Willow exhaled, blowing a few wisps of fine blonde hair out of the way. She sat up and rubbed her belly. "I sense danger coming. It's been getting stronger all weekend." Willow looked up at Aster. "I already called Sheriff Kasun to let him know to expect some trouble."

"That bad, huh?"

"Yeah, off the charts. I haven't sensed this much since the vampire massacre of '05."

Aster's eyebrows rose at the significance of the reference. She was only ten years old when Viktor Azimov, the head of the local Gothic vampires, went mad after drinking the blood of a heroin addict. Willow was in high school at the time and coming into her empathic abilities when she sensed the change in Viktor the moment he drank the tainted blood. Willow had told Aster that she didn't know what to do with the emotions she was receiving, and she didn't know who was emitting them, so all she could do was ride out the storm. Viktor decapitated a half dozen of his vampires before he was subdued. Later he was decapitated too, when he was sentenced to meet his true death as punishment for his crimes. Aster shivered at the idea of being at the mercy of the Court.

"Do you know who it is?"

"No, the signature is unfamiliar to me, so it's not someone from Havenwood Falls. Just be on the lookout. I sense the danger is near."

"Okay," Aster promised.

Since Willow refused to let her work, Aster made herself a double espresso macchiato with extra whipped cream, because she deserved it. As she unwrapped a straw, she heard the bell chime and flinched at the memory of Reeve walking through the door right before she stole Patrick. She kept her head down, angrily stabbing her straw through the hole in the plastic lid, refusing to look until she heard Willow gasp. She glanced over at her boss to find her pale as a ghost and staring at the front door. Aster followed her gaze to find a giant of a man standing in the doorway.

He stood so tall, he had to duck to step inside. The man was dressed all in black: his jeans and T-shirt—even his hair was black. He tilted his head and sniffed the air before his dark eyes zeroed in on Aster and pinned her to the spot. The hair on the back of her neck stood up as he strode toward her, his leather boots thudding on the wooden floor, which vibrated under his weight. As he approached, she noticed his eyes flash amber briefly before returning to their normal brown. Both arms were covered in sleeve tattoos that ended at his wrists, drawing her attention to his hands clenched into fists and partially covered in tawny fur. He was on the verge of shifting, and that wouldn't be good for any human patrons to witness.

"Aster, danger," Willow whispered low enough for her hypersensitive hearing to pick up, and she prayed the man in black didn't hear it, too.

"Where is she?" the man growled when he came to a stop in

front of Aster, forcing her to take a step backward, where her ass bumped into the counter.

"Where is who?" she asked, standing up straighter, refusing to be intimidated by the Neanderthal.

"Reeve. Where is she?"

"Who wants to know?" Aster cocked a hip, flipped her red hair over her shoulder, and crossed her arms over her chest.

"My name is Damian Stone, alpha of the Denver den, and Reeve is *my* mate." He leaned in closer, as if trying to make Aster bend over backwards, and she saw his canine teeth had grown into fangs. They bit into his bottom lip, drawing blood.

"Are you fucking kidding me?" She barked out a laugh, more like a maniacal cackle, as the anger toward her sister returned in full force. This was so typical. Reeve had left an alpha behind and was now shacked up with Patrick. Well, Reeve made the mess, so Reeve would have to clean it up. She ignored Willow's warning and said, "You can find her at Havenwood Village, Unit C. Two blocks that way." She pointed to the left, down Main Street.

Damian smirked and looked Aster up and down. "You're feisty. I like that. I might be back to add you to my collection. It won't be the first time I've had sisters." With that, he turned and stormed out of the coffee shop.

"Aster, what have you done?" Willow hissed. "That man is the big bad I've been sensing! He's emitting more crazy than a serial killer."

Aster's temper died out as quickly as it had flared, extinguished by Willow's statement. "I'm sorry!" She took a step to leave, to follow the man and stop him, when she was frozen in place.

"Don't even think about it, you stubborn ass," Harlow said as she approached with her hands raised like she was getting ready to catch a basketball. In between her palms, energy shimmered, clear yet tangible, like the surface of a lake. "You'll wind up getting hurt, too." Aster attempted to move again, but her friend's spell held strong.

Thankfully, only supes remained inside Coffee Haven, because Harlow could get in trouble for casting magic in public. "Let me go, Harlow," she demanded.

"Only if you agree to call your dad and let him know what's up. Willow is already calling the sheriff."

Aster stared at the front door long after Damian left. Willow's warning sank into her conscience, and worry turned her coffee sour in her stomach. *I just sent a dangerous, very large male I knew nothing about after Reeve,* she thought to herself. *What have I done?* She let out a cry when she envisioned Reeve, lifeless, in Damian's clutches.

"Okay, I promise!" The moment she said this, Harlow released the spell, and Aster almost fell over.

Without a word, Willow placed the coffee shop phone on the counter next to Aster's forgotten macchiato.

CHAPTER 4

*R*eeve woke up to Patrick lightly tracing a finger along her spine. She wiggled closer, forcing him to trail his finger down her side instead. When he hit the soft spot between her ribs and hip, she laughed. Realizing he had discovered a ticklish area, he tickled her even more, until she was breathless from laughing so hard. She'd forgotten what it was like to let her guard down and couldn't remember the last time she'd laughed like that. Then she remembered—it was before she met Damian Stone. Stone. His last name was appropriate, because she felt his weight like a boulder strapped to her back; just being in the same room as the alpha made it hard to breathe.

Thinking about Damian sobered her up, and she rolled away from Patrick, pulling the comforter over her naked body.

"Hey, what's wrong?" he asked, placing soft kisses on the top of her shoulder, which remained exposed. She knew she had to tell him about the situation she left behind in Denver and may have followed her to Havenwood Falls, but she struggled to form the words. "You can tell me anything. Whatever you're scared of, you have me now to protect you."

"What makes you think I'm scared?" she asked.

"We're bonded. I can feel what you're feeling."

"Right, I forgot about that part." Reeve closed her eyes and exhaled deeply before rolling over to face Patrick. His brown eyes were so different from Damian's. Where Damian's were hard and glinted like onyx, Patrick's were warm, like a dark honey. Yes, her mate swore to protect her, but Damian was a ruthless force. She placed a hand on Patrick's chest and ran her fingers through the coarse hair blanketing his pecs. His heart beat strong and steady under her palm.

"Talk to me, babe," he urged, placing a kiss on her forehead. "I bet you'll feel better after."

Reeve took a shaky breath and started from when she first met Damian Stone.

~

Denver, Late September

REEVE WAS WORKING for Elite Catering, which had been selected by the Denver mountain lion shifters for their Founders Day Celebration, a huge event that everyone in the shifter community anticipated each year. Since this past year was their twentieth annual party, the alpha wanted it to be special, so Reeve was brought in as the event planner. The party's venue was a warehouse that normally sat empty, providing a blank canvas every year for decorations and logistics.

When Reeve arrived at the warehouse for the first meeting, she met Damian Stone along with his beta, Gage Barrows, and Elite's executive chef. The meeting was typical—they went over the client's vision, timeline, and what to include on the menu. Reeve walked around the space, mapping out her ideas for decorations, table layout, and where to place the dance floor. The only thing atypical was Damian's behavior toward her. He came on strong and was relentless, despite her turning him down, citing Elite's non-fraternization policy prohibiting dating and personal relationships with current clients. Eventually, his beta got him to back off. Unfortunately, there were other meetings where Reeve didn't have anyone to run interference. She left those meetings disheveled from being pawed at. She asked her boss to remove her from the project, but there wasn't anyone else to take over. Reeve's boss asked her to stay on the job, and refuse Damian's advances as politely as possible. Then things really started to escalate.

Reeve had been casually dating a soldier with the Denver den. It was nothing serious—more like a friends with benefits situation—but when Damian found out, he ordered his soldier to stay away. Not too long after that, Reeve was at a club with some friends, having fun out on the dance floor. Reeve was dancing with some random guy, a human, and they started dancing pretty close. Her back was to his front, grinding to the beat, when suddenly he was gone. She turned around to see where he went, and Damian stood in his place. The poor human was sprawled out on the floor, unconscious, and by the way the bottom part of his jaw hung at an angle, she knew it was broken.

"You fucking psycho! What's wrong with you?" Reeve screamed in Damian's face. At this point, she'd had a couple of drinks and didn't think about the fact that Damian was a client. He had crossed a line, and she needed to push back.

"Nobody touches what's mine."

He said it with such arrogance that Reeve hauled off and slapped him, hoping to knock the smirk off his face. She didn't expect it to excite him, but he grabbed her by the hips, forcing her body against him.

Havenwood Falls

THE SOUND of Patrick growling caused Reeve to pause. His arm tightened around her from where it was draped across her side.

"Do you want me to stop?" she asked.

"I don't know. Did he…he hasn't raped you, has he?" He spat this question out like the very words choked him.

"No. No, never."

"Oh thank the gods!" he said with a deep exhale, and his body softened behind her.

Denver

Nobody was allowed to grab her like he did, like she was a piece of property, so she kneed him in the balls. By this time, they were creating quite the scene, and two of the club's bouncers arrived. When Damian's eyes started to glow, Reeve was afraid he would shift right there, but he managed to bring himself under control . . . barely. While the bouncers were busy with him, Reeve and her friends slipped out of the club.

The next day, her boss called and lit into Reeve about assaulting the company's number one client. Damian had twisted it all around, and made it seem like she was the one out of control—that she was the aggressor. Reeve gave her side of the story, and pleaded to be transferred to a different event, but Damian still insisted that Reeve be the event planner. Rather than be bullied and forced into a bad situation, she quit.

Two days later, her boss called, groveling. Reeve decided to go back to work not only because she loved her job, but because her boss agreed she would never have to be alone with Damian again. Her boss made sure Reeve had someone accompany her to any meeting or gathering. That worked for a few months, but Damian had a way of finding her outside of work. She'd run into him at Trader Joe's or at the coffee shop on the corner by her apartment. Fortunately, her building had security, and required a key card to get in; otherwise he probably would have shown up inside.

Havenwood Falls

REEVE SHIVERED at what she was about to tell Patrick. She'd been reliving the series of events over and over in her head since she fled Denver, and no one knew why she had returned to Havenwood Falls. Patrick would be the first to hear about her situation, and it was only fair that she tell her mate. The bond compelled her to reveal everything—to bare her soul. There would be no secrets between them. She rolled over to face him, and he must have sensed her emotional distress because he tucked her close to his chest. She breathed in his scent, and noticing that hers mixed with his helped her to relax. Feeling better, she continued her story.

Denver

THE FOUNDERS DAY event celebrated the founding mountain lion shifters who established the den in Denver. They made it possible for other supes to move into the area, and helped build a strong community. Damian was really into family history and purity of bloodlines. Every time they had a meeting about the event, he made a point to talk about his heritage and how he's a direct descendent of Ransom Stone, the founding alpha. Reeve made the mistake of mentioning her father, and that he was an alpha. When Damian heard that, he certainly seemed to perk up, but Reeve had no idea just how obsessed he was in his belief that he needed to mate with the daughters of alphas, mating bond or not.

On the day of the Founders Day party, Reeve was busy working, attending to last minute details, and Damian was busy being host, so their paths never crossed, which was a relief to

Reeve. After the party, only mountain lion shifters hung around. There was a nervous, pent-up energy in the warehouse that she recognized. The night was still young and the woods behind the warehouse beckoned. One of the Denver members asked if she wanted to shift and run with them.

"God yes," she exclaimed, relishing the perfect opportunity to unwind from a long, crazy day. On top of that, it had been at least two months since her last shift. Her skin itched with the need to let her cat out and play. So she filed out the back doors with the rest of the group, and they all stripped naked. Reeve's cat was anxious, and she shifted immediately then paced around the parking lot until everyone else had shifted.

Damian's cat was easy to spot. He was the biggest, with a square, masculine face. The dark markings around his eyes and nose looked like war paint, and added to his fierce intensity. His amber eyes locked on Reeve's before he bounded off across a small field that separated the warehouse from the trees. The warehouse was located on the border of the Rocky Mountain Arsenal National Wildlife Refuge, and provided the perfect cover for shifters. Mountain lion sightings weren't unusual and never drew much attention. The rest of the shifters followed suit, and soon Reeve was running in the wilderness, the city lights of Denver just a distant, hazy glow on the horizon.

They ran for the thickest section of the forest, to minimize the risk of crossing paths with humans. With the wind ruffling through her fur and a hint of summer in the warm night air, Reeve let the stress of the past few weeks melt away. The more she ran and her paws connected with the soft earth, the more the human part of her let go—it was such a release. She was so caught up in the moment that she didn't realize she had split off from the group and run into an unfamiliar area. She sniffed the air and surrounding trees, brushes, and rocks for any familiar scents, but didn't detect anything. She came across a stream and crouched down for a drink. The entire time her ears were at attention, twitching at every noise. In the distance she heard the cry of prey expelling its last breath. Reeve lifted her head from the cold water and looked in the direction of the hunt. Moments later, a faint trace of blood clung to the wind, and her nostrils flared with interest. Scenting her kind, she started heading in that direction.

By the time she arrived, traces of the fresh kill were all that remained. Tufts of gray rabbit fur floated in the air, while some clumps were glued to the earth with blood and guts. Multiple paw prints in the mud showed that more than one mountain lion had passed through. Reeve was also back in familiar territory. The night sky was fading into dawn when she arrived back at the warehouse, and she immediately noticed something was amiss.

Her dress and heels, which she had left in a neat pile by the door, were missing. She quickly shifted, and the moment she felt her bones pop into the right place, she stood up straight from where she was crouched. Figuring someone had mistakenly moved them, she went inside to look. There she did find them—in Damian's hands. Reeve didn't sense anyone else in the building. They were alone in the dimly lit space, and she immediately went on the defensive.

"Why do you have my clothes?" she asked, and held her arm out in a silent demand for their return. Her other arm was pressed across her breasts, where Damian's gaze had been fixed since she walked in.

"Because you're mine, and I can do what I want."

"Oh, for fuck's sake! How many times do I have to tell you? I am not yours. Now give me my damn clothes."

Reeve made it a point to stay in one place and not move toward him. He could come to her, and she had the exit at her back in case he tried anything stupid. His dark eyes glinted in the faint light, and his smirk turned into a wide grin full of sharp teeth. His canines lengthened, and he took a step closer. Reeve tensed and resisted taking a step back, not wanting him to see that she was intimidated. Instead she stood up taller and adjusted her long hair so it covered her breasts. Her arms appeared relaxed at her sides, but she was ready to fight if it came to that. Reeve didn't know Damian very well, but she'd been around him enough to know he was drunk on his power, and he struggled to keep control of his beast. The display of teeth just confirmed it for her.

"You definitely have alpha blood flowing through your veins. So proud and defiant, but you will submit to me," he said.

"No. I won't," she replied, never taking her eyes off him. Damian took another step toward her. He was stalking his prey, and she prepared to spring backwards. Her toes sought out some sort of purchase on the concrete.

He handed Reeve her dress, and she flinched at first, which made him chuckle. Glaring at him, she reached for the thin silk and fell right into his trap. As soon as she had the dress in her hand, he snatched her wrist and yanked her toward him, crushing her against his chest. She started to resist, and at first didn't register the sting in her left butt cheek. The fucker had a syringe full of sedative, and Reeve's ability to fight evaporated. She still tried, even though her arms and legs felt like they were made of lead.

WHEN SHE CAME TO, Reeve was in a small bedroom, lying on a single bed. Sunlight streamed in through the only window. It took her a few minutes to shake the grogginess off. Her eyelids felt weighed down, but Reeve wasn't about to go back under, so she forced herself to sit up, and the room spun. Finally, the dizzy spell passed, and she swung her legs over the side of the bed. Her feet making contact with cold tiles provided enough of a jolt to wake her up fully. She took stock of her situation and realized someone had dressed her—at least partially—while she was unconscious. She was wearing a large Harley Davidson T-shirt that fit more like a dress, it was so big. It also carried a scent she was becoming too familiar with—Damian's. There was a sour smell underneath the male musk that repelled her. Her inner cat had zero interest in his pheromones—they were definitely not a match.

Reeve wanted so badly to rip the shirt off, but she left it on to avoid being naked and more vulnerable. She did a quick inventory of her body to see if anything was wrong. Anything could have happened while she was unconscious, but fortunately, she found she wasn't injured and didn't have any tenderness to indicate she had been raped. She slowly rose to her feet, anticipating another round of dizziness that didn't come. There was a bottle of water on the floor next to the bed, and she drained it in seconds. Whatever Damian had drugged her with had left her with severe cottonmouth.

It didn't take her long to check the bedroom for weapons or a way out. The door was locked, and the window had bars on it. The closet was empty, and the bed was just a mattress on a frame, so there weren't any bedposts to snap off and use as a weapon. Reeve peered out the window to get an idea of where she was being held. She was on the second floor and had a view of a nondescript backyard that was surrounded by tall oak trees blocking the view of anything beyond. Sitting on the windowsill in the sunshine, she closed her eyes and listened to her surroundings.

Through the wall to her right, she heard soft whimpers like a woman crying, and to the left, someone was pacing. A male voice could be heard on the first floor. It was muffled and hard to tell whether it belonged to Damian or one of his men, or if it was just a TV show. A second male voice joined in, and the muffled conversation that followed was interrupted by what sounded like plates clanging against each other. None of this information helped Reeve, so she sat back down on the bed to think. If she was only asleep for a few hours, then it was Saturday. If she didn't show up for work on Monday, someone would come to look for her. She was last seen at the party, but she could have been in another county for all she knew. She didn't have her bag, phone, or car, since they were probably left at the warehouse.

As she sat there, more noises came from downstairs, as well as the smell of food. Her stomach growled when she caught a whiff of bacon. Minutes later, footsteps approached, and they stopped nearby. She heard a door open and close. Not long after that, the same door opened and closed, a squeak of the hinges its tell. Then the footsteps stopped outside of the room Reeve was being held in, and she waited with uneasy anticipation as a key slid into the lock and the knob turned. Reflexively, she assumed a defensive crouched position on top of the bed. A guy about her sister's age came into the room carrying a tray of food.

"Scott, right?" she asked, recognizing him as one of the den's soldiers from the party.

He didn't acknowledge her at all, or even look at her. He placed the tray on the floor by the bed and backed out of the room. It only took a few seconds.

"Wait—come back!" she yelled. His retreating footsteps paused in what she assumed was a hallway. "I need to use the bathroom." This wasn't a lie. She really did have to go, but she also wanted an opportunity to learn more about where she was being held, such as the layout and exit points.

Scott came back. He stood in the doorway and held up a pair of handcuffs. "You're not leaving the room until you put these on," he said, still not meeting her eyes. He was at least six feet tall and had a muscular build like Reeve's brother, Braden. While he wasn't making eye contact, Scott was tracking her every move. He didn't have to worry. She wasn't going to challenge him—at least not yet.

Reeve approached him with her arms held out, and he handcuffed her. Then he pulled out a gun from the back of his black cargo pants, and she gasped.

"Relax, it's a tranq gun. If you behave, I won't use it. Now, let's go." He nudged her forward with the muzzle of the gun, and they stepped out into a long hallway. There were three other doors on the right side, in addition to her room, and two doors on the left. At the end of the hallway, Reeve noticed a flight of stairs leading down. They walked until they reached the door on the left closest to the stairs.

"Here you go," Scott pushed open the door to reveal a bathroom.

Reeve went inside, relieved when he didn't follow. She closed the door and went to lock it, but there wasn't a lock available. Quickly scanning the room, Reeve was hit with disappointment again when she realized there weren't any windows. She did her business and checked the medicine cabinet for anything useful, but only found cotton swabs, a box of tampons, and a tube of toothpaste. Closing the cabinet, she caught a glimpse of her reflection in the mirror. Her hair was a tangled mess, and smudges of dirt made her right cheek look bruised. Using hand soap, she washed her face and scrubbed the makeup off from the night before. The handcuffs made it challenging, but she worked around them. Unable to stall anymore, she took a deep breath and opened the door. Scott was waiting across the hall, leaning against the wall, which was painted a light dove gray and accented with white wainscoting. Wherever they were keeping her, it had been recently decorated.

Scott herded her back to "her" room, removed the handcuffs, and left without a word. Reeve sat down on the bed and eyed the tray of food. A pile of scrambled eggs and bacon were on a paper plate, and there was a paper bowl of mixed berries on the side along with a cup of orange juice and a cup of coffee. Propped up against the glass of juice was an envelope with her name on it. Curiosity got the best of her, so she grabbed it and set the tray aside on the bed. There was a single sheet of paper inside with a handwritten note from Damian.

Reeve,

You probably think of me as some monster, but I'm not doing this for me. This is for our race. I do this to ensure our future. Our alpha blood will make our offspring stronger and faster. We've become too diluted, especially since inter-shifter marriages became legal.

Someday you will grow to appreciate what I'm building here, and perhaps even develop feelings for me. I can give you a good life as your provider, and we can create a generation of pure-blooded cats to help sustain our kind. You're strong and fierce, qualities I seek in a mate. It pains me to have to keep you locked up, but until I can trust you, this is how things have to be. I hope you choose to behave and accept your fate.

Your Mate and Alpha,
Damian

Reeve's appetite vanished after reading his note. She'd heard of species purists, but never met one. Supes weren't any different than humans. There were some who were progressive, others who were conservative, and then there were those who were resistant to change no matter what. Reeve was glad the national leadership for shifters legalized inter-species marriage, recognizing the need to align with human legislation.

Fortunately, Denver was progressive. Well, except for Damian. What struck Reeve as weird was that there weren't any warnings about Damian, so either he didn't have a lot of support in Denver, or his supporters knew how to fly under the radar. Reeve knew she was not going to be his mate, and certainly not a breeding whore. He was out of his ever-loving mind if he thought he'd control her. His note did confirm that she was dealing with a different kind of crazy, and from that point forward she needed to do everything within her power to be at one hundred percent.

Despite her loss of appetite, and while the food and coffee were lukewarm, Reeve consumed everything. She didn't smell anything off, so it hadn't been tainted, and she needed to eat to keep her strength up. Reading his note again turned the rock in her stomach into a ball of rage. Who did this asshole think he was? And Reeve already had an alpha—her dad. Even though she had left Havenwood Falls, she never swore a loyalty oath to another den.

When you're alone without anything to occupy your time except for your thoughts, it's a good time for reflection. Aside from a few friends from school and work, Reeve didn't have a huge social network in Denver—even though she'd lived there for more than six years. She'd always planned to eventually come home and be with her family and the den. She didn't realize how homesick she really was, and soon came to the realization that it could be days until someone noticed she was missing.

Havenwood Falls

REEVE PAUSED to catch her breath. Now that she was able to talk about her experience and personal revelations, the words poured out. The fact that Patrick listened without interruption was nice, too. He had stopped pacing the room and joined her in bed again. Occasional kisses on her neck and shoulders or a reassuring squeeze gave her encouragement to continue. It was hard to believe that just three days before they were total strangers yet she never felt so connected to anyone. The connection came from deep within and was more than physical, although they had spent most of the weekend in bed with the exception of eating and showering.

Reeve traced a finger along Patrick's chest and up his neck, the smooth skin transitioning to rough stubble when she approached his jawline. Her fingertip came to a rest on the dimple in his chin and she watched as the corners of his mouth lifted into a grin.

"Finish your story, love. We can play later," he whispered, lifting her finger to his lips and kissing the tip before placing her hand on his hip.

"Deal," she said with a sigh and snuggled against him. "First, I have to explain that I left Havenwood Falls for Aster. You're new to town, so you don't know how miserable Aster was being my younger sister." Reeve sighed. "I hated that she was miserable, and it wasn't as if I *tried* to be popular. I'm fairly outgoing, and in middle school and high school, people just gravitated towards me." She shrugged. "Classes were easy for me, too, so I succeeded as a student. But Aster was shy, and school was harder for her. When I tried to help, she thought I was taking pity on her. It didn't help that, with us being two years apart, she was constantly being compared to me." Reeved paused for a breath and rearranged herself before continuing. "It wasn't fair to hold myself back, and our parents were concerned that I would—and they were right. I love Aster and would do anything for her. So I thought it best to leave Havenwood Falls and began applying to colleges. My parents heard me out and were concerned about Aster, too. Braden, our big brother, was always running interference and trying to maintain peace between us. He even agreed with my plan. So, my parents made arrangements for me to leave. I'm not sure what my dad had to do in order to get approval from the Court to have a spell put on me to counteract the memory spell. He has never told me. Less than a year later, I left for Denver."

"You did that for Aster?" Patrick asked, and she heard the awe in his voice.

"Well, yeah, she's my sister. It worked too. She was able to grow up as Aster McCabe, not Reeve McCabe's little sister."

"I had no idea. Aster alluded to a rivalry of sorts, but she never went into detail."

"She wouldn't as it wasn't a good period for us. We definitely had our moments and defined cat fights," Reeve joked, earning a chuckle from Patrick that rumbled deep in his chest like a purr. It lightened the tension Reeve felt building like a storm inside her, but that was short lived. She still had to finish telling Patrick about Damian.

"So, anyway, I was reflecting on my life and what led me to being held prisoner by a whack job I swore that if I was lucky enough to escape Damian, that I'd return home and start working on my relationship with Aster. I mean, we're both adults now, and hopefully enough time has passed to heal any old wounds. I latched onto this goal like a drowning person holding onto a lifesaver, and it made me more determined than ever to find a way out."

"And then you come home and meet me. Fuck! Aster has to be hurting so bad right now. We were supposed to be going away this weekend for our six-month anniversary." Patrick was out of bed again and pacing his room. He ran his hands through his hair, which already stood up in spikes because right after his last shower, they had found their way back in bed. At this point, his hair looked like it had been through a hurricane.

"I know." Reeve struggled to swallow, her throat suddenly thick with emotion. "We can't control who our mate is, though. This is something Damian Stone doesn't understand." Thinking of the man replaced the sadness with anger. She'd been through hell for months because of that asshole.

"How did you get away from him?" Patrick asked.

Reeve returned to her story.

Somewhere Near Denver

SCOTT CAME BACK to check on her a few hours later, and after handcuffing her again, escorted her to the bathroom. She hadn't showered, and was still just wearing Damian's T-shirt. She wasn't concerned about showing skin, but didn't like feeling vulnerable. She asked Scott if she could get some real clothes, and he said he'd check with Damian. Then he locked her back up in the room again. Shadows grew longer as the day wore on, and Reeve paced the room until her legs ached. She curled up on the bed, facing the door, and stared at the doorknob as if willing it to turn. At some point she fell asleep, because she woke up with Damian curled up behind her, one of his hands on her bare thigh.

Screaming, Reeve leapt off the bed and landed on all fours in a crouch. Her entire body shuddered, on the verge of shifting, but she fought back the urge. A muffled growl came from the room next door, and something hit against the other side of the wall.

"Now is that any way to greet your mate?" Damian said. He remained lying on the bed, shirtless, but Reeve thanked God he still had jeans on. Under different circumstances, she'd probably find him attractive. He was a solid male specimen, of that there was no doubt, but his size just made her realize how much smaller she was in comparison.

Reeve didn't respond to his question and remained silent, glaring at him from her crouched position.

He clucked his tongue at her like she was an errant child, and slithered off the bed. He probably thought he was being sexy and seductive, but his movements were predatory. Reeve warily watched him approach and didn't back away. He came to stand in front of her and squatted down so they were eye to eye. "Such gorgeous green eyes. I hope at least one of our children inherits those."

Reeve flinched, and he seemed to enjoy this momentary lapse in her façade.

"Scott tells me you requested clothes?"

He caught her off guard with the change of subject. She nodded.

"You can have clothes and a shower, but only with one condition."

This shouldn't have surprised her. He had all of the negotiating power at this point. "What's that?"

"You have to eat dinner with me. We should get to know

each other. We'll eat downstairs since you've been cooped up in here all day. Do you accept?"

The idea of seeing more of the house was the hook that made her say yes. Damian, pleased with her answer, stood to go, and she slowly rose out of the crouched position.

"See you in one hour," he said, before leaving the room. Seconds later, she heard the key turn in the lock.

True to his word, Damian sent Scott a few minutes later with a pair of black lace panties and a bra. He handed Reeve a little black cocktail dress and set a pair of red heels on the floor. Apparently dinner was going to be a formal affair. He escorted Reeve to the bathroom again, where towels were laid out for her and a plush cotton robe hung on a hook by the shower. A toothbrush and toothpaste had also appeared. They were on the edge of the sink next to a wide-toothed comb.

Reeve took her time in the shower, hoping the warm water would relax her muscles, but they might as well have been made of concrete, she was so tense about the dinner. Based on the sexy, lacy underthings, she suspected Damian had her in mind for dessert. That was not happening. A knock on the door told Reeve her time was up. With a sigh, she turned off the faucets.

Damian appeared at the door to her room with a bouquet of red roses in hand. It was like he thought he was showing up at her apartment to take her on a date—not that she was his prisoner and had zero choice in the matter. Scott followed him into the room carrying a plastic vase of water, which he placed on the windowsill. "No glass until we establish some trust," Damian explained as he set the roses in the vase.

They left the room, Damian cupping Reeve's elbow and keeping her close to his side, while Scott picked up the rear. As they walked down the hallway, they passed the door for the room next to Reeve's, the room where she had heard someone growl earlier.

"That's Phoebe's room. She's a willful one, too. It must be a trait with alpha females. She misbehaved earlier; otherwise she'd be joining us for dinner."

Reeve's stomach sank when he confirmed that another shifter was being held captive. If she had needed confirmation this guy wasn't hooked up right, that would have been it, but she already knew he wasn't playing with a full deck.

"What did she do?" Reeve asked, curiosity getting the best of her.

"She tried to kill herself by slicing her wrists with her claws."

Jesus! Reeve thought. She would have had to partially shift to make that happen. Suicide among shifters was rare to almost nonexistent. It was as if they were wired for survival no matter what.

"Tamara is on the other side of you, but she's moving tonight to my house, as she finally submitted. She earned my trust, and soon we'll have a mating ceremony."

"This isn't your house?" Reeve asked.

"Well, I own it, but I don't live here. This is more of a training facility, and only a select few know its true purpose."

They reached the top of the stairs, and Damian guided Reeve forward with his hand on the small of her back. The heat radiating off his skin burned through the thin fabric of her dress, and she imagined a handprint forever imprinted on her back like a brand. For the first time, she was being taken downstairs. At the bottom, to the right, was the front door, and her heart raced at the close proximity, until she noticed the three different locks, all requiring a key. Directly across the hall, there was a sparsely furnished living room. The furniture looked stiff and uncomfortable, more for decoration than function, like a setup in a model home. Damian steered Reeve to the left, away from the front door, and down a short hallway into a dining room. The chandelier over the table cast dim lighting, and the table was set for two, with another bouquet of roses and two white taper candles as the centerpiece.

Damian held a chair out for her, and she sank down on the

cushion, the straight back forcing her to sit just as straight. An older woman appeared through a side door and poured red wine into their glasses. She kept her eyes down in deference to Damian. Her gray hair was pulled back into a bun, making her entire weather-beaten face visible.

"Dinner will be served in ten minutes, sir," she said, looking at the floor.

"Good. Right on schedule. Thank you, Marta," Damian responded, dismissing her with a nod. The woman left as silently as she arrived, and Damian lifted his glass into the air for a toast. "To the future of our kind, and that our children grow up to be a generation of strong leaders."

He held his glass out toward her, but Reeve refused to pick up hers. Like hell was she going to toast to that.

"Come on now, Reeve. We can do this the easy way or the hard way."

"Great. The easy way is to let me go." She stood up and started walking to the front of the house. Damian thundered behind her, and suddenly his arms were around her waist. Before she could react, he picked her up and carried her back into the dining room, where he forcefully placed her in the chair.

"You are not leaving. The sooner you get that through that stubborn brain of yours, the easier it will be for you. Unless you prefer being locked up in that tiny room?"

Reeve didn't say anything, but glared at him and couldn't control her lip from curling up as a growl rumbled deep in her chest. Her cat begged to be set free, the idea of captivity just as unappealing to her as it was to Reeve. They sometimes disagreed on things, but on this they were in full accord. Damian was dangerous and a threat to their independence, to their future. Reeve thought of Phoebe, the other alpha female who was a stranger to her, but her sister in this experience. She was desperate enough to attempt suicide, and Reeve refused to get to that point. Now wasn't the time to fight, and as hard as it was to do, she called to her cat and coaxed her down. *Soon*, Reeve promised her cat.

~

Havenwood Falls

"JESUS FUCKING CHRIST. This guy has more captives? What the fuck? I'm going to find him and end his ass. He's fucking done!" Patrick raged and punched the wall next to the door, leaving a fist-sized hole in the drywall.

"No!" Reeve cried out and reached for his hand, pulling him back to bed. He reluctantly sat down on the edge, but his back was ramrod straight, the muscles in his shoulders tensed for a fight. "He's lethal. It's too dangerous! But," she paused.

"But what?" He turned to look at her.

"What if he follows me here? I think he's crazy enough to do it."

"Good." Patrick stood and turned to face her, his entire naked body on display; every cord of muscle there for her to see. His eyes had turned the color of molten gold and blazed with fury. He was shorter than Damian, but only by a couple of inches and equally built. "Let him come here. He's a fool if he does. I'll die protecting you and so will your den."

"You don't understand. The last conversation I had with Damian scared the shit out of me...and my cat."

"What did he say?"

~

Somewhere Near Denver

REEVE RESOLVED to shut Damian out, and ate in complete silence. Right before he locked her up in her room that night, she broke down and asked him one question. "Is your entire den on board with this plan of yours?"

He grinned, a display of strong, sharp teeth. "Not everyone knows of the plan, and I've been challenged a few times, but I'm still here and the challengers . . . well, they're dead."

On that chilling note, he closed the door. The sound of the lock being engaged seemed to echo in Reeve's ears, putting her inner cat on full alert.

She didn't sleep that night. Instead she perched on the windowsill, staring at the stars and getting her bearings. The window faced west, and a faint glow in the distance told Reeve there was some sort of city, town, hell, even an airport or something nearby that emitted a lot of light. She hoped it was Denver, but even if it wasn't, that glow was a beacon in the darkness. If she could get out of the house, she'd make a break for it, because she was light on her paws and had always been one of the fastest runners in the den. She mentally reviewed the layout of the house over and over again, trying to recall the smallest of details that might mean a way out of captivity. Then finally it dawned on her how she could escape. She couldn't be handcuffed, though. The cuffs prevented her from shifting.

The sky was beginning to lighten by the time Reese formulated her plan. With her mind at ease, she crawled into bed and fell asleep. This time when she woke up, Damian wasn't in bed with her, and she didn't hear any movement on the second floor. A tray of breakfast food was on the floor by the bed. Knowing she needed the energy to shift, she ate everything. Not too long after that, she heard someone coming up the stairs. Based on the heaviness of the tread, she could tell it was a man. Crouching down by the floor, she pressed her nose near the gap underneath the door and inhaled. She recognized the scent and smiled, since she had factored Scott into her plan. She quickly stood up and quietly moved to stand behind the door.

Just as she planned, it swung open, and when Scott didn't see

297

her, he stepped farther into the room and made the mistake of not looking behind the door first. He had the handcuffs in one hand, which left him at yet another disadvantage. It only took her seconds to shift, and Reeve didn't even wait for all four paws to hit the ground before she pounced. He turned toward her, and she bowled him over onto his back. In one fluid motion, she locked her jaws over his throat, and hot blood burst into her mouth as she ripped his throat out. His heart stuttered once before it grew silent forever.

She didn't linger, but bounded down the hall, practically leaping down the stairs with one jump. She slid a little bit on the hardwood floor when she landed and struggled to gain traction, but it didn't matter. Her presence was still undetected. She darted down the short hallway and into the dining room, where the exit had been behind her back the entire time she was eating dinner. French doors led out to a patio. These doors didn't have bars covering the panes of glass, which shattered and rained down in a million glittering pieces when she smashed through them. The backyard was empty, but Reeve heard voices shouting behind her. They spurred her cat into action. With the lingering taste of copper on her tongue from Scott's blood, she disappeared into the woods and kept running.

Havenwood Falls

"That's how I escaped, and once I did, I ran in the direction of the hazy glow and found my way to the outskirts of Denver, not far from the warehouse. Not surprisingly, my car was gone from the parking lot. I didn't want to risk going into Denver and seeing my friends. I mean, that's the first place Damian would look for me, right?"

Patrick murmured in agreement, but didn't say anything. She coax him back into bed, hoping to calm him down. He rejoined her and wrapped his arms around her, but he was so tense, she might as well have been in the arms of a marble statue. She tilted her head to look at him and noticed his eyes glowing. The human pupils were replaced by catlike slits. Reeve could feel his anger as if it was her own. She was still not used to the bond, so it was a little overwhelming.

"Hey, I'm okay. I'm here. I stayed in the woods and in my cat form until I reached Havenwood Falls. I arrived at my parents' back door late Thursday night. They were surprised to see me standing naked on the deck, and they had a lot of questions, but I was too exhausted to answer them."

"Does your dad know about this Damian guy?" Patrick asked, his cat eyes boring into Reeve's.

"No. My dad was in a meeting when I woke up, and my mom was gone, so I headed right down to Coffee Haven to see Aster."

"And then you met me."

"And then I met you . . . and we've been in bed ever since," Reeve said with a mischievous grin, and wiggled against Patrick, getting the desired reaction.

He grinned back, and his eyes returned to normal as he rolled over so he was on top of Reeve and her legs were wrapped around his hips.

Patrick was about ready to enter her when a loud boom shook the walls. He practically flew off her, almost as if he was levitating, and he shifted midair before landing in a crouch on the floor, positioning himself between the door and the bed, ready to protect his mate.

"Oh, shit!" Reeve shouted when the bedroom door crashed open and she saw Damian standing in the doorway.

The crazy fucker had actually followed her to her hometown, onto her territory.

She watched with dread as Damian shifted, and Patrick went on the attack. The snarling, clawing mass of fur moved out of the bedroom and into the hallway. Patrick immediately dominated and forced Damian back toward the broken front door. Reeve couldn't believe it, because Damian was clearly one of the largest cats she had ever seen, but Patrick was faster and delivering more swipes. His claws dug deep into Damian's side, and blood immediately welled up, but Damian didn't even flinch.

The fight moved into the living room, escalating with each assault. Blood sprayed onto walls, and bloody paw prints covered the floor. Patrick moved in for another swipe, but Damian pivoted at the last minute, pouncing onto Patrick's back. Teeth and claws sunk in deep, and when Patrick yelped, Reeve's heart almost stopped beating. The instinct to protect her mate took over, and she dropped the bed sheet she had wrapped around her body to shift. The moment she was completely transformed, she launched at Damian, tackling him from the side and dislodging his grip from Patrick. She hit him with such force that they rolled out of the hole where the front door used to be, and down two stairs onto the front walkway.

Damian growled and hissed as they circled each other on the small lawn. Reeve kept crouched low, her gaze unwavering until movement behind Damian caught her attention. Patrick stalked down the small set of stairs to join the fray. She noticed he favored his right rear leg, which was shredded, the exposed muscle and tissue red and raw against his sandy brown fur. That momentary distraction gave Damian a window, and he seized the opportunity, knocking Reeve over and pinning her on her back. He was much heavier and more solid than her brother Braden, whom she used to spar with, and she knew she was outmatched, but she wasn't going to give up.

Damian snapped his jaws near her face, trying to access her throat, but she evaded him. Using her hind legs, she scratched at his soft underbelly, and when he wavered, this provided the encouragement she needed. Lodging her legs under him, she pushed with all of her strength and succeeded in shoving him off while deepening the wounds on his stomach.

Patrick leaped over Reeve, where she was still lying prone on the ground, and went on the attack again. At this point, they had drawn a crowd. Patrick's neighbors in the surrounding apartments stepped out onto their front steps, a gathering of werewolves, witches, fae, and humans. Reeve heard sirens in the distance, and she knew the sheriff and a containment team had been dispatched. A sharp crack followed by a loud yelp sent Patrick to the ground. Shattered bone stuck out through the wound on his previously injured leg. Damian moved in for the kill.

CHAPTER 5

*A*ster snatched up the phone and called her dad. He answered immediately.

"Aster, what is it? I'm in the middle of something." He sounded breathless, which was highly unusual. Her dad was more in shape than someone half his age.

"Dad, I think I screwed up and put Reeve in danger." He paused on the other end and grew eerily quiet.

"What did you do?" he asked.

Aster hesitated and glanced over at Willow, who was standing behind the counter listening. She nodded in encouragement, so Aster took a deep breath before spilling the story out. He didn't even wait for her to finish, but he got the gist.

"Damn it, Aster. She's your sister, not your enemy. If you only knew what she sacrificed for you."

Aster pictured her dad pinching the bridge of his nose, something he always did when he was agitated with her. "You need to stay put at the shop. There's no need for you getting in the middle. I've heard whispers about this guy and he's not playing with a full deck."

"Okay, but I want to help, Dad. I didn't know this guy was such bad news."

"Just stay there. At least I know you're safe and won't have to worry about you, too." He hung up the phone.

"What did he say?" Willow asked. She had come out from behind the counter and sat down at the table with Aster.

"He wants me to stay here."

Just then a sheriff's patrol car screamed by the coffee shop, its blue lights flashing. A second patrol car followed right behind it. They headed in the direction of Patrick's place.

"Shit," she said out loud and stood up quickly, almost knocking her chair over.

"Wait!" Willow reached out and grabbed hold of Aster's hand. "You need to stay here."

Aster reluctantly sat down again, but she was restless and literally sat on the edge of her seat, her gaze not wavering from the front picture window. Minutes ticked by slowly on the wall clock behind the counter. Her sensitive hearing attuned to the steady tick, tick, tick as time marched forward. Cell phones erupted all around her as notifications and ringtones went off. She caught snippets of whispered conversations about a fight up the street between mountain lions. That's all she needed to hear. She stood up, this time knocking her chair over.

"Aster!" Willow called after her, but she was out the door and running up the street before Harlow had the chance to cast another spell. She ran past the bookstore, and other businesses flashed by in a blur as she deftly dodged pedestrians who were in her way. An ambulance raced past, its sirens hurting her ears. Up ahead, she saw a collection of flashing lights. A patrol car was parked across Main Street, blocking traffic.

Aster slipped through an opening in a hedge and ran across several lawns to reach the front of Patrick's development, where all of the action seemed to be concentrated. She came to a sudden stop when she saw her brother, Braden, locked in a fight with the largest mountain lion she'd ever seen. She recognized her brother's markings; the tops of his ears were tipped with black fur, and he had a unique diamond-shaped patch of white right above his nose. The rest of his fur was dark and matted with blood. Fresh wounds oozed from both sides of his body.

Then Aster took in the rest of the scene unfolding in front of her. Patrick lay on the grass, off to the side like a discarded piece of trash. Reeve kneeled beside him, holding his hand as a medic treated his wounds. She wore a bathrobe that had been loosely cinched at her waist. Patrick had a surgical green sheet draped over the lower half of his body. Aster suspected they had both fought in their cat forms, leaving them naked as the day they were born when they shifted back.

Braden, distracted by Aster's appearance on the sidelines, turned his head to hiss at her, and Damian attacked. His jaws clamped down on Braden's neck, and the ensuing snap was deafening. Braden went limp, and his eyes focused on some distant point before she saw the light fade.

"No!" she shrieked, and her inner cat rose to the surface, ready and anxious to join the fight to avenge her brother's death.

Reeve's cry joined hers when to their horror, their father stepped onto the bloodied lawn. His cat bore the scars of previous battles: a clipped ear, healed-over claw marks where scar tissue prevented fur from growing. He was battle-worn, but each scar told a story of survival. He was the alpha of their den for a reason.

Sheriff's deputies circled the fight to prevent anyone else from joining the fray. Sheriff Kasun had his tranquilizer gun trained on Damian, but he didn't fire. This was an alpha versus alpha confrontation now, and the sheriff, alpha of the Havenwood Falls wolf pack, respected the significance. Aster's heart pounded in her throat, and tears spilled freely as she moved her way through the gathering crowd to reach her fallen brother. People stepped aside to let her pass, clearing a path. Jordan, an EMT and one of Braden's friends who had grown up in their family's den, was trying his best to resuscitate, but

Braden had shifted back to his human form, and his skin was already taking on a gray pallor. She sunk down to her knees on the other side of him and took her brother's hand. This was her fault. She sent that monster to Reeve, she put her sister in danger, and Braden had paid the ultimate price defending their family. Braden's hand was growing cold in hers, as if she was drawing all of the warmth out.

"I'm sorry, Aster. He's gone," Jordan whispered the words she dreaded to hear.

"No! No!" she cried out. Leaning forward, she crouched over her brother and placed her head on his chest. The sounds of the fight were drowned out as grief consumed her, yet a strange thrumming in her blood prevented her from disconnecting completely.

Her cat grew restless as if she paced underneath Aster's skin, wanting to break free, her attention focused on something approaching. Aster's sobs stilled as she concentrated on the presence drawing closer. She sniffed the air as the most tantalizing and alluring scent she had ever detected grew stronger. Her blood thrummed deep inside, and her heart beat faster. She heard footsteps coming up behind her, causing her to raise her head from her brother's chest and look.

A man stood not even five feet away. His eyes were a dark blue, like the color of the river when it reflected the sky on a clear day. He was tall and broad; his shirt barely contained the muscles straining beneath. His sandy blond hair stuck up in some areas, like he had just woken up. Her cat purred in appreciation and urged Aster to her feet. She felt inexplicably drawn to this stranger, and his nostrils flared as she approached, his eyes flashing amber briefly. Then he held his hand out to her. The moment they touched, a shock reverberated through her, like the earth shifted under her feet. Aster gasped and gripped the man's hand tighter, and she realized she never wanted to let go. He was her anchor. She felt it in her soul, and her cat did, too.

"Mate?" he asked, his eyebrows rising in shock.

"I think so," she said, breathless. "I'm Aster."

"Gage Barrows." His deep voice sent shivers down her spine, and she moved closer. Gage responded by circling her in his strong arms. She nuzzled his chest, absorbing his scent and marking him with hers. He was her mate. At this confirmation, a deep sense of contentment and belonging settled something that she hadn't realized needed settling. "What happened, Aster? I sense your pain."

The world came crashing back, her brief suspension from reality ending with his question. Shame washed over her again. Braden was dead and lying feet away, and she had already forgotten about him. *Was she always so selfish?*

"Hey, talk to me," Gage pleaded. He tilted her head up so she had to meet his eyes. She blinked fresh tears away and swallowed past the lump in her throat.

"My brother is dead. That bastard killed him." She pointed in the direction of the fight and sensed Gage tense.

"Shit! That bastard is my alpha," he growled and narrowed his eyes as he watched the bloody brawl.

"Well, he's fighting my father now, and he's my alpha." They both tensed and gripped each other's hands tight.

Aster noticed her father slowing down, and she cried out when Damian swiped at him, causing her father to stumble backwards and lose his footing.

"Not my father, too! This is my mess, and I need to fix it," she told Gage and stepped away from her mate.

Her cat whimpered at the separation. Aster ignored the urge to touch him and called her cat forward. Her muscles snapped and bones popped as she shifted into her cat form. The assault on her senses overwhelmed her at first. The metallic tang of blood that hung in the air was so much stronger, and the multiple heartbeats pulsing around her sounded like a circle of drums. Her mate's scent dominated her senses, though, and she wanted to slink around his legs and rub against him, but then she heard her father grunt as he suffered another blow.

Barreling past bystanders who cried out in surprise, she rushed the deputy who had his back to her, focused on the fight and not the threat creeping up behind him. She sprung, knocking him down, and ran past him into the fight. Damian had his back end to her, too, his focus on her father, who was uncharacteristically retreating and unable to put pressure on his front left leg. Aster charged and attempted to knock Damian over so his underbelly would be exposed, but her impact jarred her more than him, and she bounced off like a ball against a brick wall. Damian turned to face her and he grinned, revealing a mouth full of vicious teeth stained red with the blood of her family.

Aster shook off the impact and crouched down, her claws digging into the soil for traction. She hissed at the monster in front of her, goading him. Let him spring first, and then she'd slice him open once he was in the air and his belly exposed. Damian's grin faltered, and he hissed back. *Could he read her mind?* Then she noticed the crowd had quieted, reminding her of the eerie stillness before a storm erupts.

Just then, another mountain lion entered the fight. She'd never seen this cat before, but she recognized his scent—her mate. Gage moved to stand between Aster and Damian, his backside to Aster so she knew he joined in her defense. His tail flicked with agitation, and his ears were flattened as if pinned to his head. He was equal in size to Damian and absolutely beautiful. His coat glistened in the sunlight, a healthy sheen over muscles that rippled with every movement. He had a reddish hue to his golden fur, darkest along his spine, almost like a ridgeback.

Aster moved back, giving her mate space to fight. He was fresh to battle and stood a better chance against Damian. If he was his alpha, there was a good chance they'd sparred together, or at least Gage had seen him fight before so he'd know Damian's weaknesses, if he had any. On the other hand, Damian would know Gage's shortcomings, too.

Suddenly, Gage leaped, and he succeeded where Aster had failed. Damian hissed when he was knocked sideways, but he rolled and quickly regained his footing. They circled each other, teeth on full display and each emitting a low, guttural growl. Gage pounced and forced Damian onto his back, but his jaws snapped open air as Damian managed to push Gage off. Suddenly, with a burst of speed, Damian attacked, and his teeth gained purchase on the back of Gage's neck.

Aster paced nervously along the perimeter of the open space, her tail swishing and twitching when she saw Gage begin to bleed. He broke free of Damian's hold and swatted at him with a paw the size of a baseball glove. Claws sliced through Damian's fur and skin like it was made of tissue paper. Fresh blood bubbled to the surface, and as the scent hit the air, several of the other shifter spectators grew restless. Damian began to slow down, succumbing to his multiple injuries, much to Aster's relief.

Minutes later, the fight was over. Gage began to dominate, and Damian's reaction time ebbed. Taking advantage of the hesitation, Gage tackled Damian and clamped his jaws shut. He made it look effortless when he ripped his alpha's throat out. Blood sprayed in an arc and pooled beneath the prone cat. After a shudder and a series of low pops, Damian's naked, human body lay on the grass. He was dead.

The relief of tension caused Aster's cat to retreat, now that the threat had been eliminated, and she shifted back to her human form. Her clothes had been reduced to shredded bits of fabric. She should have cared about being naked or the fact that practically half of the town had gathered to watch the fight, but she didn't, because Gage stood naked before her. The mating call wrapped around them like an invisible rope. They needed to go somewhere and fast; otherwise she was going to jump him right there.

She ran back to her apartment with Gage right beside her. She caught a glimpse of Willow standing outside Coffee Haven, a big, shit-eating grin on her face. Her tinkling laugh followed them when they turned into the deserted back alley. That's as far as they made it.

Aster had her foot on the bottom step when Gage's arms circled her waist, and he pulled her against him. His erection pressed against her.

"I need you now," he growled in her ear before nipping it with his teeth, sending another wave of arousal over her body. She shivered in anticipation, enjoying the feel of his skin against hers.

He stepped away and she turned around in his arms. Face to face with her mate, she licked her lips, and his blue eyes flared with need before he lowered his head and captured her mouth with his. His tongue slipped against hers, and she opened a little wider to accommodate him, deepening the kiss. His taste exploded on her tongue. The trace of Damian's blood that lingered excited her, called to her animal nature, and she pressed her body closer, her breasts crushed against his chest. Her mate had killed for her. He defended her and her family. Nothing was hotter than that.

"Thank you," she whispered before kissing him again. She looped her arms around his neck and stood on her tiptoes, half-tempted to climb up his body. Gage saved her the work when his calloused hands moved down to cup her ass, and in one fluid movement, he lifted her. Aster wrapped her long legs around his hips as he lowered her onto him. He filled her completely, and she moaned in pleasure as their connection deepened. They didn't move, just stayed still and enjoyed the moment of their union. Her heart beat in sync with her mate's, and the rhythm pounded deep, like it was in her bones. She licked his lips, little teasing laps with her tongue until they parted, and she was back to tasting him. His scent filled her nose and she tightened around him. The stillness was broken, and Gage started to move.

Aster held on tight and rode him as he rode her. Her nails dug into his shoulder, drawing blood. Dropping her head, she licked up the droplets, cleaning the tiny wounds. Once his blood hit her throat, she was lost and exploded around him. Gage cried out, and his thrusts slowed as he shuddered, releasing deep inside her. She rested her forehead in the crook of his neck, shaking, boneless, weak, and not trusting her legs to support her if he set her down. Gage didn't, though, and he carried her upstairs to her apartment.

CHAPTER 6

$\mathcal{A}$ster woke a couple hours later, tangled in sheets and burning hot from Gage's body wrapped around her. She lay on her side and he behind her, but his right leg was between hers, effectively holding her in place. She moved slightly and rubbed against the top of his thigh, triggering instant arousal. She was sore and sticky from their lovemaking, but she couldn't get enough. It was never like this with Patrick or with anyone. Her cat and human sides were harmonious with the finding of her mate.

Gage mumbled in his sleep, and his arm that was draped across her side moved until his hand cupped her breast, then he quieted. His touch on her sensitive nipple was too much. Taking advantage of him being docile and sleepy, she rolled him onto his back and took him into her mouth. He was already semi-hard, and it didn't take long for him to wake up and tangle his fingers in her hair, holding her steady as he thrust deep. When she sensed he was close, she sat up and quickly straddled him, easing him past her tender entrance.

Afterward, she lay in his arms, sated and happy, and his fingers traced a lazy trail up and down her side. She felt guilty, though, at her happiness. It didn't change the fact that her brother was dead, her father wounded, and Patrick, too. She thought about how she would react if Gage had been hurt, and the very idea made her stomach flip and her heart ache. Is that how Reeve felt? Now that she understood the powerful and uncontrollable call of the true mate, she didn't harbor any ill will toward her sister. She needed to find her. She needed to go to her family. She needed to know more about Gage. There was so much to do. Life was too short, too precious to waste on anger, jealousy, and selfishness.

"Where are your thoughts going?" Gage asked.

Aster sat up and looked down at her mate. She had noticed the tattoo over his left pectoral, but had been too busy to ask him the meaning. It consisted of an intricate design in the background with a box featuring two crossed swords. At North, West and East points in between the sword blades, there were gold fleur de lis, and the southern point was an anchor. On top of this box was a medieval-style knight helmet. At the very top and bottom of the tattoo, there were two scrolls. The one at the bottom had Gage's surname, Barrows, and the top scroll contained two Latin words: Parum sufficit. Directly below this scroll was a stag's head. Aster traced the ink with a fingertip.

"What's the significance?" she asked.

"It's my family's coat of arms. Everyone in my family, when they turn eighteen, gets one."

"What does 'Parum sufficit' mean?"

"Little enough or a little is enough. It reminds us to stay humble and not live beyond our means or give into excess. My family dates back to the Old World. My ancestors came over from England in the 1700s."

"My ancestors came over from Ireland when the famine hit. Speaking of which, I need to go to my family. Will you come with me?"

"Of course, I'll be by your side from here on out." Gage sat up and pulled Aster onto his lap. She settled in with the familiarity of a couple who has been together for years, not strangers who just met. "I am yours," he said and kissed the tip of her nose.

"And I'm yours," she responded and with a reluctant sigh, climbed off of her mate. She needed to face her family and own up to her mistake that resulted in Braden's death. She didn't know how much damage she had caused and if it was irreparable.

They showered, and Aster dug up clothes that Patrick had left at her apartment. Gage had tracked Damian's scent to follow him, which required him to stay in cat form.

"Fortunately, I stumbled upon a plastic bag full of clothing stashed in a rotting tree trunk alongside the river. Otherwise, I'd have been strutting through town butt ass naked," he said when Aster handed him Patrick's clothes. The jeans were short in the leg and the polo shirt ridiculously tight, but she appreciated the view.

"If there's a store in town that sells clothes, I'd buy some, but I don't have my wallet," Gage said as they left her apartment.

"Don't worry about it. We'll stop at Backwoods Sport & Ski. They sell shoes, too." She looked down at his bare feet, and he wiggled his toes, making her laugh. They strolled hand in hand through the employee and delivery entrance of the coffee shop. Willow sat at one of the tables counting out the register, since Coffee Haven had closed for the day. She set the money in her hand down on the table and looked over at them.

"Well, hello, tall and handsome stranger. It's funny how I was just telling Aster to look forward to one of these in the near future . . . great timing," she said with a wink while patting her baby bump.

"Really?" Aster said, feeling the blush travel up her neck and bloom on her cheeks. "Gage, this is my boss, Willow."

She spied her bag behind the counter on a shelf beside the extra napkins and coffee stirrers. She also noticed a paper bag next to it with a little heart drawn on one side. She opened it to find two of her blueberry scones. She smiled and handed the bag to Gage.

"We have to go see my family, Willow. I'll catch up with you later." Aster leaned over and kissed Willow on the cheek.

"I understand, honey." Willow's earlier mischievousness disappeared, replaced with genuine concern. "Don't worry about work this week. I arranged it with Paisley so she can cover. You need time off for bereavement. I'm so sorry about Braden." Willow hoisted herself out of the chair, accepting Gage's assistance. "Take all the time you need." She pulled Aster into a hug and held her tight.

Aster felt the tears threaten to surface, and she blinked them away.

"Thanks," she said, her voice rough with emotion.

"By the way, Sheriff Kasun came by to talk to you. When I told him you just met your mate, he backed off."

"Thanks."

They left out the front door of the shop, which Aster locked behind them. They didn't have far to walk, since Backwoods Sport & Ski was also located on town square. When they passed by Shelf Indulgence, the bookstore right next to Coffee Haven, Aster glanced in one of the large windows and saw the owner, Sedona Matthews, sitting on her stool at the counter with her nose in a book. For a Monday, the town was busy. People were ducking in and out of shops. The beautiful, warm June day encouraged people to be outdoors. The trees lining the street and those in the town square were in full bloom, an incongruous sight with the snowcapped mountain range looming in the distance. A banner stretched across Main Street advertising the annual Midsummers Night festival that was taking place the following weekend. She looked forward to taking Gage and introducing him to one of Havenwood Falls' traditions for the supernatural community, where most of the humans were put to sleep and supes ran free.

Aster wandered through the women's section while Gage

tried on some clothes. He emerged from the fitting room wearing a green T-shirt and dark blue jeans. Hiking boots completed the outfit. Aster used her credit card, and Gage promised to pay her back.

"I'm not worried. We take care of each other. That's how this works, right?" she said with a smile as he took the shopping bag from the cashier, who subtly sniffed his hand. Gage was new to town and sure to garner interest among the other shifters.

"I guess so," he agreed.

They walked around the corner to where her Nissan Sentra was parked. It was a college graduation present from her parents, and it still had the new-car smell. Aster kept it meticulously clean, too. She didn't pull out of the parking lot right away. She sat with the car idling and her hands on the steering wheel. The next stop was her parents' house and facing full acceptance of Braden's death.

"Hey," Gage placed a hand over hers. "I'll be there. I'm not going anywhere."

Aster started to cry. "You don't understand! Braden is dead because of me!" She dropped her head and sobbed, unable to look at Gage. He had no idea what a selfish creature he had just become mated to. "I sent Damian directly to Reeve out of spite because she took Patrick away, right in front of me. But it doesn't matter now, does it?"

"Hush, shh shh shh," Gage whispered, brushing her hair out of her face. It was still damp from the shower. "If it's anyone's fault, it's mine. I had no idea what Damian was up to. Did you know he had a collection of women he kept locked up in a house? Your sister was one of them."

"What?" This startling revelation stopped Aster's tears in their tracks. Her green eyes widened, and she finally looked at Gage.

"Yeah." Gage ran a hand through his short hair, and his jaw clenched. "Marta, who apparently worked at the house where they kept these prisoners, told me. She called me after your sister escaped, and Damian freaked out. He'd been collecting daughters of alphas, so his offspring would be superior or pureblooded, or some crazy shit like that."

"Oh my God! At the coffee shop, he made a comment about coming back to get me for his collection." She shuddered at the idea of being forced to mate with that monster, then her thoughts turned to Reeve. *What if Damian had raped her?* Concern for her sister overrode everything else, so she popped the Sentra in reverse and backed out of the parking spot.

On the way to her parents' house, they slowed down as they drove past Havenwood Village and saw several witches working with deputies interviewing witnesses. Aster knew they had isolated the visitors and humans from the crowd and were casting amnesia spells to erase their recollection of all they had witnessed. Devices would be wiped of videos and photos, too. She didn't see Sheriff Kasun, so she continued driving. When Gage bit into a scone, he groaned like he had an orgasm, a sound she was quickly becoming familiar with.

"Do you like?"

"Yes! This is hands down the best fucking scone I've ever had."

"I made them."

Gage looked at her with awe. "You made these? Damn, I love you. My mate has skills." He took another bite, practically shoving the entire scone in his mouth, and Aster laughed at his enthusiasm.

Aster's parents lived in Creekwood, a development that was about a five-minute drive from downtown Havenwood Falls. McCabe & Sons Construction, the company Aster's grandfather started, built Creekwood, from the country club to the home Aster grew up in. The upscale development was nestled among trees and separated from town by Mathews River. It was a pretty drive along a winding road that ran alongside the golf course.

The closer they got to her parents' house, the more anxious Aster became. Gage must have sensed it, because he reached across the console and placed his hand on her thigh. He gave it a light squeeze. His touch and the warmth from his hand did provide some comfort, and she relaxed her death grip on the steering wheel.

Cars lined the street outside her parents' house, and Aster recognized all of them. Her grandparents' Subaru Forester and her Uncle Paul's antique Ford pickup truck were in the driveway, and her sister-in-law's minivan was parked out front. Patrick's Jeep and Sheriff Kasun's unmarked black truck were across the street. Aster pulled to a stop behind the minivan and put her car in park, but didn't get out right away.

"Hell of a way to meet my family," she said to Gage and was just about ready to tell him that Braden would probably pull his protective big brother nonsense and to ignore him. Even though she stopped herself from saying anything, the thoughts were there, a reminder that Braden was gone. Sighing deeply, Aster turned to her mate. "Ready?"

They walked up the winding driveway, lined with tiny solar lights that were still charging, as the sun had yet to dip behind the mountain range to the west. Her parents' house was a large two-story made primarily of gray stone with wood trim and features. Large windows faced the street, and Aster could see her family moving around inside. Lupines and hydrangea were in full bloom and lined the walkway that led to the front door.

She stepped inside the house to a low murmur of several conversations going on at once. The noise didn't cover up the sound of someone sobbing. Aster looked around for the source and saw her sister-in-law, Kaitlyn, sitting on the loveseat. Aster's grandmother was consoling her, while Braden and Kaitlyn's son was curled up in a ball and asleep on the other end. His thumb was in his mouth, his eyelids puffy from crying. At three years old, he was old enough to know something bad had happened, but too young to really understand. He was also the spitting image of his father, with reddish brown hair and a scattering of freckles across his nose. Her heart broke all over again seeing them, and she buried her face in Gage's chest to muffle her sobs.

He guided her farther into the house. The living room was to the right of the wide entryway where Aster and Gage stood. A large ceiling fan circled overhead, suspended from the high ceiling. To the left was the dining room that held a dark wood dining room table. At one end, Sheriff Kasun sat with Reeve, Patrick, and her father. They were deep in conversation, and the sheriff took notes in a leather-bound notebook. Aster moved to join them, but was stopped by her mom, who was descending the stairs. Her face was pale and drawn, her green eyes ringed with red. Seeing the grief etched on her mom caused Aster to cry out and run to her. Anne met her at the bottom of the stairs and pulled her into an embrace. They held each other and sobbed.

"I'm so sorry, Mom!" Aster choked out when they separated. "It's all my fault."

"Shhhh, what are you talking about? Come, let's talk." Anne guided Aster into the kitchen, and she gestured for Gage to follow. A fresh pot of coffee brewed, filling the air with its rich aroma. They sat down in a dining nook surrounded by windows, and it seemed as though the area was filled with sunlight and glowed like they were in a sun globe.

Gage sat down next to Aster and took her left hand while Anne sat down on the other side.

"And who are you?" Anne asked him.

"Gage Bellows, ma'am. I'm, uh, well, I'm Aster's mate."

Surprise and shock registered on her face before she smiled at him.

"What good news to receive on such a sad day." She reached across the table and placed her hand on top of their joined ones. "How remarkable that both of my daughters find their mates within days of each other—I'm so happy for you both. Now," she sat up and withdrew her hand, focusing her attention back on Aster. "Your father and Sheriff Kasun need to talk to you and Gage. The sheriff needs to give full reports to the Court and

Mayor Stuart. What happened today violated so many laws and risked exposing the town's secrets. Then you two, streaking down Main Street like horny teenagers on spring break, didn't help either. The cleanup and damage control are massive. Braden's death and that other shifter, well, that's the worst of all that happened. Your sister and Patrick are giving their statements now. Apparently, this shifter knew Reeve from Denver and followed her here?"

"Yes, ma'am. Damian was my alpha. I followed him here to stop him from doing anything crazy. Unfortunately, I got here too late. I'm so sorry about your son."

Anne's eyes shone with tears that she blinked away. Seemingly at a loss for words, she patted his hand and gave it a squeeze before glancing toward the entrance to the kitchen.

Mike McCabe limped into the room, and Aster looked up at him, preparing for him to chew her ass out. Instead he held his arms open. His face, already showing wear from years spent out in the sun on job sites, had aged in just the past few hours. Grief had already left its mark. Aster flew into his arms, and he wrapped her up tight in a bear hug that immediately transported her back to when she was a little girl who sought out her dad's comfort. She always felt tiny in comparison to his hulking size. At over six-foot-two, with a barrel chest and shoulders broad enough to carry the weight of the world, "Big Mike" McCabe lived up to his nickname.

"Baby girl, I'm so glad you're okay. When I saw you charge in to fight, I thought you were going to be killed, too," her dad said into her hair, before stepping away and holding her at arm's length so he could inspect her for any damage.

With the exception of a bruise on her shoulder from when she hit the ground, she was fine. Her father, however, looked like he had been in a fight with a tree shredder. His weather-beaten face was covered with scratches and nicks. A large gash over his right eyebrow had been stitched up. The black stitches resembled an insect perched above his eye. Thick brown hair, graying at the temples, curled around his ears, revealing the one missing lobe, a wound from years ago. He was a study of old and new battles. While they were shifters and possessed supernatural strength, they still healed at the rate of humans and retained scars from their injuries.

"Dad, I'm so sorry about everything!" Aster cried out. Seeing his injuries brought everything surging forth. She could have lost him, too.

"Hush, baby girl, it's not your fault. Damian Stone killed your brother, not you. This isn't your burden to bear." He held her as she cried. Her face pressed against his polo shirt, which absorbed her tears. A hand came to rest on the small of her back, the warmth instantly seeping through her shirt, and she was already familiar with this touch. Her mate. Gage wanted to provide comfort too.

She stepped out of her dad's embrace, and Gage moved forward to introduce himself, explaining his connection to Damian. "I wish we were meeting under better circumstances," he said.

"You saved Aster. Thank you. You're one hell of a fighter. It couldn't have been easy, going up against your alpha."

Gage nodded in agreement. "I own a gym called the Sweat Box, where I train MMA fighters, plus I've been Damian's beta for the past three-and-a-half years. We fought side by side countless times, but I never had to fight against him. For a split second, I hesitated, but when I saw Aster in danger, any hesitation evaporated. She's all I care about now."

Big Mike grinned at this comment. "Mates—it's a powerful bond. One look at Aster's mom, and I was done for."

Just then, Reeve and Patrick filed into the kitchen, followed by Sheriff Kasun, who was hard to miss. While not much taller than her father, Sheriff Kasun was as wide as a refrigerator and solid muscle. Reeve's right arm was wrapped in gauze, and blood had already oozed through—pinkish red stripes, an imprint of the claw marks concealed beneath. Her bottom lip was split and already beginning to scab over, and the beginnings of a black eye shadowed the left side of her face. Patrick hobbled in on crutches, his leg in an air cast, and his face didn't fare much better than her father's.

Aster wanted to run to her sister and pull her into a hug, beg for forgiveness, but she wasn't sure if that would be welcome. Reeve made the first move and pulled Aster into a fierce hug.

"Forgive me?" Reeve asked, stealing Aster's line.

"What for? I'm the one who's been such a spiteful, petty asshole." This admission made Reeve laugh, and the hug tightened.

"I did take your man," Reeve said, and Aster shrugged. Now that she'd found her mate, the hurt and anger she had experienced earlier were long gone.

They separated, but stood side by side with their arms wrapped around each other's waists, and their heads were tilted, resting against each other. With less than a half-inch difference in height and similar builds, and with their hair the same color, they could have passed as twins.

"Can we go talk?" Reeve asked. "I have something to tell you, something I should have told you a long time ago."

"Of course." As they left everyone behind in the kitchen and climbed the stairs, Aster tried to puzzle out what her sister had to say.

Her bedroom hadn't changed much, and it was like stepping back in time. Her old twin bed still had the sea-foam green comforter and matching bed skirt. Framed pictures of her senior year were mounted on the wall, and miniature pompoms, in Havenwood Falls High's silver and blue, hung on the bedpost, a memento from a homecoming game. One side of the room had a poster for AFI, her favorite band, and a family portrait taken when she was twelve, Reeve was fourteen, and Braden eighteen.

Seeing her brother's smiling face and mischievous eyes made her heart ache. She sank down on the side of her bed, and Reeve sat next to her. She, too, was looking at the picture. They were all happy and whole then. Reeve had just started high school, and Aster was in middle school. This was taken before they fought all the time and before Aster's jealousy turned into resentment. It didn't even matter now, and looking back, all of it was so stupid. She had lost so much valuable time.

"Aster, I want us to get along. I really want to try. Now that Braden is gone," Reeve's voice cracked, and Aster looked over to see her sister crying. "It's just us, you know?"

"I know. I want to try, too, and I'm done being jealous of you. I was an asshole."

"You already said that." Her laugh was shaky, but it was a laugh and a positive start. "I left Havenwood Falls for you. That's what I wanted to tell you."

Aster's eyebrows rose, and she stared at her sister in amazement. "What are you talking about?"

"I knew you were miserable, and we fought constantly. I originally had planned to stay home and take online classes after graduating high school, but thought going away for college would give us the space we needed. So, Dad asked for approval from the Court for me to leave to attend UC Denver, but he petitioned to have the memory spell lifted so I could still come home and not forget anyone. I swore an oath to never reveal Havenwood Falls or bring anyone back without the Court's permission."

"Reeve . . ." Aster started, but didn't know what to say. Her sister's leaving was an act of selflessness, which made her feel all the more selfish. *It doesn't matter anymore,* she reminded herself. She leaned over and rested her head on her sister's shoulder. "Despite how I acted, I always loved you," she admitted.

"I love you, too."

They sat together like that in silence, enjoying the moment.

"Braden would have loved to see this," Aster said a couple of minutes later. "He was always stuck in the middle, trying to broker some sort of peace agreement between us."

"Right? Like we're the Middle East or something . . . brave

soul for getting between two redheads, though," Reeve said with a chuckle that faded into a sigh. "I can't believe he's gone."

"Me, either." This time they leaned against each other for support as they wept and mourned over the loss of their brother.

This is where their mates found them. Aster looked up when they walked into the bedroom. This was her first time really seeing them next to each other, and she marveled at how similar they were in build and coloring. They could have passed for brothers, with their sandy light brown hair and height. Gage's upper body was more muscular and defined, but Patrick wasn't that much smaller. Gage sat down next to Aster, and Patrick sat down next to Reeve.

"I gave my statement to the sheriff," Gage told Aster. "Are you ready to talk to him?"

She nodded and stood up, grabbing Gage's hand in the process so he'd go with her. She turned back to address her sister. "Thank you. See you downstairs?"

"Anything for you, sissy," Reeve responded with a wink and teasing smile when she used the nickname from when Aster was really little. "We'll be down in a bit."

Patrick had a hand on Reeve's thigh that kept creeping higher. The higher it went, the redder her cheeks became.

Aster rolled her eyes and tugged on Gage's hand.

"We're so out of here!" she yelled over her shoulder before shutting the door behind them.

Sheriff Kasun was waiting for Aster in the dining room. She took a seat across from him. The table had been recently polished, and the faint lemon scent clung to the wood. She clasped her hands in front of her, and they cast a blurry reflection on the finish. The sheriff regarded her with his piercing blue eyes that she had long been convinced could see right into people's souls.

"Aster, first I want to tell you I'm sorry about your brother. He was a good man."

Aster looked away, blinking fast to keep the tears at bay. Her throat ached from crying so much, and her head felt like it was full of cotton, her sinuses were so jacked.

"He . . . he was." Aster winced when she said this, hating to refer to Braden in the past tense.

"Can you tell me when you first encountered Damian Stone?" he asked, his pen poised over his notepad.

CHAPTER 7

Court of the Sun and the Moon, One Week Later

The Court of the Sun and the Moon held their hearings in the basement of City Hall in a windowless, soundproof room. In homage to the founders, the only lights used were candles. Large glass globes hung suspended from the wood-paneled ceiling, and each held white candles. Flickering flames cast shadows that danced on the walls, which were decorated with murals depicting a timeline of Havenwood Falls' history.

Aster sat at a table facing the Court, who sat on a raised dais, set up similar to a regular courtroom. Having all of the members of the Court, representatives of the town's Old Families, elevated before her was an imposing sight, and Aster licked her lips nervously. She tried not to stare too long at Willow's great-grandfather, Elmsed, who was the fae representative on the Court. He had lowered his glamour, so the arrow-shaped tips of his ears were clearly visible, poking through his silver hair. His nose was almost flat, and his long chin almost touched his chest. He had frosty blue preternatural eyes, even more piercing than

Sheriff Kasun's, and Aster felt pinned to her seat when his gaze fell upon her.

Aster was flanked by her dad and Gage, and Reeve and Patrick sat on the other side of Big Mike. They'd endured their inquisitions earlier, and the Court, anxious to not draw the proceedings out and potentially delay the Midsummers Night festivities, called them all into the room together for the verdict.

They all faced punishment for violating the rule prohibiting shifting in public. They had also been charged with engaging in a public fight in their shifter forms. Their actions had resulted in enlisting extra witches and mages to wipe devices and memories of any evidence.

Since Gage didn't register when he first arrived in town, he was originally going to have to face punishment for that offense, but he didn't know the rule, and he registered as soon as he became aware, so they threw the charge out.

"Aster Marjorie McCabe, please stand and come forward," Elmsed ordered. Gage's hand had been on her leg, and he gave her thigh an encouraging squeeze before she stood. On unsteady legs, she walked the few steps to stand in front of the court.

Mayor Barbie Stuart leaned over the dais; her body cast a shadow over Aster. The mayor was allegedly pure human, but the town's comedians speculated that she had giant genes in her DNA. She was almost the same size as Sheriff Kasun, and everything about her was big, from her hair to her chest.

"Aster, what do you and Gage plan to do now? Are you going to stay in Havenwood Falls?" she asked.

This question surprised her. They'd been so caught up with Braden's funeral and then the inquisitions that they'd never really talked about it. Gage was expected to return to Denver to restore order to his den. Since he was the one who killed Damian, he had inherited the leadership. The very thought of Gage leaving her behind while he took care of this business was as unpalatable as eating cockroaches. She turned around and looked at Gage. He, too, appeared surprised at the question.

"What happens if I choose to leave and go back to Denver with Gage?" she asked, facing the Court again.

"We discussed this. Eloise Sinclair predicted you would choose to go with your mate. However, this won't excuse you from any punishment." Eloise was a powerful psychic who owned Into the Mystic New Age Books and Gifts. She did psychic readings at the back of her store and ran a psychic fair every year. She had a steady clientele, because her predictions were accurate.

"If you leave Havenwood Falls, you can't come back for two years, and we won't remove the amnesia spell like we did for your sister. Your friends and family can't contact you either, not that you'd remember who they were if they did make an attempt."

Aster gasped and spun around to look at her father. His expression didn't convey any emotion, but his hands were clasped in front of him on the table, and she noticed his knuckles turning white. Leaving now that her family was still reeling from Braden's death was wrong, but staying behind and being separated from her mate wasn't right, either.

"You know the rules, Aster, and you broke them. We can't be lenient with anyone. Order needs to be a constant, otherwise we devolve into chaos."

"What's the punishment if I stay?" she asked.

"Gage engaged in a public fight in his cat form before even registering here, which sets a poor precedent for his den. He'll be banished permanently, and you, Aster, will serve a three-month sentence in jail."

Elsmed stared down at Aster with his frosty eyes. Sweat gathered under her hair as he stared at her. Beads slid down her neck and underneath her blouse, to collect at the small of her back. Neither option was ideal, but punishments weren't meant to be easy. She did fuck up. On the surface, the second option seemed to be the better one. Being separated from Gage would suck and possibly be physically painful, like withdrawing from a drug, but how bad could three months be? His permanent banishment was an issue. She'd want to be able to come back for holidays and family occasions, especially once they started having children. She wanted Gage to be included. Two years away from her home and the only place she'd ever lived was a long time. Sure she went on vacations, but always returned within the first twenty-eight days, before the amnesia spell took effect. What if after her two years was up she never felt the call to return to Havenwood Falls? Her family and her memories would be lost to her; all she'd have would be a new life with her mate. This was a risk with either option, though. Once she left Havenwood Falls and the amnesia spell kicked in, there weren't any guarantees she'd ever make it back . . . unless someone compelled her to return.

"You have twenty-four hours to choose the punishment, Ms. McCabe. I think we've been more than generous, considering."

She had a lot to think about, but didn't have the time right then, as the Court had moved on to reading off the other punishments. Elsmed called Gage to the front of the dais, and Aster gave his hand a reassuring squeeze when he stood up.

"Mr. Barrows, you're new to Havenwood Falls and therefore not familiar with our rules. The circumstances of your arrival are extenuating, however, secrets have been revealed, and a life taken in public. Granted, a wild animal attack story is plausible and easy to sell, but the supernatural community knows better. From what we've learned about Damian Stone, many have argued that you performed a service. Stone killed one of our own, and his punishment would have been death."

Aster's heart jumped at that statement. *Did the Court plan on sentencing Gage to death—a life for a life?* She squirmed in her seat, ready to leap up and protest if that turned out to be the case. Elsmed peered down his flat nose and bided his time, like he enjoyed drawing out the suspense.

Aster barely breathed as she waited.

"You won't have the same fate," Elsmed finally said, and

Aster exhaled in relief. "Gage Bellows, the Court sentences you to pay a penalty of fifty thousand dollars, and you will be held in jail until the fine is paid. Additionally, the memory spell will ensure you have no recollection of your visit here. We expect you not to linger once your fine is paid."

"Understood, and thank you for your fairness. I can make payment arrangements immediately." Gage bowed to the Court before returning to his seat.

"You have fifty grand lying around to pay that fine?" Aster asked. Her eyebrows rose in surprise.

"I've done all right for myself," he answered, giving her a coy smile that revealed the adorable dimple in his left cheek she had grown to love. "Let's just say that the fight nights at my gym do really well."

The past couple of days had been days of discovery, and there was still a lot she didn't know about her mate. Since he didn't get sentenced to death, they had their whole lives to learn about each other.

Next, Reeve was called to the front. Aster pulled her attention away from Gage and his dimple. Her sister had dressed demurely for the occasion in a simple gray suit with a white shirt underneath. From where Aster sat, she could see Reeve shaking with nervousness, and Aster knew why. Reeve took full responsibility for bringing Damian Stone to Havenwood Falls. After sharing a bottle of wine and several crying jags following Braden's funeral, Reeve had revealed to Aster that she blamed herself for their brother's death. If she hadn't been followed, Braden would still be alive.

"Reeve McCabe, you know your crimes. Are you ready to accept your punishment without complaint?" Mayor Stuart asked.

"Yes. I will honor your decision," Reeve said, her voice so soft that Aster could barely hear it.

"Good. We will proceed. You are being charged with shifting and fighting in public as well as bringing a stranger—a dangerous stranger at that—to Havenwood Falls without seeking prior approval from the Court. You took an oath of secrecy before you left, and you broke that oath. For these crimes, you and your mate, Patrick O'Shea, will be sentenced to banishment."

"No!" Aster yelled, jumping up out of her seat and launching herself across the table. She shook off both her dad and Gage when they attempted to pull her back. She came to a stop next to her sister and reached for her hand. "Reeve never told that psycho about Havenwood Falls, and she was running for her life. How was she supposed to know that he would track her here? Plus, Patrick was acting in self-defense. You can't banish them!"

"While I admire you being loyal to your sister, she agreed to accept. Our decision is final."

"No," Aster whispered, more to herself than in protest, and she turned to Reeve who remained stoic in front of the Court with her head held high, but the glimmer of tears in her green eyes told another story.

Barbie rapped the gavel and told them to take a seat, then their father was called up. He faced the Court with his back straight, hands joined behind his back and his legs hip-width apart.

"Michael," Barbie began. "When you approached us six years ago to call in the favor we owed you, you do recall we were hesitant to honor your request because of something like this happening, correct?"

"Yes, Mayor, I know you all took a risk, and it was greatly appreciated."

Aster didn't like seeing her dad so acquiescent. He usually commanded the room and demanded respect.

"Clearly we all failed when we allowed the memory spell lifted from Reeve, but you called in your favor, so we had to honor it."

Gage leaned over and whispered in Aster's ear, "What did your dad do to earn a favor?"

"I have no idea, but I'm determined to find out," she replied and hoped the adage "curiosity killed the cat" didn't hold true.

"The Court has decided that having both of your daughters banished, on top of losing Braden, is punishment enough. Court adjourned." With a crack of the gavel, all members of the Court stood and silently filed out of the room through a side door that appeared in the middle of a mural depicting a dragon shifter melting down gold from the mines. The door disappeared once all of the members had passed through.

No one else moved. Mike McCabe had sunk back down in his chair and now stared off into the distance, his expression once again unreadable.

"Dad? What was this favor you had called in? It must have been pretty big."

"Not now, Aster," he said and pinched the bridge of his nose.

"Come on, Dad. I think we deserve to know, since all of our lives have been impacted. Besides, we're all adults now," Reeve pried.

"Fine!" he snapped and threw his hands up in the air. "I can't give specifics, but I will say that the Court has a lot of secrets and a lot of power. In order to protect our town, and our own kind, sometimes we have to make sacrifices and do things we don't want to do, but must. Anyway, because of things I've done for the Court, they bestowed one favor for me to use."

"They sound like the mafia," Aster said.

"Be careful what you say, baby girl. You're in enough trouble already, and you never know who is listening."

"Why did you risk telling us anything?" Reeve asked.

"Because you're all going to be leaving and will forget this information as well as everything else." At this admission, her dad's emotionless façade broke. He pulled Aster and Reeve into a hug, and they all sobbed. When they regained their composure, Aster wiped her eyes and had a thought.

"Dad, why do you assume I'll be leaving? I haven't given the court my decision yet."

He smiled at her and reached out to brush an errant tear from her cheek. "Baby girl, I know because you won't be able to leave your mate. As much as I know you want to be loyal to your family, you'll be miserable. Gage is your fate and your love. As Patrick is yours, Reeve," he said as he patted Reeve's knee. "I am going to miss you both so much, but I know you will be happy."

Aster turned to look at Gage, who stood off to the side watching her. Wordlessly he walked over and took her hand in his.

The next day, Aster delivered her decision to the Court.

GAGE DROVE Aster's Sentra through downtown Denver, pointing out landmarks along the way. Night had fallen by the time they hit the city limits, and the skyline was lit up like Christmas. Aster marveled at the height of the skyscrapers that had been built around older buildings like Union Station, its bright orange sign visible for miles.

"Oh, there's my work!" Reeve announced from the backseat. Aster looked in the direction her sister pointed and saw a sleek three-story building. A giant monitor in the front glass window displayed images of fancy events. "I'll talk to the owner about hiring you, Aster. Your scones will be a huge hit."

While the Court had banished them from Havenwood Falls, they didn't put any restrictions on where they had to go. Maybe the loophole was intentional or an oversight, but Aster and Reeve saw it as a gift. At least they could be banished together. After a tearful farewell, Aster, Gage, Reeve, and Patrick were on their way. When they left Havenwood Falls, Aster had looked in the side view mirror at her parents. They had stood in the middle of the street waving goodbye, and Aster watched until they faded from view, then she focused her attention on the journey ahead.

Gage had Damian's mess to clean up, and he needed to assert himself as the new alpha quickly. How deep the faction of species purists ran in the den remained to be seen. When Reeve described her time as a captive and mentioned that other women were being held prisoner, too, it chilled Aster to the bone. Historically, species purists went to great lengths to achieve their goals, and Damian wasn't an exception.

As if she was thinking the same thing, Reeve asked Gage why Damian had never told him about his breed purity project.

"I don't know," Gage answered. Aster noticed he made eye contact with Reeve using the rearview mirror. "But, I think he knew I'd object to his plans and challenge him. He also knew that he stood a good chance of losing to me."

They dropped Reeve and Patrick off at Reeve's apartment. Her sister's landlord had made arrangements with the doorman to let her in since she'd lost her keys. With a promise to meet up for dinner the next day, Aster and Gage continued on to his house. She looked over at her mate as he concentrated on the road and navigated through traffic. She examined his profile— the straight nose and long lashes, how his lower lip stuck out a little bit in a permanent pout that she loved to nibble on. His big hands were loose and didn't grip the steering wheel tightly, indicating his confidence with driving. She had only known Gage for a little more than a week, but she already knew him to be a strong leader and fierce protector.

Whatever lay ahead, they would face it together.

We hope you enjoyed this story in the Havenwood Falls series of novellas featuring a variety of supernatural creatures. The series is a collaborative effort by multiple authors. Each book is generally a stand-alone, so you can read them in any order, although some authors will be writing sequels to their own stories. Please be aware when you choose your next read.

Other books in the main Havenwood Falls series:

Forget You Not by Kristie Cook

Old Wounds by Susan Burdorf

Covetousness by Randi Cooley Wilson

Coming soon are books by Lila Felix, R.K. Ryals, Belinda Boring, Heather Hildenbrand, Stacey Rourke, and more.

WATCH FOR HAVENWOOD FALLS HIGH, a Young Adult series launching in October 2017.

IMMERSE yourself in the world of Havenwood Falls and stay up to date on news and announcements at www.HavenwoodFalls.com. Join our reader group, Havenwood Falls Book Club, on Facebook at https://www.facebook.com/groups/HavenwoodFallsBookClub/

ABOUT THE AUTHOR

E.J. Fechenda has lived in Philadelphia and Phoenix, and now calls Portland, Maine home. She is the Amazon bestselling author of The New Mafia Trilogy and is currently working on the Ghost Stories Trilogy. She has a degree in Journalism from Temple University and her short stories have been published in *Suspense Magazine* and several anthologies. E.J. is a member of the Maine Writers and Publishers Alliance and co-founder of the fiction reading series, "Lit: Readings & Libations", which is held semi-quarterly in Portland.

You can find her on the internet here:
Facebook: https://www.facebook.com/EJFechendaAuthor
Twitter @ebusjaneus (https://twitter.com/ebusjaneus)
Tumblr: http://ejfechenda.tumblr.com/

ACKNOWLEDGMENTS

I need to give a huge shout out to Kristie Cook for coming up with the incredible concept of Havenwood Falls and for keeping the crazy train on the tracks. Keeping all the stories and elements straight, plus herding multiple authors, is serious work, and she makes it seem so easy. This is a tremendous opportunity, and I'm excited to be included. It's been a blast collaborating with the other authors on this project such as Kallie Ross, Kristen Yard, Randi Cooley Wilson, Belinda Boring, and so many more. Some of their characters and businesses are mentioned in Fate, Loyalty & Love. I'd like to thank Liz Ferry for working her proofreading magic. My husband deserves huge props because I basically ignored him on his birthday to work on revisions. He always helps to keep me on task, and at one point said, "Go pursue your passion!" So, yeah, he earned this acknowledgment. To all of my family, friends, and fans, thank you for your support and enthusiasm. When my tank is running on empty, you help fill it back up. Much love!

Printed in Great Britain
by Amazon